ALSO BY PETER HELLER

FICTION

The Dog Stars

NONFICTION

Kook: What Surfing Taught Me About Love,
Life, and Catching the Perfect Wave

The Whale Warriors: The Battle at the Bottom of
the World to Save the Planet's Largest Mammals

Hell or High Water: Surviving Tibet's Tsangpo River

Set Free in China: Sojourns on the Edge

The Painter

PETER HELLER

THE PAINTER

ALFRED A. KNOPF   NEW YORK   2014

THIS IS A BORZOI BOOK
PUBLISHED BY ALFRED A. KNOPF

Library of Congress Cataloging-in-Publication Data
Heller, Peter, [date]
The painter : a novel / Peter Heller.—First Edition.
pages cm
HC ISBN 978-0-385-35209-3 (hardback);
EBK ISBN 978-0-385-35208-6
1. Artists—Fiction.   2. Abstract expressionism—Fiction.   3. Ex-convicts—
Fiction.   4. Life change events—Fiction.   5. Psychological fiction.   I. Title.
PS3608.E454P35 2014
813'.6—dc23   2013045522

Manufactured in the United States of America
First Edition

To all the artists in my family

And to Jim Wagner and Nancy Carter

And Kim

BOOK ONE

Mayhem

OIL ON LINEN

40 X 50 INCHES

COLLECTION OF THE ARTIST

I never imagined I would shoot a man. Or be a father. Or live so far from the sea.

As a child, you imagine your life sometimes, how it will be.

I never thought I would be a painter. That I might make a world and walk into it and forget myself. That art would be something I would not have any way of not doing.

My own father was a logger, very gentle, who never fought with anyone.

I could not have imagined that my daughter would be beautiful and strong like my mother. Whom she would never meet. Or that one afternoon at the Boxcar in Taos I would be drinking Jim Beam with a beer back and Lauder Simms would be at the next stool nursing a vodka tonic, probably his fourth or fifth, slurping the drink in a way that made ants run over my neck, his wet eyes glancing over again and again. The fucker who had skated on a certain conviction for raping a twelve year old girl in his movie theater downtown, looking at me now, saying,

"Jim, your daughter is coming up nice, I like seeing her down at the theater."

"Come again?"

"Long legged like her mom, I mean not too skinny."

"What?"

"I don't mean too skinny, Jim. I mean just—" His leer, lips wet with tonic. "She's real interested in movies. Everything movies. I'm gonna train her up to be my little projectionist—"

I never imagined something like that could be reflex, without thought: pulling out the .41 magnum, raising it to the man half turned on the stool, pulling the trigger. Point blank. The concussion inside the windowless room. Or how everything explodes like the inside of a dream and how Johnny, my friend, came lunging over the bar, over my arm, to keep me from pulling the trigger again. Who saved my life in a sense because the man who should have died never did. How the shot echoed for hours inside the bar, inside my head. Echoed for years.

I painted that moment, the explosion of colors, the faces.

How regret is corrosive, but one of the things it does not touch is that afternoon, not ever.

I

An Ocean of Women

OIL ON CANVAS

52 X 48 INCHES

My house is three miles south of town. There are forty acres of wheatgrass and sage, a ditch with a hedgerow of cottonwoods and willows, a small pond with a dock. The back fence gives on to the West Elk Mountains. Right there. They are rugged and they rise up just past the back of my place, from sage into juniper woods, then oak brush, then steep slopes of black timber, spruce and fir, and outcrops of rock and swaths of aspen clinging to the shoulders of the ridges. If I walk a few miles south, up around the flank of Mount Lamborn, I am in the Wilderness, which runs all the way to the Curecanti above Gunnison, and across to Crested Butte.

From the little ramada I look south to all those mountains and east to the massif of Mount Gunnison. All rock and timber now in August. There's snow up there all but a few months a year. They tell me that some years the snow never vanishes. I'd like to see that.

If I step out in front of the small house and look west it is softer and drier that direction: the gently stepping uplift of Black Mesa where the Black Canyon of the Gunnison River cuts through; other desert mesas; the Uncompahgre Plateau out beyond it all, hazy and blue.

This is my new home. It's kind of overwhelming how beautiful. And little Paonia, funny name for a village out here, some old misspelling of Peony. Nestled down in all this high rough country like a train set. The North Fork of the Gunnison runs through it, a winding of giant leafy cottonwoods and orchards, farms, vineyards. A good place I guess to make a field of peace, to gather and breathe.

Thing is I don't feel like just breathing.

Sofia pulls up in the Subaru she calls Triceratops. It's that old. I can hear the rusted out muffler up on the county road, caterwauling like a Harley, hear the drop in tone as it turns down the steep gravel driveway. The downshift in the dip and dinosaur roar as it climbs again to the house. Makes every entrance very dramatic, which she is.

She is twenty-eight. An age of drama. She reminds me of a chicken in the way she is top-heavy, looks like she should topple over. I mean her trim body is small enough to support breasts the size of tangerines and she is grapefruit. It is not that she is out of proportion, it's exaggerated proportion which I guess fascinates me. I asked her to model for me five minutes after meeting her. That was about three months ago. We were standing in line in the tiny hippy coffee shop—Blue Moon, what else?—the only place in town with an espresso machine. She was wearing a short knit top and she had strong arms, scarred along the forearms the way someone who has worked outside is scarred, and a slightly crooked nose, somehow Latin. She looked like a fighter, like me. Sofia noticed the paint splattered on my cap, hands, khaki pants.

"Artist," she said. It wasn't a question.

Her brown eyes which were flecked with green roved over my head, clothes, and I realized she was cataloguing the colors in the spatters.

"Exuberant," she said. "Primitive. Outsider—in quotes."

"You're kidding."

"I went to RISD for a year but dropped out."

Then her eyes went to the flies stuck in the cap.

"Artist fisherman," she said. "Cool."

She asked how long I'd been here, I said two weeks, she said, "Welcome. Sofia," and stuck out her hand.

I said I needed models.

She cocked her head and measured me with one eye. Held it way past politeness.

"Nude?"

"Sure."

"How much?"

Shrug. "Twenty bucks an hour?"

"I'm trying to decide if you are a creep. You're not a violent felon are you?"

"Yes. I am."

A smile trembled across her face. "Really?"

I nodded.

"Wow. What'd you do?"

"I shot a man in a bar. You're not going to back out the door like in a horror movie are you?"

She laughed. "I was thinking about it."

"My second wife did that when she found out."

She was laughing uninhibited. People in line were smiling at her.

"You're married?"

"Not anymore. She ran off down the road."

"I'll do it," she said. "For twenty-five. Danger pay."

Took her a while to rein in her mirth.

"Nude modeling for a violent killer convict. That is a first. Twenty-five, right?"

I nodded. "I didn't kill the guy, I just shot him. I was a little high and to the left."

She was laughing again and I knew that I had made a friend.

Now she shoved open the door like she always did, like she was doing some SWAT breach entry. Tumbled into the room.

"Morning."

"Hey."

"Your muffler is getting worse."

"Really? Tops is balking at extinction. Poor guy."

She sat on a stool at the long butcher block counter that separates the kitchen in this one big room. I pushed aside a bunch of sketch paper and charcoal and the fly-tying vise where I'd been tying up some Stegner Killers, invented by yours truly, which the trout couldn't seem to resist the past couple of weeks. I set a mug of coffee on the counter between us, poured myself another.

"What are we doing today?"

"An Ocean of Women. Something I've been thinking about."

"An ocean? Just me?"

"On my way up here from Santa Fe a good friend told me I can't always swim in an ocean of women. I saw it. Me swimming, all the women, the fish. I thought we could give it a try."

"Forget it."

I set down my mug. "Really? No?"

"Just kidding. Fuck, Jim, you ask a lot of a girl."

"Want an egg with chilies?"

Shook her head.

"You just have to make like an ocean. Just once."

She cocked her head the way she does, fixed me with an eye. The light from the south windows brushed a peppering of faint acne pits on her temple and it somehow drew attention to the smoothness of her cheek and neck.

"Stormy or calm?" she said.

I shrugged.

She leaned forward on the counter, her breasts roosting happily in her little button top.

"How about choppy and disturbed? Dugar told me yesterday he wants to move to Big Sur." Dugar was her hippy boyfriend. "I'm like how fucking corny. Plus nobody lives there anymore, it's so damn expensive. He read a bunch of Henry Miller. Are you a *teen-ager*? I said. You like read a novel and want to move there?"

She stuck out her mug and I refilled it.

"It wasn't a novel it was a memoir, he says. Jeez. He says he is a poet but between you and me his poems are sophomoric. Lately, since he's read up on Big Sur, they are all about sea elephants which he has never seen. I have and they are not prepossessing, know what I mean? They would never even move if they didn't have to eat. I said there is *no* fucking way I'm moving to Big Sur with the sea elephants, or even Castroville, which is like the closest place a normal person could afford to live. I mean, do you want to live in the artichoke capital of the world? Be grateful for what you've got right now, where you are right now. Then I unleash the twins."

I am laughing now.

"That's not fair, is it?"

"Not by a long shot."

"I'm young," she says. It's a simple statement, incontrovertible, and it stabs me with something like pain in the middle of my laughter.

We begin. Sofia is a champ of an ocean, a natural. I paint fast. I paint her oceaning on her side, arched, facing and away from me, swimming down off a pile of pillows, breaststroke, on her back over the same pillows willowing backwards arms extended as if reaching after a brilliant fish. I paint the fish as big as she is, invoking him. More fish, a hungry dark shark swimming up from the gloom below with what looks like a dog's pink boner.

The shark has a blue human eye, not devoid of embarrassment. I am lost. In the sea. I don't speak. Sofia has the rhythm of a dancer and she changes as she feels the mood change.

I love this. I paint myself swimming. A big bearded man, beard going white—I'm forty-five and it's been salt and pepper since I was thirty. I'm clothed in denim shirt and khakis and boots, ungainly and hulking in this ocean of women, swimming for my life and somehow enjoying it. In my right hand is a fishing rod. It looks like the swimmer is doing too many things at once and this may be his downfall. Or maybe it's the root of his joy. My palette is a piece of covered fiberboard and I am swiping, touching, shuttling between it and the canvas, stowing the small brush with a cocked little finger and reaching for the knife, all in time to her slowly shifting poses. I am a fish myself, making small darting turns against the slower background rhythms and sway of the swell. No thought, not once. Nothing I can remember.

It is not a fugue state. I've heard artists talk about that like it's some kind of religious thing. For me it's the same as when I am having a good day fishing. I move up the creek, tie on flies, cast to the far bank, wade, throw into the edge of a pool, feel the hitch the tug of a strike *bang!*—all in a happy silence of mind. Quiet. The kind of quiet feeling that fills you all night as you ready the meal, steam the asparagus, pour the sparkling water and cut the limes. Fills you into the next day.

I wouldn't call it divine. I think it's just showing up for once. Paying attention. I have heard artists say they are channeling God. You have to have a really good gallery to say that. I am painting now without naming any of it, can name it only in memory, and I become aware of a tickling on my neck. Sofia is leaning into me, standing on her tiptoes and watching over my shoulder. I turn my head so that my bearded chin is against her curly head. She is wearing the terry cloth robe she leaves here. She doesn't say a word. She is behind me, but I can feel her smile, a lifting and tautening of the pillow of her cheek against my chin. I was painting more fish, and women, and these crab-like things at the bottom that had men's eyes and reaching claws, and had somehow lost the fact that my model had vanished in the tumult.

"It's been three hours," she whispers. "I'm gonna go." I nod. She tugs my beard once and is gone. Somewhere in there among the ocean of women and the darting fish and a man happily lost at sea I hear wind over water and a heart breaking like crockery and the bleating roar of a retreating dinosaur.

II

I came to the valley to paint. That was four months ago and I am painting, finally. I came up from Taos which is getting more crowded and pretentious by the minute. I was looking to find a place that was drama free. I am pretty good, somewhat famous, which means it gets harder to be quiet. A quiet place. There are two books about me. One I admit was commissioned years ago by Steve, my dealer in Santa Fe, as a way to boost my cachet, and it worked: prices for the paintings almost doubled. That's when I traded in my used van, the one with the satellite Off switch that the collection agency in Santa Fe could activate if I missed a payment. Leaving me stranded by the side of the empty desert highway.

The other book is a fine and true scholarly study of what the author calls a Great American Southwest Post-Expressionist Naïf. I've been called a lot of things, but naïve was never one of them. It must have been because I couldn't stop painting chickens. Farmyard chickens in every frame: landscapes, adobe houses, coal trains, even nudes. There was a chicken. They make me laugh, their jaunty shape all out of balance—like a boat that was built by a savant boat maker, you know it shouldn't float but the fucker does. That's chickens. Naïf.

So I bought this what? Cabin, or cottage, up against the mountain. Bought it because it was made of real adobe bricks by a poet no less—a good one named Pete Doerr, I read his stuff—who had to go back East because his sister contracted cerebral palsy. Wait, I don't think you contract that. She contracted something that as he described it to me halted her gait, confined her to a wheelchair and turned her into a Christian fundamentalist, which he said is like watching someone turn into an idiot before your eyes. I laughed so hard and liked the guy so much I bought the house without negotiating. Plus, he said I could have the books, which I appreciated. For a poet to do that. I asked him if he was going into this deal of sound mind, giving away his books and all. He laughed loud and long. I really liked this guy. He said Yes, I just don't have the time or the energy or the money to box them up and send them. I offered. Nah, keep 'em, he said. Maybe one day I'll come out and pick a few favorites and we can drink a bourbon together. Do, I said. I really wish you do, and I meant it. Thirty months of sobriety or not.

He was big into Pablo Neruda and Rilke. I read some of them. Seemed like very different guys, to me, what do I know. Neruda making little doves out of his lover's hands and wheat fields out of her stomach and stretching out like a root in the dark, he made me horny he really did. Made me want to find a Latin lover, Spanish or Chilean, not too young, one with hips and eyelashes and a voice like dusk rubbing over a calm water. Read enough Neruda you can't stop.

Rilke on the other hand did not make me horny at all. He walked around like a man who had been skinned alive, didn't know what to do with all those acute impressions and so made his poems. I can see why Pete Doerr was fascinated by him. I mean Rilke wrote the *Duino Elegies* in three weeks in the so named castle. I paint fast, but not that fast. Anyway, I admired Rilke as I read him and loved some of his poems, especially the part in the *Elegies* where he talks about animals, and the one poem about the panther in the cage which has to just slay you:

> *As he paces in cramped circles, over and over,*
> *the movement of his powerful soft strides*
> *is like a ritual dance around a center*
> *in which a mighty will stands paralyzed . . .*

The cell phone rings. The house has no phone line, it's off the grid, all the electricity comes from four solar panels on a pole off the northeast corner. Doerr was probably some sort of an environmentalist with this solar power, the woodstove, these thick dirt walls that absorb the sun coming in from the big plate windows on the south side. No phone, no grid, a little propane, the poet was an idealist and an environmentalist and so probably mostly miserable.

The phone rings. It's Steve. He's my dealer in Santa Fe. Has been for almost twenty years. The Stephen Lily Gallery. Very high end.

"How's my clean and sober genius?"

I wince. How does a guy who has known me for twenty years talk to me like this? Hmp. Maybe exactly because he has known me that long, I think.

"You are, aren't you?" Edge of anxiety.

That's his big sweat. I am one of his top earners. The gambling addiction, the costly divorces, these things he can absorb with epic calm, without even a little pit stain on his immaculately pressed madras shirt. Those times, the chaos, they actually serve him because when I get hard up and desperate I paint faster. But when I binge, forget it. He might not see a canvas for three months. That makes him nervous. I suspect he has payments on things even his wife doesn't know about.

"Huh?" I say. All muffled and growly. "Who the fuck's jis?" I slur it.

I can almost hear the sharp intake of breath.

"Jim? Jim?"

Poor bastard. I relent.

"Oh, Steve, it's you. Christ. I thought it was the collection agency."

His relief is a cool wind through the airwaves. "You're not in trouble with the car payments?" he says hopefully. "Or the rent?" His good cheer is truly obnoxious. How can I love a guy I want to strangle most of the time? I do love him, I don't know why. Maybe because he knew I was good before anyone else.

"I've got good news and better news," he says.

I notice that his attempts at fraternal concern have been forgotten, thank God. When he just acts like the ruthless predatory sonofabitch he is I can respect him.

"You there?"

"Barely."

"Effy Sidell bought your *Fish Swallowing All Those Houses*. What were we going to title it? *The Continuing Housing Crisis*? Well it was perfect. The timing. He came in and saw it just as we were hanging it. You have to dream about timing like that. I saw the gleam in his eye, how he pretended to move on, how his eye kept flitting back to it. He was rattling on about this and that, covering his excitement, then very casual he says, What is Jim working on these days?

"Well, we didn't want to pique his interest in anything else did we? So I said: A series of dung beetles I think. Whatever the shiny ones are. Jim says they are his best bug work yet. Definitely worth waiting for!

"Sounds like it, Eff said drily. Then he gestured at the Fish House thing and says very offhand, That's interesting.

"Yes, we love that, I said. Several collectors have expressed interest already. But I told everyone we hadn't even set a price yet.

"Why haven't you called me? he shot back angrily. I mean he tried to sound suave, but you know Eff.

"Oh, well. I mean. Two regulars just dropped in this morning. It was leaning against the wall.

"Pim Pantela, he almost snarled. Well? Have you priced it?

"Yes, I said without thinking. Instinct, Jim, instinct. I tacked on two thousand plus the ten percent consideration I would take off because he was so decisive.

"Twenty-two thousand, I said.

"I'll take it, he said. Have it sent up to the house today. Tomorrow is Margaret's birthday.

"Can you believe that? He told me he loves you like a brother."

"No shit."

"He said that if you have anything that isn't a goddamn bug to call him first."

Pause while he catches his breath.

"Don't go out and get hammered to celebrate?" he says with sudden seriousness.

"Wouldn't think of it."

"Well, there's better news," Steve said.

I was looking out the window. Heavy clouds were blowing in on the mountain ridges from the southwest. No wind here though. And the air had that darkening, heavy, pressure drop feel. If the wind didn't pick up it would be a perfect afternoon for throwing some flies up on the Sulphur. We were in a gibbous moon if I was remembering right. They might be feeding at night, might not be too hungry, but if it spat a little rain so much the better. Hadn't been fishing in maybe four days.

I have to admit that the prospect of thousands of dollars pouring into my Paonia State Bank account via instantaneous electronic transfer right now was appealing. I would not bet on horses or even a baseball game, and I certainly wouldn't play online Texas hold 'em. I mean only a stupid compulsive idiot would do that.

"So?" I say into the phone. "And?"

"The aforementioned Pim Pantela wants to fly you down here for a week. He is commissioning a large portrait of his daughters. We talked about size and came to fifty by eighty."

That woke me up.

"What do you mean you 'came to'? I don't recall you asking me."

"Jim, your phone has been off for ten days."

He had a point. I just found the charger in my truck last night. It was down in a clutter of Backwoods cigar pouches and old tippet spools. Tippet is the thinner gauge fishing line you tie on the end of your leader. I had lost the charger that plugs into a house outlet. I only had the one for the cigarette lighter, so I had to charge it driving to the coffee shop and back.

"A week? I've met his kids. They came in that one afternoon right? In matching polka dots?"

"Right!"

"I could paint them in two hours."

"He wants you to cut loose, Be Jim. Really be yourself. You know, throw in some chickens if you want. Or a coal train."

"For fuck's sake. *Be Jim?* A coal train?"

I was now officially steamed. Steve had already said yes.

"I'm just getting to work here, Steve. I'm doing good work. Tell him another time. Anyway I need to get off now."

The silence now was stony. Slight clearing of the throat. "He has offered thirty-five grand. Since I made the commitment without asking you, I admit, I am willing to take a forty-sixty split." His voice was cool the way it almost never is.

"I'll think about it. Gotta go." I hung up before I could blow my top.

I dug out a cigarillo from the foil pouch and stood out on the ramada. Cool wind now pouring down off the mountain, smelling of ozone and juniper. The way the clouds were. That's how I felt. The mountain formed a long ridge, higher peak swooping to lower, left to right, east to west.

The clouds massed in from the south, dark bellied and brooding. They hung against the ridge like a herd of deer afraid to cross a fence. How I felt. I lit and sucked on the stogie. If the anger I felt now—if I let it cross some line, let it spill, I probably wouldn't have a gallery.

The cigars are little rough-ended cheroots, made to look hand rolled like the stubs Clint chewed in *The Good, the Bad and the Ugly*. Vanilla flavored and irresistible. Limit myself to two packs of eight a day. The wind tore away the smoke. Maybe too windy now to fish the creek, I didn't care, I'd go up anyway and get the fly into the water. I could always fish a weighted wooly bugger, let it drift down on the current and strip it back up like a wounded minnow. The thing was to get in the water, feel the cold press against my knees, smell the current.

Steve, the fucker. I hated this part. Just when I am moving on something good and true he throws out some bullshit like a commission for two panfaced little girls in polka dots. And makes it clear that unless I spend a full agonizing week on the thing the guy writing the check won't feel he's getting his thirty grand worth. Thinks it's okay because I have full creative freedom to throw in a chicken. Fuck. Fuck that. If I finish in a day they can take it or leave it.

The *Ocean of Women* painting was the first big piece I had made it halfway through since I'd come up here four months ago. I'd made a bunch of smaller paintings, but it took so much energy in just figuring out who to pay for the water bill, etc., where to buy the cigars, find a model. Sofia was a good one, a great one. She didn't need much direction, she was creative, she knew what painting was and she allowed for departure, the kind we had this morning, where eventually she disappeared. I loved that.

I smoked and breathed. I was standing there. The floor of the outdoor ramada was rough sandstone flags, inexpertly laid by the poet probably, with sand between. Basic. The stones were reddish, ruddy to ochre. The roof just shade, latilla poles covered with a rush of young willows, haphazardly piled, tied down with cord. The simplicity. Something about the sincerity of this partial shelter. I was standing there and I thought of Alce, my daughter. That she would be eighteen, that she would be a better fisherperson than me now. Very damn good at fifteen. When I could get her to go out, get her away from that crowd. That she could have come

with me this afternoon, fished with me up into the night, the rain.
Relax, Dad, she'd say. Steve is a pain but he loves you. I know, I
know, she'd insist, the commercial part of your painting, what a
pain in the ass, but relax. Everybody's gotta serve somebody, right?
Sometimes we just pay the piper. Get our meal ticket.

She loved using a string of clichés, making them go where she
wanted. Just one week, she'd tell me now. Finish this beautiful one
you're working on, then go down there. Go grateful. Grateful you
have a job, doing what you love. Right, Pop? Uncanny wisdom for
a fifteen year old who had been so tied to her own tugging needs.

Right, Alce.

Her flashing smile, dark eyed like her mom, Cristine—the high
cheeks, my fine hair. Not too tall, no longer gangly, filled out, long
legged. Always graceful. Moved like an animal I thought. Moving upstream away from me to fish ahead, the next bend. Moving
upstream away, away. You went around the turn of the gravel bar
looked back once, raised your chin. And gone. Gone. Alce.

I have an iPhone and now Steve can get to me. I don't text, don't
get email or sports news on the fucker. It is little, too small for my
hands, I'm always pushing the wrong button, losing the call, calling the wrong person. Steve made me get it so I can take photos
of my new paintings—he showed me how—and then I message
him the image. That's why he got it for me, he said.

With the phone I get to talk to people I might not have talked to
again before I died. Some upside. I don't read the thing while I'm
driving like I see so many do, even around here. Or teens, walking
down the sidewalk together, each one on a phone, working their

thumbs. Probably messaging each other, one foot away. Leads to an evolutionary loss of the vocal cords. Alce didn't do that, she didn't have a phone. I know she wanted one.

The last time we spent together, just the two of us, was the summer before the fall she started getting into trouble. Cristine's sister Danika was dying of lymphoma up in Mora County outside of Las Vegas, NM, and Cristine went up for two weeks to be with her. It was summer and Alce and I took a couple of flannel sleeping bags and some meat loaf sandwiches and cans of Hawaiian Punch and fished her favorite pool below the falls at dusk. We both caught a couple of browns, nothing big, and then she made a small twig fire on the gravel bar the way I had taught her and we unrolled the bags under the stars. We were happy, I think, I mean glad to be together fishing, and before we went to sleep we named all the constellations we knew, and then I said, "See that cluster over there, above the Bull?"

"Yeah."

"That's you."

"You are so corny!" Her fist came down on my shoulder. "That looks like a bunch of zits."

"Ouch."

"It's alright, Pop, you are a dreamer. That's why you paint."

"Huh. Okaaay."

"I'm a combination of you and Mom, a dreamer and a fighter."

"Whoa."

"Yup."

"Hold on a frigging minute."

"Glad you didn't say fucking. You always want to."

"Given my record, I kinda thought I was the fighter."

"Nope, you react. That's why you're in the ER all the time."

I laughed out loud. "No shit."

"Yup. Mom's a fighter."

"You are so damned smart. I'll be damned."

I watched the stars beside my daughter feeling as proud as if she'd done something great and ordinary, like won the state track meet. I remembered I had felt the same way when she came home from her first day of kindergarten and declared, high spirited, that the teacher couldn't pronounce her name. "I told her: *AL*-say! *AL*-say! *Al* like Al, *Say* like say! Now she says it right."

Alce. "Don't worry, Pop," she had said that night. "We probably need dreamers more than we need fighters."

Four months later she was dead.

I know. I stand out here now in the wind watching the clouds mass and I know. That Steve in his greed is feeding me and will kill my art if I let him. That my daughter died for nothing. That I better go fishing before my thoughts start to spiral.

I drive into town. Down the hill, cross the tracks, no coal train, no seven minute wait as it clatters by. Good. I don't have to pack the truck because it's perma-packed for fishing. I keep vest, waders, rods, boots in the backseat or in the bed always. I turn at Brad's Market, honk at Bob who is changing a tire in front of his station. Good guy. He runs the Sinclair gas and service station with his old father and his son. Three generations of Reids. I met Bob my second day in town. I pulled up to get gas and he saw the rods in the truck bed through the windows of the topper. Saw the unlit stogie in my jaw, the cap paint spattered and stuck with flies. I guess he was curious.

"Going fishing?" He unspun the gas cap without looking, placed it on the roof of the topper over the truck bed while he reached for the pump handle, looking at me the whole time.

"Thought I better get after it. Been in town two days."

He grinned.

"You moved into Pete Doerr's place."

"How—?"

"Small town," he said. "You know how it is. Can't fart without it coming up at some church breakfast."

I liked him right away. The way I took to Pete on the phone. Bob watched the spinning clicking numbers on the pump, stopped dead at thirty-eight ninety-nine. Gave it an extra click. Recradled the handle, the metallic double cluck.

"You have a spot you were thinking about?" he said. He turned, spat a stream of tobacco juice on the concrete apron. Pushed his cap back. He was a short man, strong, in a grease smudged t-shirt (North Fork Archery Club), about my age, with a lively humor in his eye.

"I was going to go to the Pleasure Park down at the confluence. Everybody says how it's Gold Medal and all."

He nodded. I'd read about the place in magazines, where the Gunnison meets its North Fork. A rock canyon hole, clear water, three pound browns not uncommon.

I handed him two twenties. "Go upstream," he said. "Go up the Sulphur. Gold Medal is good but what is it? Saturday? Be full of fuckwits from Aspen. But there won't be a soul on the creek. One dirt road. The only person who goes up this time of year is Ellery who has the ranch above, and Brent the deputy who rents a trailer from him. Son Mark was up there Wednesday night, said it was hitting real good."

He snagged a dollar out of his breast pocket, handed it to me.

"Let me know how it went. Never seen that dry fly you got on the front of your cap. The one with the orange body."

I grinned. "That's a Stegner Killer. I just made it up. The orange is baling twine. Seems to be working." I took off my cap and worked the hook free and dropped it into his palm. "I'll make you some more," I said.

That was mid-April, before snowmelt. The creek was running low and clear. I liked it a lot. I liked it better than any place I had fished in years. The quiet of it. The nobody of it. The elk tracks in the silt and, lately, the piles of bear scat, full of the seeds of berries. That part of it.

Now as I drive by, Bob looks up from the tire he is changing, waves. Sometimes I think that's all you need. A good man with a fishing tip, a wave. A woman once in a while. Some work to do that might mean something. A truck that runs, that some faceless bastard two hundred miles away can't turn off. It's not much, but plenty when you don't have any of it.

I turn up Grand Avenue: hardware store, two cafés, pizza shop, Mexican restaurant, ice cream, barber. A throwback. The town is half a mile off the county highway, so there's only local traffic. I pass the gravel company, the trailer park by the river, cross over the bridge and accelerate up the hill past the high school sign EAGLES AAA CHAMPS!, up to the highway and turn right east. Five drops spatter on the windshield and I don't care. I can already feel the excitement of stepping off the rounded stones of the bank into the clear green water. The wind from upstream will be in my face, wanting to screw with my cast. I can feel the cold current against the light waders, the warmer rain.

Elbow out the window, I smell the downpour that's already passed cooling the pavement, the ozone. I drive through Stoker. It's a town of fifty houses, small and grimy, crammed between the river and the tracks. Coal town. Heaps of it, a small mountain piled in a cone on the slope across the river. Conveyors and silos climb the side of the canyon. Above the coal are broken rock ledges and oak brush all the way to the ridgetop. Mountain lion country.

Out the other side of town and now there is just the river. The canyon opens up and the river is wide and riffled, running low and clear. The road straightens and I floor it. I can see the high rugged wall of the Sheep Mountains still streaked with snow. When I get to the green tanks of the gas well I turn sharply off to the left, cross a bridge and the road turns to dirt and follows the Sulphur. Something in me relaxes. I can see from the darkness and shine of the clay that it has just rained. Nothing now. White patches of cloud moving fast and a mobile shifting sunshine. Everything in this whole country is getting ready to move. Archery season's in two days and Bob tells me the woods will be thick with bow hunters from Arkansas and Texas and I might have to fish in an orange vest. Never happen. If some sonofabitch from the Ozarks mistakes my white beard for the ass of a deer, well.

I cross another small wooden bridge with a clatter of boards and am now on a rough track with a small clear creek running below me. Across the creek is a fancy log lodge and cabins, the last group of houses before there is nothing. A lifesize bronze bear stands in the forecourt, up on two legs and arms spread to the sky as if he were calling down a rain of locusts.

I can already smell the change. The darker spicier scents of spruce and fir. They come right down to the road. Big tall trees, heavy boughed, the branches trailing little flags of dry Spanish moss. Leaning and dark. And the creek below gathering the light as it gathers the water. The water is nearly blue, greener in the pools, snowy in the rapids, a living pulse reflecting trees and sky and cloud and ducks and crossing elk, and soon yours truly as it runs. My own pulse quickening. The excitement that never changes, of getting wet soon. Of facing off with a bunch of wary fish who may or may not be smarter than me.

The afternoon is somber under cloud, then the edge tugs away and the water sparks in a sudden sweep of sunlight. Can I say that

I feel happy? First time in how long? No. Won't say it. Shut up and inhale and drive.

Up ahead there's a horse trailer in the middle of the road, horses, men. A short man in a big hat, leather vest pushed open by his belly, holds up a hand. Cowboy mustache. I can see the round of the chew tin in his breast pocket. The lace up cowboy boots called packers. Dirty and cracked. Up ahead a big man with a bigger gut and another big hat, liver colored, is trying to load a little strawberry roan. The horse's head is strained back, the lead line from the man's hand to the halter is taut and he is jerking on it hard. He is also yelling which is scaring the mare, I can see her sweatsoaked belly now as she wheels, the slack teats. Her eye back in her head.

"Goddamn it! Rockheaded piece of shit! Yaaaah!"

He jerks hard on the lead, the whole weight of his upper body in the twist of his torso. At the very end of his tug the horse rears. The fat man, more bulk than fat, is at the end of his rotation, he has nothing left, and the rearing mare tears the rope through his hand which I notice is bare. No glove.

The man yells. Or roars like a bear. Too bad the mare doesn't get all the line and run. She doesn't. I am staring. The short cowboy who has approached my window is half turned and staring too. The horse didn't get all the line and before it is out of his palm the man dives for it with both hands and hauls. He is screaming now. He ties it, three fast moves, to a ring at the back of the trailer. The mare's mouth is foaming. She is hauled back stiff legged, neck extended, trying to get as far away from everything at the other end as she can. She can't.

"You good for nothing balky shit factory."

The man's voice is lower. He doesn't have to scream, the horse is tied. He can do what he wants. He reaches into the back of the trailer, into the corner by the door, and tugs. Unhitches whatever it is, a wood stave, no, some kind of club, looks like a two by four, polished dark, maybe oak, lathed down, but the corners still on it. The first strike is both hands, from back and behind like a slugger swinging for the fences. The club comes down beside the withers and the mare screams, a sound like a choked whimper amplified, and it fells her, partly. Her front legs buckle. Now I am out the door. I shove it hard against the short man and he stumbles back with a surprised shout and lands on his butt in the dirt. I am jogging, hitching, trying to run down the road on my bad knee and yelling.

"Hey! Hey! What the fuck!" Running, limping, blind. I am blind. That part of me. Same as in the bar that day. Just a red blindness.

"Hey what the fuck!"

Too late. The man hauls back and swings again, this time against the architecture of the mare's ribs. A thud and blow like the thud of a hollow drum. And crack. The horse, eyes rolling, white foam at mouth screaming, a madness, high, beyond whinny or snort, something human almost. I am on the man. I topple him and he is under me and we roll into the ditch. There is water in the ditch. Cold and it shocks. He is beside me flailing his arms trying to get back and I am hitting him, I feel something give, the pulp of his nose and he is pushing up and back scrambling.

"Hey what the—" He is scrambling back fast then standing above me on the road blinking, his nose trickling blood. Trying to digest. The meteor, the surprise of it. A stranger. "What the fuck was *that*?" His back to the mare who is still standing, I can see beyond the lip of the ditch, standing and shaking like in convulsions. The big man is looking down at me, holding the club. He must have picked it up. The little man has run up and he is staring too, they are looking down at me, as at some animal they never in this world have seen.

"Buddy," says the big man. "What the hell was that?"

I stand slowly in the ditch water. Try my left leg, don't know if I can weight it. Pick up my paint-spattered cap. It's soaked. They are staring.

I look at him. His face meaty like a ham. He does not look particularly perturbed which makes him a dangerous man. Unconsciously he dabs his nose with the sleeve of his forearm. He's done it before. I'd rather not talk. I'd rather tear his arms loose from his heavy shoulders like the wings of a cooked duck.

"You were going to kill that horse," I say finally.

"Well. Maybe. My horse not yours. Headed for the glue factory anyway, that one."

I stand there. Watching them, not the horse. The two men watching me. I cannot put a name to the hatred. The small one looks back to the trailer.

"Dell? What are we gonna do with her? She won't load."

"Cut her loose. She can starve if that's what she wants. Let the coyotes eat her I don't give a shit. I'm done." Looks back to me. "Mister I suggest you mind your own goddamn business. Now and evermore." They turn, walk away.

The big man called Dell stops in the road as if he just remembered something, turns back. Walks to the edge of the ditch, looks down on me. His eyes are small and colorless, without pity, flat with contempt. He gauges the distance. Then he snorts, a loud hawk, and spits. A heavy dark jet. I flinch back, too late, the phlegm hits the side of my neck, hot, a stink of tobacco. The trickle into my collar. Then he shows me his back.

I hear the horse whimper as they approach, like a child's mew. I hear the metal door of the trailer clang shut, the slide of the bar. Two doors slam, the truck revs, the grind of first gear, the rattle as truck and trailer go on up the road.

I clamber slowly out of the ditch, hitch myself onto the gravel. The little mare is where they left her, standing, in shock, quivering. I wipe my neck with my sleeve—gobbet of snot, trickling tobacco spit, blood. Well.

The mare mews when I approach her. Doesn't move just shakes. She's cut, slashed across the back, a wonder he didn't break her spine, and she's cut deep, welted over ribs on her left side where the skirt of a saddle might lie. I speak just above a whisper, soft as I can and come slowly. She's frozen in a paralysis of terror. When I touch her shoulder the quiver and tremor spread outward from the sweatsoaked hide, spread up and back like something seismic. She flinches away from my hand but doesn't step. As if her hooves, small hooves, shiny and black, newly shod, are glued to the dirt. The lead rope hanging from her halter.

I almost cannot contain—the rage and the tenderness together like a boiling weather front. I stand beside her and breathe. The two of us just stand there.

CHAPTER TWO

I

The Digger
OIL ON CANVAS
20 X 30 INCHES

What I did was gentle her over to a tree by the pullout and tie her there and drive back out to the highway where I got two bars on the stupid phone. Called my neighbor Willy. He's an elk rancher just east of me. Friendly but not intrusive, neighborly. Bachelor at the moment like me, maybe ten years younger. Told me when I first moved in: If I ever needed anything. Repeats it every time I see him. So I called the number I'd managed to store in my phone and he told me to wait and forty minutes later he pulled up in his own diesel pickup, his own blue six horse trailer, and when he swung down and saw the state she was in he went back to the truck and loaded a feed bag with oats and spoke to her gently like a person who has been aggrieved and injured, and got the bag over her ears and we leaned against my truck and let her eat and calm down.

Willy was in no hurry and neither was I. Now that my chance at fishing was shot for the day. He didn't seem like the other ranchers I'd met around here. He wore a twisted copper bracelet on his left wrist and he gave off the kind of intelligence of someone who might have read a shitpile of books but would never talk about it. We were in the cool shade of the spruce, smelling the breeze stirring downstream, and he told me he'd grown up in New Hampshire. He took off his raggedy straw cowboy hat and ran a scarred hand through his thinning hair.

"When I first came out here I must've stuck out like a finger on a foot," he said. "But I had good neighbors."

"New Hampshire? Never knew anybody from there."

"You can't move to New Hampshire," he said, "but you sure as shit can move out of it. First frigging chance you get. You can move there, but. My folks did. From Germany. Don't ask me."

He coughed, spat.

"State has a Berlin and a Hanover, maybe enough for them. You know what the closest neighbor gal told my mother when she saw her swelling with her first baby bump? *You can have kittens in the oven but that don't make 'em biscuits.* Jeesh."

Willy said he went to Harvard for a semester, in engineering, he liked to build things, dropped out. Came west and built houses, then cabinets, bought a small farm here and supported it by building kitchens for rich people in Aspen.

"Custom stuff," he said. "How I got to doing that was I always loved horses. Wanted to be a cowboy all my life. Grew up in Sandwich, New Hampshire, reading those Louis L'Amour books. You know them? About the Sacketts and all? And I loved boats. Went out with some of my buddies and their families in the summer. I liked small sailing boats. How they were built, how everything fit together tight like a puzzle, a place for everything."

He laughed. Took a can of Red Seal chew out of his vest pocket and pinched a sizable dip, tucked it up under his upper lip, held it to me.

"Thanks." I waved it away.

"That was gonna make life difficult, huh? Horses, mountains, cowboys and yachts. Never did make anything easy for myself I've come to find out."

He spat on the road, glanced to the mare who was finally eating. It was nice to stand there in the deep afternoon shade, lean against a truck, let things settle. I could hear the creek below and a deerfly buzzed around us. I didn't mind.

"I was a good woodworker," he said. "Like my father, and I started out retrofitting big horse trailers, turning the forward end into living quarters, all finished wood, just like the cabin of a boat. Cherry, teak, walnut. Rich people were impressed. Figured I was house broke, I guess. Invited me in for a beer. Started asking could I make their kitchens like the inside of a yacht, too. There's a dozen breakfast nooks over on the Roaring Fork with chart tables and dedicated weather radios I shit you not. So you can pretend you're drinking coffee on your sloop. You couldn't make up the shit I've seen."

"Weather radios?"

"Yup. And VHF type radios, mounted overhead like in the nav station of a yacht, with mics on pigtail cords they unhook and call like the pool deck or the guesthouse or whatever. Everybody a captain in their own dream. Long as they pay me."

He spat. We watched the mare.

"I'd like to see your paintings sometime," he said. "Won't hurt my feelings if that's not something you do."

"You come over any time," I said.

Willy watched the little mare shaking the feed bag for the last oats, raising her nose.

"Why don't I take her for a while? Till you get set up. I got an empty stall, we'll throw some hay down, let her heal up, calm down. Don't want her getting excited and hauling the mail into a bunch of barbed wire. I got a bunch of horses, and I feed every day anyway. And you can sort it out with the outfitter. He'll have to give you her papers or the brand inspector will be climbing your backside. Nobody wants the good Inspector Madriaga in their face."

"Dell," I said. "His name is Dell. The outfitter."

Willy's eyes went blank. His face got stony. He didn't look at me.

"Don't know him," he said.

When it came time Willy talked to the mare and stroked her neck and she followed him up and into the trailer like a heeling dog. Go figure.

■

I can't get it out of me. My head. The heat of it in my blood.

The picture of the man swinging the club. The man in the picture in my head much bigger than the little horse. The man swinging with a hatred, to kill or not he doesn't care.

■

I call Sofia tell her not to come tomorrow. I take the *Ocean* off the easel. The bearded man swimming happily with his fishing rod through an ocean of women, that seems like a different man than me. The swirling women, the fish, the glad waters, they are in another universe than the one I am in now.

I think of *Guernica*, the painting. The knife in the horse. A story I read once by one of the Russians, maybe Chekhov, a man beating a horse. How seeing it happen is so much worse. A big man wreaking his anger on a tied horse who cannot even beg.

II

The door of my bedroom opens onto the ramada. The clap of the screen door behind me and a nightjar, startled, flutters out of the little arroyo that feeds the pond. Flutters without sound into the light from the window and on into the dark. Love those birds. They fly up off the dirt roads at night through the beam of the headlights, fly up from where they are roosting in the heat of the ground, a muffled rising like a giant moth, softer.

I light a cheroot and smoke, listen to the burble of water falling through the crease. I was so rattled tonight. Didn't eat. I followed Willy into his yard and helped him bed down the mare. She seemed to know. Willy handled her with such a sureness, so gentle, she seemed to know that this two legged at least would not beat her to death, probably.

We cut the strings on two bales of musty hay and spread it on the floor of the box stall, gave her grain in a bucket and water in the cut round of an old tractor tire. Willy dabbed her cuts with a salve like auto grease and we left her to sniff out her new circumstances. Whoever the fucker Dell was, I didn't give a shit if he signed over her papers or not, there was no way I was going to give her back. It was the one thing I knew, maybe the only one. I also decided I would give Willy a painting. Not sure of what, but the other thing I knew was that Stephen Lily would never hear about it and that I would know exactly what to paint when I got to it.

Now I smoke and breathe trying to shake off the fight. Cloudy tonight like a lid, down over the top of Lamborn. Smell of dampness. The rain that didn't fall this afternoon is gathering up there. Maybe tonight. Maybe the sweep and drum of it on the metal roof, a sound so loud and whelming and sweet it turns the bed into a little boat and thoughts into a wind that blows on northward. What they should do in psych wards to calm everybody down: build a steel roof over the beds and wash it with hoses, and pump in the smell of wet sage.

I had pulled down one of Pete's poetry books tonight, the collected T. S. Eliot I've been reading, and opened again to the *Four Quartets*.

Time present and time past
Are both perhaps present in time future,
And time future contained in time past.
If all time is eternally present
All time is unredeemable.

I read the lines and I put the book down open on the counter. If that were true about time. Then. Then we could be together again, could be now. It *was* redeemable. I couldn't follow the logic, he was saying it wasn't, but it was somehow comforting anyway. Can't explain it. My daughter was not gone, not completely ever. Nor Cristine, her mother. We were held somehow in our circle and would be always. The river flowed around us.

It didn't feel that way. Not really. It felt like what? A hollow bell. A bell that poured sound like water, the sound of our three lives together, but when you went to look in there was nothing.

Less than a year after Alce went and Cristine left, I remarried; trying to fill the bell, I guess. It didn't last long.

I divorced Maggie just over a year and a half ago, part of the reason I moved up here. She was a wholesome Minnesota redhead who had once been a Playboy bunny, very by the book in all things. We got along, moved back to Taos together, and I wondered fifty times a week why I married her. Like when I came back from fishing and found my studio cleaned up, the canvases in progress set in order along one wall according to her estimate of their chronology, my paints, which tubes I leave scattered over a giant walnut table we inherited with the house, all laid in a row according to the Koala Paints color chart. The chart she left square on the table also in case I needed refreshing.

Coming to the Valley and living by myself for the first time in two decades, and letting the ache for a woman settle on my memories like a fine mist, greening them too, I realized that I hadn't loved Maggie, not once.

Isn't that strange? To be able to feel so much tenderness for a person, and I did, and powerful attraction, sometimes, and yet feel no love. It seems cruel, almost monstrous. I mean I can love a bug. I have watched a spider weaving her web in the evening, in the young alder branches along the river, and I have loved her. Truly. Or a small moth trying to beat her way off the water of a dark pool, her soaked wings stuck to the surface as if by glue. And gently slid a leaf beneath her and lifted her to the ground, praying that her wings would dry without damage. I've done that. And yet I could not love my wife. Not that wife. As many knitted wool hats and back rubs later.

This is one of the things I ponder when I think about stuff, which I try not to do too much.

The other is how I could have loved Cristine so fiercely, who was such a world champion bitch, who even came after me once with a kitchen knife.

This was supposed to be a time of peace. Not a Holding Pattern—a Gathering Period.

Well, I pretty much fucked that up this afternoon.

It was supposed to be a time for having both feet on the ground and drawing breath. That's what Irmina my fortune-teller–healer friend in Tesuque told me before I came up here. She said: "Jim, in every life there are seasons. You are a planet you know."

"I am?"

She has black, almost violet eyes, not so serious, full of lights and humor. Of course I loved her. I really loved her. Anyone who looks like she does and puts her hand on your knee and heals it from a tweaky soreness you've had forever, that's a person to adore.

She lived in a small adobe house shaded by one old willow and a few piñons in the middle of miles of rabbitbrush and mesquite. She had lost her husband to a car wreck very young. We had been lovers off and on for many years, before Cristine, and were both wise enough to know that our limit was a day and a half. Then she got breast cancer and had a mastectomy and I moved in with her for almost a year, to take care of her while she went through the treatments. We remained close, and after Alce died and Cristine left, we saw each other sporadically and it was always like coming home and we always kept it short. She was the one to teach me that this was not a bad thing, just a thing, something to honor that allowed a friendship to flower. It was a great lesson, one I have used in every kind of relationship since.

"You are a planet and you have a magnetic resonance," she said, "and spin, and gravity. You have an atmosphere and a hot core. You do. I've told you that. Others have a core that is cooling. You have seasons and tides and one or two moons who will circle you for life."

"I do?"

"Give me your hands."

She held my big rough hands, hands I have always thought of as awkward—I'm missing half the right ring finger and the left hand is covered in scars—she held them in her round little ones, very warm, and squeezed them.

"You can't run all the time. You can't create all the time. You can't always swim in an ocean of women."

"I can't?"

When she said that, my eyes got wet, I don't know why. The way she was holding me and looking at me so steady and warm.

"You can breathe. Sometimes just breathe. Go ahead."

I breathed.

"You are holding Alce so tight. That's okay. How many years has it been?"

"I don't know. Three."

"It's not possible to hold that much pain."

Then there was a silence, and then she said, "Jim, even the earth rests. The moon swims up, thin as grass, and the stars, and you can see every one. It is a much quieter song."

She had this way of talking in pictures which I also loved.

"You rest now. Rest for longer than you are used to resting. Make a stillness around you, a field of peace. Your best work, the best time of your life will grow out of this peace. And don't worry, compa, you will be rowdy and out of control again. You will throw off every kind of light. You can't help yourself."

She leaned forward and kissed me, warm and lingering, and my rowdy aurora borealis self was like Fuck the field of peace, I want to bed Irmina right now, and then she pushed her little hands against my big shoulders and said, "Go now." Smile. "Next time."

And I thought, How long do you need between times to make one Next? Like could I drive out to the county highway and turn around and come back?

That was just over six months ago. I had been trying really hard to do what she said, until today.

After Willy and I had gotten the mare settled earlier this afternoon I drove back down to town and stopped at Bob's gas station. The time was beer-thirty, just after closing, and he was sitting on the torn couch on one side of the front office with a twelve-pack of Bud Light, what else. A fat old redneck in suspenders with three days of grizzled beard was on one of the metal chairs—the man stood when I pushed open the door, stretched, crumpled his can in a ham fist and tossed it perfectly into the corner trash can with a neat ring of steel, said to Bob,

"Keep the dirty side down." Nodded to me once and went out the door.

"Do I look scary?" I said. "Scared him away?"

"You don't look that good to tell you the truth." Bob pried a can out of the torn box and held it out.

"No thanks."

He cracked it, took a long swallow.

"I forget you're on the wagon. I should do." Smiled. "Never happen."

I sat on the vacated metal chair, still warm from the man's big butt.

"You see a ghost or just didn't catch any fish? I saw you go by. You were driving a little too fast so I knew you were going fishing."

Being in Bob's front office always settles me. Something about—I don't know what. Always having enough time for whatever needs doing. Taking it just as it comes: everything's fucked up, might as well meet it halfway and see what happens, that was Bob's approach. And laugh about it if possible.

I said, "I went up the Sulphur. You know the second pullout, by that flat where people camp?"

He nodded, drank. He was watching me and his face was serious, like it rarely is. Could see I was somehow shaken, I guess.

"Somebody was setting up some wall tents, had the road blocked with a horse trailer."

Bob's new beer was already done. He crumpled the can, set it in a fruit box to the side of the couch.

"You met Dellwood," he said. "Big guy with a gut? That could ruin anybody's day."

"Dellwood?"

"That's where Dell puts his bow camp every year. He's an outfitter out of Delta. Camps there and rides his hunters up into the basin every morning on horseback. Ask me, it's a back assward way to do it but that's Dell. He gets a lot of return hunters so they must like it. Kinda like cowboy camp. For folks from Alabama."

The compressor rattled. Bob cracked another beer.

"He doesn't do too bad on bulls neither. I think he's got salt licks but I can't prove it. I gather you traded words."

"How—"

"You got blood on your shirt."

"Huh."

I told him. The whole thing. The horse, the fight, Willy.

"You knocked Stinky into the road? Opening the door? Well shit. Goddamn, Jim." He couldn't contain his laugh.

"Then you took Fats into the ditch? Pretty good for an artiste. God-damn." Shook his head. Pried a tin of Skoal out of his breast pocket with one finger, took a dip that would make me faint. Offered it. This time I took a pinch.

"He won't forget you, Dell. He's a mean SOB."

"I won't forget him."

"Yeah, I can see."

Spat. Handed me the cup.

"He's a different cat. Last fall I found one of his horses lying down by the creek. Curled up like a dog. Whimpered like a baby when I came up. Like I was gonna hurt her. Saddest goddamn thing I ever saw."

"Ouch."

"His hunters think he's John F. Wayne I guess. He can spin a story that's one thing. And they get their elk. So."

He spat.

"Are they poaching up there? Who knows? If they are, they get the animals out at night. And he sure as shit is not easy on his stock. Half his horses are so broke down at the end of the season he ships the whole bunch down to his brother in Arizona where he sells the used up ones to the killers, is what I heard. Guess they make more money that way than feeding them right and working them to what they can handle."

He spat. "One way of doing it, I guess. Not the right way."

The compressor rattled, hissed. A truck rolled through the pumps, dinged the loud bell, a driver in a baseball cap leaned forward in his seat, waved, rolled on through.

"Alright," I said. Stood. "I'll let you go."

"You don't gotta run off. Soon as you do I gotta go move cows."

I grinned. Bob had about four jobs when I stopped counting. In another week he'd start driving a school bus.

"Bob?"

"Yeah?"

"What's his last name?"

"Dell? Siminoe."

"Thanks."

"Be good."

Bob probably reading my mind. Be good. Be good.

█

I stood on the ramada and tried to shake off the pressure of Dell's body pressing me into the cold wet of the ditch, the sound of his grunt. I smoked the cigar down to the root, crushed it on a flagstone, lit another. The smell of rain.

What I'd noticed was that here, in the windshadow of the mountain, it often smelled like rain. It might be raining up on the ridge, I might see the veils and rags of rain hanging down out of the scudding clouds, I might see shrouds of rain hauled over the country the way a fishing boat might drag a net, but—no rain here. A spatter, maybe, then nothing. Willy told me when I first moved in that it was like living in a strip bar. So close, looks so good and you never get laid.

Virga. That's what it was called. Alce told me that once. Came home from school one day and told me. Rain that falls and never hits the ground.

"C'mon I'll show you," she said.

I told her we might as well go fishing while we were at it. It was the first afternoon she ever caught a fish, I don't know how old she was. Little. She was small for her age. She pointed up at the veils over the west rim, the water in the pool smooth, without a drop.

"Virga!"

I gave her a thumbs-up and threw a caddis for her and let it drift and gave her the rod and as soon as she touched it the trout hit and almost pulled it out of her small hands. *Oh God! Oh God,* I yelled. *Way to go! Keep the tip up! Like that! Yeah!* She was holding the rod straight up with all her strength and it was all she could do and she was in hysterics, laughing, as much from shock as anything. Her hair was blowing across her face and the jerking rod was shaking the counterweight of her body and the fish was whizzing out the line. I wanted her to catch it herself, I was almost as panicked as she was, I had an idea. *Run backwards!* I yelled. *Try and hold around the line, yeah like that, slow it down, go! Run up the bank!* I was awed that she could even shift her grip. She ran. Half backwards, half sideways, trying to hold the rod high like a broadsword. Ran up into the dried stalks of mullein the willows and the fish came with her up onto the rocks and was flopping, thwacking the stones, a big brown, God, big. She dropped the rod and ran like a puma down over the stones and pounced. Both hands. The trout got away from her and she chased it, bent double, trying to wrangle it, landing on it again with both hands, it squirted out like a watermelon seed, slipped over the rocks, she was after it, I was laughing. Yelling and laughing. She got to it and grasped it and then fell on it, covering it with her whole body like a punt returner covering the ball, screaming with glee, laughing and crying too. I reached under her, and I picked up the heavy fish and thwacked it on a rock and it was finally still and the colors dulled the way they do and then she burst into tears. Her print dress stained with fish slime and algae and blood. She was inconsolable. Not for her clothes, for the fish. All the way home I held her in one arm as I drove and told her about the spirit of the trout, how he was probably swimming now among the stars and would be happy to feed her and her mother and father tonight and how proud I was of her, and I was surprised when a few days later she wanted to go out with me again, and that's when I bought her a seven-and-a-half-foot four weight and began to teach her to cast.

After she died I moved from Taos to Pilar, closer to the Rio Grande. Cristine wasn't coming. She had her own history there and she was no way going back. She had a bodywork business going, massage and pressure point, a good trade among rich steady clients who appreciated her strong capable technique and her no bullshit attitude. One Silicon Valley transplant tried to paw her breasts once and she told him politely that was not part of the service so he tried again and she squeezed his balls so hard through the towel he screamed. She was laughing when she told me. If I could get Cristine laughing I was probably good for at least twenty-four hours.

Anyway by then it was just the two of us and we needed a lot of space, from each other.

Back then I went fishing. Every day. Alce was suddenly gone and I didn't know what else to do. I fished the dawn and I fished the evening. Down in the canyon of the Lower Box. Down under the rushing drop where Pueblo Creek comes in. Down in the yellowing leaves of the cottonwoods, the box elders. Yellowing then falling leaves. Then the nights when my fingers got numb, and toes. The October cold numbing more than my hands. I cast way across the river and let the fly tumble down the edges of the far pools, pulling line off the clicking reel as fast as I could. So much line out, so much current it's heavy against the rod, my arm, stop the line, let the fly swing across the current to the middle of the river. And— Bang! They hit.

They were twenty, thirty yards downstream and mad and full of autumn vigor, sleek and fat with summer bugs, with crawdads, frogs, with colder water, and then I had to fight them against the current all the way back up, thigh deep in the dark water, sucking on the stub of cigar, not sure if it's even lit, three stars, sweet smell of fallen leaves, raising the rod tip against all the weight trying to feel the limit, the limit of the tippet and the knots, the break-ing point, then dropping the rod fast and stripping in the sudden slack, foot by foot, and the trout, if he was big, suddenly deciding too that that's enough and putting on the jets, get the hell away from here and running *zing*, every foot I'd just fought for gone in a flash in the willed charge of a fast-tiring trout. Running with my line. The song of the reel. I loved this.

I would be moving in the cold of the settling evening, the few stars in the chasm overhead, the only way I could still myself at all: move.

The only time I could forget myself, forget Alce. Lost to anything but fighting the fish. And if I got him in finally and he had fought and fought and if he was beautiful which he always was I reached down and cradled him in the current with one hand and with one twist of the other slipped the hook out of his lip and cradled him some more. Cradled and watched him idling there, tail slowly finning while he caught his breath and strength. Like me, I thought. Idling, barely able to breathe. And then a wriggle and slip against my palm and he was gone, lost among the green shadows of the stones and I said Thanks. Thanks for letting me live another evening.

I drank sometimes. I had quit maybe two years, pretty much, off and on, but sometimes I went to the Boxcar and sat at the bar, sometimes the same stool where I had turned and shot Lauder Simms, maybe wishing the bastard was there again, insinuating the unspeakable things he wanted to do to my daughter. Wishing that I could shoot him again and relive a year in Santa Fe State, so Alce would still be here. I drank, drank steady like it was a job and Johnny nodded to Nacho and Nacho drove me home. More than once he carried me inside and laid me down on the couch and I remember him whispering *Dios, Jim, He is looking over you, you don't need to join your daughter, not yet compa.* This from a cousin of Cristine's who had spent more time inside Santa Fe than he had out, who *ran* the cell block when he was there and saved my life just by being incarcerated same time as me. God is looking over you. I remember it like it was whispered by an angel. And it didn't feel like that, not one bit. Like anything else was looking over me, like some kind of bad weather.

That engine. Grief is an engine. Feels like that. It does not fade, what they say, with time. Sometimes it accelerates. I was accelerating. I could feel it, the g-force pressing my chest. I wrecked my truck. Definitely a one car accident, nobody else to blame. Me and a rock. But somehow I was up to date on the insurance—because I had paid it all in a lump sum that spring, sometimes I did that after I sold a painting—didn't even know if I had insurance but I did, and the adjuster knew my work, had seen it in an airline magazine, a story about the art scene in Taos, and it turned out he had lost a son at four to a heart defect and he rigged it so the truck was covered, total loss, and I got a new one, and I knew that I would wreck that too, knew it like I knew winter would come and I didn't care, and I drank and then one morning the door shoved open and in walked Irmina carrying an overnight bag and a string of habaneras and an unplucked chicken carcass I shit you not and it was the only time since I'd left her house that we ever stayed together more than a few days.

She stayed for three months. She rescued me. She made me go to AA meetings. She drove me and sat next to me at the open groups. She cooked me food so spicy every meal was some kind of battle. She made love to me again and again until I was sore and gasping like one of those trout, and then she cradled me like a trout and let me catch my breath and then she let me go into sleep.

This is how I healed. Or didn't. One evening I took her down to the river. We turned off the highway and rattled slowly up the gravel road and into the heart of the canyon. The walls closed in above us, the high blue of the sky deeper, deep and dark like a river is deep. The highest rock at the rim was a strip of fire, holding the last long sun. The old gorge was a vessel and it was filling with shadow, slowly, and with wind. We drove upstream. We drove with the windows down and the wind came down against us bringing a night's cold and blowing the last rattling leaves off the cottonwoods. They blew into the river and floated slowly in the pools, pushed by the wrinkles of the wind, singly and in sad fleets. I pulled over when we got to the end of the road, where the creek poured in from above. Now we could see the first few stars above the walls, smell the smoke of some fisherman's fire, someone who had hiked up into my favorite stretch and was unwilling to leave with the thickening darkness. Got out. Tang of smoke and the sweet decay of leaves. I could smell my past.

These were the smells of a devotion and of a history and they carried the touch of my daughter. Her voice. The way she was when she came with me here.

"Did I tell you that she was a better fisherperson than me? Would have been?"

Irmina smiled at me in the dusk, breathed.

Alce was curious, down at water's edge faster than me, turning over smooth stones, looking for bugs, standing in the wind with her long dark hair blowing around her face and squinting at the hatch, the cloud of mayflies backlit like some blizzard, smiling like that, the pride of knowledge, knowing: that is a mayfly, maybe number 18, that is a stone fly, a gnat. Before I had even tied my shoes she would have decided on a strategy, what she would use and how she would fish it.

Was I speaking this to Irmina or talking to myself or thinking it? Didn't know.

Now next to Irmina I stood on the high bank and smelled the dusk and watched the white thresh of the rapid pouring over the rocks that spilled out of the mouth of the creek. The thrashing water, the rush like some pounding prayer. *Deliver me, Oh God, deliver me, not out of but into, further into what is here.* I felt Irmina's hand slip into mine and she was beside me, up against me but not leaning. Her hand was warm. We stood there. A pair of ducks angled fast out of a luminous sky, just shadows, veered hard last second and dropped into the long pool below. Their wakes silver on the dark water. Years of getting shot at. They waited until very last light and came in fast and turning.

"We fished here together, here most of all."

"But she stopped fishing?"

"Yes, the last year. Just after she turned fifteen she didn't fish at all."

"She got angry?"

"Unh huh. And I don't know why."

I knew. I think I knew it was because her mother and I were angry at each other. Alce wanted peace and she couldn't make it, tried, couldn't, got mad and surly. She got sick of hearing doors slam. How I blamed myself. Why she disappeared into that crowd, into the drugs, etc. Because I wasn't big enough to make peace with her mother.

Squeeze. Irmina squeezing my hand now, relaxing. Holding it, warm, almost hot in the chilling air.

She said, "She was a teenager. Every teenager has to do that somehow. It is how you become your own person. And every marriage has those times. You know. Jim?"

I watched the current, the tailwater rolling out of the bottom of the falls, white and fast and pushing through the little haystacking waves and quieting into the darker water of the pool, the smooth stretch where I could see the pair of ducks drifting, dark against the dark silverblue of the reflected sky. That luminous night that is not yet true night. Why couldn't we be like ducks? Make the decision to be together and be together forever without argument, flying wing to wing into and out of the seasons year after year. Drifting on some slow night current, muttering each to each.

"Jim?"

"Huh."

"You know. You have to let her be her own person. Before and now."

I stood and breathed. Grateful for the ice in the air. Frost tonight down here, down in the canyon, maybe already forming.

Her own person. I watched Alce in the dark. As if she were here. I saw her step down to the river and begin to cast. Letting out the line smoothly in longer and longer throws, the loop up high over her head and behind her growing longer, a graceful animal coiling and straightening, lengthening and lancing far downstream, right along the slackwater of the eddy line, fishing a streamer the way I would have. I watched her in the dark, fishing past when we could see as we did so often, the trout able to see the flies on the surface against the lighter sky, I heard us laughing and cursing as we stubbed and stumbled over the rocks of the bank when we had finally given up and were climbing back to the road.

Pop?

Huh?

I got a sixteen incher. A cutbow. I put him back.

You're fibbing.

She clambering behind me, poked me in the butt with the rim of her net.

Heard rock scrape as she stumbled.

Ow. I wish I had owl eyes. Or was just an owl. We could fly back to the truck.

Why would we need the truck then? I said. *We would just fly home.*

Carrying all this junk? The rod. We couldn't fly that far in our waders.

If we were owls we could, we wouldn't need rods, we could just— Nah.

What? What, Pop?

Owls don't fish do they? I don't think they like water much, only snow.

Miss Pettigrew told us that they can sit in a tree and hear mice in a field under a foot of snow. Those ones that turn white.

No shit?

Fifty cents.

Ouch. Shit.

A dollar.

Damn!

A dollar fifty. Pop, if you keep swearing you'll go broke.

Silence.

If we were osprey, Pop, we could fish and fly back to the truck and fly home because we wouldn't need any of this crap.

Climbing slowly. On a smoother trail now. Walking with some rhythm, she and I. The scuff of our wading boots, tick of the swinging nets, loud croak and squawk rising from the river below, a heron complaining.

Back to a dollar, you said crap.

Crap is not a bad word.

Are you the bad word dictionary now?

Silence. Knew she was nodding her head.

I painted that. The first and only good picture I made in the year after. She and I over that canyon, ospreys. Carrying our rods, the fish teeming below us.

I stood with Irmina and watched my daughter Alce fish into real dark. Past when we would have ever fished. Watched her fish until even her imagined shadow was swallowed by the night and the rush of water.

Good night beautiful. Fish on.

What got to me was the thought that maybe she did not want to fish on, into the full darkness alone. That she was tired and alone and cold but didn't know what else to do. That she couldn't stand for us to leave. That I couldn't bear.

Felt Irmina's hand again squeezing.

"She can go wherever she wants now. If she is here it is because love holds her here. Because she loves it."

"Okay," I said. The tears were streaming into my beard. We got back in the truck and drove home in silence. The next day Irmina left.

That was the other lesson Irmina taught. It is okay for people you love to leave. For them to come and go. She taught it to me over and over.

I stood on the ramada and smelled the rain that hadn't arrived and thought about the little horse. I prayed she could recover. She would never be the same, certainly. None of us ever are, the same. I lit another cheroot. Smoking seemed to lessen Dell's residual stench. I wished it would rain tonight. I felt what? Unmoored. Felt like I was just getting my feet. Like I had a friend, two, in town, had a good spot to fish mostly alone. I was just starting to work again, good work, which was anything I could get lost in. And then Steve called with his stupid commission, which meant climbing back into the truck and driving back to Santa Fe to paint something I didn't at all want to paint. Two things. Two little girls, I'm sure were nice enough, I mean how bratty and screwed up could they be in six short years? Even in the House of Pim. And then the horse. The horse happened. Dell Siminoe happened, all over the road, all over the creek where I had found a certain refuge, all over me like a scum.

Nothing ever happens just how you want it to.

III

Next morning Sofia came over. I had told her not to come. We'd left it I would call her if I needed a little more Double U O M A N in the picture but thought I had plenty, more than enough. I said I needed maybe a giant halibut to model for a day. I'm not a funny person, have long accepted that. I was just trying to enjoy my first cup of coffee in the Adirondack chair on the ramada, the first little stogie, I felt hungover—I wasn't—but groggy, edgy, and I heard Tops rumbling and coughing up the drive. Car door slam, counted to ten: front door flew in, could hear it hit the antique school desk where I drop my keys, heard a yell. *Hey! Where are you?*

"There you are! Smoking away your breakfast."

"How do you know I haven't already eaten a stack of pancakes? Were you raised in a barn?"

She pulled over the other chair, just scraped it over the rough rock, plopped down beside me. Tossed her curly hair off her face.

"You mean not knocking? I'm always hoping I'll catch you— what's that Latin—*in flagrante delicto*."

"With whom?"

"A muse. An angel maybe."

"You should knock." And I thought to myself: If I were in a better mood that would be my next painting. Me in the arms of a muse. A dangerous proposition. I mean getting that close to the one who brings the gifts.

She turned bodily in the chair and looked at me. Then prodded my calf with the toes of her sandaled foot. "You're serious today," she said. "What's the matter?"

I let out a breath, stubbed the cheroot on the stone. "I got in a fight. Sort of."

"Yeah? Like the Jim of old? The violent felon I've heard about?"

"Kind of."

"Sorry. I don't mean to joke. If you got in a fight you must have been really mad."

"I guess. I was blind. The way you get."

She shook her head.

"Everything goes dark at the edges. Kind of tunnels down to the target. A good fighter, a real brawler has to open up that vision. Use the anger but open up the field of view and stay relaxed. My friend Nacho used to tell me that. Don't just charge in swinging like a crazed bull, Jesus, compa, you are going to get yourself killed. That was never me. I was the one rolling around in the spit on the floor."

"Wow."

"That's what happened yesterday."

"It did? Jeez."

I told her. The whole thing: Dell beating the mare, the rolling wet in the ditch, bloodying Dell's nose, my talk with Bob. I told her and we watched a harrier, a big hawk fluttering low over the sage, beating its wings over a bush, lift then glide, scaring up the mice, methodically hunting.

When I was done she was looking at the mountain. A flash of blue and four small birds tore by the edge of the porch and down past the pond. Mountain bluebirds. Early to be here, maybe they just stayed all summer. When I was done I lit another cheroot. She didn't say anything.

"Don't you want to kill the bastard," she said at last.

"It had occurred to me. Mostly I just want to get his stench out of my nose."

"No kidding. Fuck. I'm not even a violent felon and I want to tie him to a post and shoot him. How do people even get like that? Like a stain."

We sat side by side, watched the big hawk. It had a white rump that flashed as it rose. A cool morning, the sky over the mountains washed clean. Something touched my arm below the rolled up sleeve. Her hand. Her small fingers. Brushed the skin lightly and lay over my forearm. Don't know why it surprised me. I watched them, her fingers, the way I had just been watching the bird, happy to see them there, a little awed.

Her fingers migrated down toward my hand, rested on a scab of dried green paint, picked at it, moved on, covered my paint spackled knuckles, one finger sliding down over the stub end of my half finger. Resting there a second, pushing on the end.

Slipping to the side, onto my thigh. I was wearing baggy khaki shorts, enjoying the chill, and her warm fingers wriggled under the hem and her touch on my bare thigh raised instant goose-bumps. We were both watching the transit of her hand as if it were another animal. She stopped, let it rest and curl on top of my leg.

"You see me naked all the time," she said. "Does that do anything for you?"

I lay the half cheroot down across a lip of flagstone for later. She was very pretty. Head tipped downward, quarter profile. The length of her eyelashes. Maybe the prettiest angle for a human head, a woman.

"Yes."

"What?"

Didn't answer.

"What?"

"Sometimes I get— When you were a mermaid. Arching back-wards and all."

"You get a boner." She lifted her head and smiled at me, open, guileless, her eyes suddenly as faceted and sparkly as gems.

I nodded.

"You have a boyfriend," I said lamely.

She pursed and twisted her soft lips, like: That is really stupid.

"Dugar is a certified airhead. The official documents just arrived. He wants to go live with sea cows or whatever they are. Plus, I have suspected for a while that he's been banging the hippy girl from the orchard and now I know. I told him we were coasting, just coasting, no more gas. He asked me if he could use that in a poem."

Her hand stirred, woke up. Crept stealthily up under the loose leg of the shorts, worked inward, found me. I don't wear underwear unless it's like some formal event.

My dick was as surprised as I was. Kind of embarrassed. She brushed it with the curled backs of her fingers then pounced. Squeezed and tapped. Amazing how fast an embarrassed cock, one with ethics, social sensibilities and all sorts of reasons to just stay home, amazing how fast it can forget everything and lunge for the prize at a hundred miles an hour. Must be how a vener-able, canny trout feels when it triggers on an elk hair caddis— somewhere in its pea brain it knows, *knows*, this is probably not a good idea, but Fuck it. *Bang!* Also, she was—what? Ten years older than Alce would be, but still, she was young. I shuddered. She— It wasn't right. Any of it.

"Uhh," I said.

"I want you to see me naked. No painting. A person seeing another person."

"Uhh," I said. "I haven't had much luck lately."

"You don't need luck, dummy. I just want you to look at me. C'mere."

She gave the head one more friendly squeeze and took my hand and led me through the screen door into the bedroom.

▪

Context is funny. How things hit you. Like on one planet there is gravity and you are walking along, then there is no gravity and you are airborne, sort of flying in slow parabolic leaps. I had seen Sofia undress probably a dozen times. Had seen her stretch out naked. Had paid attention to the curves and the colors and living heat of her body, the potential for movement there, and rhythm, even when she was very still. She was never still. Even immobile she had the sprung tautness, the restrained leap of a deer, one at dusk who lifts her head from the grass and is—listening. For threat I suppose.

With Sofia it was as if her body were listening, but it was for some inner laughter. That's how it seemed when I painted her. That thing where color and form become almost like a music, something rhythmic and flowing, and somewhere in there I lose myself. When I am really painting, when I am painting well. I lose myself and may not wake up for hours, for most of a day. What I loved was how Sofia understood that and gently took her leave. And in that, when I was really painting and in it, and if she was modeling for me, I would see her and not see her. I would not see her as a young woman, naked, open, waiting for me to make love to her. I would not see her as a nude girl coyly, just barely covering, enticing the next move in the game. It was not a game, ever, it was completely, wonderfully serious, and it was never about sex. The boner thing was when I needed a break, got hungry, snapped out of it.

As she tugged me into the bedroom the screen door clapped behind me. I thought: Punctuation. A period on the last long paragraph of my life.

"You look like you are being led to slaughter," she said.

She turned and pulled off her thin jersey blouse, unclipped the bra from the front and loosed her generous breasts. Wriggled out of her cutoff shorts, let them fall. Pushed down on the elastic of her little thong and worked it down to her knees where it relinquished itself also to the floor. She smiled up at me, as open and guileless as before. Her eyes about five different colors, blues, grays, greens, warm browns. Then she took my hands as she had before, hers small and warm and assured, and she placed them open on her collarbones, still smiling, and stood straight and still and closed her eyes. Something about that gesture. So simple, so joyful, so trusting. I felt a surge of something simple and clean, something like happiness. Felt myself rouse and reach with a sympathetic attention. I was up against her, my dick was touching her belly and she reached and pushed it down so that it was against her, her crack, sort of sprung against it, and I could feel the brush of her curly hair, the pressure where she clamped me there. And we stood. And we looked at each other and laughed. And my hands moved along her collarbones, the delicate bird-like architecture. And down over her breasts and back up to her slender neck, the perfect ears. Over her strong shoulders. And her hands down over my hips, around to the front, stroking and pressing me into her, up against her. I lost myself again. But this time it was to a euphoria with a different gravity. I think I was laughing. She pulled me toward the bed and fell backward and suddenly all the angles were right and she was moist and open and I was in her and it was that shock. The shock that never dulls. Of being inside another. And her laughter was overtaken by breath and we rocked together in a pure and simple delight. That's what I remember: the simplicity, the lightness.

How often is anything that simple?

We lay in the coolness from the open door. I could hear the burble of the water running through cattails down into the pond. A cricket warming to the morning on the ramada. Her head was in the crook of my arm and I thought she might be asleep. This much peace vouchsafed to any one man. The luck of it. That's what I thought. Drifting in it. And as I drifted I was open and careless in my thoughts and I bumped up against something barnacle sharp and ugly. Dellwood Siminoe, swinging the club against the little mare like she was a piñata. The candy spilling, and I knew the candy for him was the pain and terror of the other. Clotted and dribbling, then pouring onto the road in a shiny gush. How many terrified horses like that? Enough to make a business of shipping those broken to Arizona. What Bob told me.

Fuck it. I pushed it away. Pushed my nose into the warm mass of Sofia's dark hair, breathed it, pushed everything else away.

I made omelets and we shared a trout, fried in butter with a little salt and pepper, lemon. Made another pot of coffee. Sat on the ramada.

She said, "I thought of doing that a few times." She smiled, her hand curled on my thigh. "Doing *you*."

"Really? When?"

"When you were painting me."

"Workplace harassment."

"I know, that's why I didn't. I knew on some level it would have made you mad. I almost didn't care."

We made love again. This time it was me who asked. Lying there again, on the bed, this time with heat, almost an oven heat, coming through the screen, and sweat instead of tears, I wondered how simple we really are. That we can do the same things again and again and again and find them interesting, even fascinating, and seek the repetition with a hunger as avid. How fishing was like that, and painting. And this time as we lay quiet and listening, our pulses coming through now and then like the drumming of a distant village, this time I kept the boat of my thoughts sailing along from one tack to the next on a course I could control.

Somehow the day passed like that. We made more food, went for a walk to the far pond, I read her the lines from the *Four Quartets* I had copied down and stuck into the breast pocket of my Carhartt barn coat:

> You are not here to verify,
> Instruct yourself, or inform curiosity
> Or carry report. You are here to kneel
> Where prayer has been valid.

I don't know, it made me feel better. Another way of saying, Keep it simple. You don't even have to pray, just kneel where there's prayer and I'm beginning to think there is prayer everywhere. I had written down another bunch of lines and tucked them in there, too—about how crazy hard is the journey of getting to where you have never been. That too rang bells for me in this new place, trying to paint something good. Sofia's cell phone buzzed a few times and she finally picked it up and I heard her telling Dugar she wouldn't be coming home for a couple of days, he could move in with that hippy chick from the orchard he'd been banging for who knew how long, she didn't give a shit, and I stared at her, checking the checklist, was any of that okay with me, I mean she hadn't said she was staying *here*, had she? But come on Jim, this is not your first rodeo, you know exactly where she's staying tonight, but she hadn't telegraphed or acted in any way like she wanted anything more than this, not one inch past what I could give freely. Right? Why don't you try trusting her for a second?

She rummaged through the fridge, the cabinets, began putting together a spaghetti dinner. Said her mother was half Italian. I took a small pre-stretched canvas from the stack against the wall, about two by three, and propped it on the empty easel. Picked up a piece of fiberboard and taped a flipped for sale sign over it and squeezed out turquoise, cobalt violet, white, a stiff white close to the lead white I can't get anymore. Yellow. I wanted cool yellow. My favorite lemon yellow was used up, so I put out cadmium yellow light, which is not as sharp or cold. Good for now, maybe better. Terre verte, cobalt blue. Joyful colors.

While she chopped garlic and heirloom tomatoes, while she hummed and sang, I painted a house. A small adobe house on an ochre hill, like this one, like mine. I painted a blue pond and sailing glad clouds, and I mixed the terre verte with cobalt violet and tinted it in half with the white to make the delicate undersides of the cumulus. I began to feel that gladness that can only come when I paint. I painted a crane-like bird hunched at the edge of the pond fishing. Then I painted a man in the garden, also hunched, leaning to a shovel digging. An intensity in the man. A garden? Yes. No. The dirt he threw grew into a pile. As I painted, I myself grew alarmed. The pile grew and grew, the man dug, until the hole could only be of a certain size, could only be one thing. I squeezed a tube of Mars black onto the palette and I painted birds: one two three four large night colored birds. Like that Carl Sandburg poem I had read the other day *They have been swimming in midnights of coal mines somewhere.* Except they were not crows. They were bigger, they were ravens, but big as vultures. Four in a line looking down off the roof at a man digging a grave. A man like me.

I painted fast. Sometimes I painted so fast I did not see how it could be done. If I happened to look at a clock. Sometimes a big painting with a lot of elements in four, five hours. Or one. Or half. Sofia was humming, I could hear the bubble of boiling water. Smell sautéed onion, garlic, simmered tomatoes. In the time it took her to make dinner.

We had no Italian bread, she had popped two slices of Sara Lee into the toaster. Could smell that too. Out the open double doors the mountain was catching the full brunt of the lowering sun. Every outcrop and rockslide, the quilt of the forests: spruce and aspen, juniper, oak, lit to sharper detail and warmed by the honeyed light. Sharpened and softened at the same time. One reason I could spend so much time alone up here, happily: could sit and absorb the two hours before dark every evening as if it were a pageant.

But the picture on the easel. Somehow it spawned itself and somehow it felt, what?

I felt guilty. Like the man digging the grave. I got myself, the bulk of me, between the painting and Sofia behind the long counter. As if I could cover it. She glanced up now and then as she worked and she seemed happy—happy that she was cooking, happy that I was painting, happy that it was a lovely evening and that we were doing whatever we were doing, happy maybe that it wasn't at all defined. She did not seem to be focusing on the painting in particular when she looked, on the details, maybe it was a little too far away. It was a landscape with a figure, like so many. I stepped to the canvas and quickly lifted and flipped it and leaned it against the wall frame out, against a large piece of fiberboard I tore up for palettes. Leaned it at enough of an angle that the paint wouldn't smear. And straightened.

"Smells good," I said a little too loud, a little too hearty. Her head came up sharply and she studied me for a second, curious, then went back to laying out plates. I went onto the ramada, lit up. What the hell was going on with me? I had never hidden a painting ever. A bug, a freight train, a trout, they had all seemed born more out of themselves than me, they deserved the simple respect of being. I could not remember hiding a painting from anyone, much less myself. Even the nudes that had so pricked Maggie. Because that's what it felt like—hiding. I had turned the picture's face to the wall so fast as much to hide its guilty expression from my own eyes. Strange. That's one thing, I murmured. One thing we are learning to be sure of: life does not get less strange.

"*Ding ding!*" she called happily. "Ding a ling. Pronta!"

"Great," I called. I called Great and didn't feel so good.

Watch it brother, I said to myself, and set the cheroot carefully on the arm of one of the Adirondack chairs. Watch yourself. Start lying this early and. It can't be good.

■

We hit the hay early, soon after full dark, must have been close to nine, and I asked her to rub my shoulders, and she did, and we fell asleep curled around each other. Me around her, looking out the screen door to the broad shadow of the mountain. She slept, the even breathing, deep, the twitches, sighs. A content sleep I envied. I could not. I lay awake, elbow against her hip and hand cupped over her breast. The weight of it. I lay awake and watched the heat lightning. Wondered what good would come of it. Had found a model I could really work with and now look: complication. Well. It worked for Wyeth and Helga, for decades, wasn't it? Had never worked for me. I never needed a subject that badly. Fuck, Jim, way to go.

I watched the heat lightning and small fleets of clouds sail over the mountain ridge, lit from underneath, pale hulls and dark in the rigging. The lightning shimmered and boomed without sound, a far off battle. Heat lightning is a funny name. I guess because it comes this time of year, in the heaviest, sultry nights. But the glimmers seemed cold, part of the same cold distance as planets and stars.

Few stars tonight, just noticed. And then a minute later I saw why: as I watched the clouds scudding over the mountain's shoulder, a bright white light flashed on the eastern ridge. Like hunters playing with a powerful spotlight up there. It wasn't a spotlight, it was the moon. It flashed and then domed and it backlit perfectly the trees on the ridgeline, made of them a finely drawn fringe. I sucked in a breath. I hadn't seen this, not since I'd been here. It rose, the moon, so fast it seemed to lift off like a big bright bird. Like a great egret rising out of the cattails, too big too white too slow. Too pure. The moon in that instant brought the mountain close, close enough it seemed I could reach out and touch the bristle of trees.

The same moon was shining down on Santa Fe, on Irmina with her losses, who harbored nothing it seemed but compassion, on Steve, on whatever deals were hatching like red birds in his head. On the Box of the Rio Grande where the river was threshing pale and loud over the big drops, in the long pool where I had spread Alce's ashes. On the bends of the little Sulphur where I had found some peace in the past weeks. On bow hunting camps and bronze grizzly bears.

I lay watching the moon detach and distance itself from our troubled topography, and sail, it seemed, with some relief into the absences of space.

The trout were probably wide awake like me tonight, finning the current at the edge of the riffles, feeding on the bugs haplessly lit.

That is where my heart went. To them. To the cool water. The unburdened sounds of water flowing over rock, smooth water over smooth rock, roiled into a rough edged rush and burble that was also somehow soothing. Under the moon the whitewater would be rips and tears in the darkness, the pools black, or maybe black with the bright moon reflected there, the trout lost to sight but looking up themselves into a bright firmament. I cannot name it but my heart felt like that. All those reversals, rough to smooth and back again, light erupting in the dark and subsiding back to a blind flow where sound and smell and cold were more important. Where touch was. The thing about night, about dark: touch is most important. And lying there against the heat of Sofia I could feel the stones underfoot, the press and cold of the current.

I, we, used to fish at night. Alce and I. Under a moon. We did well when we could rouse ourselves to do it. When we could be bothered to put on sweaters. There was something so magical about the two of us fishing a run together in the dark, barely visible to each other, throwing flies for fish we would never see until they leapt into the sere gaze of the moon.

I slipped out of bed. Slipped my arm from under Sofia's, kissed the back of her head, held the quilt in place as I moved out from under and felt the cold earth of the floor. Found jeans thrown over a rocker, the flannel shirt, dressed fast, stepped into clogs. Poured what was left of the morning's coffeepot cold into a travel mug and went quietly out the screen door. Night warm enough, end of summer, but with a chill scent of fall. How can it be both? Cold and warm, I don't know but it can. The five weight rod was in the back of the truck with the old felt soled boots, vest behind the seat, light waders over the side mirror where I had hung them yesterday. I felt between the front seats for a packet of Backwoods cigars, good, the foil pouch was fat, held four or five. I'd smoke them while I fished, one after another, and I looked forward to that as much as the fishing.

Don't remember much of the drive. Bumped over the railroad tracks at the edge of town. Turned along the length of the fruit packing shed. I remember glancing down Grand Ave, the short route out to the county highway, and that the digital bank clock read 11:32 and the town was dead. And I remember: straightening the wheel and continuing on, out toward the orchards. I shivered. I skirted the main street and instead went a mile further out of my way and took the black bridge over the river to the highway, took the windier, the prettier way around. Just wanted that certain quiet, I guess, that peace.

There was one house along the road there, before the bridge, a big house, the doctor's, and the rest was dark with orchards, and farms with long drives. The staccato tumps of the bridge a sudden drum-roll as the tires rolled over the planks, the sudden smell of water.

That smell always stirs me. I felt excited the way I always am before a session fishing, also angry, also a little scared. What was I scared of? I would never say.

In twenty minutes I turned off the highway and dropped down to the creek bottom where the lodge stood darkly, the reaching bear. Right there I turned off my lights. Because this is where the road turns to dirt and it gets beautiful, and there is the moon, and I like to navigate in natural light, acclimate eyes for fishing. Night vision. I also slowed, to make less rattle and rev, and I was careful not to touch the brakes, not to pulse the brake lights.

Because at night there is a comfort in moving darkly. In slipping through, shadow to shadow. Can't say why. Maybe because we were hunters, all of us. The way a cat moves in the shadows. Or a wolf. The instinctive safety in that. I know that when Alce and I went fishing at night I often did that: turned the lights off as we clattered along the river, eased off the gas. Maybe hoping to surprise a herd of bighorn or deer, or a great horned owl in the road.

I wanted a drink. How many days, months now? I thought counting days in AA was obsessive, but could see that it might have saved my life. Well.

The creek at night under the moon was just enough like the creek in daylight to be reassuring. There was the deadfall spruce that sieved the current with skeleton branches, churning a line of pale foam. There was the long pool above, a dark mirror of tree shadows and beacon moon. There were the gravel bars, chalky, shaped to the banks and swept into low moraines that divided the water. There the sky, softened as if by a thin fog of moonlight, filling the canyon. For a moment I forgot my preoccupation with the dark and drove up the road with that awe I felt before certain paintings in certain museums, the awe in which I disappeared.

There was a pullout I had come to use when I wanted to fish this stretch of creek, just a widening of the road, but tonight I turned off just before it. I swung right into a rutted opening of thick willows into a small clearing where people had camped. Tonight I parked here, hidden, and tonight I pulled on waders and boots quickly and shut the door carefully with a quiet click. The warm comfort in moving like a ghost, being part of the night. Tonight I took the already strung rod out of the truck bed and barely checked the two flies, a Stegner Killer on top, a shiny copper John on the bottom, I didn't really care. Pushed through the willowbrush holding the rod high over my head and out of the snagging branches like a brandished sword and stepped over the smooth stones and into the dark water with a relief and sigh. Stepped in up to my knees. The cold. Smelled woodsmoke trailing down from upstream with the current. Began to cast.

Time past and time present. Whatever kind of time ruled the earth receded into the night shadows. I cast and cast and walked carefully upstream, sometimes the slow current of the pools up to my waist, sometimes taking to the bank to get a better angle on a piece of slackwater, throwing into the fast funnels between rocks, the boulders bleached by the moon and marking the course of the creek upstream the way a scattered herd of humped and silent beasts might mark a twisting trail.

I followed them. Lost myself and followed them. Sometimes I saw the bushy little fly hit and drift, sometimes I lost it in a silvering of current. When I got a strike—sometimes I heard it first. In the calm places. A gulp. A blip, the double note, nose and tail. And the rod tip bent hard, the shiver. And then the old euphoria. I know I talked to myself, to the fish—*that's it, you're alright you're alright, come up come up, off of those rocks, careful careful, that's it*—to him and me the same. I loved this, and in the lost time I worked in a trout I forgot the preoccupation of the predator, with stealth, with melding into the night, forgot myself, which is maybe how a true predator disappears, I don't know.

Released them all easily, no deep swallowed hooks, no snags, fishing as well probably as I have ever fished in my life. I reached into a side pocket of the vest and pulled out the foil pouch, unrolled it and dug out a soft cheroot, the vanilla scent heady, and stuck it between my teeth, just sucked it. Content with that.

It must have been close to a mile. Around the third bend as I worked upstream I saw the firelight. It was thrown across the creek onto a backstop of shaggy trees, a high shifting flicker cut with shadows. And heard the laughter. Fuck. Of course. It was what? Friday night. Tomorrow the first morning of archery season, deer and elk. Everybody would be amped, nobody exhausted yet, cutting the edge of their excitement with booze and loud talk. I fished up. I fished. That's what I was here for. Fished up until I could see the campfire through a scrim of willow and alder. Could see the three pale wall tents, the trucks, shapes of horses on a taut line. Could smell smoke, manure, burnt meat. A shout, raucous laughs,

That was not a cunt it was mud wallow!

Aw crap, Les wouldn't know the difference if he was up to his neck in either one!

The fire popping, crack of a limb on rock, a stirring of sparks as someone threw it on.

If you fuckers are on good behavior we just might see what Les knows about cunts. Maybe Sunday.

It was him, the voice. The shiver inside like hooking a trout but icy.

A couple of those gals from the Mill might come up and party with us. You seen 'em. Spirited. Do about anything after the fourth round. This is the pussy you dream about tonight while you got your dicks in your hands. Damn.

Dell. It was him talking, a booming voice, coming up out of a gravel pit. Ugly, a little slurred. The image hit the group, one-twothreefourfive . . . counted seven, hit them like a gust of wind: the prospect of young women in tight skirts, tight jeans. Maybe that's how he got so many return clients. For about a second, the quiet, and then the uproar, the overlapping claims and yells calling bullshit, calling out the shit they would do with a girl that would do anything, more loud laughter. I scanned and found him at the edge of the group, a hulking shadow on the creek side of the fire, bigger than I remembered. He was shaking his head. I saw him tip it back and drink, pass the bottle, holding a beer in the other hand.

Dell! one called from the other side of the fire. A sallow face, unshaven, hollow in the cheeks leaning into the uneven light. *Kip thinks you should call one now. One or two. Call that one called herself Trina. That skinny one likes to dance.*

Laughter.

Another voice, deeper, out of the shadows, said, *You all need to take a chill pill and focus. Get some rest. Goddamn.*

Use the sat phone, another said, ignoring the voice of reason. *The one we got for emergencies. Like this.*

More laughs.

Dell gestured with the can like he was swatting away a fly.

You all just fill your orders this weekend. You'll get it when you get it.

He hitched himself tall. *Jason,* he said, almost shouting. *Keep an eye on Tyler will you? Make sure he don't fall in the damn fire? I'm gonna piss in the creek, see if I can make a trout drunk.*

He turned and swaggered away from the light.

I couldn't keep my eyes off him. I went still, barely breathed. You are fishing, night fishing, fish on. Before he sees you. No. I couldn't move. It was like I was paralyzed. He was a big man, even bigger than I remembered, bigger than me, which few men are. He dropped the can of beer as he walked and I could hear by the sound of it hitting the stones it was partly full. A big man in a dark colored Carhartt coat, unzipped, a baseball cap. Broad shouldered, a gut, heavy in the legs, walking with a hitch. I have hunted a little and I did not watch him that way, moving unevenly to the bank, his shadow thrown on the rocks by the moon and thinned by the fire. The way you watch a deer moving or an elk. And my heart was not hammering the same way, the way it does when you are hard against a tree, pressed into the bark for steadiness. The stillness, the long drawn breath, the leaning into a future where the gun bucks and the deer falls. Not like that. Not expectant, not excited. The ice of my focus took the heat out of it. For once I did not feel blind.

The scrim of willows went almost to the water. I watched his progress through the leaves more the way a cat watches a bird. Utterly stilled. The line between us a thread of simple attention, as taut as a line can be without breaking. He got to water's edge, a cutbank maybe two feet above the current. He cleared his throat, coughed, spat, shrugged up his shoulders to unzip. One of the hunters was yelling *C'mon! You ain't never come near that and don't say you did!* Peckerwood accent, probably Arkansas. Laughter. Someone turned on a boom box. Old Little Feat, *Dixie Chicken.* Well. Pretty good music. He was less than fifteen feet away, partly turned, I could see his back, his right ear, the curve of his cheek. The oak leaf pattern of the camo on his cap and hear the stream of urine hitting the slow water. Slide guitar, taunts, bottle breaking.

The whimper of the mare like a human baby, eye rolled back, absolute terror.

Leaned the rod against a branch, squatted, felt the fit of the smooth rock in my hand and stepped out fast.

He turned and the piss spattered against the leg of my waders.

"Matt? What the— Oh—"

Face lengthening in recognition.

"You!"

He couldn't wait to finish it, me. His hand went to his waist and came up with a hunting knife which flashed with firelight and in the same instant I swung. I swung as hard as he had swung at the little horse and the rock caught the side of his right eye the temple and a crush louder firmer than breaking eggs and a warm prickle pattered my face and I shoved with my left hand and the knife clattered onto stone and he splashed into the creek. Face down.

I pivoted and threw the rock as far as I could downstream and heard it plash, and before I picked up my rod I made sure he had washed to the bottom of the pool, into the rocks there half submerged and that he was still face down. I thought I saw his arms moving, spastic. Not too late. I could. I stayed. I watched until I was sure the only movement was the back and forth rocking of the pulsing current.

Slow, slow down. Breathe. I stumbled back of the brush and made myself take my time. They were all drunk with cognitive abilities further smitten by dreams of easy women. They wouldn't bother about him for an hour probably, then figure he hit the cot in his personal tent early, was it early? No it was late, and he'd be the first up, rousting the cook and graining the horses. If he did that. Probably not, probably fed them only dusty second rate hay. Anyway, if he wasn't in his bed and someone noticed they'd figure he was tugging it off in the trees, or passed out on a hummock, he was a big boy, let him sleep it off. Wouldn't miss him till morning. So I hiked downstream slowly, the last thing I wanted to do was twist an ankle.

I kept to the game and fishermen's trail along the bank. The trail pushed through the thick brush and dark open groves of virgin firs and pines, footfall soft on needles there and scented. Threaded back to the bank. At a long pool with a flat and stony bar I knelt and dunked my head in the icy water, scrubbing and scrubbing my face and hair with both hands, dunking again. The fine patter had been his blood. I waded in up to my waist and let the current wash the waders. Picked up the rod again and walked. Wanted to light the cigar bad but didn't. Wanted a drink, didn't have one. Was tempted to throw some casts and fish the bottom of the pool, like if I fished, like if I picked up the routine where I'd left it off, fishing under the moon, watching the molten light twine in the flats and unravel in the riffles, if I did that then I could pretend that thing between hadn't happened. Did I want that? To pretend? No. I wanted to hoof it downstream and get to the truck and didn't know beyond that.

I did. I must have dropped the rod in the truck bed less than twenty minutes later. I climbed in, wet wading boots and waders and vest and all, and started it up and backed around in the little clearing where the reverse lights wouldn't be visible from the road and rolled slowly out onto the packed clay of the track, accelerated smoothly and not too fast, and hit the pavement in ten more minutes and goosed it. No lights at the lodge and cabins but security lights. Desolate. Not another car. Lit the vanilla sweetened cheroot with the dash lighter and drew on it hard and let the smoke get sucked out the open window.

At Stoker no one. Just the strung white lights of the coal conveyors, the towers. It was well into the graveyard shift, no one coming from town. Pulled my shirt up to my chin anyway, lowered head and cap brim and drove through. Passed the turnoff to Grand Ave and took the back road again over the black bridge, and where the sign at a drive said OLD BRIDGE ORCHARDS and the woods in the bottom were thickest I turned in. Just a hundred feet. I had been here last week to buy peaches and remembered a tractor yard on the right, a Mexican filling up a spray tank from a hose and hydrant. I pulled in, shut the lights, the motor, listened for the barking of a dog—none. Could see the orchard house up the hill above the rows of apple trees, one window lit. Could smell late summer roses, a hedge here somewhere. Everything still, all at peace.

The moon was settling now into the western quadrant, settling in for a long sail, casting the fragrant valley in something between dark and dawn, a midway limbo that suited. In its benign light I could make out the fruited trees, the boughs heavy with black apples. I saw the hydrant and the hose as if it were morning, and for a moment I just stood there, wishing that this stillness, this limbo, could last forever. It couldn't. The ugly man intruded again, his image face down washing against the boulders, moving a little with the rhythm of the stream.

I pulled up on the stiff tap handle, felt the gush swell and weight the hose. A spray head at the end. Moved it over the truck, from hood to bed, bumpers, back up the other side, remembered the roof. Crouched stiffly down and washed the undercarriage as best I could, re-coiled the hose, took one more deep breath of flowers and pulled out. Pulled on the headlights: reminded myself that if seen now in town it would look worse with the beams off. I turned back onto the pavement that led to the edge of Grand Ave and as I did my headlights swung and a bright shape filled the windshield, splayed across, big as the night. Owl. White owl, wings wide as the truck, soundless swift and gone. Jesus. Heart hammering now, booming. Had kept my cool before, but now— It was spirit. I had not one doubt, not one doubt in the world. And it was not of the man because it was beautiful and it flew and was silent, it was Alce. That's what I thought, said: Alce.

Thanks or warning or just company, reassurance, I didn't know. Alce. Out of the twilit limbo of this night that was both night and day, deeply peaceful and profoundly violent. In a night that was between everything, came my daughter flying. Thanks, I said as I drove.

I crawled into bed and curled around Sofia. Sleep came stubborn and slow but came, carried me into the dark. Sometime between falling asleep and morning a storm swept in and it rained. Hard. Then cleared just as fast. Monsoon season.

BOOK TWO

Road

OIL ON CANVAS

24 X 36 INCHES

Road Home

OIL ON CANVAS

24 X 36 INCHES

I woke with the rain. Woke with the first halting tattoo on the metal roof *tap tap taptap taptaptaptap tap* fingerdrumming, tentative, a few scattered drops, pause, then a clatter like someone throwing a handful of seeds, speeding up until the beats ran together, then the onslaught. A rush, a dark flood that silenced all thought.

Inside the roar I spooned her. Cradled her breasts in my left arm, pressed my cheek into her hair, curled around her warmth and let the wind that came through the screen door wash me. Inside the roar and the dark and the currents of cool wind we floated.

I could die now. My one thought. Somehow complete. With the *Ocean of Women* back on the easel and the dead man in the creek and my friend in my arms and the rain at last reaching the ground and drenching the country.

I

Woke again with the knocking. Not tentative. I woke and I realized I was expecting it.

I untangled myself, slipped to the floor, pulled the Hudson's Bay blanket that came with the house over Sofia, pulled on a pair of paint smattered khaki shorts that were hung over the rocker.

Two of them this time. The last time, when I shot Lauder Simms, it was just the sheriff. Well. He had been my friend. This time evidently they were not here to arrest me. He was very polite. He was a rangy thirtyish detective in a green soft wind jacket, the kind sporty outdoor people wear, I remember thinking it was a beautiful color, something between sage and grass, looked supple, thinking it would be perfect for fishing on a night like last night. Last night. The man was thin, with the drawn cheeks of a runner, with red spots flushing the cheekbones; gave him an impressionable sensitive look the way adolescents can't quite control their emotions. Steady hazel eyes, a smile. A man you could trust.

To lock you up forever.

That's what I thought. Of Rilke's panther. In the first instant, opening the door, taking in the man and the uniformed deputy behind him I thought, Careful Boy, say the wrong thing and this man will put you away to die in the zoo like Rilke's cat.

"Jim Stegner?"

"Yah."

"Sorry, did we wake you?" Very polite. Held up a wallet badge. "Craig Gaskill, Delta County Sheriff's Department."

"Nah. I mean, yes, but it's okay. The rain in the middle of the night. Slept better than I have in a month."

Clear conscience. Something a stone cold murderer probably wouldn't say. Much less feel. I was standing holding the carved door open with my right arm, kind of leaning into it, and smelled my fishing vest. It was hanging on a hook two feet from my head. I could smell it because often if I was just keeping dinner for myself, I would slip one or two trout into the zipper pocket high on the back. If it was a hot afternoon I would unshuck the vest and tear a bunch of grass and horsetails from the bank and wet the fistful in the creek and stuff it in the pocket with the fish to keep them cool. Made the vest smell fishy but I liked it better than carrying around a slung creel. The vest was two feet from my face, hanging on the wall right where the open door swung into it, and I could see that it was spattered with blood.

Icy grip in the guts. The sporty detective saw it. I know he did because he said, "Mr. Stegner, are you okay?"

"Yah," I said fast. "Just haven't had my coffee yet."

And in the rush to cover for myself I heard myself saying, "You boys want some coffee too? I'll just make a pot."

And heard Sport say, "That is very hospitable. I certainly could use another cup, you, Dan?" And I heard Dan say he was just thinking they better get down to the Conoco out on the highway and get a refill. And I saw myself stepping back and opening the door wider and they came through the screen door with a clap and I heard Sofia call out, "*Jim?*" And I said, "It's alright, honey, we have guests. Gonna make some coffee." *Honey?* I must've been really frazzled. And I saw the men come to the long counter and pull up two stools and I went behind it and reached for the old pot and rinsed it in cold water and refilled it all the while talking about how bad we needed the rain and how fresh the country looked already like it had been rinsed in green, and saw myself clutching the little grinder to my chest like a secret and compressing the sprung top in my hands while the motor triggered and the blade bawled and shredded the beans that rattled then whined.

Heard the door to my bedroom which opened onto all of us slam and that snapped me out of it.

She had slammed the door. She didn't want to talk to cops, to anyone this early. That was one lucky break the way I saw it. She was not social this early in the morning. She did not wrap herself in the blanket and come out stretching and purring and being polite to the nice policemen and go into the bathroom to pee and brush her teeth and throw on a wrap and join us for coffee the way some more finished hostesses might have done. Finished like finishing school, not her. She slammed the door. The two men raised their eyebrows, I shrugged, it was a male bonding moment, all good, but more important it let me pull myself up. Kind of reined me up short and put a loud period on my rambling.

I heard the slam and stopped stock still and thought Jesus, Jim, get a grip. You are a cooler cookie than this. Take a breath. I did. Went to the sink at the west end of the counter, put my back to them, and rinsed out some cups, covered myself, my loud thoughts, with the running water and the clatter of ceramic and thought, Slow down. You were here all night, sleeping the sleep of the dead, not the dead, Jesus, the newly rained on, the sleep of the new monsoon, and if your fishing vest is spattered with blood and hanging there right by the front door, well. No big deal. When you let them back out, lead them away from the vest to the French doors in the south wall, follow them around the house to their cars, you go out that way all the time, it is a natural motion to exit out toward the big view, the mountain, talking the whole while about how you haven't seen the foothills this green since June. That's what you will do.

I gave Sport the elk mug. A bull elk in the fall in a tawny field, yellow aspen losing leaves, overcast about to snow, he is lifting his head to bugle and from his muzzle a stream of fog in the icy air. Seemed right.

"You get the elk," I said. I was going to say bull but I didn't want to encourage him. To the deputy I said, the NASCAR cow or the loon? The NASCAR cow coffee cup said WISCONSIN and had the head of a happy looking Holstein framed by a border of what looked like black and white racing checks.

The deputy grinned. He was a beefy kid with a fade and flattop, probably played high school ball for Delta and was the luckiest man in the universe when he landed the job with the county. Could tell he was the type who appreciates what's appreciatible, really loved his wife, etc., which I admire and like in a man, in fact liked them both and had the circumstances been different I would have relished pouring the two coffee and sitting down to bullshit.

"NASCAR cow every time," said Dan the deputy.

There was no stool on this side of the counter so I stood, leaned back against the drawers next to the stove said,

"Anything in those? Sugar?"

Sport said, "If you have cream and honey, otherwise fine." I smiled at him. Because it was clear that he was getting me in the habit of getting him what he asked, the more specific the better. Honey. Exactly what I took in my coffee. The kid shook his head. Polite. A blunt instrument. Hadn't learned the use of subtle tools yet, probably never would, it would probably fuck up his general sense of gratitude. I am not at all a simple person but I like simple people, I admire them.

I put out the half and half and honey, took mine, alternating with Sport, our spoons tinking in happy duet, picked up my Ugly Mug and leaned back, crossed my arms. The mug by the way is a bad picture of an ocean liner, don't ask me. I was awake now, felt ready. Sport sipped, nodded, smiled, said,

"You often fish in the middle of the night?"

■

This time I did not let myself get thrown. I did not babble. I took a long sip of strong coffee looking at the greening base of the mountain out the window and thought, Virga. Not last night. Last night the rain reached the ground with a will, furious. Furious and glad. The way I would be feeling right now if Sport didn't scare me. Well. Don't be scared. Be yourself. Be honest. About the things you can be honest about.

"Yes. Once in a while. My daughter and I used to do it pretty often. When there was a moon."

"Where's your daughter now?"

I put down the Ugly Mug.

"She was murdered."

Sport's mug stopped halfway to his mouth.

"I'm sorry."

"She was fifteen."

He nodded. He drank, didn't say anything. We all looked into our mugs.

"There was a moon last night before the rain?"

"I guess there was."

"Did you go fishing last night?"

I shook my head, sipped. "Last night I slept."

"Your wading boots are puddling by the front door."

I blinked.

"Rain," I said. "Remember."

"They're in under the roof, in your vestibule. Nothing else wet."

"That's right," I said. "After it poured I remembered I'd left my whole kit lying on the grass and over the stump. From the other day. Boots, waders, rod. Sometimes I just let it all dry out there. I thought fuck. In the middle of the night when I woke up to pee. So I went out and put them away. I mean it won't hurt anything but it's better to let everything air out."

"Good coffee," Sport said. "What is it?"

"Folgers. New whole bean."

He raised an eyebrow, grinned.

"Tastes better when you take it out of a fancy jar."

"I'll have to try that. Huh. But you brought your vest in?"

That stopped me. Cocked my head, turned, slid the pot off the hot pad on the coffeemaker, gave us all a refill, the three cups, elk, cow, *Titanic*.

"The vest by the door that's flecked with old blood," he said.

Everybody stared at him. Everybody being me and Flattop.

He sipped, little smile. "Fish blood, I'm guessing."

I turned, slipped the pot back onto the burner, mind jumbling. Turned off the pot's red-lit power switch, flick, now brown and dead. Off. Same as blood. Red going on, then brown. Dell's blood. DNA, all that. The picture of the man raising the club to strike the little roan for the third time probably to kill it. Hitching up the road fast as I could to take him down. Down into the ditch. I straightened, drew a breath, turned.

"That's a man's blood to tell you the truth. Recent."

Flattop's mouth actually opened.

I wanted to see. If I could make Sport stop in his tracks. Reciprocate. Make him tick into a facial expression he hadn't planned on. Catch his breath. Drain some of that runner's blush from his boy's cheeks.

It worked. He had the mug coming down from his lips and he almost choked. Everybody knew what everybody was after, this wasn't anybody's first rodeo except maybe the kid deputy who, I noticed, had been watching the whole interview with a kind of awe.

"Man's blood? You don't say?"

"Yup. Outfitter named Dell Siminoe."

Now the kid actually choked. Hid it in a big cough, took a white kerchief out of his back pocket and wiped his brow instead of his mouth, stared at me, then his mentor. Like he was watching a tennis match. I smiled at him. A big honest smile, the first one since the two arrived. I wanted to laugh, but, funny thing, I didn't want to embarrass the kid in front of Sport. Instead I topped off his cup, leaned back against the far counter, against the drawers next to the stove. Through the French doors onto the ramada, which were open to screen, I noticed the sun breaking over the cottonwood leaves, the big trees up on the ditch, the morning was cool and fresh and soon it would start getting hot. I loved this. The morning. The smell of the damp ground coming through the screen doors after night rain. Even having visitors, these visitors. I felt happy. Which was fucked up, thinking about it now.

It was Sport's turn to collect himself. He was too smart not to know what was coming. He just had to drink his coffee and watch it play out. I thought.

"Dell Siminoe?" he said.

"Yah. The reason you all are here. Because of the fight. Because I assaulted the man day before yesterday and gave him a bloody nose and I guess he's just a big pussy and now he's filing charges. Probably didn't tell you he was in the middle of killing a little horse."

They stared at me.

■

I thought he would say, Why don't you start from the beginning. Thought now we could stop the foreplay and he would pull out a steno pad, one of those flip notebooks, all official now, and start writing. He didn't. He said,

"Dell Siminoe isn't filing any charges. Dell Siminoe is dead."

Pause.

"Murdered in cold blood."

Pause.

"Thirty steps from seven bow hunters and a campfire."

Pause.

"In the middle of last night."

Pause.

"Would you mind telling us where you were last night? *All* of last night."

"RIP," I said. I said: "Not really. Dead? Kinda hope he's in the bad place. You think I killed him because I was mad enough to give the man a bloody nose?"

All the time I was thinking, I wasn't wearing the fishing vest. When I tackled him, when we fought. I don't dress until I get to the creek. Thinking, wondering if the cowboy Stinky would remember that, the one I knocked into the road. Probably not. I'd have to go with it anyway. That was a gamble. I was not averse to gambling when I didn't have to, so it was no stretch at all to roll the dice, go all in when I had no choice.

"I don't think anything," Sport said. "We'd just like to eliminate you as a suspect."

"Huh," I said. "I'll bet." Everybody's gloves off now.

"Why don't you just tell us what you were doing starting, say, Thursday morning."

This is going to be fun, I thought. And wished Sofia wasn't in the next room, just beyond that door, about to hear everything I was going to say.

I was getting good at telling the story, this my third telling in two days, and I told it. A good morning painting. The girl leaving.

Knocking the man into the dirt with my door and running as best I could up the road before the big man could kill the mare. Rolling in the ditch, Siminoe's nose bleeding— He stopped me.

"You say you were grappling and rolling when you felt his nose break?"

I knew what he was after. The blood on the vest. It was flecked, spattered. Just like if you hit someone on the head, say, with a rock. A bloody nose rolling in a ditch would probably streak and smear, blotch. Well, you do the best you can. What if there were brain matter flecked there too? Well, I'd probably get good at learning how to order grease pencils and watercolor paper from Cañon City or Walsenburg, if they let you do that from max security. There wasn't, wouldn't be brains. Right Jim? Right. I'd hit him once with the flat side of a rock, hadn't like smashed his head in, he probably died of drowning. Same as thwacking a trout: sometimes there's a spray of blood, but never any brain. Probably because their brain is the size of a pea. Well.

"Yes," I said.

Sport nodded, writing it down, taking me at my word, nobody lying yet except about when exactly we went fishing.

"The girl?" he said suddenly shifting tack. "In the bedroom? She's the model you mentioned you were painting Thursday morning before you went fishing? Let's see." Began flipping back the pages of his pad.

"Sofia."

"Sofia, right. Last name?"

"I don't know."

He raised an eyebrow, wrote.

"You said she left these premises some time around midday on Thursday, she was modeling for a painting and left, and when did she return?"

"Yesterday morning."

"You called her?"

"No."

"She came uninvited?"

"Yes."

"Is that the painting?"

"Yes."

"Can I take a look at it?"

"Sure."

He got up. The young deputy got up. I moved around the counter fast, not sure why, to overtake them. Got to the easel first. Stood beside it like a kid at a judged show waiting for my ribbon. Sport smiled, genuine. His eyes moved over the canvas and I watched the picture overcome him, exactly the way the light that trails a cloud shadow overtakes a hillside. For a moment he was off the job, he was a spectator, an appreciator, he looked years younger. He smiled, said,

"Have a name yet?"

"An Ocean of Women."

Smile to a big grin.

An Ocean of Women was maybe a great painting. It took the viewer to a lot of different places at once which a great painting can do. The first impulse on seeing the painting was to laugh, but at the same time a queasy feeling rose out of the depths, rose with the big sharks, swimming up to the surface: a tinge of fear: would the man make it? He looked pretty happy swimming but he also looked lost. He looked very far from anything like a boat or a shore, he looked a little like a man taking his very last swim.

The kid stood uneasily before the easel, his hand on his holstered gun, blinking. I could tell he wanted to laugh, maybe the first time he'd seen an original painting ever, one that wasn't painted by an aunt that had taken a How to Paint a Western Landscape by the Numbers class and hung it in the den next to the flat screen, he glanced at his mentor and relaxed, twitched a smile, studied the painting, dove into it, couldn't help himself, his eyes roved from woman to woman wondering maybe how many the swimmer could fuck and still tread water. A good picture should do all of that. Invite the viewer in from just wherever he stood, lead him on a different journey than the person standing beside him. I loved that, watching different people watch a painting at the same time. Because that's what it turned into: in front of a fine painting a viewer stopped looking and started watching, watching is more specific, watching is a hunt for something, a search, the way we watch for a loved one's boat on the horizon, or an elk in the trees. Before a good painting they started watching for clues to their own life.

Abruptly Sport straightened, sort of shook himself off, took two steps behind me to the wall, bent down and lifted the turned-back canvas. Flipped it around and held it arm extended, nostrils flaring at the fresh paint. The man hunched and digging a grave, four vultures or ravens watching.

"Wow," he said. "Diverse. When'd you paint this?"

The stark and surprising shock of being violated, as swift and sudden as a hawk stooping out of the sky and *strike*.

I let go the breath. As if Sport had been gently gyring, wings extended the whole time, lazy circles and *siiiiiiiiiiiii*—WHAM. A dangerous man. Far more dangerous than I'd thought or given him credit for. No point in lying.

"Yesterday," I said.

"About what time?"

"Maybe it's time I get a lawyer."

He cocked his head and looked at me. The first time level. No BS, squared off, measuring. "That's your right. Is that something you want to do?"

"I don't want to do any of this."

We looked at each other. He nodded.

"Understood," he said. "Could you ask Sofia to come out and talk to us for a second?"

"No."

He nodded.

"I think you two better leave," I said.

He nodded. Took one more long look at the painting, glanced at me again, this one honest and bleak, like: *I have just looked into the heart of a murder and it raises the hair on the back of my neck, still—as many of these as I work I still can't get used to it.* Then he set the painting back down, carefully flipped it backside-out, fastidious, the way you do something distasteful and guilty, leaned it so the paint wouldn't smear.

"I wanted to be an artist growing up," he said. "Then I got married."

He said it like he thought maybe he had made the right choice after all.

"Thanks for the coffee," he said, and went through the door. The big kid followed him, ducked his head at me, didn't say a word, didn't know what to say, looked like he'd been hit on the head with a cow.

■

Sofia flew out of the bedroom. The second they left. It's a small house. The bedroom is just off the main room with the long counter, the kitchen, their stools weren't twenty feet from her listening head. The door flew open and she burst out naked.

Most women would have dressed, armored themselves somehow with clothes. She felt stronger I think without them. She came out of the bedroom like a whirlwind, all tossing dark hair, all curves, all huge eyes flashing the five colors, and scents and something like a hum, a breathed song, a sigh, like someone singing to herself.

She wasn't singing to herself, she was finding her rhythm. She did that when she modeled, very low, didn't distract me, and she did it now with an urgency. I was rooted to my spot between the painting and the front door.

"You killed that sonofabitch? Last night?"

She stood just more than an arm's length away.

"When you got up in the middle of the night? I felt you, I went back to sleep. Thought you were peeing. Heard the truck, thought you were gone a long time, too sleepy to wonder about it, figured you might be an insomniac, next thing I felt your arms around me."

She stopped, cocked her head the way she does, listening for something it seemed inside her. She was more beautiful right then than maybe any woman I had ever seen.

"You *killed* him?"

Not really saying it to me. To herself. Listening inside for how she felt about it. Then eyes on me. The eyes different colors, the colors shifting, the way pebbles on the bottom of a stream, the way the fast water is constantly moving the lances of sunlight.

She said: "He didn't say *how*. I guess he wouldn't. That'd be giving a suspect inside information. *Fuck*. With a *knife*?"

She shook her head. Like trying to clear her ear of water. She looked straight into me. Not only with her eyes, with all of her— her eyes, her breasts, hips, the sparse thatch of dark hair.

"Well you better have a good fuck." She said it exasperated, as if she didn't know whether to laugh or scream. "You better store them up, who knows how long it will be when they get serious about you."

I stood there. Kind of transfixed. Watched her turn and walk bare-ass into the bedroom.

Falling. Falling into her. Like stepping off a cliff and spreading arms and flying downwards. Didn't matter to where. Because she would swoop up under me and carry me down. With Irmina maybe once or twice like this. Maybe not. Because she was always trying somehow to heal me, to make me better. Not now. Sofia let me fall. Met and wrapped and covered me and we went down together and I cracked open, not like hitting the bottom but like a chrysalis maybe, shuddered open all light and weightless and winged, blown skyward, hearing her with me with me—a cry— whose? No names no words, lost and falling upwards with her in blinding light. Like that.

When it was over she touched her nose to mine.

"You didn't kill him did you?"

I didn't move.

"You got up to pee once. And to get the gear from the truck, out of the rain. To hang it up. I heard you say that."

I didn't move.

"You were here in my arms all night, weren't you? I don't remember much about it do I? *Do I?*"

I shook my head. Barely.

"Because we were sleeping."

"We were sleeping."

II

The search warrant was executed that afternoon. The bloody vest was enough for any judge and I knew it was coming. But I was careful not to touch it. Before they came I stood next to the hanging vest that smelled like fish and studied it from inches away, didn't look like any pieces of brain. Like I said, I was pretty confident that the one blow hadn't gone that far into the Simian's brainpan. The blood? Where did all the blood come from? Must have hit and broke that vein that throbs on the temple.

A squad car, a white van, and a plain white Crown Vic with Sport driving alone. Seemed like a lonely man, to me. Twice as smart probably as anybody in the sheriff's office, twice as sensitive. Wanted to be an artist. Well.

They didn't take much. The vest, my rod, boots, waders. The light nylon sack with shoulder straps I sometimes use to carry lunch, a water bottle, extra pack of the cigars if I am going all day which I hardly ever do. They took photographs of the two paintings, first separately then side by side which I thought was pretty sophisticated. Evidence of a sudden shift in state of mind would be my guess. Premeditation. Sport asked us politely to stand outside, formal now, friendly still but making no effort to hide that this was a contest, a match and we were on opposite sides and he, beg your pardon, had every intention of winning. Watched him direct the tech to sample the clay under the truck in the frame, take an imprint of the treads on the tires, all four.

Took maybe twenty minutes, the whole thing. When it was done he walked up to us where we were standing in the shade of a young cottonwood on the west side of the house. Not wearing the green shell anymore, too hot, had on a short sleeved button shirt but not business, more like what a surfer or climber would wear at a barbecue, but tucked in, a wide checked pattern olive and soft yellow, and brown loafers, all very casual. He walked up, nodded to Sofia, to me, a frank not unfriendly look as if we had been friends for a long time and didn't have to pretend anything, said,

"All done. They were very careful. Didn't toss the place."

I said, "Am I under arrest?"

"No."

"Can I go fishing then? Up where I fought with Dell?"

"Sure. But I wouldn't recommend it. Five of the hunters stayed on. Said they'd paid for nine days of hunting, they were going to hunt nine days. Dell's brother is flying in from Tucson this afternoon. Grew up here too, knows the country better than his brother. I'd rather not have any more fights."

I took the mostly unsmoked cheroot I'd just had time to light when they showed up, took it from behind my ear, lit it, inhaled. For a second the three of us stood in the shade and looked at the mountain, the sage hills beneath it flushing pale green with last night's downpour.

"How about New Mexico?" I said.

His head came up sharply.

"You planning on going there?"

"I have a commission in Santa Fe. A portrait."

He chewed that over. Let out a breath.

"I can't keep you from going anywhere. But do me a favor: call me and tell me where you are. I've got your cell too. Better if we can get this whole business cleared up and I can keep you posted."

"Right," I said.

He handed us both a card. Turned to Sofia who was expressionless.

"Would you come down to the office and make a statement? Say tomorrow morning?"

She turned her face up square on to his.

"No," she said.

He recoiled, as if struck and trying not to show it.

"No?"

"Unh unh. He was with me all night and that's all I've got to say. We fucked twice. Once pretty fast, slept. Spooned. You know?"

He blinked at her.

"Then we both woke up and fucked once really slow and long. I had two orgasms. I mean two more. That hasn't happened in a while. Then we were exhausted, wrung out, just drugged kind of, the way the sweat, the musk of sex, the fatigue it just takes you out. All tangled up in each other's arms. Then we woke up because some assholes were knocking on the door. That's my statement."

She handed back his card and walked back into the house.

III

That evening I tried a new fishing spot, the one I'd heard about for years, the stretch where the Gunnison emerges from its gorge. I was agitated and I wanted to fish and I had to buy new gear anyway, a whole new set, thanks to Sport. And down there, right at the confluence of the North Fork and the main river, there's an outfitter's base with a full fly shop. It's called Pleasure Park which sounds like an adult theme-o-rama. I drove through Hotchkiss, just a row of false fronted shops and a cowboy bar lining the county highway, crossed a deeply shaded creek, climbed a couple of switchbacks up onto the prettiest mesa, a high bench of orchards and green fields overlooking the West Elks and away south the hazy and high snow peaks of the San Juans. Say what you want about Santa Fe and Taos and the clean light, they didn't have this. Kind of washed the dirt off me, just seeing it. I don't know if truth is beauty or not but I have always put my stock in beauty every time, the real thing, the one that comes with cold rain and hard stories, and I had never seen a place like this.

And then the road dropped down to the railroad tracks *thump thump* and it was all desert out ahead, a hundred miles of rolling saltbush westward, and I took the turnoff on my left, south, and wound down to the river.

It was a real hole, a burst of lime-green old cottonwoods with high rock walls sheltering a run of dark smooth water. The water reflected the tall reeds and cattails, the willows and box elders along the banks. On the other side of a big gravel parking lot was a low building with blue river rafts stacked on trailers.

I parked and pushed open the glass door. A bell on the door tinkled. It was dim and cool inside. Polished wood bar with high stools, fishing shop behind. They had their priorities. A Discovery Channel fishing show was on the two TVs, a handsome guide directing the casts of a pretty celebrity into a wide blue river. The sound was up and I got from the guide's accent and the helicopter on the gravel bar that this was New Zealand. I thought that was funny: this was Gold Medal water, fishermen came from all over the country to fish here, and they had New Zealand on the TV. Behind the bar a guide with a gray waxed handlebar mustache, and a cap stuck with flies, dunked two tumblers in rinse water and gave them two shakes and placed them in a row of others. His eyes were on one of the TVs while he did it. He finally turned to me.

"She sure can fill a pair of waders, huh?" He took a tug from a sweating green beer bottle, put it back down on a cardboard coaster. The coaster was stamped with BELGIAN CREAM ALE and a picture of a cow. His eyes were blurry. Well. It was after five and it was hot out.

"Your shop open?"

"Sure. What can we do you? Need some flies?" He let himself out a low stall door on the shop side and came around. Stuck out his hand. "Ben."

"Jim."

"Jim Hemingway? You look like Hemingway, anybody ever tell you that? Really. The eyes, the beard."

"Thanks. You have rods?"

"Sure."

Judging by his breath that wasn't the first or second beer of the day. Well. He stepped back, gave me a quick once-over. Touched his stiff mustache. He seemed to perk up. A rod was a big sale. I wasn't just some dude coming in to ask what was hitting and buy a dozen two dollar flies.

"Leroy's not here," he said. "But I can sure sell you a rod. Follow me."

"Great. You have light waders?"

He stopped. Turned around with some effort, reminded me of a boat moving in uncertain currents. "Waders, too?"

"Yah. And boots and vest, flies, tippet, forceps, Gink, lead, strike indicators, leaders. Oh yeah, and a reel and backing and maybe let's try some of that snakeskin fly line."

"Sharkskin? You mean Sharkskin? Scientific Anglers." He swayed a little where he stood, and now he reminded me of a tree.

"I guess that's it. Yeah. Or maybe it makes too much noise. I've heard it makes a real zing as it goes out."

He studied me, his biggest catch of the week.

"Maybe," he said. "Yeah, some people say that." He squinted his eyes at me and thought about it. "Can cast a lot longer though." He said it like he was confessing something.

"Distance," he said and lifted one hand, palm up. "Noise." Lifting the other, making a balance in the air. Stood there, balanced himself in the middle of this conundrum. He seemed to forget we were on our way to the rod section.

"You all have time to wind the reel? Like to go fishing tonight if I can."

"Oh sure sure, we can do that. Take just a few minutes. Jake is back there. Jake can do it. He's just a kid."

"They still name kids Jake?"

He was walking ahead of me, walking like into a stiff wind, he put his chin back over his shoulder, barked, "Ha!"

I tore through the store like a contestant in one of those shopping game shows. Pretty quick it was Ben who was following me, murmuring, "Sure, sure, Good choice, That's a good one, Pretty much the best you got right there, Hemingway knows what the hell he's doing, Nope this ain't Hemingway's first rodeo no it isn't," trying to keep up with me, carrying one of the shopping baskets he decided at one point to haul out of the back. I really really wanted to go fishing. The more time I spent in the dim store that smelled of beer, with the running commentary of the fishing show blatting in the background the more the pressure mounted inside my chest to blow the fuck out of there and get on the dark flowing river.

I bought a Winston rod, a five weight. I'd always wanted one. I hefted a nine footer, gave it three false casts careful not to tangle with a steel beam above, and handed it to Ben who raised his eyebrows, said, "That right there is the best there is, no doubt about it." Then he muttered, "I think Leroy has that at eight hundred dollars, lemme check. Ah, how were you thinking of paying for all this Mr. Hemingway?"

Trotting after me as I tore through the vests, fly boxes, flies, me thinking: I'm paying for it with a painting of a fish gobbling up houses and another of two little girls in polka dots and probably a chicken, how else?

And then we got to the waders and sticky rubber soled boots and I had to stop the flow of picking and gathering which had really become like some harvest dance and sit and try them on, the boots. I pried off my sneakers and was pushing my big bony foot into the unlaced top when Ben spilled my gear into a pile on the floor and sat on the wood bench beside me with a bleary sigh and said, "This is just like Christmas. Should call you Santa Claus instead of Hemingway, ha. Wait, I should get that reel started so's you don't have to wait."

He got up again, fished the reel out of the pile and a box of expensive yellow fly line and disappeared into the back. Came out again a minute later and sat down, this time holding a new green bottle of sweating beer. It looked very good to me, could taste my own mouth watering. Good sign to get into the river pronto.

He said, "You hear they killed a man up on the Sulphur last night?"

I wedged in my foot.

"I think someone mentioned it."

"Cold blood. With a rock is what I heard. Went to piss in the creek and someone crushed his head in." Ben shuddered dramatically and took a long pull from the bottle.

"Dellwood Siminoe. The outfitter. Hate to say this, but not a lot of folks will be crying."

"Don't say."

"Nope. Even his daughter-in-law has a restraining order." He shook his head. Pulled from the beer, gave a meditative twist to the end of the waxed mustache.

"Anyways, they say they know who did it."

"Don't say." I shucked the boot, said, "These'll work." Stood, said, "Can't think of anything I'm forgetting."

Ben was tugging at the leg of my khakis. He wanted to tell me something. I wanted to swat his hand away.

"It was a fisherman," he said real solemn. "A *fly* fisherman. Got in a big fight with Dell just Thursday right at the creek."

"Yeah, really?"

"Yup. Big guy, I heard. Newcomer from New Mexico. Big guy with a white beard, a painter they say. Paints naked ladies. Now that's a great job, don't you think? That's a job I'd like. Think I'll try that one."

He grinned lopsided, took a long drink from the bottle, then his eyes seemed to settle and focus on the colored spatters on my pants. I could almost hear the gears clicking in the wash of beer inside his brain. He looked up at me. He blinked. His mouth opened just a little under the mustache. For a second I could see a little kid, the kid he had been, trying to make sense of all the things that overwhelmed his understanding.

"You paying with a credit card?"

"Yup."

"You got ID?"

"Sure."

"Is it from New Mexico?"

"Yup."

He was sitting on the bench and he looked up at me. This time he swallowed hard with no beer. He blinked. Then he shook his head.

"Gimme a minute," he said.

"Take your time."

He drank from the beer, leaned forward, stared straight ahead. Put his hands on his knees. He was adjusting to the new information, taking his time. He was a fisherman.

"Dell was scum," he said finally.

"Sounds like it."

He nodded to himself, glanced up at me again just once, said, "Well let's ring you up. I bet you want to get the fuck out of here and go fishing."

I smiled.

"I'll check on the reel."

At the register he wouldn't meet my eye. His hand trembled as he picked up the little matchbook of twist weights, the dropper bottle of silicone, ran the scanner over the bar codes. I looked past him and in back, hanging just back of the doorway to what must have been the shop, I saw a young man in a baseball cap watching us. Jake. Ben said, "Back in Hotchkiss they got a fly shop, too. If you need flies. Raymond's."

"This one is pretty good," I said.

"Well." He scanned a pair of forceps with handles speckled like a brookie. "Well," he said again.

"Like I might scare away the other customers?"

He wouldn't look at me.

"I don't see any other customers," I said.

"It gets real busy sometimes," he snapped defensively, and started putting my gear into a flimsy plastic bag.

IV

The sun had gone over the canyon, the top of the red wall upstream was lit to a strip of fire. The hole gathered the cool dusk. I smelled tamarisk, sweet, heard the ripple of the current against grass banks, the descending slow notes of a canyon wren somewhere across the river.

Behind me the clunk of two car doors closing, chafe of a starter, tires on gravel, all muffled by distance and the thick cottonwoods along the bank. Here, the wide run of slow water reflected the green banks, and all across it, silvering the dark surface, and silent, spread the faint rings of trout rising.

I counted four other fishermen staggered in the mile above me, two on the far side, could see their blue raft nosed into the willows. Plenty of room to be alone with the evening.

I stepped into the water, tested it, thigh deep here and black along the grassy undercut, waded out, soft sand bottom, waded until it firmed to gravel and got shallower, a covered bar. I wanted to cast back from here and fish the edge of the bank.

Before I unhooked the little pheasant tail from the keeper above the cork grip, before I pulled a few feet of line straight off the new reel with a well oiled zing—before I did anything I stood knee deep in the cold water and closed my eyes.

In the silence of the evening I could hear the tiny blips and gulps of fish rising. One behind me, then one to my left, close. A chortle of current. The breeze was lazy upstream and carried somebody's charcoal. Another fainter tick, this in air. Bats. I knew that when I opened my eyes I would see a bat flitting the dusk over the water. Rising fluttery, the antic turns like a leaf getting blown about. The leathery wings ticking. Bats and trout, everybody having dinner, everybody going after the same bugs. Nobody leaving any wake.

Do you *leave a wake?*

No. Maybe.

Do you leave anything important? Worthwhile?

A few paintings.

Huh.

I was a father.

But now you're not.

I still am. I just. She would be here tonight. She would love it.

You are a killer. Now the wake you are leaving is absence and pain.

I stood stock still. I listened to that, the accusation, the way I had been listening to the bats and the fish.

I don't feel like a killer. I feel pretty good. Now I do. I didn't like what Ben said at the end, but now I am just standing here listening.

You are a killer twice over. First time you escaped by a few inches. Happenstance. You missed. But. You have the heart of a killer.

I do?

Answer that yourself.

You are myself.

Silence.

I stood knee deep in the cold water, eyes closed, and listened to the end of day over the river. Then I opened my eyes and pulled the line and began making long casts upstream just off the bank. The new rod was light and alive in my hand, it was beautiful, and the line sang out fast and smooth with a whisper like scratching a guitar string. I didn't mind the sound at all.

V

In cop shows they always talk about motive and murder weapon and hard evidence and eyewitnesses. I mean, to build a case beyond a reasonable doubt you need to assemble some facts. Facts that are beyond dispute. Like bits of a man's brains on another man's clothes. That's the thing I worried about most. But. I kept telling myself no way. I didn't puncture Dell's skull, I cracked it. Didn't beat it to a pulp. I hit him once, KO, and he fell into the creek and drowned. Crack.

The other stuff seemed under control. Murder weapon? None. One rock in a million like any other in the bed of a stream, already probably gathering algae or the pupa shells of caddisflies. Motive, sure. It sounded like lots of people might have some motive. The mother of his grandkids for one. Hard evidence aside from brains? Sulphur Creek road dust on my truck, patches I hadn't washed off? My tire treads along the creek, just downstream of the camp?

I fished there almost every day. I had never needed to wash off the dust in the first place. That was an adrenaline move, something you do in the middle of the night when you're so pumped and you don't realize it and you do unnecessary and stupid things.

Blood on the vest? What if Stinky said I wasn't wearing the vest during the fight? Then Dell's blood came at another time. What if the pattern of spots was deemed in no way consistent with a bloody nose? Stinky could fuck me.

Alibi. I had one. Rock solid, right? What if she got mad at me? What if she turned on me the way she did on the big dumb hippy boyfriend? Maybe that was her MO. Or the other way, what if I left? I was never going to be hostage to an alibi. A spurned woman can do crazy things. What if. What if.

But I didn't hear from Sport. I figured I'd wait two weeks, not be in too much of a hurry, then drive down to Santa Fe and do Steve's stupid commission. I figured they'd run the tests on the vest pretty fast since it was a hot case with a suspect at risk of flight, etc. And they had probably interviewed Stinky already, so. I figured if they had any kind of a case they wouldn't fuck around, they'd nail me. I don't know why, I felt confident. It's not like they had to carefully construct a case. They would have only so much material with which to build a prosecution and I figured either they had it or they didn't.

Sofia went back to the orchard house she shared with Dugar and kicked him out. She told him his poems were moronic and it was time he went to California and became the sea mammal she always knew he could be. He objected with a string of *b-buts* she said sounded like a machine gun. When she asked about the orchard girl he'd been screwing for months, playing her, Sofia, like a fool, he got sheepish and shut up for a minute.

We were drinking coffee at the counter again, she on a stool, me on the kitchen side, and I was happy that we had fallen back into our old ease. She had brought a baguette, a jar of peach marmalade, a wedge of triple cream Brie, and we were devouring them. She smiled, her eyes all the colors you see on the bottom of some clear creeks, and she said, to me, "You know I hold your nut sack in my strong little fist?"

"I know I know."

"I don't want your nuts." She opened her fist and shook her palm in air. "No matter what you ever do or say to me your nuts are your nuts. I will never change my story."

I looked at her and I believed her. As much as I could believe anything.

"What did Dugar say? At the end?"

"He said he thought we were the perfect couple. Not that he loved me more than marine wildlife or poetry, but that we were perfect together. 'I, Dugar, have a strong back and a huge heart,' he said, 'and you are smart and great with people.' Can you believe that? He carefully rolled us each a Drum cigarette and said we should start an organic farm. Then he took the little feather out of his left ear, the one he's had since he apprenticed with the Arapahoe, and he gave it to me. Tried."

"He apprenticed with the Arapahoe?"

She slid her mug across the butcher block, allowed me to refill it.

"Maybe it was the Cheyenne. Or the Shoshone. I can't remember. He was like nineteen. He lived on the rez in a willow stick thing covered in blankets and he was boffing the shaman's wife so they kicked him out. Put a curse on him. Come to think of it, that explains a lot."

She drank from the full and steaming mug and looked at me past the tilted rim. She put it down lightly on the counter.

"Do you want to paint today? It's been a while."

"No. Maybe. I don't think it will have a woman in it."

"No?" She leaned forward. She was wearing one of her signature spaghetti strap tops. She squeezed her biceps into the sides of her chest and her breasts did that thing where they dominated the universe for a minute. I held up a four and a half fingered hand.

"Not this morning."

She relented.

"I can't tell if you need me to help you get your mind off of things or if that's exactly what you need, to focus."

"Tell you the truth I'm not sure either. Think I need to be alone this morning."

She pursed her lips at me. Her eyes were serious. Shadows of big trout swimming along the bright pebble bottom. "I bet you do," she said. "Call me later if you want to swim with beautiful naked girls."

She came around the counter and tugged my beard, kissed my temple and strolled back out the front door.

Roar of Tops, then silence. Me and two crickets, and the morning air already hot, breathing at the screens.

I walked over to the west end of the house and picked a twenty-four thirty-six out of the stack of pre-stretched canvases leaning against the wall. Put it on the easel, squeezed ten measures of pigment onto a piece of plastic covered fiberboard, lifted a medium stiff brush out of a glass of spirits and began.

I painted a road. Cracked tarmac running over the desert hills west of here. Burnt brush, cracked clay, washes of white alkaline in the low places. The road climbed a hill, there were piñons at the top of it, a ridge, the road disappearing into them. It curved left into the shadows of the pines. Hot. Hot on the road, not much relief in the shade. Along the road grew flowers. Small asters on the shoulder, purple and blue, breathing out the last colors, the last moisture in the whole country. My hand moved from the spirit jars holding the brushes to the palette, to the canvas, the palette knife, a rag. Moving, it seemed, faster, without pause. The loaded brush carving a single living cloud in the washed sky. Then a big bush by the pavement, rabbitbrush, fading its green, and in the laced shadow of the bush a shape.

Brush to palette to canvas: an arm sticking out from under. On the arm, bracelets. A girl's arm. A girl's body at the base of the bush.

And then. On the rock, in the trees, on the hill, the four birds. Not together now, perched and watching from their separate distances. Black and huge. On rock, on tree, on another branch. Saw them appear with a dread. Could not make them not come. Not not come, they were already there like the road and the sky and the dead girl. They had been there always, with the unrelieved heat, the relentless sky.

Phone rang. Jarred me out of the place. How many hours? Wasn't sure, it was hot in the house, already afternoon. Rang four times stopped. Began ringing again.

Okay okay. Too much going on probably not to answer. Put down the brush, board, rag, lurched over to the counter. Stiff, wrung out, like I'd been shoveling all morning, swinging a pick.

"Yah."

"Stegner?" Static on the line, wind. Voice scratchy, deep. Familiar.

"Yah."

"I want my horse."

Pause. Hair on my forearm standing up.

"Whoever this is, it's not your horse."

"Why? Because you think you killed me dead? In the creek?"

Static.

"With a rock? While I was taking a leak? Cracked my skull and left me for dead?"

Neck prickled, goosebumps: "Who the *fuck*?"

"Well you did. Good job. Dead as the rock you used and tossed into the creek."

Heart hammering, could feel my pulse racing in the thumb I was using to grip the phone.

"Who the fuck is this?"

"Tough guy. Using lots of grownup cusswords. Nice." Gravel laugh.

Then: "You wanna know Who? The *fuck*? Well it sure as shit ain't old Dellwood is it? Thanks to you."

"I'm hanging up."

"No. No you won't. You hang up you'll be dead. Promise. Cross my heart. Be joining Dell."

I hung up.

Immediately the phone rang four more times, I let it ring. Nothing on the caller ID. Blocked number. Ring ring . . . silence.

I hobbled over to the armoire in the corner—felt like I'd run some race, knee sore, legs stiff and tired. Hobbled over trying to unkink my lower back and opened the fragrant pine door, reached under a stack of wool sweaters and pulled out my .41 mag. An ugly, heavy, black Smith & Wesson revolver I'd had since I was a teenager, the one I'd shot Simms with, the one the state let me keep because I pled down to misdemeanor assault, the DA allowing it because they wanted Simms the fucker behind bars more than they wanted me. I took out the gun and thumbed the cylinder twice around. Loaded. Good.

I lay it on the counter next to the tubes of paint. Walked to the little guest room on the other side of the woodstove. Pushed open the blue painted door. Small room with a quilted bed, one window with a view west to the uplift of the Black Mesa. On the bed lay a pile each of khakis, jeans, flannel shirts. My walk in closet. In the corner behind the door was a soft camo gun case. Lifted it onto the bed on top of the shirts and tugged the heavy zipper. Wrapped the grained wood stock with my right hand and pulled. Out of the flannel lined sheath slid a shiny stainless short barreled shotgun. A twelve gauge pump, triple plated Winchester. The Marine. Made for boats. I'd never had a boat, but I liked the idea you could drop it in the swamp.

What else? Check if it's loaded. I turned it side down toward the bed and worked the pump six times, kicking the shells out onto the quilt. The sixth pump empty. I gathered the cool plastic buckshot shells under my palm and thumbed them one at a time back into the sprung door of the magazine on the underside of the receiver. Five. I racked the pump once more to chamber a shell, leaving space for one more. Where? On the rough painted bed table was a box of Fiocchi dove loads. Well. At close range it would ruin someone's day just as bad as buckshot. Tore the cardboard top and fished one out, loaded the sixth. What else?

I lay the shotgun on the counter next to the handgun, picked up the iPhone that still lay there, punched in Sofia's number.

"Hullo!"

"I was just threatened. On the phone. I don't want you to come by today."

"Wha—?"

"In fact, you have any friends in Telluride or Aspen?"

"Crested Butte."

"Go there. For a couple of days. I mean it."

"Jim what the fuck? What did he say? Who was it?"

"Dunno. It was bad. Just go to Crested Butte. Soon as you can. I'll call you."

"Did you call the police? I mean, like the detective what's his name? The one you call Sport?"

I didn't answer.

"Yeah, I guess that's a dumb question. Jim?"

"You gonna go? You gonna promise me?"

"Okay okay. Be nice to get up there anyway, it's so frigging hot down here. Okay."

"Okay, go."

"Okay okay. Jim—"

I hung up.

What else? I wish I had a dog. I needed a damn dog. I wasn't going to let whoever it was run me off, that's just not me. But I'd be vulnerable tonight. So would Willy. I pressed on the phone again, hit his number.

"Hyell-o."

"It's Jim. I think I better come get the horse."

"You too? Everybody wants that poor little horse today."

"He called you too?"

"Yep. Just now. Said he was coming over to take the mare."

"Who?"

"Dellwood Siminoe's brother Grant. I told him his brother, RIP, lost all rights to the horse when he tried to use it for batting practice. He said he had the papers and that all their horses were owned jointly and he was coming over. I told him I already called the sheriff and let them know the mare's condition and that I had her until it was sorted out. I said if he set foot on my place I would take it as a physical threat and put a new buttonhole in his shirt. He didn't like that too much. He said I would dearly regret my attitude. I've been regretting my attitude my whole life. I keep wishing I'd thought to tell him that."

Pause.

Willy said, "Somebody killed your pal Dellwood Friday night up on the creek. I guess you heard."

There was a new tone in Willy's voice. It was not gruff and hearty. It was like the words would be whatever they would be but the tone underneath was speaking a truth no one could alter.

"I heard that."

"I didn't hear your truck start up in the middle of the night. Didn't hear it rattle back down your drive about three hours later."

Pause.

I said, "What do you do awake in the middle of the night aside from not hear things?"

Willy said, "Draw pictures. Horses and such. Campfire scenes."

Willy wasn't being cute, he was dead serious.

I said, "They sound nice. Did you show the pictures to Sport? The detective. He seems to be very curious about art."

"Nope. Gaskill came by to talk to me. I didn't much like his attitude, to tell the truth. For him I was sound asleep all night. What'd you call him? Sport? Ha. He's curious about fishing too. He kept asking me if you were wearing your fishing gear when I rolled up with the trailer. Waders, vest."

I cleared my throat. "And?"

"I thought a minute," Willy said. "Seemed to me if they were so concerned with them they must be some kind of evidence. Where

I come from clothes that are used as evidence in a murder have blood on them. I chewed it over and I said Yes, pretty sure he was. And that vest had blood all over it from where he gave Dell a bloody nose. That shut him up. He got kinda pissy after that. I told him to be sure to write that down, because come to think of it the blood on the vest made a deep and vivid impression on me and I would be sure to mention it in court."

I didn't know what to say.

"Jim?"

"Yeah."

"Dell was a snake."

"You knew him then? You said you didn't."

"Yeah, I know him. I caught him and a client poaching a Pope and Young bull pre-season once. He threatened Dorothy, my wife, and I let it go, didn't call the warden. Didn't seem worth it then. Her safety. That was a mistake."

"Hunh."

"Probably makes me a suspect as much as you."

Pause.

"Jim?"

"Yah."

"Take a vacation. Go bonefishing in the Keys. What I hear, Grant is a meaner snake than Dell. The police don't have anything on you. They did, you'd be in county right now."

■

I didn't take a vacation. I pulled out another canvas. I cut two pieces of the baguette Sofia had brought, it was stale but I didn't care, and I sliced a thick wedge of the sharp soft cheese and moaned as the smooth cream hit my palate and crumbs from the crust broke onto the counter. I ate another, drank a tall glass of cold water, poured my ugly mug half full with tarry bitter old coffee from the morning, and began again.

Another canvas, another road, this one coming toward me over the shoulder of the mountain, my mountain, Lamborn. How do you know if a road is coming to you or going away? I knew. A summer evening like this one. Coming out of the oak brush and junipers and dropping into the sage meadows. No black birds in this one, but a single horned owl perched in a long branch of Russian olive by the pond. The pond with fish, swirling here and there with the quiet feeding. Russian olive fragrant in its rags of dusty leaves. On the road a horse, small, reddish, the little mare trotting along the shoulder, coming almost jaunty, head high. Next to it another, a little bigger, spotted, the big antic eye patch of an Appaloosa, an Indian horse, spirited. Evening, like now, shadows thrown eastward in the long light, toward the mountain, the ponies' steps in tandem, matching gait, the rhythm of their coming, the thudding of the hooves and the play of the late light all as if set to music, and the closeness of their flanks like a dance and then I see why they come together: across their withers bundled, balanced, is the body of a girl. I seize. Brush halfway to canvas: breathe. And then I paint through it. Paint the young girl bundled and joggled on their backs, not even tied to the ones who are carrying her, balanced in the swift loping, balanced I see now only by the complete attention of the horses, by love.

■

That a painting could bring her this close.

A week before she died I was painting in the many-windowed shed that was my studio. She hung in the doorway and watched me for a while saying nothing, the way she had done since she was a little girl. Except now she was stooped over her own lankiness, her hair hanging in her face. Tentative, brooding, the way she never was. She had been suspended from school three days before for smoking in the girls' room, her grades were failing in three subjects. I was not pleased. Plus Cristine and I had been fighting for days and I was sleeping in the studio. Alce watched, I painted, drank from a can of PBR, finally she said, "It's good, Pop. I like the clouds that look like birds."

I grunted, didn't answer.

"I know you're mad."

I painted.

"Jeremiah lives ten miles out of town. I don't know, Pop. I really like him. He's into some stuff, I get confused sometimes, but he's a good person. Boys are weird. You know?" I turned. She pushed her hair out of her face and with great effort looked up at me. She had changed. She was no longer my little girl. I saw that like a stroke of bad lightning and it conjured a rage that shocked me.

"I'm trying to figure stuff out," she said.

I turned back to the canvas, the loaded brush, forced myself to paint.

I heard her huff out her breath behind me. Heard her summon her strength, her stubbornness.

"I wondered if I could have a phone? You know, so I can coordinate with him."

Could feel my breath quickening, hear the palette knife like sandpaper enacting its coarse rhythm. Finally, turned:

"You have got to be fucking kidding me. How old are you? Is this the guy who gave you ecstasy? Are you even using birth control? Have you remembered that school involves *studying*? Jesus fucking Christ."

She wouldn't look at me. I had never spoken to her that way. She really loved him, the boy Jeremiah, that's what she had told her mom. She trembled where she stood in the doorway, then left. She wouldn't look at me all the next week, or speak.

Then she was gone.

That day when she left the studio I went to the cupboard and found the bottle behind cans of turpentine and downed half a pint of Jack and threw the knife that was still in my hand against the wall.

■

When I finished the painting of the horses on the road it was almost dark. Dusk gathered in the quiet room. I heard in the distance dogs barking and I smelled smoke.

Smoke. A horn blare long and urgent. Yelling. Dogs barking.

I tossed the brush the tools on the counter, stepped outside. A plume of white smoke billowed from behind the hedgerow between me and Willy's. Twined in the gusting pillar were blowing strands and boils of black.

Oh, fuck. The sonofabitch. The fucker.

I hustle to the truck, overcrank the starter in my hurry, wince at the loud rasp, back up too fast, slide in a damp patch on the gravel, throw the shifter into first and peel out.

It's a minute to his ranch: I bounce up the steep drive to the county dirt road, sharp right at the top and two hundred yards to his gate which is open. Now I can see it: his bigger barn, the one flush against the line of old elms, is burning. The south side of it. The flames are consuming the tack room. It's a lower extension of the barn proper, and they are licking at the eaves of the main roof. As I skid to a stop I see Willy, hatless, framed in the main doorway and fighting the haltered head of a huge gelding, a chestnut, who is rearing, eyes rolling back. Willy is hauling with all his weight, taking the hard jerks with his bent right arm.

He gets the horse clear of the door and unclips the lead rope with one thrusting motion under his chin, yells *"Yah!"* The horse bucks once, throws both rear legs out in a tremendous kick, and bolts for the dirt track to another open gate and the sage hills. Willy whirls, a wild dervish, and disappears back into the maw of the burning barn. I am running. As best I can. I nearly collide with him in the door. He is leading the little mare. She is whinnying, different now than the cries of her beating, this is terror, not the piteous wail at a merciless universe but a cry for help. It breaks my heart open.

"Here!" Willy yells. "Here! Take her!" He thrusts the jerking rope into my hand and spins and dives back in. I back up. Transfixed by the mare who is bellowing now almost like a donkey, transfixed by the flames that are eating the far wall, backing, pulling the rope, and suddenly she lunges for the opening and I am clinging, hanging on, arm about ripped out of its socket, somehow catching up with her and unclipping the lead and watching her bound, unhampered, soundly gaited, watching her with huge relief run for the fields and the still galloping chestnut. Oh God, go. Nothing broken, running like a horse should run.

I wheel around and plunge back into the barn. Willy is in the back, too close to the flames, struggling with the latch on a stall door. The black smoke gusts and rolls upward from the far wall, half obscures him. I can hear the thuds of hooves, breaking barnwood, the terrified kicks. I slide beside him into the searing smoke and grab the door and yank and we almost fall back together into the rushing sparks as the door frees and swings. No thought of safety, of bones, Willy dives into the stall. He yells, thud, a swat I can hear over the roar, and another big brown with a starred forehead bolts, jumps clean over me no shit and I can hear the clatter on concrete and she is out the big door and gone. "That's it! That's it! Others already out! Go! Go! Go!" I feel his grip on my upper arm, tearing at my shirt, tugging me after him and we are running. Running down the aisle between stalls as something behind us cracks and thwomp! collapses, running in a blizzard of sparks and sudden heat on polished concrete and my right foot comes down on a thatch of hay, hay slipping on the smooth floor and I am down. Willy's hands now—can't see him in the black smoke which is pouring toward the wide opening, sucked toward open air, can't see him but feel his hands clawing into my armpits, hauling, pulling me again to my feet, a great shove in my lower back and I am spilling, tumbling out into the dirt yard and the night and the heat and wind is at my back and I land flat out on the stones and clods and look straight up into a sky luminous and clear as a spring, into a rash of rising sparks freeing themselves from the smoke and losing themselves in the paler stars.

■

Two red pumpers, sirens wailing, screamed up the road, jounced into the yard. The volunteers in yellow slicker suits and helmets, six to a truck, were out and swarming the hoses. There within ten minutes of me and two minutes later they had four heavy streams shooting into the flames, the roof of the barn, the part unburned. Willy had his hydrant going and was spraying down the side of his wood and tool sheds with a garden hose. The pillar of smoke on the south side of the barn went black to gray to a violent steaming white that exploded and rolled. It flowered inside out in the blossoming of its own death. A crack of timber like a shot and the roof collapsed on the south end, showering orange sparks straight up into the dark. Within an hour they had it all out. Half the barn stood unharmed. The other half steamed in a blackened ruin that burned the nostrils with acrid and sodden char. Willy stood in the yard. He held the triggered end of a garden hose as if he'd forgotten he held it. He watched the firemen spray down the hot spots, the backup man pulling and hauling the heavy cloth hoses over the yard, the nozzle man bracing and working the bale trigger in bursts, the rush and billow of steam.

I limped over to Willy. My lower back spasmed with shooting pain, trick knee screamed. I had to stop sprinting and rolling in the dirt every other day.

He was standing holding the little hose, his thin hair sprung out, a lick of it sweatstuck to his forehead, his face smirched, shirt torn. He stared at the remains of his barn. I stood next to him.

"I lost my hat," he said.

I clapped it against my leg and handed it to him. A fraying palm-straw wide brim Resistol stained by sweat and rain.

"It was by the door."

He looked at me first, straight into my eyes and I shuddered. There was a cold emptiness there I had never seen. Then he shifted down to the hat, no change in expression. He dropped the hose to the dirt and reached out and slowly took the Resistol. Deliberate and slow he set it on his head and snugged it down.

"Thanks." Then he smiled. It was like the man I had recently come to know had just reinhabited his body.

"I'd say Grant Siminoe chose to mess with the wrong people," he said. He spat. A spit that hawked up and ejected an entire swatch of the universe.

"But then smarts were never the Siminoes' most obvious charm."

As he said it headlights swung across his face. A pulsing blue followed. In that light he looked ill. A squad car pulled in, and the white Crown Vic, unmarked. Sport got out of it. He was wearing the soft shell wind jacket, hiking boots. Before he closed his door he took in the smoldering barn, the firemen, me and Willy. It didn't seem to surprise him. He looked like a man coming to an event he had on his calendar. Out of the patrol car stood a broad shouldered, white haired officer in a badged green jacket. His face had the bitter not unhappy set of an old war general: the sheriff himself. Must be. He reached back into the car for his hat. Surprised me when I saw in the moving lights it was a hunter-orange baseball cap. The sheriff walked over to an unhelmeted and bearded fireman who was talking into a cell phone. Must be the chief. Sport came to us.

Willy looked at him with undisguised distaste.

"Gentlemen."

Sport turned his body to watch the mop-up, the clouds of steam. Three spectators in a line. "Any ideas, Mr. Kesler?" he said.

"You know, Craig, the *Mr.* really bothers me. My barn just burned down so I guess I shouldn't sweat the small stuff, but I do."

"Willy."

"Nope. No ideas. No guesses. I *know.*"

Sport took out his flip notebook.

"Grant Siminoe called this afternoon, said he wanted his horse. When I told him it wasn't his horse anymore he threatened me."

"Can you recall the exact conversation?"

"Sure."

Willy told him. When he finished he said, "Jim got a call just after me. It was a little less polite."

Sport took it all down, the approximate times. When I told him that the caller said I'd be dead he stopped writing. He said, Just a sec. He walked over to the sheriff and the fire chief, pulled the sheriff aside, talked to him for a minute, came back. Asked about suspicious activity before the fire, headlights, etc. Nothing. The sheriff walked up. He scanned our faces.

"You lose any horses, Willy?"

"No. Almost lost Jim, though."

Sheriff worked his jaw. "Got a dip?"

Willy hooked a finger into his breast pocket, took out the round tin.

"Thanks. Swore to Lee I wouldn't buy another can. Turned me into a beggar. Christ."

He pinched about a quarter of the can and stuffed it in his jaw.

"Cluster fuck," he said.

"Well, yeah."

The sheriff spat. A black stream that splatted over the dirt like wet cow shit.

"You all are giving me a headache. Willy?"

"Sheriff?"

"Grant's at the camp. I went up there as soon as I heard the fire call come in. Him and five hunters swear on their wives' coochies he was there all day."

"And?"

"And you and I know he's done this before. He didn't go ahead and drop his driver's license next to a gas can. We won't find a thing." Spat again.

"I want this to stop," he said. "Now. I don't want any more bodies."

He turned his head and looked straight at me. His eyes were black and dark blue in the flashing lights and they were empty of kindness. "You fish the Forks today?"

I think I must've shaken my head to clear it.

"No?" he said.

I nodded.

"How was it?"

I stared at him.

"Good," I said. "It was good. Pretty."

"Windy though, huh? And hot. Catch anything?"

"Pretty big brown."

"On what?"

Now I felt like I was in a dream, a weird dream.

"Bead head prince on the bottom. That's what he hit. Had a royal coachman on top."

The sheriff nodded, spat.

"Hit it on the swing did he?"

I must have been looking at him like he was speaking a foreign language. Hearing the words but trying hard to understand the meaning, the intent.

He pretended not to notice. He said, "I fished down there this morning early. Used a streamer just because I felt like it. Didn't catch shit. Couple of little rainbows. I blamed it on the moon." He smiled without mirth. "Always good to have a big fat moon to blame it on. You gonna do any creek fishing in the next few weeks?"

"Sure. If—"

"If you're not in jail? We're trying our hardest. Tell you the truth, the quality of witnesses isn't what they used to be." He glanced at Willy.

He spat a clean jet onto the gravel. "If you're fishing the mountain creeks I'd get one of these." He patted his neon orange cap. "Don't want some asshole from Alabama thinking you're a muley."

I didn't know what to say so I said, "Thanks."

"I'm posting a deputy at your house tonight for your protection. Another will come tomorrow. And I'm taking the horse."

Willy started as if someone had touched him with a lit match. "Mark—"

"Until we get this sorted out that horse is going into the witness protection program. She'll be well cared for."

"Marly's—?"

"No not Marly's for chrissakes. You know about Marly. So does Grant. Don't concern yourself. Why don't you go get her. Keep her back in the corral if you want. Just a few minutes. I just called Eckly, he's on his way with a trailer."

"She needs a vet's attention. He clubbed her, nearly killed her."

"She'll get it, you have my word."

"I don't want a deputy," I said.

"I can't post one on your property without your permission."

"Then don't," I said.

He studied me. "Okay." He nodded to all three of us, lumbered back to his car. Leaned against it and began talking on a phone.

■

Willy called in his big gelding and hopped on him and hazed the other horses back into the corral. When Eckly arrived, Willy led the little roan slowly from the corral and she was unsure and trembling, and she shied when she neared the barn and there was a sudden hiss of steam. She was frightened by the sliding snake of a hose getting rolled in, but she never balked as he led her. He walked her right up the ramp of the sheriff department trailer, talking to her low and gentle the whole time.

■

I lay on top of the quilt naked and I cried. For the horse. Who was being moved to another strange place, into the tenuous care of more strangers. For myself, who couldn't seem to stop spreading trouble wherever I went. How the violence seemed to follow me, and it was wildly undiscerning and it hurt the things around me: horses, friends, neighbors. I cried. Jesus, Jim, Irmina was right, you need to get calm, make some peace around you, not mayhem. For everyone's sake. How did you get like this?

The three quarter moon rose over the shoulder of the mountain. At some point I heard the diesel pumper trucks roar, the air brakes, the fading growl as they went back down the road. At some point I stopped feeling sorry for myself, for everyone. The horse was in much better hands than she was a few days ago. Willy's barn burned, but not all of it, he hadn't lost any animals, and he told me before I left not to lose any sleep over that—he was heavily insured. He said the tack room was getting way too small anyway and that he had insured the building for so damn much he was sure they would think he burned it down himself. I got up and went to one of the poetry shelves set into the wall at the end of the bed. I flicked on a light switch there that lit only the books. Picked out a thick volume of Derek Walcott's collected poetry and scanned the titles. *The Schooner Flight* caught my eye.

> *In idle August, while the sea soft,*
> *and leaves of brown islands stick to the rim*
> *of this Caribbean, I blow out the light*

by the dreamless face of Maria Concepcion
to ship as a seaman on the schooner Flight.

It's an old style sea tale. Reminded me of the *Ancient Mariner* and *Moby-Dick* and "The Secret Sharer," all those poems and stories I'd read in school. It lulled me. I thought: Maybe that's what I need to do, go back to the coast, go past it, get washed by salt fog. Or. I had no idea what I needed to do. I reminded myself that I never had.

The next morning I loaded the new paintings and my dovetail jointed paint boxes and my new fishing gear and drove to Santa Fe.

On my way through town I stopped in at Bob's to fill up. He came out of the station slowly, snapping his jacket at the waist and hunching his shoulders like a man going out to do a chore he didn't much like. He unspun the gas cap and hit the lever on the pump without asking me how much, and as he cleaned the windshield he didn't look at me. I leaned out the window and opened my mouth to ask him how his cows were doing, then shut it. I'd never asked him that before. Fuck. I got it. He stopped at forty zero zero, no need for change, no extra conversation, and cradled the pump handle with the same remoteness. I held out two crumpled twenties. I felt nauseous. He took the bills, turned away. Stopped. He took a deep breath, turned back.

"Jim, if anyone deserved an early demise it was that sonofabitch. But you know, we can't just go around killing each other. Just saying.

"Be good," he said again, the way he does.

A partial reprieve. It was fifty miles of state highway before I could breathe normally again.

VI

Just Before Fishing?

OIL ON CANVAS

20 X 30 INCHES

PRIVATE COLLECTION

I have never painted in plein air. Never set up on some hillside, on some shore, in a big hat. But I did on the road south of Saguache. I made the right turn off the state highway onto a smaller paved road that went over a swell of grass hills and dropped down to a little creek limned with willows that ran off through open hills and pinewoods. The stream along the road ran dark and clear. It ruffled to white then smoothed almost black again. I slowed the truck, leaned out the window. I watched the creek, the purple stemmed willowbrush, the redwing blackbirds rising out of it, and I had two urges: to fish and to paint. Also, I wanted to shake off the scene with Bob.

As I studied the trout stream, the painting won out.

I turned a corner around a ruddy rock outcrop and saw the creek fan into a plain of willows, beaver dams, tannin dark pools. The pools stepped down the valley and cloud shadows tugged across them and the still water was touched with the quiet rings of feeding trout. In almost every one was a stick lodge. The beaver lodges were covered with a spotty packing of dirt, as if the animals had tossed shovelfuls of mud onto the roofs of their houses. How did they do that? Where did they carry it? I pulled over in a widening of trammeled tire tracks. The bank looked over the braids and pools, the thick low brush. A worn trail cut down to the water. For the first time in maybe my life I didn't take it. Kinda blinked at myself. Gee, Jim, are you growing up? Or old? Art over life?

I could paint, then fish. There was plenty of daylight and I was in no hurry. Nobody would bother me out here.

But just in case, I set up the easel, swung down and latched the narrow shelf for brushes and stuck the .41 magnum in a hole meant for a jar.

The sheriff hadn't been taking any chances, either. When I pulled out of my driveway this morning there was the young flattopped deputy who had admired my nudes. He must have been there all night. His beefy face in the open window was blotched with lack of sleep. He waved, very friendly, I waved back, then he started up and followed me down the county road. He followed me through Hotchkiss, past the turnoff to the Pleasure Park, all the way through Delta. We passed the little airport and the salvage yard Black Jacks where I had stopped a month ago to get a side mirror and the proprietress had fed her big Rottweiler watermelon gumballs. We passed the propane yard, and a mile after that he blasted his siren, one long two shorts, and I crossed the county line. The sign said,

LEAVING DELTA COUNTY
CANYONS RIVERS MOUNTAINS

I looked in the mirror and he was pulled over and his arm was out the window and he was waving. I waved back.

Now above the open creek I unwrapped the brushes from their rag, flipped open my folding knife and scored then broke off a rough square of fiberboard. I pulled out a for sale sign and taped it white side up onto the board. I'd use a similar palette to *Ocean of Women*. A tremor of anxiety and I realized I was thinking about Sofia. She was safe, right? I dug my phone out of my khaki pocket, no reception of course. Grant Siminoe wasn't going to go after an innocent woman, a bystander. Nah. Well. He did try to burn up a couple of horses. Panic like reflux rose in my throat. She said she was going to Crested Butte. She wouldn't have thought of it, but the road to the old mining town went right by the Sulphur, the steep turnoff where the bow hunters had their camp. Well. She was going to go in the morning, they'd all be in the woods hunting. Right? Grant didn't even know I had a girlfriend. Right?

I almost packed up everything right then, almost got back in the truck and turned around. Whoa. Cool off Jim. The sheriff would be all over Siminoe. If he was watching me he was sure as shit staking out the Sulphur road and keeping an eye on who was coming and going. He sure as shit didn't want Grant burning down any more buildings. Or assaulting girlfriends. Is that what she was? Calm down. Breathe.

Hey, Pop?

Yeah?

Don't get so excited about everything. That's what always gets you in so much trouble. Just leaping all the time. Like a chicken. A rooster. Right?

Right.

Always striking at a bug, another rooster, chasing a hen. How do those little hearts handle all that all the time?

Hunh.

Try just sitting still for a sec. Want to?

Okay. You sound like Irmina.

I like Irmina. Okay, meditate.

Sure.

Pop?

Yes, Alce.

You have three speeds, huh? Like that antique station wagon we used to have. With the shifter on the wheel? Remember?

Sure.

That's you, right? Kinda: crawl, fast, stop. Right?

Right. Laugh.

Maybe you should stop now. For a sec. Paint the picture. Everything will work out.

It will?

Sure.

I stood by the empty easel looking over all those mirrored beaver ponds and thought, That is some advice coming from my girl. My girl who one morning didn't have a chance. I stood and breathed and then I pulled the jars out of the jointed box and filled them with turps and walked down the steep trail to water's edge and splashed my face with tea colored water.

I had put five small canvases in the back of the truck with the new paintings. The unused canvases were wrapped and tied in an old piece of rubber tarp. I pulled out a twenty-thirty and set it on the easel and began. I painted what I saw. The braided stream threading the green and red willows like a little delta, the blackbirds flying. Three black birds of life. Not the deathly watchers. Could hear them as I painted, the peculiar exuberant buzzing call like an electric cable. I painted the Cooper's hawk that circled high, the clouds above him on their own compelled heading. I painted fish jumping out of the water though they weren't really jumping they were sipping the surface but fuck it, let's not be too literal, and I refrained from putting in a chicken or any death anywhere. Funny, but it was very freeing just sticking to the landscape. You'd think it would be the opposite. A certain kind of pressure was lifted, one I realized now that I'd always felt in the limitless blank outer space of total freedom. Which is a vacuum of sorts and has its own imploding force.

I thought it was ironic that now, with my assignment in front of me—paint the creek, the whole creek and nothing but the creek—now I felt released. My spirit flew. I painted like a child, without thought, one color to the next, one bush to one pool to the next to the birds to fish to a June bug about as big as a hummingbird who landed on my cap. Fun to paint like this. I mean it wasn't much different than painting an ocean of women except that I had forbidden myself that kind of license and I hummed and sang and my imagination rested, not frightened at all of any sharks coming up from the deep or any malevolent birds.

I was happy painting and suddenly envied my friends who built houses and cut down trees, the gypo loggers like Pop, the ones in Mora County who were Irmina's friends, Bob at the station: fix the transmission, change the oil. Or build a foundation, cut down the tree and the one next to it. What Irmina had said: *Jim you burn so hot.* What felt good was to cool. To paint simply and to feel a cooling, the calmness of craft, of being a journeyman who focuses on the simple task: pin this one corner together and make it fit in an expanding universe.

Not a single car passed in not sure how much time. A katydid pulsed out of the grass on the shoulder. The blackbirds buzzed and shrieked in happy territorial arguments. The sun climbed over the low ridge behind me and threw my shadow down to water's edge. After a while the beaver in the closest pond emerged and cut a faint wake across the still water. Came back. Some woodless errand. I could hear too the slow current pouring over the closest dam, sifting and burbling in the pool below. I painted. Painted the pace of it, the sounds as much as anything. The calm. It calmed me. That thing happened where I disappear. Except this time it was not into the poised energy of a woman, or into some watery interior landscape, but into instead the quiet creek in front of me, into the raucous commerce of corvids, the inscrutable transit of a beaver, the slow breathing of the morning. It was different and soothing and freeing and I didn't even know that I'd disappeared until I heard the higher vibration of an approaching car, still a ways off.

It wasn't a car it was a truck. A tall long-nosed blue semi with a shiny V grille like a cowcatcher and a high load of hay. Downshifted as it came around the last bend into view, the loud stuttered growl and cough and pitch into a higher octave.

The hay was in square bales and stacked tight and green. He passed at maybe 40 mph, blasting me with a sweet grass-smelling wind and then I heard the air brakes hiss, the double downshift and he stopped along the shoulder. Grind of gears and he backed up, neatly slotting into what was left of the pullout ahead of me as if it had been made for him. The high door clucked open and he swung down, the idle of the big diesel somehow growling benignly, fitting nicely with the other sounds of the morning.

I thought of "Phantom 309" the way Tom Waits sang it, I loved that song. *At the wheel sat a big man / and I'd have to say he must've weighed two ten / As he stuck out a big hand and he said with a grin / "Big Joe's the name . . ."*

He was—big. Not sure about two-ten but he was like six feet, heavy in the shoulders. Wore a camo cap and a full beard like me, but dark. Aviator shades, Wranglers, brown leather shitkickers. His boots scuffed the ridged dirt as he walked the length of his rig, unconsciously checking the straps and the load as he came. He moved with the loose jointed rhythm of an athlete. Hand came up in a wave, still twenty yards off. Country. I noticed that most country people hail you from a decent distance, city people wait till they're right up in your face. Then he stopped at the end of the trailer, looked up at the high stack of bales, put a hand up on the wall of hay, patted it. Fished a tin of chew out of his breast pocket, twisted off the lid and put a plug in his upper lip. Extra polite. I smiled. I raised my chin: c'mon. He came.

"Morning."

He stood off twice the length of an extended arm. Somehow I knew right then that he was a hunter.

"Hey."

"Dip?" he said.

Shook my head. "Took me five years to quit."

He nodded, spat. "Don't want to interrupt."

"Not at all."

"Sure?"

"Yup."

"You a painter?"

He broke into a wide smile at his own question, showed white teeth, surprisingly white for a guy who chewed.

"I mean as opposed to a hobbyist. I mean you sure as shit look like you know what you're doing."

"Well I don't know how to do much else if that's what you mean."

"'Cept fish?"

That surprised me.

"You got two rods leaning against the cap of your truck. I noticed as I passed. I thought fisherman-painter, this guy's got the life."

He took off his shades, folded them and hung them off the same pocket the chew came out of. He glanced at the canvas, shyly, as if he were sneaking a look at something very personal which I guess it was.

"Nice," he said.

"Thanks."

"I like the fish."

He looked past the bank at the stepped and spreading ponds.

"The way you made 'em jump even though they ain't jumping. That takes something. Maybe *balls* isn't the word. Spirit."

"Huh."

He was looking at the creek but addressing the painting, politely.

"The thing moves. The picture. I like that. The birds, the fish, the beaver, the clouds, the water. Sorta like looking at music. You know if it had colors. Nice."

Nodded to himself.

"Jason," he said.

"Jim."

"Pleasure."

"Likewise."

"I fished this stretch before. Why I stopped, partly. Brookies a course, but last time, it was fall, I got a cutthroat about as big as a tuna. Surprised the shit out of me. Didn't even know they were in here."

He glanced over. "You expecting company?"

I put the brush I was still holding back in the murky spirit jar, set my own cap back, rubbed my forehead.

"No. Don't think so."

I looked at him puzzled.

"You got a .41 magnum stuck in your easel."

"Oh shit." My hand went instinctively to the gun, stopped halfway. I shrugged.

"Maybe for bear," he said politely.

I didn't know what to say. Suddenly my whole predicament, the one I'd happily forgotten for a few hours, came tumbling down. He must've seen it.

"Or lion," he said more helpfully. "Lotta lion coming back into these hills."

I rubbed my face. We both looked down at the creek, at the molten rings of the sipping trout touching the black surface with the delayed rhythm of a very slow rain.

"You like to fish the Sulphur, huh?"

"What?"

"Me, too. I fished it just the other day. Hay delivery. I never fished it in the middle of the night, though. That must be interesting. With a moon and all."

He was looking down at the creek, very casual. My hand went to the shelf of the easel, rested there.

"Amazing that's legal when you think about it. I mean fishing and hunting, they're pretty much the same. Going out to stalk something in the dark like that. Maybe kill it."

He patted the tin of snuff in the breast pocket of his snap shirt, thought about doubling the size of his plug, decided against it. Maybe trying to cut down. A phone rang, his. The ring was coyotes yapping. He pulled it out of his jeans, glanced at the ID, at me, and silenced the ringer. Put it back.

My hand did not move from the easel. Inches from the gun. I was very still.

"You must have Verizon," I said.

"What? Oh. Yeah, only way to go around here. If you don't have it you need it." He spat, hit a clod with a neat jet. He said, "Not good to be out in the middle of nowhere with no way to, you know, get in touch."

Turned his head, looked at me full on, expressionless. "I was thinking of fishing this, take a break for an hour. Take a chill pill. You?"

I didn't answer. *Chill pill.* I'd heard that expression recently and then I remembered where: at Dell's camp, two minutes before I'd killed him.

Sometimes in a bar fight, just before it erupts, you feel the way things are going, they can't go any other way, and you strike. Preempt. Maybe you don't even want to, but you've been here before

and you know how it will go if you don't. Now I didn't. It teetered.
I watched him.

"You deliver hay to a hunting camp? Half a dozen guys?"

"Eight guys. Well. Seven. Now it'd be seven, wouldn't it?" Spat.
"Yeah, one on the slab makes seven. I never was too good at
math."

"Maybe the fishing isn't too good here right now."

"Maybe not. I got things I got to do anyway just down the road."
He turned his head, worked the plug in his cheek with his tongue,
looked at me, steady. His hair was very dark, almost black, but his
eyes were mineral blue. They were mineral hard and the calmness
in them tightened my wires more than any anger.

"Dell is family," he said.

I didn't move.

"Well, we don't choose 'em, do we?" he said. "Too bad." Spat.
"Whoever fucks with them. The law might not take care of it, but
one of us always does."

He looked down at the creek.

"Second thought, I think I will fish," he said. "Could use a stretch.
You? An hour?"

It was a bald challenge.

"Sure," I said. It was the only answer. I said, "Hold on."

I took the canvas off the easel with both hands, then thought better and put it back on the stand. Picked out a smaller brush and dabbed it in black on the palette. Scrawled in the lower right corner: *Just Before Fishing with Jason*—Jim Stegner.

"Here," I said.

"You want me to hold it? On the edges?"

"It's for you."

"Me?"

"It's for you."

He stepped forward and his hands closed around the sides. Strong and scarred. He stood there with the painting held straight out and too gingerly the way a man who is unused to it holds an infant. His eyes went from me to the picture and back. A flicker of confusion. He wasn't exactly back on his heels, but it was where I wanted him.

"Do you have a place you can lay it flat for a few days? While it sets up?"

"Oh yeah sure. I can lay it in the sleeper."

"Might wanna crack your windows. You know for the fumes."

"Well shit. No one ever gave me anything like this." He just stood there. Finally he turned his wrist so he could read his watch.

"I got an hour, better get after it."

He grinned and suddenly he looked like a kid. He held the painting out in front of him with both hands and trotted back along his load of hay.

We fished. He snugged together the four pieces of his rod and strung it and hopped down the steep trail of the bank with a natural's grace, his eyes sweeping the braids and picking his spot as he fell into the brush.

I put on hip waders and took the gun out of the easel and shoved it into my belt on the inside of my pants, just back of the hip the way I used to wear it, took up my rod and pushed through the scratchy trees. A redwing flew up from the willows and whistled and buzzed and made a commotion. Landed in a Russian olive that overhung the beaver pond. I knew he would supervise the rest of my session with a restless disapproval. The sandbar was yellow in the murky tea water and welcoming, maybe a foot deep where it extended into the pool and through the short watergrass I saw minnows darting. I could smell the perfume of the olive tree and feel the cold of the water through my waders. Sometimes you just fish a spot because it makes you welcome. Under different circumstances I would have felt happy. I can say that. Even the territorial blackbird clicking and hopping: as agitated as he was, he would have seemed auspicious. But there was zero traffic on the road and now as I fished I was aware of the weight on my hip and I kept one eye on the trucker who was casting into a braid maybe sixty yards downstream. Fished his own braid and thought his own thoughts.

We fished for over an hour. Don't know how long. Long enough that a tamarisk on the far bank was throwing its shadow across the pool. Long enough that I had released a mess of little brookies not a whole lot bigger than the streamer fly itself, which always made me laugh—the bravery!—and landed a two pound cutthroat that surprised the shit out of me and which I also let go. I'd usually cook that one, and sometimes carried a camp stove and a pan in the truck with me, but this time I didn't, and didn't care to build a fire. I was happy to watch him fin with what looked to me like great dignity back into the tea colored murk. At first it wasn't fun. I was watching Jason. There was a cold grip in my gut and I was aware of how vulnerable I'd made myself. We were in the middle of nowhere and now we were off the road. It came down to proximity and angles and the knowledge that I had a gun and that he might or might not. Well. After a while I relaxed a little and just fished, fishing has a way of taking care of things, and I kept one eye downstream and found I could pretty well do the two things at once. Jason was more than forty yards downstream, he'd been working up. I was sight casting after a rise and I'd let myself get lost in thought when I looked up and he was gone. Nowhere. Panic sounds like tearing paper. I remember thinking that as I backed further out into the water and scanned the willows. He might have circled upstream. I would have. If I wanted to surprise me I'd get to the bank and circle fast. I turned, stepped in up to my knees and searched the bend above the little pond. Fuck. Scrape. Whisk of branches, the knick of stone, and I spun around.

He was right there. Out of the brush, on the shallow edge of the pool. He was less than fifteen feet from me and he had something in his hand.

I stepped back careful of my footing and shifted the rod fast into my left hand and let my right drop to the gun in my belt. *"Whoa!"* I said.

He stopped, took it in, measured the distance.

"Whoa, Pops." His eyes were dancing. "I just caught three in a row on this thing, ugly little fucker, I tie 'em myself. Thought you might wanna try it."

He held out something that looked like a big ant, but wasn't, with a half dozen rubber legs. Ugly.

The proffered fly, the hand out, down here off the road in the brush. I cleared my throat.

"Think I'm done," I said.

Was that a smile? Not sure. He could be amused, I wasn't. If the ugly fly had looked less like an ant and a little bit more like, say, a Glock, I might have plugged him. I backed up two more steps and retrieved the line and swung the fly back in and hooked it to the keeper. I kept my eyes on him the whole time. I wanted him to wait because I wanted him to go ahead of me up the steep trail, but not too far ahead to where he could ambush me. He had sussed it, too, and he got it. He waited for me, very civil, and then he turned and led me back up to the road.

Before he got back in his rig he said, "You did pretty good." It wasn't a question. Then: "Thanks for the painting. I'm sure I'll see you down the road. Can pretty much guarantee it."

I didn't say anything.

"Wait a sec," he said. He trotted back to the cab, threw in the pieces of the rod, swung up, and a minute later jumped down in his jeans, and stuck something in his mouth as he came.

"Here," he said. "One of my ranchers gave it to me a week ago. He and his wife went on a cruise last winter."

It was a cigar, a Montecristo Number Two, a classic, a great Cuban. Steve had given me a box once after I sold the entire Dung Beetle Series.

"It's pretty good I guess," he said. "Never had anything to compare it to, so what do I know." He pulled out a lighter and lit my smoke. As he did his blue eyes met mine. I shuddered. They were warm with more than mischief. You aren't the only one who can play at this, they seemed to say.

"We might as well enjoy ourselves," he said. "One of us for sure is going down."

He turned in a wreathing of gray smoke, walked back to his cab and climbed up. I put my rod in the bed of my truck. I glanced up once, and in his big driver side mirror I saw him talking on his cell, looking back at me and talking. Then the grind of a low gear, the loud rev and he pulled out.

■

Threats are threats, violence is violence. In my experience the two don't go together more than half the time.

I shook myself off and drove slowly. I was in no hurry to get to Santa Fe. I was driving down the prettiest rolling road with the window down smoking a Cuban cigar. What the hell. It didn't get better, not in my book. I mean if you weren't looking too hard at what had just happened or who might be down the road or at some of the other stuff. Maybe living well is the art of not looking at that, at the other stuff, when you don't have to. Or being okay with it. What the fuck do I know. I wasn't sure that I was okay with much in my life at the moment, and I felt shaky, like when you haven't eaten in a while, but I felt almost happy.

In no hurry. I wasn't looking forward to the painting, the portrait commission. Not because the little girls I had met seemed mostly bewildered by the extravagant world of their father: I remembered them moving tentatively and always hand in hand, as if they were orphans brought into the great house straight from heatless dormitories—I wasn't looking forward to it because I had gotten excited by painting outside. I had painted a lot of landscapes, had stood before many while they burned their remote beauty into my skin, but had never done both at the same time. Don't know why. I was comfortable painting indoors and I liked best to retrieve those images from memory where they might be stained by awe and jumbled together with other things I loved. Now that I had tried the other, I wanted to do more. And I liked being on the road. The important thing was to be moving. As it had been so many times before. So after fishing with Jason I decided to take it slow, spend the night on the highway. Probably only four more hours to Santa Fe, but it was late afternoon by the time I got going again, and I figured I'd stop at some little town along the way. Also, it wouldn't hurt to throw an unexpected stutter into my schedule in case some blue eyed trucker was waiting up ahead.

I drove down along the bulwark of the Sangre de Cristos with the sun riding the ridge, past the turnoff to Creede and out into the flat expanse of the San Luis Valley. I didn't drive fast. The big pivot sprinklers were sending their jets out into the fields of garlic and peppers and the mile long rows strummed my vision as I passed and the sidelit plants throbbed green and the arcs of spray misted with rainbows. Almost stopped to paint again, look at me go, but I was too tired. Too pleasantly exhausted.

When I was young, just in grade school, growing up on the Oregon coast, I used to surf with my friends. I wasn't the greatest surfer but I was unstoppable. I didn't mind getting hammered. In fact, I actually loved getting tumbled and drubbed. Something about being lifted and slammed and wash cycled by such a force, such a force that was so powerful yet soft. I mean it wasn't a rockslide. I loved it. We used to put on short wet suits—they should have been long and thicker than they were, but we were tough and turning blue seemed to be a badge of honor—and we'd go out before school. My friends called me Knotty. I guess I wiped out more than I rode. Knotty was the name of Lane's retriever's favorite toy, a long knot of rags the dog shook and shook until we thought he would dislocate his neck. That's what the waves did to me. The name followed me to college and stuck until I dropped out, and friends there assumed it had to do with my muscles, or maybe some attribute of my private anatomy. The way nicknames are. Why did I start off about surfing? Oh, because one of the best things I remember about it was the pleasant exhaustion that could stick with me all day. Not pleasant, more than that. A muscle fatigue, a relaxation, a post-adrenaline wash that hummed in the body. Like an easy smile that ran through every cell. Often, if it wasn't too windy, and even sometimes when it was, we would go out again in the afternoon, and then that physical well-being thrummed me to sleep. Now, driving down the wide green valley smoking the stogie with the warm air pouring through the open windows, having painted well, having fished, having met a man who could have been my friend, I felt almost like that. Almost as good as that tired teenager, but without the nibbling anxiety of wondering if Jenna Larson would go out with a fool like me, or what kind of music I would face for not doing any of my English homework. Instead I wondered if Jason or Grant were going to try to kill me in the next few days. What we give up, what we gain. For some reason, maybe the afternoon fishing, I didn't feel consumed with dread.

Somehow the towns don't make a big impression on me and I went through Alamosa almost without realizing it. Steeped in images of the fields and in a daze of memory. Thinking about surfing and my friends whom I left in eleventh grade for California, and Jenna who was the first girl I ever slept with. Which took three attempts, no shit, to figure out what went where and how to get everything there before it was over. There was a stupid joke going around then: What's the secret to comedy? And before your straight man could get out an answer you interrupted: Timing! It was stupid and funny. Guess you had to be there. Anyway, after that first time making love she passed me a note in geometry that said *Timing!* And smiled with me as I read it, a goofy smile that I came to love more than anything on the planet.

She was a great girl with a big belly laugh, and what started as a crush became a real friendship and for me my first love. Timing! was our code for anything that didn't quite work out. We would say it under our breath, a catchphrase for anyone who meant well and couldn't help fucking up. Seemed to sum up most of the world. When I ran away to Santa Rosa, I swore I would sustain us and marry her once we got to the same college, and the night I was seventeen and called her from a pay phone in Monterey where I'd been surfing and Jenna broke up with me—it was the worst night of my life, till then.

Till then.

If we all knew what was coming, maybe we wouldn't even stick around for it. Time present and time future.

The afternoon I heard Alce died, I was feeding her pig Mittens. He didn't have mittens, he had a big dark stain on his side that I told Alce looked like Gondwanaland. She was about five when she first got him and he wasn't much bigger than what she could cup in her two hands. He was a rescue pig. His mom had died of some hemorrhage induced by labor, had lived a couple of weeks very sick, enough to give her piglets a start, and then we adopted the little guy with the grayish saddle that seemed always to be slipping off his side, and Alce bottle fed him five times a day for a month.

"Why do you want to call him Mittens?" I said. "There is nothing on him that looks remotely like a mitten. He looks like a tiny ancient continent floating on a little ancient pinkish sea."

Alce moved her mouth around the way she does and said that one of her friends had a huge fat red cat named Mittens and another had a horse called Socks. Well. That made enough sense to me. She bottle fed him in the beginning, and for a year I bought him feed, but once she was in first grade she stopped on the way home from school—we lived in town, on a dirt street with horses in the yards—and picked up slop from two restaurants. The girls at Chayo's especially loved Alce, and they would sit on the back steps of the kitchen off the alley and smoke and gather around Alce and her bucket and show her all the special things they had saved for Mittens that day, like stuffed sopapilla and posole. The big girls with their dangling earrings and smokes huddled and squatting around the little girl with her bucket almost as big as she was, and Alce looked as excited at each bit of food as if she were going to eat it herself. It was at a time between lunch and dinner when it was very slow and almost always one of the girls helped her carry the bucket home and accompanied her to the back to meet Mittens where he would be waiting at the fence with an expression of delirious anticipation, I swear, snorting and squeaking, leaning into the wire fence, his big ears unable to stand and flopping in his eyes. We scolded her but Alce let him out often anyway and he followed her down to the creek behind the yard where they would both swim. She would swim, he would lie happily in a shallow pool in the gravel and snap at minnows. On several occasions it was suggested that it was time for Mittens to meet the fate he was bred for, he was getting really huge, but Alce always said she would kill anyone who harmed him and I knew she meant it. She would try. So Mittens became family, the only one of us who could use his flat nose in the dirt like an excavator and loved mud and would follow Alce anywhere.

That week she hadn't been home for two days, she had been suspended and she was very mad at me, me and her mom both, and I noticed Mittens was forlorn and agitated, and it occurred to me that no one had fed him. I went to the shed for a bucket of backup feed we kept in a trash can and when I came to the fence he saw it and surprised me by barely getting up from his wallow in back of the pen.

"C'mon, Mits, dinner time. C'mon."

With great effort and grunting he finally roused himself and came to the fence head down like it took all his will, and when I lifted the bucket he looked up at me and I swear his beady black eyes looked like they were crying. There were no tears, but that's how they looked. I dumped it and he looked up at me again and nosed the food and barely ate. I was turning back to the shed when I heard the tires on the gravel and the cruiser pulled in. It was Finn, the sheriff who had arrested me once before. He looked ashen, stricken, and he took off his hat and stood like a man who had been hit by lightning and was just coming out of it. I thought he might need help.

He really loved Alce. He was the one who had picked her up when she was caught shoplifting a few months before, and he was the one who told me that her boyfriend was distributing X and other pills to his friends, if not exactly dealing, he was worried about her. Everybody in town loved Alce. She loved to laugh with you and listen to what got you excited and then she got excited, too. She protected kids in school who got picked on. She gave away trout she caught to the old Chinese woman who lived alone down the block and couldn't speak more than five words of English and looked forward to Alce's fresh fish more than anything in her day or week. Alce was good to the bone.

He stood there in the yard and I asked him if he was okay and he said No, Alce is gone, and I said What do you mean *gone*? And he said she had been knifed to death trying to buy pot in the lot on Mission and I stood there then and couldn't move. He put his hand on my shoulder, he tried to lead me inside but I was stone and he finally touched my beard, reached out and touched it the way a parent would and got in his car and left me in the yard. The next day I went out to feed Mittens, I wasn't going to forget her best friend in my blind grief and he was lying out in the middle of the sunbaked pen, the part without shade where he never rested. Hey Mits, I said. Just the sight of him, her friend since she was little, was too much. I unlatched the gate and went over. He barely lifted his head off the dirt and he looked at me again, straight into my eyes, his eyes like wet black pebbles, like he was trying to speak to me, speak out of his animal muteness of something too big for his heart to bear and then he lay his head down again with a huff and he hardly moved the next day or the next, and two weeks later he died.

■

In Antonito there was a billboard for a railway trip along the Toltec Gorge, a painter's rendition of a steam engine coming around a piney bend above a narrow rock canyon and it woke me up. Hey, hey, you are driving, it's getting late, it's dusk.

I had fished the Rio de los Pinos before. It's the little creek that runs through the gorge. How those little streams make such a big impression. I had driven the long washboarded dirt road down off the plateau and parked at a little bridge. I had walked up into the walled canyon. I had fished with a peregrine gliding the wall just over my head, and later with the sun slanting down and backlighting the biggest hatch of mayflies I had ever seen, the light coming through a candescent mist of wings, and I caught more fish in an hour than I ever had before.

Some creeks you simply loved, and seeing the railroad sign with the craggy gorge reminded me that we can proceed in our lives just as easily from love to love as from loss to loss. A good thing to remember in the middle of the night when you're not sure how you will get through the next three breaths.

I pulled off at the road I remembered and switchbacked down to the bridge and unrolled my sleeping bag just on the other side in some ferns. I fell into a dreamless sleep under a cloudy sky that smelled like rain. It sprinkled before dawn, barely wetting the bag. I folded the ground tarp over me and went back to sleep. Didn't fish at daybreak. Threw my gear back in the truck and under a sky cleaned of clouds I drove to Santa Fe.

BOOK THREE

CHAPTER ONE

In Hostile Country

OIL ON CANVAS

20 X 24 INCHES

Once an interviewer on a radio show right on the dock in San Francisco asked me why, coming from a family of gypo loggers in Oregon, I had decided to paint. He was sitting on a stool beside me, and we were beneath a large window that looked from the Embarcadero out onto San Francisco Bay.

I used to get drunk before interviews like this, but this was eight a.m., a little too early for even me. The interviews tended to make me feel like a rabbit or a lamb caught above treeline at nightfall. Steve, who had just become my most important dealer and sort of my manager, swore he would cut me off and send my paintings back if I ever got drunk again on live radio or TV. So I was stone cold sober except for a one hitter I did openly in the green room with the window looking out to Alcatraz, and I shivered and tried not to follow the progress of a small white sailboat and a big white ferry moving obliquely toward each other on the choppy blue water—what a cool place to have a radio interview, right on the dock—and I tried to think seriously about the man's question. He was a good interviewer, warm and really interested and he seemed to have actually read some of the coffee table book about me that I was now promoting. He must have looked carefully at the images of my work on the gallery's website. I could tell by his questions.

But this question stopped my wildly beating heart for a moment and stiffened my bristles and raised hackles I suddenly discovered I had. Maybe I was not a rabbit after all. If I was a little stoned before, I was not stoned now. I blinked. I turned from the imminent and beautiful sea tragedy that was unfolding out the big windows and stared at the man.

"What did you ask? Why does the son of a simple logger paint?"

"Yes," he said smiling. "Why choose to be an outsider artist with all the vagaries of a fickle art market, the stormy uncertainties of creativity? I mean it is practically asking to be poor, at least for a decade or two in the best case, isn't it? And your family can't have much money to help, I read that you grew up in a trailer in the woods. Why choose art when you might have a decent and rugged living as a logger like your father?"

I stared at him and thought about my father who died on a forty degree slope under five tons of Doug fir when a choke cable snapped. For some reason right then I thought about his red Jonsered chain saw which had a thirty-six inch bar. How he had set it down still running on a big stump and turned to lift a canteen filled with tap water when he died. What his buddy Egger told me as he handed me the saw.

"I sharpened it," he said. I thought about that. All Egger could say after sketching the scene was: I sharpened the chain.

"I think a lot of our listeners would like to know," the interviewer was saying. "It seems terribly brave. Or reckless? I mean where you came from. Your father was practically illiterate."

That I could tell was the question of the day. Was it reckless for the son of a gypo logger to aspire to be an artist. It was the recklessness that informed this *visceral, muscular, exuberant, outsider* art. How he had described it in the intro. I got it. How the art world worked: it was okay to be an outsider as long as you carried your spear and wore your loincloth, stayed primitive. Didn't get any uppity ideas. He widened his smile until it was pressing against his cheeks.

I looked at him. I knew he would never ask the same question of a RISD grad. I had spent nights in jail because of men like this, men who condescended, who impugned. Getting in fights. I had paid fines, been on probation.

I said, "Is this show live? It is, right?"

Now it was his turn to blink. He didn't understand, I could see it. But he held his smile.

"Yes, of course. That's why we call it *West Coast Live,* ha!"

A flash of fear appeared in his eyes, there and gone, like the flank of a trout catching sunlight.

"Okay." I nodded, in some kind of complicit agreement. I stuck out my hand, like for a handshake. He hesitated. He seemed relieved.

"Okay, a handshake," he said. "Let's shake on it. To the recklessness of the artist who is truly down out of the hills, and to the recklessness of live radio!"

He held out his long slender hand and I took it warmly like the fish that it was, and gripped it the way you grip a big brown to get the hook out, and then I squeezed. He chirped. Like a chipmunk. Then groaned. I squeezed.

He pulled away, then tugged, then he was half laughing half crying *Owww!,* okay okay *uncle!,* then he was kind of rearing back out of his stool and then he was howling and then I felt a bone snap, one of the knuckles in the first joint and he screamed, an unbridled uncensored live radio shriek, and in his panic he had knocked over the stool and two soundmen or whatever they were, stout guys in baggy jeans, shot across the floor and smothered me. They pulled me off and just half ushered, half shoved me out the double doors that led onto the bright atrium gallery and the wide steps. Nobody followed. No cops, nothing. I stood at the top of the steps with the blood pounding in my temples and looked down at the bustling crowd milling through the indoor market, the coffee shops and bookstores and restaurants, and felt the sun through the skylight warm on my shoulders and let the anger wash through me like warmed oil. A fine skim of anger on every working part until I didn't feel it at all, except that I moved smoother, cleaner than I had in weeks.

I felt as if the ghost of my father were standing next to me, and he was laughing. Pop, I said out loud. Fuck the fuckers. Let's go get drunk. And I bounded down the steps.

■

Why I remembered that now, driving through Española and onto the last stretch of highway into Santa Fe, I don't know. Maybe it was because I was about to see Steve. For the first time in more than six months. I had been painting pretty well, through the move to Paonia, and had been shipping the canvases from Delta, a few a week, mostly small, so he had been mollified, then happy, then thrilled, and he stayed off my back. The pictures were selling. I painted, sent off the canvases, didn't think of Steve much. But now I did. Driving into the outskirts of Santa Fe and onto St. Francis Drive and down the long hill with the view of the town spreading its pink adobes under the piñon hills, driving like an arrow straight toward the gallery—now I did. Think of him and remember that fucked up and wonderful scene on the pier after which he called me and screamed into my ear, *You crazy motherfucker. You total embarrassment to the Taos School, whatever the hell that is, you blight on the community of artists of the American Southwest, you—you—you*—stammering, spitting I'm sure all over his phone—*you goddamn loose cannon, you—you—can dress him up but better not take him out—goddamn it, you basically redneck fucking freak—I LOVE YOU!*

He loved me because all of San Francisco sat up and took notice. All of California. All of the Internet and the news channels and then the networks and CNN. They YouTubed and Twittered and the interviewer's howl went viral. They replayed the scene on nightly news and I was a sensation and suddenly you couldn't find a Jim Stegner painting anywhere, couldn't touch one for less than five figures. I was a hero. Apparently it wasn't only me who had been offended by the condescending, snotty tone of the man's questions. It was class warfare, it was authentic, hardscrabble, bootstrap Truth vs. entitled, pedigreed, monopolizing bullshit. It was everything wrong with the art world, with the whole goddamn society for that matter, exposed in a raw scream. People loved it. They loved me. They bought my paintings. Steve was putty. It was right before I met Cristine and when she listened to the interview later she laughed out loud, and I could see that she was impressed: it was something she would do.

I pulled right up to the gallery two blocks off the plaza in Santa Fe. Didn't bother to drive through the alley to the parking lot behind, just backed into a meter space in front and walked in. Because it was one p.m. on a weekday and the meter people take their lunch at one. They are mostly Jimenezes and their cousins and I know two of them. The Stephen Lily Gallery squeezed between a J.Crew and the Fazil, a very high end gallery that focuses on Edgy Contemporary, which mostly means erotic and cruel. One whole wall of the Fazil is always taken up with Ransteen's painstakingly detailed engravings of torture. They are in the de Fereal School of naked and splayed girls being flayed alive by Inquisition machines and are rendered in the most fawning detail. The pictures are smallish, because they can accomplish what they are after in a small space and there is something alluring and creepy about the implied discretion of such scenes in small frames. *My private collection, come this way.* They must be very popular because they go for shameful prices. Also, boasted Ignatius Fazil with a little ruffle of his feathers, each one takes at least a *hundred* hours. Wow! I said. No shit. He knew he was talking to the slapdash king.

I walked into the front room of the Stephen Lily Gallery. Carla was hanging my *Ducks in Heat*. Carla stood on a small stool and she half turned from the wall and her mouth rounded into a hollow O, and her eyebrows hit the roof, and I couldn't tell if she wanted to laugh with joy or scream in terror. She probably didn't know herself. This seemed to be my present effect. But anyway she was mute. She bent down and I kissed her on the cheek and told her that there were two new paintings in the back of the truck. Steve was standing in front of a Max Ramirez, one of his series of Demolition Derbies, a folky Mora County scene of partying Chicanos under the summer lights—a fiesta in bullfight style but instead of bulls there were colorful-cars-destroying-each-other kind of thing. I liked them. He, Steve, was interpreting the painting for a well heeled older man in a navy blazer and a bow tie. Very Ivy League maybe, but the man wore lizard cowboy boots which were disconcerting. Steve glanced over his shoulder at the sound of the door, the electronic chime, the sound of maybe money, and the color rose instantly into his boyish cleanshaven face, he looked apoplectic and relieved at the same time. This was fun. I had never ignited such powerful opposing emotions.

Steve's whole head was beefsteak red. Beefsteak tomato red. He gulped like a fish in air. He excused himself from Boots. He must have been beside himself because he almost shouted as he left the man, "I actually adore that painting. I actually won't sell it unless I get a written guarantee that it will hang where lots and lots of people will see it!" It was an asinine thing to say, kind of a violation of Gallery Salesman 101 First Rule: "Remember you are *not* a car salesman. You are an arbiter of popular culture, a High Priest, your value and the value of your work depends upon an unassailable disregard as to whether anyone ever actually buys the work or not." Gallery owners, the good ones, seem to float magically above the trenches of commerce, and if they are among the best they are also authentic in their absolute love of the work and of their artists, and their clients grow to trust that love. Steve was one of the great ones, which is the only way I could have stuck with him all these years, and I never doubted his true and real passion, his love for me, but he had just shown a breakdown in his bedside manner and I thought it was hilarious.

He was not in a hilarious frame of mind. He grabbed my arm and refused to meet my eyes and ushered me briskly into his back office. I felt like a bridegroom who had shown up late at the church.

"My *God!*" he whispered when the door had clicked shut. "Jesus, Jim, the *police* were here!"

He was right next to me. He stepped back. He wanted to hug me, I could tell. He didn't know where to be. I fought off a moment of panic: the police were already here. Why? Did they come to arrest me?

"Apparently you are a suspect in a *murder*!" Steve continued breathlessly. "And the Pantelas thought you would be here *yesterday*! The girls had their *hair* done!"

Amazing with Steve, how the two things, the more universal and the purely self-interested, could be thrown onto the same level of importance. I found myself very glad to see him.

He finally looked at me, but wincing, glancing, as if he were looking into the sun.

"It's good to see you," I said.

"It is?" he stammered. He seemed surprised.

"Yup. Despite all my best instincts. I'm not a suspect in a murder. I am a person of interest."

"I see, these are fine distinctions. I'm just an art dealer not a lawyer. A very nice fat detective came in two hours ago and asked where you were. He said you were supposed to be here and where were you? How should I know? I said, I'm his dealer not his mother. It seems that this morning I am *not* many things. I am not the artist's manager who feels wonderful about calling Pim and telling him that his homely daughters can take out the bobby pins in their hair. What the hell Jim, what have you gotten your hairy self *into*? I just know you didn't kill anyone, I mean we both agreed you'd gotten past that part."

He let out a long breath, sucked in another. Apparently he was not finished.

I thought: Why are the cops looking for me here? Now? Did they find something damning and new? Bits of brain?

"If you did," Steve went on. "I mean kill some sad sonofabitch, it could destroy you. The art I mean. The prices. Many examples. The establishment washes its hands of you in disgust with a We told you so. We tolerated Jim Stegner because he was brilliant and dangerous but now he's over the top, now he's just repulsive. It's fickle fickle fickle, Jim, like a pickle."

He loved to say that. I had no idea what it meant. Except that in his mind I was sure the pickle was a big fickle penis. Jesus, Steve was a trip. I would let him yammer all morning if he wanted to. Except that I wasn't sure what to do about the cop. What could I do? Running was out of the question. I'd be like one of those hangdog idiots who always got caught just over whatever state line, buying a six of beer in a convenience store with his Wanted poster plastered all over the wall. I shivered.

He heaved, collapsed in his bright teal ergonomic swivel chair. Steve's desk was a bean shaped spaceship sort of console made from materials not of this earth. The phone was the only thing on it aside from a razor-slim screen and keyboard, and it, the phone, was titanium gray and shaped, come to think of it, like a pickle. One afternoon I came in with my kit and I painted blackbirds all over it, the desk, New Mexican kitsch—which I started, by the way. Now you can't buy a stick of furniture between Santa Fe and Taos that doesn't have a magpie or a coyote painted on it. Steve threw a fit. He was so mad he couldn't get the words out, a real feat for him. But an hour later Severin Ricefield came in to settle a purchase and just about screamed at how delightful. The mix of Danish space futurism and manito folk, it just about stretched the universe out taut between its two poles, didn't it, Steve? How marvelous. Severin was a woman, an extremely erudite, also rich socialite who was one of the few in town, it seemed to me, who had more money than God and also had read and thought deeply about more than, say, landscaping. And had great taste in clothes, and cheese. I knew, I had been to many receptions and parties at her institutional sized adobe on Ravens Ridge. I mean the house was the size of a regional art museum, which I guess in its way is what it was. I was always very honored when she bought one of my paintings, and honored again when I saw it hung in a coveted and prominent spot on her wall.

Still, Steve hired a specialist to strip the blackbirds off his desk.

"*Did* you murder someone?" He looked up at me, very serious, face exhausted and wiped clean of expression, a very rare moment for him. A desert landscape washed after storm.

I thought about that. I couldn't really answer him. His honesty of expression seemed to require an honest answer. Which I wasn't sure how to give. The more I waited the more an idea seemed to intrude on the wonderful clean country of his face, like the shadow of the next storm.

"You—You didn't murder anyone, did you?" A little desperate.

"No, Steve no, I didn't murder anyone."

It was the compassionate thing to say. After all, he had just had to let the father of two little girls know that they had had their hair done in vain.

Not sure if he believed me. He looked relieved if still uncertain.

"Well, good. Good good good. Great. Three goods make a great."

I knew he was going to say that. I mouthed the whole sentence along with him.

"So I can call Pim and tell him that one of your always unreliable cars broke down in the desert but you are safe now, thank God, and here and ready to paint his beautiful spawn tomorrow." He reached for the phone which was his way of saying, Right? Daring me to challenge him.

"Right," I said.

"Okay, good. I've put you up at the St. Francis. Pim has. He's being extraordinarily generous about this whole thing. And anyway, we'd love to have you with us, but our guesthouse is being renovated."

That was a lie. He said it every time I came to town and my behavior for one reason or another frightened him. Which was more than half the time.

"Don't even think about killing anyone while you're here," he demanded as he turned his attention to the voice that was now answering the phone. He offered me one last wispy wave, like a passenger fluttering a handkerchief at the rail of an ocean liner.

I like the St. Francis. I have stayed here often and I am known. I walked across the broad streetside porch and the door was pulled open by a smiling young man in green tails with brass buttons. I hitched my tattered self to the front desk and the pretty Chicana behind the desk lit up—"Mr. Stegner! How wonderful to see you again"—and I thought she truly meant it. Well, the whole experience of the St. Francis is scented with memory. Steve always gets me the same room when someone else is paying for it. It's called the Artist Suite, has a little brass plaque by the door proclaiming it. Two rooms about as big as my cabin in Paonia. Distinguished by prints of Georgia O'Keeffe's least suggestive flowers, and by a slew of Rauschenbergs, go figure, I suppose because they are bright and active and only faintly suggestive of the end of the world as we know it. Seems like a half crazy curatorial choice, but I have to admit I like it. Makes me want to paint, if only to help rectify the tippy imbalance. And I have to think that in a cage fight between these two almost perfectly opposing artists there would be some parity of energy and weight. I had left almost everything in the back of my truck, had never had a single problem with theft in the hotel's back lot, and now threw the one small duffel on the big Mexican four-poster.

Mexican furniture must be built for earthquakes, or civil wars. A stray bullet would not even traumatize this ten ton ship of sleep. Stray bullet. I shivered. I needed a bath. I went straight to the oversize bathroom, to the whirlpool tub. There were scented candles in screwed down sconces at the head of the tub, little lighthouses, I mean they were made to look like lighthouses, set in a blue tile sea where even a pyromaniac child couldn't light anything on fire. Smart, I thought, in a world full of arsonists. I turned the hot tap, tossed my cap in the corner, began to strip off my shirt, stopped, pulled it back down. Fuck it. I needed more than a bath. I needed Ten Thousand Waves spa and hot spring.

■

Susurant pines. Susssss. Dirt parking lot, half empty on a hot early September weekday afternoon.

I dug a twenty out of the wallet under my seat and slipped the .41 magnum under there alongside it. Don't know why I was being so paranoid. Was I? Who was going to come after me here? Jason? Grant? Maybe.

Ten Thousand Waves. Cristine and I used to call it Ten Thousand Steps. The treads were stone and wood, the path winding up through the trees. In the evening simple lamps marked the trail. The gate was Japanese, heavy red fir, the top crossbar longer than the one beneath it, like a kanji character. It probably is a kanji character for something concise like Peace and godliness to the one who enters here after a hard journey, hot bath and naked people up ahead. That's what it always felt like to me anyway, whatever mood I was in when I parked at the bottom. Maybe it was the wind in the long needles of the pines. Maybe it was the rhythm of the path, the steps, the winding contours, the simple wood bench placed beside a lichen covered rock just off the trail. It felt a little like you were climbing the mountain like the wandering poets of old. One of the two books of Pete's I had tossed in the bag before I left and was becoming my favorite was a slim thing called *Two Hundred More Poems from the Chinese,* translated by a poet named Kenneth Minton. There was one I loved, made by a guy named Chen Bo in like the eighth century:

> On the snowy mountain
> even the crows are silent.
> My horse shakes his bridle.
> Where are the songs
> you and I used to sing
> in the hillside garden?

You might shed a little of the dusty earth on the way up. Between the grit of everyday life and the cold silence of death are jingling bit rings and singing and love. I loved that. Maybe where Frost got the notion for his own snow and horse poem.

The lodge was weathered dark wood and shoji screens, built in the style of a Japanese lake house. A German girl sold me my robe and key. She had a finely boned face and red rimmed blue eyes. She asked me if I wanted a tour and when I said No thanks, I'd been here before, she seemed crestfallen. She said, "You are an artist?"

I said, "How do you know?"

She smiled. "For one, we get many artists, so the odds are especially good." She laughed sadly. "For second, you have green paint on your cheek."

"Ahh. Ach. I always miss a spot."

"Well," she said, "let me at least show you the new meditation room." She wouldn't take no for an answer, she led me to a glass walled house with tatami mats, told me she was a conceptual artist from New York City reassessing her life. I thought she maybe wanted to be asked out, and when I didn't oblige she became sullen. She was very formal at the end and looked like she wanted to cry. Maybe she was just having a bad day. I shook her hand and thanked her warmly and realized that I could not save everyone. I could not, it seemed, save anyone, except maybe a small strawberry roan.

The coed pool was clothing optional, a round bath cut into a cedar deck out under the full sun. A few big pines leaned over it and the sparse shade was in high demand, crowded with supine nudes, mostly men. The rest soaked and lay out on the hot fragrant boards heedless of melanoma. I liked the bodies, both men and women. Some reclined in poses of flagrant exhibitionism, others looked as natural as a stump.

I hung up my robe and eased my scarred self into the hot pool. I sighed and leaned my head back and watched a long needled limb brush a scratchless sky. What could be better than this? The Japanese and Chinese poems back at the house shared an appreciation for the simplicity of nature. I thought the collections of ancient Chinese poetry were the most beautiful in my whole new library, and the most accessible. The government official who was steeped in politics and the luxuries of the court renounced it all and rode his horse, or walked, into the mountains. Or maybe he was exiled. He endured swollen river crossings and rain and snow and nights caught out alone without shelter. The relentless and steepening path. He was rewarded with: leaves falling. Blossoms blowing. Cranes and redwings croaking out of the rushes, flapping off down the valley. Mornings of frost and mist coiling on the river. The rustic hut of an old friend, nights of wine and song in the bamboo. Dawn parting, a poem left at the gate. Whenever I read them, I wanted my own life to be like that—simple, wandering the mountains from friend to friend, painting.

Well, many of the great Chinese poets like Wang Wei were painters as well.

"Jim!"

Knocked out of reverie. A toe prodding my shin. Who—?

It was Celia Anson, wife of the renowned gallery owner.

"Prodigal Jim, wow!"

Her husband, Happy Anson, had famously died a couple of years ago and left the store and his entire collection to this twenty-seven year old massage therapist who cared most about White Russians, not the men, the drink. Well, I knew about massage therapists and clearly had nothing against them, until they came after me with a kitchen knife. Celia was naked, of course, and when my eyes came down out of the trees and registered probably surprise, she slid over on the underwater bench and leaned in and kissed me hard somewhere between my cheek and the corner of my mouth and let her ample breasts float like happy ducks against my shoulder and collarbone.

She pushed herself off me, and her left hand slipped into my lap, which, in the buff, and the way things float around, was not just a lap but something more.

"Oh," she said, a little surprised. "*Sorry.* Maybe not!"

She smiled, goofy. I always liked her. I always felt a little sorry for her when I saw her at openings and parties, the way the art society treated her, the snotty razors of nuance she never seemed to understand but always felt, I was sure. She was very pretty, and she always dressed as a stunner, and she was much younger than the patrons, so of course many of the women hated her. But she tried. She was a sunny open soul from Half Moon Bay, a part of the north-central coast I knew well, from a hippy family as she described it, that ran an organic orchard and farm right along the bluffs south of El Granada. She tried hard to be forthright and friendly and she wore her hurt in a bewildered half smile. Where she came from, if you planted seeds and watered them, they grew. If you rubbed and kneaded a cramped muscle it uncramped. Cause and effect. Why, now that she was Happy Anson's wife, did kindness and offerings of friendship produce wilted plants year after year?

I think there should be tribunals for social cruelty as there are for physical assault. Calculated cuts in the first degree. Snobicide or its reverse. I always talked to her in those crowded rooms, took her on my arm from painting to painting when I could, and discovered she had a sensitivity and intelligence toward the works that might have surprised even her husband. Clearly she had been listening. And she was always so relieved at this attention, she split open like a milkweed and her laughter floated into my eyelashes.

Celia cheated on him of course, after a while. He had one of the best eyes for new work in the country and he was very busy promoting his artists. So not much consoling there. The rumor was that discovering her with one of his painters triggered the stroke that brought on his demise. He managed for more than a year, on a quad cane, and slurring out of one side of his mouth, but he had been a tall, upright, vain man, the kind of gallery owner that talked with a cultivated vaguely British accent he must have learned by replaying Alistair Cooke specials over and over. A real asshole. He didn't give his new condition time enough to teach him anything like real humility or gratitude, he shot himself with an engraved Italian sixteen gauge worth forty thousand dollars. Messy. Made a Jackson Pollock of his brains on his study wall.

Well. He left her the store, anyway. Must have, in his reptilian way, forgiven her and understood how much he had asked of the guileless, very young girl he had married, and how much he had damaged her.

"So damn good to see you," she said, smiling into the sun.

She was genuinely glad, and she grabbed a fingerful of my beard and kissed the side of my face again and let her breast swell against my shoulder.

"Are you back?" she said. "Please say yes."

"A week or two."

"Will you call me?"

"Sure."

"You're not married again are you?"

"Nah."

"Steve told me you threatened the last one with a chain saw."

I laughed.

"Word gets around," I said. "I told him I felt like it."

"We all have those feelings, Jim. You don't know how many times I wanted to shave off Happy's eyebrows while he was sleeping off one of his binges. That would've been tantamount to murder wouldn't it? He was such a peacock."

"Ha."

She was such a sweetheart. I thought she was going to say she wanted to cut his nuts off or put an ice pick through his ear.

"You know," she said, "you are the best artist in the whole joint. Happy always talked about stealing you away from Steve. He said you were a modern-day Van Gogh, how you are self-taught and all, and kind of have two left hands when you draw, and are such a wild hair half the time, and are a plain old, old fashioned genius."

She grinned. "So there."

She blinked at me, at me and the sun. She looked as pleased with herself as a kid who has just tied a bonnet onto her cat's head. Oh man, I loved her. Right then she had to be the cutest sweetest girl on the planet. What was wrong with me? An ocean of women. Is that what murder does? Some endocrine reaction?

"Call me," she said, and gave my ear a heartfelt squeeze. She rose out of the water. It poured off of her breasts. It ran its watery hands to her waist and down over the spreading round of her hips and the smooth flat of her lower belly and. Venus on the Half Shell. Celia rose out of the sea of Ten Thousand Waves a glistening magnificent thing, slowly, slowly turned, stepped one long tapered naked leg onto the bench and the deck, did not look back. Grabbed her robe off the peg and shrugged it on as she went. Good God.

"She did that on purpose," murmured an awed shaved-headed man to my left. "If I weren't unreconstructed one hundred percent all American gay I would go for that."

"Whew. Me too. I mean—"

We looked at each other and grinned. He had a bone in his right ear and a snake tattoo running down the side of his neck. "You're Jim Stegner. Couldn't help overhearing. Anyway I recognized you. Philippe Sando." He put out a fist to bump.

"Rocks right? You paint rocks hanging from strings," I said.

"You got it. You might wanna put that thing away."

He glanced down through the water. The bath was not sudsy or murky, it was very clear.

"Around here," he said smiling, "it might get you in trouble."

We surveyed the deck littered with muscular tanned oiled bodies and we both burst out laughing.

I felt oddly exuberant now and I needed to paint. I did not want to use the usual studio up at Steve's, the one he kept for me. I did not want to tangle with Steve or the cops. I took an ice cold shower and drove up the mountain past the state park lodge, up away from the creek into the aspen on the backside of Lake Peak and parked at the overlook. I put the straps of the easel over my back and carried the wooden box and a small canvas and a can of turpentine and walked up the old logging road a few hundred yards until the path toward Hobbitville forked off to the southeast. That's what I called it. They were crude tipi-shaped shelters of dead wood spaced down through the forest like a tribal ruin. They were artfully hidden from the trail. Most were wrecks, skeletons of once proud lodges, but others had been freshly woven with boughs and stuffed with leaves and looked like they might shed water, and they were all haunted with the inaudible vibrations of questionable practice, ceremony and ritual of God knows what. They were creepy. The hills of northern New Mexico are riddled with sects, orders, communes, religious cults of every stripe, so who knew. I liked them. I set up next to the one that felt most dangerous, a tall tightly woven lodge that reeked of recent embers. I stuck the .41 magnum in its cup holder on the easel, unscrewed a can of turps and poured a jar full of spirits for the brushes and began to paint.

I painted mountains. Blue. A disappearing powdery cobalt blue—mixed with alizarin crimson and lightened up with a bit of titanium white—like those I could see through the opening of the trees ahead of me. I painted a dry valley and along it the one river, in some spots just an arroyo riven in the rocks, I painted a trail and two figures toiling. One led on the narrow trail, hunched against the burden he carried in a sack. He turned, reached a hand back for the larger figure who was also having a hard time navigating the rocks. A harder time. The men were in league, the gesture was familiar, familial. They were brothers. It was clear. Clear to the silent woods on the slopes, clear to the clouds that massed and were not friendly. Clear to me. They were close in age and they had been traveling like this their whole lives. They were Dellwood and Grant for certain. Twisted and hunched and making their way together in a hostile country.

I painted like my own life depended on it. Can't remember when I painted in such a frenzy. The shadows of the big mountains. Where was the sun? Who knew. Where were the birds? There, hidden in the trees, not inclined to show even a little beauty. There was zero compassion in the valley, none anywhere. Traveling like that, season to season. What was it like to lose a brother? A little like losing a daughter.

I had. I had killed a man, someone's little brother. I stared at the picture coming alive in front of me. How could that be true? I had killed both him and my daughter in some sense. What I felt. Not what Irmina told me, but what it felt like, the certainty I could never talk myself out of. Who the fuck was I?

I stuck the brush in the jar, lay the palette across the open travel box on the ground and walked twenty feet to a lichen covered rock with a view down the valley. Up here the aspen were already start-

ing to go tender with the pale greens that presaged the yellows of
death. Some leaves had already fallen.

Sat on the rock. Up here not desert. Up here it was cool. When the
wind came through it spun the leaves like a million chimes, they
ticked and turned their pale undersides back, so that the wind
swept through with a brightening of the canopy, a wave of light
that carried the sweet smell of dying leaves. Already some blown
down, littering the ground. This time of year. He had beaten a
horse nearly to death. The horse. Focus on the horse. The little
bleating terrified roan. He was a drunk, who wasn't. He bluffed
and blustered. Who didn't? His older brother was his partner.
Likely his only ally on earth. He loved him somehow. Who knew
what tribulations growing up, the two of them, what threats Grant
had protected him from. What vicious fights. Maybe Grant's only
true project on earth, to protect his little brother. Well. He had
failed. We knew about that.

I needed a drink. Alce, I need a drink. Little one. I can taste it in
the back of my mouth.

Silence. Wind.

What are we here for? Surely not to purge others who have no clue
either. There would be no one left. Urge rose up like bile to drive
straight down to the police station next to the courthouse and confess everything. It choked me. I swallowed it back.

I thought about leaving the canvas up here in this unholy spot as
kind of a tombstone, but then I thought, Screw it, Steve will love
it, I know him. He will scrunch up his lips and digest it and look at
me sideways wondering what the fuck is going on with me, what's
true, and he will sell it for seven thousand dollars.

I backed out of the parking spot at the trailhead and swung a U-turn onto the two-lane and did a double take on a black El Camino parked on the shoulder across the road. The driver window was down and he looked straight at me, a dark bearded man in a trucker's cap and aviator shades. The shock of recognition. Fucking Jason. He looked straight at me, made sure I saw him, saw him speaking emphatically into a cell phone. Fuck.

Steve called me as soon as I got back to my room.

"Do you have a camera in here?" I said.

"No, I have Kimberly at the front desk. You know, the gringa. Who, by the way, adores you."

"Kimberly. You. And the cops."

"A Detective Hinchman is on his way to see you. Very courteous. A bit fat. What time will you be at the Pantelas' tomorrow? The canvas is already there, you know, since we expected you yesterday. I set it up in the piano room, remember? Off the courtyard with all the hollyhocks. Remember that big spacious room with the north light, where Julia serenades us with all that awful Bach. Imagine! Taking up piano at forty. Should be illegal. I always felt like I was at a kid's recital. Why couldn't they just let us tipple in peace? What time did you say? Ten a.m.? That seems perfect to me. Give the hairdresser time to get the girls up to running speed. Did I tell you they hired a hairdresser? Who specializes in kids?"

No he hadn't told me, and I hadn't said a time in the morning, but this was Steve and ten sounded right.

"Steve?"

"Yeah?"

"I better hang up and wash the blood off if Officer Hinchman is coming."

Silence. Shocked probably.

"Ha!"

Steve was always nimble, never took him long to recover.

"Ha! Some joke. Speaking of which. You know I've been revisiting your last two paintings. The ones from last week."

That usually meant he was reconsidering whether he should show them. Or that they hadn't sold and he was going to offer buyers a further consideration or find other ways to discount them.

"Yeah."

"They are disturbing, that's all. Not really like anything you have ever done. Ah—"

"Wait till I show you the one I did this afternoon."

"Really?" Excitement back in his voice. "You have another? Already? Well, you're Jim Stegner of course. Wow. I—" He stopped like a car coming to a clanging railroad crossing.

"Is it dark and disturbing? I mean the paintings—something is going on with you. I thought you might want to talk about it. Do you?"

He couldn't help himself. His tone now was completely free of affect. Kind of in awe.

"The phone is probably tapped," I said.

"Oh oh. Of course. Okay." He was flustered. "Okay, go up tomorrow at ten! Whoa."

I hung up. I waited for Detective Hinchman. I waited for three minutes.

He called from the lobby. I invited him up. Don't know why, but I placed the fresh canvas next to the hearth in the sitting room, face out. Maybe because I didn't want him turning it around a la Sport, and because I knew he would see it eventually since I was going to let Steve show it. It could hang next to the others on the Wall of Confession.

A spirited double tap at the door, ta-da! announced Detective John Hinchman, homicide. He was fat and wheezed like a bulldog, and was the most cheerful man I'd ever met at death's threshold. He seemed to be, anyway. Seemed about to drop from a cardiac at any second. He maneuvered through the door and was genuinely glad to meet me. His blurred smile was infectious. I say blurred, because it was hard to see him sharply through the cloud of good cheer he brought with him the way Pig-Pen brings his dust.

He said, "Been an admirer for years. Did you know you were the first man to paint magpies on furniture? I did the research."

"Ouch."

"I know, huh?" He chuckled. "You have a true creative impulse and within no time at all the market turns it into kitsch." He shook his head in mirth. I offered him a seat in a wingback and he waved it away.

"May I?" he said.

"Be my guest."

For such a big man he moved pretty smoothly, a little like a parade float. He studied the new picture.

"You paint that today? Still smells strong."

"You must be a detective."

A goofy smile stretched to his sideburns.

"One thing I love about this job. Nobody knows anything about being a detective except what they see on TV and in movies. So they talk like that. The dialogue, it usually runs along those lines. Even in interrogation. Makes it easier that way, everyone knows the protocol." He laughed.

"What is it?" he said, bending down and looking more closely.

"Two guys. On a rough road."

"Yep. Anyone you know?" He straightened.

"Probably Grant and Dellwood."

His eyes widened.

"Well. Off script," he said.

"Not really."

"You're a pretty straight shooter. I thought you would be. You can tell a lot about a person from his paintings."

"You want a beer? That mini fridge is stuffed. I think there's some fancy German beer in there."

Waved it away again. "Any reason you'd be painting Mr. and Mr. Siminoe?"

"They've been on my mind a lot."

Again his eyes. His smile at his own astonishment. Can a man really move through the world like this, with such droll good humor? I thought he was Buddha-like.

"How so? On your mind?" he said.

"Well, let's see. Dellwood almost beat a horse to death in front of me, then fought me, then got himself murdered so everyone thinks I did it, so that's Dellwood. Grant, well, he threatened my life a week ago and burned down my neighbor's barn. Because of aforesaid horse and brother. So maybe that's why."

He nodded. He looked serious for the first time since he'd come through the door.

"These guys, in the picture, they're having a really rough time." He frowned. "The older one in front, that must be Grant, he's trying to take care of his brother, protect him, like he's done ever since the two of them went to foster care."

It hit me like a blow. I felt dizzy. Not even sure why. Of course they were raised in foster homes. I guess of course.

He was watching me. I liked him. He seemed to be just about wincing, feeling my pain.

"They always went together. Since they were like ten and twelve. Couldn't separate them. They tried, the state, but they always ran away and came back together. Child welfare just had to make allowances."

"Right."

"You don't look so good."

"I'm not."

"You see Grant lately?"

"Never met him."

"But he's in the painting. Wrong scale, though. You've got him smaller than Dell. I'm assuming that's Dell right? Yeah, Grant's even bigger. Hard to believe he's bigger, huh? Given how massive Dellwood is. Was."

He looked at me. He wheezed. "The painting is real sad. Kinda makes me choke up. Don't even know why. Sign of a great artist."

He was watching me. "Want to sit down?" In a reversal he was offering me the same chair.

"Yeah, sure."

"Think there's a Coke in there?"

"Probably."

"We could use one."

He went to the mini fridge, pulled out two Cokes, cracked them, handed me a blessedly ice cold can. I drank half of it in one gulp.

"Grant took off Tuesday. Headed this direction. Sheriff had him at the Delta County line, then a witness saw his truck going through Saguache. Hard to miss a diesel two tone blue F-250 with a gooseneck hitch and spotlight. No reason for him to come this way except to come after you. A dangerous man, very pissed off, already threatened you once. Why I'm here."

"You're worried about me."

He smiled. "Right now I think I'm more worried about him. You look like you want to hurl. Want me to call reception and get you some Pepto?"

"No."

"I take these." He pulled a prescription pill bottle out of his jacket pocket, twisted off the cap, tipped the bottle up like a can and shook some into his mouth. "Sad thing is even a Coke can give me acid reflux. Sucks being fat." He smiled.

"Mr. Stegner."

"Call me Jim."

"It can eat at a man. The stuff we do. Secrets make you sick, isn't that what we say?"

"Being in prison makes you sick."

He nodded. "You have no idea where Grant Siminoe might have gotten to?"

"Wherever it is, I'm sure it sucks. I'm sure it's no fun at all within about a three mile radius."

He nodded. He dug in the pocket of his overcoat, pulled out a piece of clear plastic. He held out his palm.

"This belong to you?"

It was a small Visqueen envelope with a dry fly in it. A number 18 hook, tufty elk hair wings and an orange body made with strips of baling twine. It was a Stegner Killer.

"Yes? Take it, take a closer look. None of the fishermen we interviewed had ever seen one in these parts, but somehow you've got a shitload of them in your fishing vest. Excuse my French. Ten or twelve. And a couple on your kitchen counter. Must catch a lot of fish."

He stared at me.

"That yours, Mr. Stegner?"

"I'm not sure. Probably."

He nodded.

"Think you can patent something like that? I mean if it's just head and shoulders better than anything else?"

That twist in the guts. A sharp pain in my stomach that cut through the queasiness.

"Forensics found this by the creek," he continued. "Right where Dell was bobbing in the water. They missed it the first morning, but there it was in the second sweep, wedged in the sand between two rocks, right there, like a marker."

"I fish that stretch all the time," I said weakly.

"We know that," he said.

"It's funny," he said, standing, wheezing with the effort. "The longer I do this, the less I'm sure who the bad guys are. Ever feel like that?"

His candor landed on my shoulder like a lost bird.

"Not really. I have a pretty good idea who's really bad."

"I found something else in my travels," he said. "Something I read."

He brought two folded pages out of his inside jacket pocket. Handed them to me in the chair. I took them, my hand was shaking a little, I unfolded them, read:

She had the bag. I say to Hen, "Hey, Bug uses those black bags." "Fuck Bug. Let's grab it," Hen says. I say, "You fucking grab it." He says, "What're you afraid of pussy? She's about the size of a Chihuahua."

I gagged. *She* was Alce. It was the transcript, from the DA in Taos. I'd read it before, three years ago. Alce coming at them with her bag of pot. I read it now. The whole thing. It was the last thing I wanted to do and I couldn't help myself.

She went to buy an ounce of pot. Something any kid might do. That last year she started skipping school. Began dating a druggy. One afternoon the manager of the pharmacy off the plaza called to say that Alce was in the office, could I come pick her up, she had been caught shoplifting. Beto Salazar went to school with Cristine, he wasn't going to call the cops, but could I please get the girl to just apologize. She never did. She walked out of there tight-lipped and proud. The next time the sheriff Finn drove her. Then the meeting with the vice principal, the slipping grades. Her smoldering silence. Cristine and I were too caught up in our own fighting and our own work to offer much in the way of radical change at home.

Then she came to me to ask if she could have a cell phone and I unloaded on her. Thinking about it later, I saw that she was trying to talk to me. Trying to tell me about her first boyfriend and the stuff they were into, trying to get me to help her sort it out, and I just unloaded on her.

That week she went to buy pot from Bug and there was another buyer in the parking lot, parked at the south end in the mouth of an alley. Two. Two men in their twenties waiting. One described the whole thing to the DA, the one who hadn't been stabbing, he dished it for a lesser charge. The big one got out of the car and grabbed her bag and she wheeled and roundhouse kicked him in the face and he went berserk. He cut her all over. The coroner said her right hand was cut nearly in half: she had been holding the blade. The men fled and she bled out, there in the alley.

She died because she fought back. Like she'd seen me do her whole life. Throwing caution and sense away and hitting the fuckers. Like her old man. Fuck the fuckers, fuck the ER, fuck the cuts and concussions—strike. How else was she supposed to react?

She died because she was just like me.

And what if she'd had the cell phone she'd asked me for? What if she could have called for help from the alley? How long had she lain there? I always wondered. I could feel Wheezy watching me. I couldn't read the rest and I couldn't not keep reading. She died in the ambulance, what they told me. Choking and trying to tell them her mother's phone number.

I let the pages drop.

"I get it," Wheezy said. "Why you'd do almost anything to protect a little beaten horse. We hardly ever get it right the first time around. Don't even kill maybe the one that really needs killing."

Wheezy nodded, looked at me with real concern. "Thanks for the Coke. Don't get up, I'll let myself out." He smiled sadly at me, wheezed.

"What we always say in the movies. Back to the script at the end," he said and left.

∎

Vertigo. What time was it? Would this day ever end? Time did that thing it does, when it uncurls and lengthens like a rattlesnake patiently sliding after a mouse.

I reached for a plastic lined wastebasket next to the wall and vomited into it. As I threw up I ejected the images. Shut and locked the steel doors behind them. What the fuck else did he know, Wheezy? He knew I had failed as a father, what else was there?

I leaned over and vomited again. Nothing but Coke. When the Coke was gone I gagged and heaved. The world splits open when you vomit, you kind of untether in space, get tiny as a mote. A baby. Why there is such an impulse to be held, held down, embraced. Well. There was no one here to hold me. I convulsed. *Mom!* A grown man still cries the word. That was something Mom always understood. When we threw up she just came behind us and cradled us in her arms and whispered it'll be okay, it'll be okay, and stroked our foreheads.

When my father died, I orphaned myself. My sister had already graduated high school, married her boyfriend, and moved down to Santa Rosa. Mom was tall and strong and people said beautiful. She loved my father fiercely I am sure and she cursed him his carelessness. How could he let himself be cut down in the prime of both their lives? It was the measure of her loss, I think, that determined the fury of her renunciation. I understand that now. But not then. She wept and cursed and drank and I came home from school on my bike one afternoon and found a big pickup in the yard. I was sixteen. I knew the truck. It belonged to Gus Hebert, Dad's foreman. Not just the boss of the cutters, but the ops guy for an entire lease—roads, cutting, transport—a compact, hard man who had worked his way up from choke setter as a teenager. I'd met him before, and I could tell that if Pop didn't exactly like him, he respected him.

They were drunk and half dressed—she in a robe, he in boxers and a t-shirt—when I came through the door. They were sitting on the couch in the trailer watching the cooking channel. The cooking channel. Instead of being abashed, Mom went after me, yelling at me for surprising her. *I thought you were surfing,* she yelled. I stammered that there was no swell, I was stunned, more than hurt by the whole scene. Gus watched me. I remember him blurry drunk, but there was something in his look that seemed sympathetic, like *I have a clue what you're going through and I'm sorry.* I didn't want his fucking sympathy, and I didn't want my mother to be a slut and I didn't want my father dead. Okay okay, I kept repeating and disappeared into my room, and filled a rucksack and said on the way out the door, I'm spending the night with Eddy. She came after me as I hit the outside steps, grabbed my arm, spun me. She was a strong woman, physically strong.

She said, "Jimmy, you—I—"

Her eyes were red rimmed and afraid. I remember thinking for the first time that she might get old one day. That scared me as much as the scene inside, and also how much I loved her. Way too much. I couldn't stand any of it. I couldn't take it all in and I tore myself from her grip and fled.

I didn't spend the night with Eddy. I stuck my thumb out on Route 1 and I ran away. Is that what it is when you're sixteen? I guess. Not really. I went to my sister Caila's in Santa Rosa and when I told her the story she let me stay with her for the rest of the school year. Mom visited twice, she had cooled down, and she did not contest this strange custody. I wanted to tell her how much I loved her and didn't know how. Truly, I was not myself that whole spring. I know what it means when they say *beside yourself* with grief. That's what it felt like. Like I was standing always a few feet away from my body as I went through the motions. Remote. From my feelings, from a clear view of anything. All I cared about was reading and surfing and drawing. I turned seventeen and bought a motorcycle. I could carry my shortboard on it. Caila lived on the west side of town and it took about twenty-five minutes to get to a break, and I finished the year and dropped out. I had a clue enough to get my GED before I hit the road and went down to San Francisco. I thought of Mom often, I forgave her, I loved her more than I could bear, and she died in a car wreck on the Arch Rock Cliffs, drunk, before I could tell her any of that. I was shell-shocked. I was living with Caila and Silas and I wandered around like a zombie. I'd go down to the city and just walk and walk and get stoned. Two weeks after the funeral I got into a fight downtown and with my head pounding I wandered into the San Francisco Museum of Modern Art and saw a painting on loan from Boston called *The Fog Warning* by Winslow Homer. It shocked me. This was a shock of life. The fisherman in his black slicker rowed through a rough gray sea, the stern of his little boat weighted down with a couple of huge fish. The man is in mid-stroke, climbing the back of a wave, and he cranes his head to get a better look at his distant ship and the coming wall of fog bearing down on it out of an ominous evening. He is completely alone and a little alarmed, and capable. If they—the ship, his rowboat—are overcome by fog before he can close the gap he may be lost at sea, forever.

I knew water. From years in the waves surfing I knew how it acted, how it felt. And I felt this windchop. And the groundswell underneath it, and the weight of the stern-heavy boat and how sluggish it would be to row. This sea was alive and the colors, they came through my skin and they were cold. The slates and silvers and grays. And how the man was pinned on the sea between life and death: his catch meant life, for him and his family. But it also weighed him down in a dangerous sea with the fog coming. He had nothing to do but put his back into it and pull another stroke, and another.

How I was feeling, I guess in my own life, why it hit me so hard. The fog meant oblivion, but it also meant respite. I was seventeen and I was already exhausted.

I leaned into the painting and placed a bruised cheek almost to the canvas and eyed along the brushstrokes, trying to fathom how he had done that, made the sea so cold and wet and dangerous with only swipes of pigment. I could feel too the almost metallic scaly cold of the fishes' flanks. A guard in a blazer told me to step back. I'd had enough anyway. I'd only seen a few rooms and I'd seen enough. I wanted to do *that*. Make stuff come alive like that. With the wall of fog bearing down on my own life, that one painting gave me a reason to row like a motherfucker. Six weeks later I enrolled at the San Francisco Art Institute. I didn't graduate, I didn't even make it halfway through, but I didn't need to.

I finished gagging, the pages of the transcript on the carpet where I had dropped them. I sat in the wingback chair patterned with lilies that were no doubt supposed to rhyme with the Georgia O'Keeffe flowers, and I shuddered and breathed. Wiped my mouth on the back of my arm. Quivering. I felt empty, empty as a dead shell.

I should eat. No wonder I'd gotten sick, hadn't eaten anything all day, and I had put my body through a bunch of stresses, including heat, Celia Anson naked, and interrogation. Hot bath, then I'd hunt something up for dinner.

I had a better idea. This was all on Pim wasn't it? I pushed myself out of the chair, stood unsteadily, went to the phone by the couch.

Picked it up, dialed zero. The front desk answered, it was Kimberly the smiling gringa. "Hi, Mr. Stegner!" she sang. "It's Kim. What can we do for you tonight?"

"Is it night?"

"Nearly. Figure of speech I guess."

"May I have room service?"

"Certainly. In the future just dial six. Or call me, anytime. I'm here for you."

"Thanks."

It occurred to me that one of the problems and the perks of being somewhat famous is that you are connected everywhere, to almost, it seems, everyone. Which is not as sweet as it might seem, when hardly anybody you are connected to really knows you. Seemed that with killing I felt a little more remote from the world. Isn't that what Fatty said? Wheezy? Secrets make you sick? Well, they were already making me feel lonely.

■

CHAPTER THREE

Horse and Crow
OIL ON CANVAS
36 x 48 INCHES

I'm sure the designers of the Artist Suite didn't intend for their patrons to actually paint there. But they must have had enough stained carpet that they wised up and left a circular patch of floor tiled beneath the cove window looking out on Don Gaspar Avenue.

I turned on the TV and watched a cop show, one of those reality deals with videos of car chases that usually end with the suspect crashing his vehicle and fleeing on foot across a median where he is leveled by a German shepherd or three beefy cops with Tasers. In the one I watched it wasn't a shepherd but a big black Lab that took down our perp while he tried to get through a backyard cluttered with plastic playground equipment. He was a Hispanic kid in a white wife beater and neck chains and he vaulted a little slide set like a pro but the seesaw got him, tripped him headlong and then the Lab was on his back and tearing at his neck. I ate a bowl of tomato bisque and a slice of lasagna off the rolling tray as I watched, and drank a ginger ale on ice and felt a lot better. I didn't know Labs had it in them.

Then I digested with a segment on the Military Channel where they pit a squad of virtual U.S. Marines, say, against a Roman legion. In this one they had a SEAL sniper team, just two guys, against fifty Comanches on horseback with Henry rifles and bows. The SEALs had to enter the camp and free a white woman captive. I can't remember why they didn't get to use their whole SEAL team of five men. They had some good reason. The episode made me sad. Half of the Comanches looked Chinese and none of the horses had the handprints and suns painted on their flanks, what the Comanches were famous for. There was a lot of mayhem in the final assault and the spotter got killed by an arrow as they ran across the shallow river with the girl. I turned off the TV. I set up the easel on the tiles by the bow window and took out another twenty-four thirty-six stretched canvas from the tarp-wrapped bundle, and my paints, and I painted a horse covered in blue and red fish and I put the horse on the edge of a cliff and I put a crow with a blue eye on a rock watching him. The crow's bill was half open. That's all. I liked it. The crow was not exactly disinterested, and though a dead horse would mean a big feast, a crow potlatch, the bird I think was telling the horse about choice, that he didn't have to jump. The horse it was clear was supposed to jump for some reason and had never encountered the concept of choice. Everything in his life had come in a certain order and he had always been told what to do, or knew what to do in his bones, so choice had never come into it.

His instincts and what he was supposed to do were now at war and the crow was weighing in. I felt a little sorry for the horse.

I poured another ginger ale and thought about putting a coal train in the desert beneath the cliff but knew that was just a self-destructive impulse. It would add too many elements, complicate the simple proposition between the horse and the crow. I had fucked up all my life, especially when things were going well, going smoothly with a lot of clean light in the picture, but I had fucked up very few paintings. I seemed to always know just where to stop, I was not a painting wrecker at the end like a few other good painters I know.

Looking at the painting, I wasn't sure the crow was doing the horse a favor. One of the things I had read about crows somewhere is that they are much smarter than their station in life. I mean, unlike other birds, it takes them about two hours every day to secure enough food to survive and the rest is play time, electives. They are so clever and they get easily bored. I had read about crows in California that ate the eyes out of baby seals and sea lions, for fun mostly. Because they could. Seemed more like something a person would do. I imagined Dugar, in the Big Sur landscape of his dreams, witnessing such a thing. So crows must spend a lot of the day wondering what they are supposed to do now, what they are here for, and that seemed like a cruel existential dilemma for anyone who didn't have TV. It made me look at the painting in a different light: that the crow was more mischievous than he seemed at first. He was handing off this idea of choice to the horse the way the serpent handed off the apple. Poor horse. It was leap and die or live and be haunted by the ability to choose. Which when I think about it, might be one definition of consciousness. I pitied just about everybody.

I lay down on the big bed. Flat on my back. Smelled like starch. The cover was starch white. Like lying down in a snowstorm. Which is another way to give up all choice is what I've heard. Once my doctor friend in Taos recommended it to me as a way to kill myself if it ever came to that. He was trying to be helpful. Mitchell Gershwin is a very good ER doctor and probably a better fly fisherman. A devout Buddhist with a good sense of humor and a crazy great poet wife. I met him when I came in late one night with a small knife gash on my forehead. Don't ask—I used to get a fair share of those. He sewed me up and he bought a bunch of my paintings and we fished together sometimes in the Lower Box. Another friend of ours, a sculptor named Duff, was dying badly of pancreatic cancer and I told Mitchell that I would just shoot myself if it came to that, and he said, "Hey, don't leave a goddamn mess for your friends, just wait for a fine cold clear winter day and have a few drinks and take a shower and go out and stand wet in the wind or lie down in the snow. You'll chatter for a few minutes and then you'll go numb and warm and it's really peaceful."

I thought about that. I said, "What if it's summer?"

"Use the gun. Stand in a pond."

Never thought of that. Standing in a pond. I loved how he didn't even hesitate and I chalked it up to that acceptance thing Buddhists do, the way they are supposed to look at everything straight on, but I know he was just a great guy and he would have said that even if he were a Baptist. Funny, but I couldn't help thinking of the crappies and sunfish in the pond eating my brains.

I lay on the bed and I wasn't sleepy. I was exhausted to the bone but not sleepy and didn't feel a bit like offing myself, so I got up and shrugged on my barn coat and went out onto Don Gaspar Avenue.

Just then I wished it were winter. Winter nights in the mountain towns of northern New Mexico can have a stillness like nowhere else. I craved that right now. The stars like rivets, the air cold and absolutely motionless, the snowbanks like stone. I would not have it, not tonight.

Early fall here is full of movement. Everything is shaking off a summer languor. Harvest, tourists, storms, the leaves that never rest, gusts from the southwest that shudder the windows. It was night when I crossed the wide porch of the hotel and stepped onto the sidewalk. And breezy. I breathed it. It felt good and I felt drunk. Not woozy anymore but leery of time: what time was it? Not what it was supposed to be. And: fuck it. I don't care if it is yesterday or next year. Walk. Tighten your cap down on your head and walk.

It can be a dangerous place to be, for me. Displaced in time. I am not fully responsible for the now because the now has repudiated me, and one way to get its attention and to nail myself back into the moment is to crash a truck into an embankment or knock some condescending asshole's head against the bar. Like that.

So I knew myself well enough not to drive and not to go into a bar. I walked up into the plaza. Music spilled from the balcony of the Marble Brewery. I walked under the covered gallery where the Navajo sat on the ground along the wall in daytime and showed their silver jewelry to the tourists, and now there were two Indians curled up asleep in a pile of quilts on top of their jewelry boxes. Couldn't tell man or woman, shocks of long black hair and blanket. The cops left certain families alone and were merciless with others. Some ancient feuds. The breeze blew leaves out of the few big cottonwoods and chased them up the street.

I walked up to the dark cathedral and followed the high adobe wall down to Alameda. At Paseo I turned south into the wind, and at a bronze sculpture of two dancing sheep, I turned left up Canyon

Road. Did I just want to get mad? Maybe. Now it would be solid art galleries both sides for the next quarter mile. A half dozen restaurants but otherwise a relentless gauntlet of art. Maybe I thought it would make me mad enough to shake the weird vertigo I was feeling. Because most of this art was made with brazen pander. The sight of one blue coyote howling at a blood moon was enough to arouse my pity. The sight of a dozen made me furious. Same with fall landscapes that include an adobe house with smoke coming out of the chimney and a red 1935 International pickup parked in the drive. Strings of red chilies hanging from the porch. I didn't get it. Why didn't these people just deal drugs or something? They could make more money with less work. Once I went into a gallery with one of these nostalgic cartoons in the window and found a young clerk who wouldn't know who I was and asked about the picture with the house and the truck. She was very excited and tried to sell it to me. Apparently one of the most wildly popular artists in the Southwest. Value increasing by the week. I didn't know. I went home and researched the artist and found out he was a former stockbroker from Connecticut who had changed his name from Wiggins to Garcia Vega. Well. Wasn't Gauguin a stockbroker first? Didn't matter. Once you got to the work it wasn't supposed to matter, and I guess a painting was a painting and I suppose I might have loved Wiggins/Garcia Vega's pictures if they had been any good. Or even just a little brave.

I walked, breathed. Why was I so hung up on anyone being brave? So what if 90 percent of artists, or people for that matter, were meek? Just wanting to get through the day without getting yelled at or run over? Just have a good meal. Most people wanted to do one thing today with a small portion of pleasure like maybe weed the garden and pick tomatoes, or make love to a spouse, or watch a favorite TV show. Maybe they wanted to sell a painting. So what? What did it matter to me?

In Penstemon's there were blocks of color bisected by strips and geometries of other hues a la Diebenkorn but without the merciless compression that led somehow to freedom. I dug in my pockets and found an old pouch of cigarillos and, thank God, a lighter. I stepped into a doorway and lit up. Better. The smoke ran into my head and shirred along the veins. In Mariel's there were eagles made from bone and feather and tin milagros, the little stamped metal devotional charms shaped like trucks, legs, houses, cars. They were ragged, Catholic looking birds, maybe good at praying but not too good at flying. And life size bronzes of mountain lions, lynxes, curled fawns out front. I could imagine the conversations between them in the middle of the night when no one was looking. The gallery was perfect for the ski chalet crowd that needed something indoors and outdoors, something a touch folky but ironic as well as something a little awesome but safe like a bronze cougar who will never tear your throat out.

In the Stern-Gallietta someone was making hay with massive watercolors of trees in fog. I kind of liked them until I put my face against the door and saw an entire room full of them. I had thought about the art market way too much to be healthy. And why wasn't my anger clearing up the vaguely seasick feeling of not knowing what time it was or what day or what year? Which of course I knew, just felt like I didn't.

At the top of the street I stepped into El Farol, the low ceilinged tapas and music joint. I had told myself I wouldn't but I wanted a drink badly and knew I could settle for a nonalcoholic beer, it would help. As soon as I opened the door I was hit with the heat of a crowd and food smells and electric flamenco. I almost stepped back out, it was a little sickening. The bar was in the back and I scanned it for a seat and saw a young couple with salted margarita glasses leaning into each other and laughing, and they looked happy and in love and uncomplicated, and for some reason it clenched my heart. The possibility of simple happiness.

Cristine and I used to come here when we were first dating, and we enjoyed dancing, we were good together, and the nights we didn't get totally shitfaced, the nights I remembered, we'd had fun.

Further down the bar a tall honey blonde in a tight skirt and stilettos perched on a stool and I recognized Celia Anson. I moved toward the bar and then stopped. A man was leaning into her, a broad shouldered cleanshaven darkly handsome dude in a polo shirt, he was saying something insinuating it looked to me, and gesturing at the bartender at the same time, and she was waving his offer away, and he leaned in closer, right to her temple and she stiffened and picked up her keys on the bar and made to stand. His hand came down on her shoulder. She shrugged it off. He straightened tall with an angry half smile, looked down at her once like she was a recalcitrant caged bird who had maybe just struck and drawn blood and he stepped quickly behind her and out the front door. My hackles rose, those ones I never know I have. She didn't seem to notice. She stood a little wobbly on her heels and took a deep breath, smiled and waved at the bartender and made her way through the tables and sound toward me and the door. Damn. She hadn't seen me yet and if nothing bad was about to happen, the last thing I wanted right now was to get into a conversation with Celia. Let it play out, I told myself, see what happens. I knew this place well. I had been coming here for twenty years. I stepped quickly to my right into the dining room and made my way fast to where the bathrooms were in the back and out a service door just shy of the kitchen, pushed through it into the gravel alley at the side of the building where I used to go sometimes for a smoke. I could read it all without thought the way a fisherman reads the water. He would be watching the front door. He was. I saw his car, a silver Lexus parked in the back of the dirt lot across the street, under a big cottonwood in the deepest shadow, waiting. That heat in my blood: I had no doubt that wasn't an accident. Mr. Polo Shirt liked to park in the shadows just in case. Then I heard the jingle of her bracelets and the *tap tap* of her stilettos on the wood steps and she came into view walking with a mission, a little unsteady, but with a will to get the fuck home, another quiet drink that didn't work out, get me home. She crossed the narrow street, hardly looked for traffic and tottered down into the dirt lot, her long legs scissoring pale in the streetlight. Her car was toward the back, a new Toyota Highlander, also silver, three spaces to his right. When she got to it, she leaned into the driver door for a second, back to the other cars, and then looked down and sorted her keys with both hands, feeling for the right end of the opener and at the same time he was out of his car and moving fast and closing the distance with a practiced grace. He came around the front of the cars, his eyes locked onto Celia. Then his hand was on her right shoulder, not the touch of a friend but a stealthy grab and his back was to me. Okay, *now.*

I came across. Angled to my right to stay at his back and crossed the street in two seconds and came through the cars using them as a screen, fast and pretty quiet and as he pulled her around I was two steps back. She was turning, startled—*huh?*—and he said *Hey, I just wanted to* and his other hand came around toward the back of her head. At the same instant she saw me and her eyes widened, he couldn't have read it, I clenched my right fist in left hand and from full height *slam.* At the base of his skull. His grunt, his hands released her and he collapsed to the dirt like an ox shot in the head. Even then, even as she cried out, pressed back into her car in horror and her face crumpled into tears and she fell into my arms and sobbed, sobbed violently, even then I knew that it was the same fucking move as with Dell, the same strategy and timing like a practiced signature, parking lot vs. creek, but this time it was clean and right and somehow as I squeezed

her tight in both arms and let her cry, somehow something balanced, something bad was balanced and countered with—I can't
say good. With something necessary.

I made sure he was on his knees, grunting, working his way to
standing, and then I drove Celia home, it was only blocks away.
On the way her crying subsided and her hand came onto my thigh
and she said, "He was an old boyfriend, Jim. You shouldn't have
done that."

I turned to ice.

"He's an asshole and he gets crazy, you never know what's going to
happen, so I appreciate the gesture, Jim, but." She had a Kleenex
at her eyes and she began to cry again. She leaned and then keeled
into my lap and cried. It was hard to drive like that. I went numb.
I'd just gone berserk on one of her boyfriends. What the fuck?
What the *fuck*, Jim? You are losing it, buddy. Who *are* you?

At her big house on Camino Santander she kissed me hard on the
mouth and asked me in and I said I had a big day ahead of me,
sorry, sorry for everything, and I was, and then I walked back to
the hotel. Miserable. The bone misery like when you hit bottom
drinking. It was cold enough to see my breath which was a little
reassuring.

The horse and the crow were having a conversation when I fell
into the room. The longest day on record. Weeks and weeks long.
I went over to the painting and looked closely. It had changed in
my absence, something paintings liked to do.

The crow was now telling the horse that he, the crow, never had to make a choice about jumping off of any cliffs because he had wings. He never had to worry about leaping off of anything. He told the Indian pony that there was a horse once that had wings, too, and never had to worry about such a choice. And the horse in the picture painted all over with red and blue fish, my horse, was all ears. The crow had his full attention. The crow said the horse with the wings was named Pegasus and that he was the horse of gods and a god himself. The crow began to tell the horse the story and the horse put his ears forward, he was interested, then in thrall, and he forgot to be frightened about the cliff or anything else. He began to be like any horse listening to a great story. That's what it looked like to me, anyway.

I lay down on the big plush down pillows and fell asleep, sound and deep, a sleep of the gods, the gods that are always in trouble.

CHAPTER FOUR

Sisters

OIL ON LINEN

50 x 80 INCHES

PRIVATE COLLECTION

Two Boats

OIL ON CANVAS

20 x 30 INCHES

COLLECTION OF THE ARTIST

The phone rang loud in my room at eight, and I woke and took the down pillow from under my head and put about half a goose between my ear and the receiver, and listened to Steve crow. He wasn't going to let me sleep in.

Pim's house was up Double Arrow Road, a twisty washboarded dirt road with a locked gate for the big houses at the very top. There was a Buddhist stupa up there that few people knew about, a tall gold cross-legged Buddha off in the pines. He had serene, all loving eyes, and I admit that after Alce died I drove up there more than once and knelt before the Lord of Compassion and looked into those eyes and wept. I didn't know what else to do. I would park below at the gate and walk up the last steep mile. Once it was during a snowstorm and I lost myself in the trees and almost froze to death like a polar explorer. I can't even remember now what color his eyes are, blue agate I think, or green, but I remember feeling that they were without judgment and without the desire even to comfort, and so they were naked in the conviction that everything would unfold as it was supposed to. I took great comfort in that.

This morning I didn't have to walk to the top of the road, I had the code for the gate and it slid open. I was on time. I was already breakfasted, I was coffeed, I was a good boy.

From the road there was a long driveway that climbed to the highest knoll of the ridge. A circular drive pooled before a two story pueblo with latilla fences and stick ladders on the stepped roofs. Here was a massive front door carved with suns and corn. Pim's wife Julia came to the door. Yoga pants and a ponytail. She was sunny and brisk. She had a French accent, but she was not French, she was Canadian, from Montreal. She had been running a health club and I guess Pim was on business there and went for a workout and presto. She gave me a great big hug and I could tell she wasn't holding my truancy and the girls' hairdos against me. She understood the unpredictability of art. Yesterday I told Steve to tell Pim: No more hairdos, I wasn't Rembrandt. Please have the girls come as they were on a normal day, if there were such a thing.

Sailor suits, it would turn out. White with blue trim. I guess that was normal.

Julia ushered me into a great open room with a grand piano that looked straight down on the campus of St. John's College in the valley below. Church, adobe dorms, soccer fields, almost like looking down from a plane. And the steep wooded ridges behind it. My easel was already set up, the light from the north facing windows was clean and tempered. Perfect.

Julia asked if I wanted an espresso. I said, Please.

"Come into the kitchen. The girls are almost ready."

She walked briskly ahead of me down a tiled hall covered in Persian and Indian runners and lined with paintings. I was there, two of the beetle series, as was my friend from Vermont, Eric Aho. Also an early Alex Katz from when he spent a lot of time out West. Good mix. Down two steps and through a dining room with big windows looking out on the same mountain view and featuring a table that must have been sliced from a redwood. One solid slab. One tentacled candelabra in the middle made from handworked black steel, vines that flowed to each corner of the board, flowered with small yellow candles. Pretty nifty. I could imagine having dinner here as long as there were a butler to carry the ketchup. Julia stepped briskly, talked briskly over her shoulder as she went. We pushed through the swinging door into a red saltillo tiled kitchen bright and warm with a round table in a corner cove. The table was backed by tall windows outside of which bloomed the oranges and yellows of fall flowers. The room smelled of toast. On the brushed steel of the double fridge were taped the artistic endeavors of the girls, watercolors of Mom and Dad and dogs and trees and some animals that might have been moose. There was a newspaper spread on the table, and crayons, and there was a tiara on the bench and a plush baby seal and a doll face down on the floor in the attitude of a bomb victim. I understood that this was the heart of the house. It was the only room where anything was out of place and the only place that was alive. I thought of Alce, how she had never felt kinship with dolls, human dolls, and had left them scattered on the floor like this one; her favorites were birds and dogs, which I had taken as an early sign of good values.

Julia made us both espresso in a fancy machine, going through the motions with practiced ease, barely looking at the cups, talking all the while in high spirits, about I'm not sure what. I liked her accent. She said that Pim had to go to Detroit on business, he was sorry to miss me, I said I didn't know Detroit still existed, except for baseball, she laughed, she said You look good, Jim, better than when you were married to that playmate. Bachelorhood is good for you, maybe. I said, maybe. I said that I wanted to paint the girls in the kitchen.

"Here? You mean in the kitchen?"

"Yes."

"Why?"

"Because it smells like toast."

She laughed. "Well, paaw! Okay! Or if you want we can bring the toaster into the big room and make toast in there!"

Shook my head.

She smiled. I could see what she was thinking: Artists! Already the project had taken a delightfully surprising turn.

"I can help you move the easel."

"I can do it."

We polished off the little cups and I moved camp. I got everything ready before they came so the twins wouldn't tire as fast. I set up the brushes and jars and spread a palette of bright oranges, cadmium and transparent, and yellows and blues. I wanted them next to the table with the flowers in the background. She got the girls. They were six, in sailor suits, and nervous. They gripped each other's hands like a lifeline. Celine and Julie. They were tiny. Seemed smaller maybe than I remembered Alce at six. Julia shuffled them sideways two feet to their left so they were framed in the windows. They stood holding hands by the table and chewed their lips and watched me wide eyed as if I were the polar bear at the zoo. Like there were no bars on the cage, just this moat, and wasn't this supposed to be safe but maybe the bear would jump?

I went to my coat which I'd tossed over a chair and dug in the pockets and pulled out three candy necklaces. They took theirs without letting go of hands and without taking their eyes off me.

"Go ahead," I said. "Maybe let's try eating all the blue ones first."

They couldn't open the plastic wrapping without letting go of a hand, so this presented a dilemma. Probably couldn't open them anyway. Here, I said, I'll open them. The tiny hands holding the candy came up in unison and they relinquished their prizes without protest and without taking their eyes off me. I tore open the cellophane and the hands came up again.

"I brought one for me, too," I said. I opened the third one.

"I eat the blue ones first for good luck." I began to chew on one blue bead at a time, like a parrot high-grading the seeds of a fruit. "Yum!" I said. "The blue ones taste cool somehow."

They were watching me. I thought I saw a growing light of fascination in their brown eyes. They looked down finally at the candy necklaces in their hands and moved their lips around. Quick glance at each other and the hands came up and they began to chew on the candy, the blue beads, still watching me.

"Good?"

Nods.

"Wanna see if the pink ones taste different?"

Nods.

"Okay, let's go." I sorted through my own beads for the pink ones and bit them off one at a time.

"Which is better?"

"Pink!" said Celine. Julie nodded. They let go of each other's hands and began to eat with gusto.

"Now green?"

They nodded. In three minutes nothing was left of any of our necklaces but stained and ragged elastic strings. Their mouths and cheeks were sticky with color, the tunics of their sailor outfits smudged with their own palettes. Their hands fell together again. They continued to watch me with unwavering vigilance, but now it was more anticipation than fear.

"Want a gum cigar? Can they chew gum?"

Julia nodded. "Bien sûr." She was sitting on a stool at the counter and clearly enjoying herself.

I went to the coat and got out three pink bubble gum cigars. I unwrapped these too and the hands came up and I said, "Let's chew half." We did. They were sort of smiling through their chewing.

"Don't swallow, right?"

They nodded, chewed.

"Okay, maybe we better give the other half to Mom for later." They chewed, looked to their mom who nodded. "It's okay," she said. "Sautez!"

They broke ranks, ran to their mother, leading with their half cigars, and all three began chattering happily in French.

I polished off my own stogie, chewed. Occurred to me that a real one would be pretty good right now.

"All done," I said. "That wasn't too tough, was it?"

"What?" Julia called happily out of her huddle.

"Got what I need. That was perfect. They can go do whatever."

She straightened. "You what? I don't understand."

"I'm going to paint this at Steve's. Get out of your hair. That was perfect."

Her eyebrows were two perfect high arches. She was poised between disapproval and delight. All of this dealing with an artist was a bit strange and so unpredictable. But fun.

"I love Celine and Julie. They are perfect," I said. "Terrific models. Best I ever had."

I meant it.

"Steve brought up this big easel?" I said. "He'll send someone to get it later. Give me a couple of days."

"Well! Paaw. Well, okay. Wow." She released a long draught of laughter. "I believe I get it," she said. "Do you want some toast before you go? Another espresso?"

"Sure."

Before I drove back down the mountain we all ate cinnamon toast, and Julia and I drank espresso and talked about fishing, which, it turned out, she used to love to do with her father in Quebec. The girls played girl Legos on the floor. I didn't know they made girl Legos but they do. I packed up and all three of them waved me off from the front door.

■

I drove straight to the hotel. I asked the manager at the desk if there was a room I could paint in, not my room. Still didn't want to deal with Steve's place. I said I was planning one rather large canvas, like five by seven. Probably three days. He said, yes, of course. In fact the conservatory room on the roof has just been redone, it would be perfect. I asked for a drop cloth, a small folding table that could be stained. I called Steve and explained that I needed the canvas, the easel from Pim's. He was used to this from me, he was eager and quick, happy as long as I was working.

"Julia just called me," he said. "She was a bit giddy. She said you all just had the most remarkable portrait session. She said you didn't paint at all, you just sat around and ate candy cigars. The girls adore you, apparently."

"Candy necklaces. The cigars we chewed."

"Ha! You are not acting like a murderer. You are acting exactly like the old Jim."

Silence. The old Jim didn't feel like the old Jim. The old Jim didn't even know who the old Jim was. Or the new one.

"Sorry to bring up a sore subject," he said.

"It's not a sore subject. Can you just bring me the stuff?"

"Be there in an hour. Miguel is on his way up."

"Thanks." I hung up.

The thing about old friends is that they never want you to change.

I knew I couldn't paint the girls without painting something else first. Not sure what. But something was pressing the way it does sometimes. And I knew I couldn't paint it in the big sunny room on the top floor. I took another small canvas out of the bundle and put it on the easel in the room. I cut off a piece of fiberboard and made a small palette. I wouldn't need many colors. I began to paint an ocean. It was a cold sea. There were no swimming women this time, no fish. There was a single boat. It was sailing away, not sailing, drifting. In the center of the boat was a pile of sticks, and the sticks were on fire. A plume of smoke rising into an overcast sky. Inside the pyre was a mass. I painted a second boat. It was much smaller, much further away on its journey, but the smoke rose faintly from it, too. It was almost to the horizon and around it circled a flock of birds, and others trailed after it, the way they do after a fishing vessel.

That was it. I signed it. When Miguel came to tell me everything was set up I gave him the picture of the brothers in the valley but I kept the one of the boats, not sure why. I told him to tell Steve to price the brothers however he wanted and to hang it beside the new ones on the west wall. Then I took the elevator to the top floor.

■

I spent two whole days with the girls, much longer than I'd planned. I painted the garden outside the window first, and I painted in more detail than I had been used to lately. I painted an emerald hummingbird and a finch. I painted mums and holly-hocks, black-eyed Susans. I painted them framed in the windows and then I stepped back, felt the pressure of the windows in my chest and got rid of them, the frames and glass. I painted some sparse grass and a doll in the grass and a seal. The seal seemed alive and somehow happy to be there. That's what I painted the first afternoon. For some reason I wanted to make a world first, a safe and good world for the little girls.

The second morning I woke feeling clean and energized. First time in a while. I had walked once around the plaza the evening before, bought a silver bracelet for Sofia from the Indians in the gallery, fought the impulse to call her, knew I didn't want any news, turned my phone off, then I'd eaten a bowl of minestrone in the hotel dining room. Back upstairs I watched two hours of a reality show about sheriff's deputies in the bayous of South Louisiana called *Cajun Justice,* and fell asleep. I would have watched more had there been more episodes, I could listen to that muddled French accent all night long. Like the Quebecois, like Julia, the Cajuns were full of beans and mischief and humor and even the bad ones, the ones that were stealing copper and poaching gators, they seemed to be having more fun than the rest of us.

So I ordered room service on Pim, with a double espresso and an extra carafe of coffee, and I took the elevator to the bright room on the roof and I painted the girls. I painted them face on in their sailor suits, holding hands. Their tunics were smeared and streaked with colors. They were a happy mess. On Celine, on the left, on top of her head I put a chicken. A very content chicken roosting in a shaggy nest. On Julie I placed a nest of baby birds and a mommy bird. They were shaped like blackbirds, but they were wildly colored. The girls had forbearance. They were clearly in this together and they were willing to undergo the ruckus on their heads because they thought it was funny and necessary. The nests in their hair did not at all detract from their dignity, they enhanced it.

I signed the painting. It was late afternoon. It had taken much longer than most of my pictures and it was perfect.

Now what? What I came here for and it was done. I wanted to take it off the easel and run it right up to Julia and the twins, just to see their faces. But then I thought I better let it sit for a day or two so no one thought I'd blown through my assignment. Nobody, not even artists, understood art. What speed has to do with it. How much work it takes, year after year, building the skills, the trust in the process, more work probably than any Olympic athlete ever puts in because it is twenty-four hours a day, even in dreams, and then when the skills and the trust are in place, the best work usually takes the least effort. Usually. It comes fast, it comes without thought, it comes like a horse running you over at night. But. Even if people understand this, they don't understand that sometimes it is not like that at all. Because the process has always been: craft, years and years; then faith; then letting go. But now, sometimes the best work is agony. Pieces put together, torn apart, rebuilt. Doubt in everything that has been learned, terrible crisis of faith, the faith that allowed it all to work. Oh God. And even then, through this, if you survive the halting pace and the fever, sometimes you make the best work you have ever made. That is the part none of us understand.

The reason people are so moved by art and why artists tend to take it all so seriously is that if they are real and true they come to the painting with everything they know and feel and love, and all the things they don't know, and some of the things they hope, and they are honest about them all and put them on the canvas. What can be more serious? What more really can be at stake except life itself, which is why maybe artists are always equating the two and driving everybody crazy by insisting that art *is* life. Well. Cut us some slack. It's harder work than one might imagine, and riskier, and takes a very special and dear kind of mad person.

So anyway, best not to tell even your dealer that some masterpiece took you a few hours.

Fuck it. I couldn't resist. I hadn't felt this way about a painting in a long time, that almost bursting urge to show it, why shouldn't I? The oil was set enough. I'd put the canvas carefully in the truck bed on top of a drop cloth on top of my gear and make sure all the sliding windows of the cap were shut tight to protect it from dust. I'd surprise them.

That's what I did. I carried the painting by the stretcher bars in back, down the elevator and through the lobby and out to the truck in the back lot. I loaded it into the bed. I got in and felt under the seat. The .41 magnum was there, wrapped in a rag. I kept thinking about the talk with Wheezy, the cheerful Buddha-like cop. It set me on edge. It was like he was trying to pressure me into a slip about Dell, but also like he wanted to warn me about Grant, warn me to be careful, to maybe even keep a gun at hand. But I also believed he didn't want any more fights. He was complicated. I couldn't get a bead on him, as fat and simple as he seemed.

I drove up Double Arrow, let myself in at the gate, parked in the gravel circle and knocked. In a minute Julia answered. Her face was lit with surprise. She laughed, the high bell-like laugh that must have been one of the reasons Pim married her.

"You are back? So soon? Do you need another look at the girls or did you just come for some more espresso?"

She was wearing running shorts and shoes and a St. John's College t-shirt that must have been Pim's. No makeup, mother of pearl stud earrings, she was lovely.

"I have a surprise for you."

A flicker of uncertainty crossed her face.

"What? Another surprise? I don't know if I can take any more, Jim." She laughed. "Did you bring more candy?"

"No, something else."

I went to the truck. Her eyes followed me. I unlatched and raised the door in the rear of the topper and lifted the painting out of the bed.

"Oh, pawww! Jim, you can't be serious? Come in, come in, I'll get the girls. You remember the kitchen—"

She was off. There, then gone like a bird off a limb. I held the canvas by the stretchers and carried it into the bright kitchen and leaned it against the table where the girls had posed. The bomb victim doll was now head first behind a banquette pillow, and the tiara was under the table, but there were new toys, a pink princess convertible on the table edge about to pull a Thelma and Louise, and a large plush dolphin, about a quarter scale, in the middle of the floor. The girls were into sea life. I heard a clatter, an excited clamor of conversation and the swing door pushed open and in tumbled the three of them. The girls were wearing matching lilac capri pants and plaid light cotton hoodie jackets. Like something you'd wear after a session surfing. Everybody seemed ready for action. They saw me and squealed. Couldn't help themselves. With delight. Ran to me, skidded to a stop a foot away and yammered over each other. I have to say that just then I felt happier than I had in years. Better. I felt good, I mean like a good man in a good world, like the sunlight slanting through the big windows was also warming our spirits. I turned my pockets inside out.

"No necklaces, no gum."

The girls exchanged a quick look as if seeking permission to forgive me. The answer was simultaneous and seemed to be Yes.

"But. I have something else."

I pointed behind them. They turned. They had their mother's panache with exclamation. They released a high chirr like startled birds, then stood stock still and their mouths fell open in unison. Their hands came unconsciously together and their eyes widened. For a perfect moment they took it in, their delight about to take wing. Then *Crack!*

A clay pot shattered off a shelf above us.

Stung cheek, raining bits, sharp, pottery clattering over the floor, another pot exploding off the shelf, crack, gunshot, unmistakable. The airless hum. My hand to face, bloody, blinking, the girls screaming out of the sudden caesura and two neat holes in the plate glass in front of us, the garden sunlight altered there, swirling, tiny vortexes of shadow. Holy fuck. All this in a flash and I bent and grasped, picked up both girls as I spun and hunched and covered them, covering, on my knees now and pushing all of us back behind the granite island, down onto the floor and sliding backwards, somehow pulling Julia down with us. The girls wailing, Julia making a breathy keening, a stream of questions in French I didn't understand, her hands everywhere, under us, on the heads of the girls. Everyone shaking, pushed back now into the farthest corner of the room, pushed over the clay tiles with a bunching runner carpet and shards of blue pottery, back behind the counter, one tiny hand clutching my beard, another poking my right eye trying to hug my neck. Okay okay. Above, down the wall I saw a portable phone.

"Stay, stay!" I breathed. "Stay, just a sec." Released them all long enough to lunge up for the phone, grabbed it and back, punching in 9-1-1 as I covered them again.

"Talk to them," I whispered to Julia. Why was I whispering? I pressed the phone to Julia's ear, her eyes just focusing.

"Talk to them. Stay here. I'm going to get this thing away from here."

"Non! Non!" She almost hysterical, pleading, gripping my shirt.

"No, please. It'll be fine. He's not coming back. Talk, talk to them, now!"

Her tearstained face, nodding.

I half stood. The line of fire from the window could not touch them here in the corner. Plus the counter. Okay for the moment, they were safe. Fuck. I moved fast, as fast as I could, through the swing door and down the runnered hall and out to the main entrance and pressed into the jamb of the front door and shoved it open. Nothing. I could see the flower garden at the corner of the house outside the kitchen, all golds and yellows and flecks of blue, and a stretch of buffalo grass lawn gently sloping away from the house to the pines, he had been shooting upward, barely, he had missed because of the angle probably and the hard reflections of flowers and sky off the window.

From where I stood to my truck in the drive, from where he must have been, there was no angle. Except the first ten feet across the gravel. I took a breath and ran. *CRAACK!* Thud into stucco behind me. You fucker. You're getting old and slow goddamn you. Goddamn you for hurting those little girls. Trying to.

I pulled open the door and clawed out the .41 under the seat and grasped the grip and shook off the rag and moved back to the rear of the bed and gripped the pistol in both hands, edged to the corner of the tailgate and looked around it. Flash in the trees, off glass his scope just at the expected spot. Forty yards. I jerked back, took a breath, visualized the target and then swung around the tailgate and pulled off two shots. Silence. A lazy shirr in the pines like distant water. Could smell the tang of them, the warm-bark afternoon peace of them. Silence.

The fucker maybe didn't expect me to be armed. Why not? I waited, put one eye around the back of the truck. He would have to cross open space to do more harm, to get to anyone in the kitchen. He would be counting down, he would know there was a call to 911. Silence. The fucker. Three ways off the mountain from below the gate. I counted to two hundred, more, and then I heard the cough of a starter, rev, the rattle of a truck through wind and trees. And then I saw the dust rising through the pines down at the end of the driveway. Diesel. It was diesel, the growl. It was him. Not an El Camino but a big diesel pickup. Barn burner, assassin. I looked down at my hand, the hand holding the gun, and it was shaking like an aspen leaf and my heart was pounding in my ears like a bongo and I could feel a trickle of blood running off my cheek into my collar.

Cold rage. Cold and dry and sharp, a honed and frozen blade, unstained by pity, by any sentiment at all.

The cops came. I heard them three minutes before they arrived, in a snaking convoy. My gun was a revolver so there was no brass in the driveway. I wrapped the gun and tucked it back under the seat. Five cars, an ambulance, a fire truck. Wheezy got out of his own unmarked cruiser. He still had the air of a man who can't get over the antics of the species, but now he had an edge of real worry, the first crack in his impeccable jocularity. He went straight to Julia and when they were done talking he came to me where I was leaning against my truck. I told him everything in four minutes except— Some instinct. Didn't want him to know I had a gun. So I didn't mention the part about me shooting back and he wrote it all down and licked his lips and glanced up at me and said,

"Why did you run to your truck? To get something?"

That got my attention. He saw it.

"Nope. To draw him away from the girls."

He nodded, studied me.

"You in possession of a firearm?"

"You mean, like my .41 magnum?"

I thought: Might as well, they would know I had it anyway, bought and registered in Portland, Oregon. My other guns were back at the house, which they surely also knew.

"That one, yeah."

"I got rid of it. A while ago."

He moved his lips around, seemed disappointed. In me. That hurt, ow.

"Happen to remember when and where?"

"Nope. Must've been one of my drunks. I lost it."

He nodded. He mustered a smile, seemed sad.

"Wherever it is, maybe it should stay there. I don't want any more killing in my town. I have too many other fun things to do."

I didn't know what to say.

"Mrs. Pantela says the first thing you did after shots were fired was cover the girls."

He nodded. "That makes sense. Other stuff doesn't add up. Know what I mean?"

I didn't say anything.

"Okay," he blew out at last. "You want to go, huh?"

I nodded.

"You want security? No? I knew the answer. That self-sufficient streak. I'd like to lock you up right now, Mr. Stegner, for your own good. For everyone's."

That stung.

"I wish you'd call me Jim."

"You can go whenever you want."

I went back into the kitchen. The girls, thank God, and Julia, had not been hit by any shards of the pots, at least not anywhere exposed, and when the twins saw me I had a moment of panic, I thought they would reject me, the horrible cause of everything, but kids' minds don't work like that, they tore themselves from the ministrations of two women paramedics and ran to me and hugged my legs.

"You guys okay?"

The nods in unison.

"That will never ever happen again. That thing is gone forever."

I didn't say That Man is gone, I didn't want them to attach a specter to the things that had happened.

"I'm going away for a couple of days, I'll see you after that, okay?"

Nods okay, still clutching. I lifted them up one at a time and squeezed them, and kissed them on the tops of their heads, the places where the happy birds should have been.

Julia was shaking. When she met my eyes her own welled with tears and she hugged me so hard, and I whispered into her ear, "Don't be grateful. That was because of me."

"I know I know," she said. "But."

"He's gone, he's not coming back. He wanted me, not you all."

She kept saying I know I know. I got in my truck and drove off the mountain onto the paved road and onto the pavement of the Old Santa Fe Trail and I didn't stop. Fuck. Fuck Jim. You will kill everything good in your life. Kill it always. You always do. You pull the storms after you like hellhounds on a leash. What the fuck is the matter with you? You should maybe shoot yourself and end it before someone else you love dies.

I thought that. Knew I would never do it, never stand in that pond. Or freeze to death. Ever. Knew my curse was that I had to see whatever havoc I wreaked, always, everywhere. Goddamn.

I drove the black two-lane straight through the outskirts of town, straight into the juniper hills, straight north through Española and into the ranch country of Rio Arriba County. Already late afternoon, maybe an hour to dusk. I didn't call Sofia, I didn't call anyone. Didn't even know what the fuck I was doing really, except getting away, getting the blackness and threat away from everyone else. I'd stay away for a couple of days. I'd hit 285 and drive back to the Rio de los Pinos and fish it. Far enough away. Everything was in the back of the truck as it always was. I'd sleep out.

Julia wouldn't have counted the shots, wouldn't have known who fired them if she had. Nobody had to know I had a gun. I pulled over and felt under the seat. Beside the pistol in its rag was a box of ammo. I pulled it out, heavy with fifty bullets minus the six, and I tugged out the gun and thumbed open the cylinder and ejected the brass of the two I'd fired and threw them off into the weeds. I thumbed in two fresh bullets and put everything back. Drove.

Already late. I drove up into the open country south of the San Luis Valley, back toward Antonito and the los Pinos gorge. The instinct to go someplace I loved, someplace of peace, someplace where there would be no one. Especially no one I cared about.

Vast grass and sage plains, wooded hills. Something about the wide openness of it, the nothingness of it, the sun touching the hills off to my left. I breathed, felt the piano wires in my limbs relax. The windows were rolled down and poured warm air and the tangy scents of Mormon tea and sage. I breathed. Settled.

Everyone was okay. They were okay, no one was hurt, he wouldn't bother them again, not his game. Right? Right.

And you have all your limbs, your legs, your arms, they all work, right? Right. There are bad things in the world, bad people, not you. Okay? Okay.

You are *All Right*. Lighten up. You have made mistakes but getting rid of a very bad man may not have been one of them. If his brother is bad, too, well. Cross that bridge. Whew. Tomorrow you will go fishing. Fish one of the prettiest canyons in the world.

The sun was gone and the country ahead had more trees and the air coming through the window was suddenly chill and smelled of pines. The trees and the asters scattered along the shoulder of the road and the boulders sitting on the slopes all rested in that moment when every line is sharp and things seem to radiate color from within themselves. That perfect balanced moment between day and night. My absolute favorite time.

I slowed. Backed off the accelerator and took a left turn down a dirt track that ran through an open park of sage and grass beneath a ridge of pines. In that moment the sky also does something wonderful. It shines too from within, on its own, without help, a radiant blue sea, as clear and dark as the clearest water. Up there, ahead, sitting over the furthest purple ridge, sat a single star. Faint but irrepressibly alive.

Alce.

It blurted out of me. It was good to be alive and I was okay inside myself, for once I seemed to fit inside this quiet dusk, seemed okay, seemed okay to be alive and. She wasn't. But in my heart.

She lived. Lived as irrepressibly as that star. I slowed almost to a stop because I could barely see through the blur of my memories, and then I did stop, I pulled over into the grass, not sure why, nobody would drive by all night probably, and I turned off the engine and sat, and when my eyes cleared I saw a herd of five elk in the meadow feeding heads down just below the trees.

It was a bull, with a rack like a tree, and two cows and two calves. A family of sorts, and the strange alloyed happiness welled up again.

They fed, they ignored me, they were in the middle of their reprieve. Bow season not here yet on this side of the New Mexico border, the calves in their first autumn, before the beginning of the hunting season that would bring who knew what terror. I felt the terrible vulnerability of everything, and the depthless peace of the evening, and I wondered that God could have made such a doubleness, allowed it all to exist together so that we might feel so helpless. I swallowed the grief this time. Took a deep breath, wiped my face with my sleeve, and thought, It's just how the universe is, one big food chain, from galaxies eating other galaxies down to the tiniest shrimp, and it is a wonder we get to be here at all, in the middle of it.

I was certainly in the middle of it. Fuck Grant, fuck his brother, fuck their posse.

I shoved open the door and got out, stretched. The elk lifted their heads, turned them my way, lowered them again. I listened for the sound of water. I wanted to sleep out under the stars, now I could count two then three. Seven. Ten. More the more I looked, faint but burgeoning in the waveless blue. Like a perfectly calm sea, like minnows, who knew how deep.

I listened for the sound of water because it would be nice to sleep beside a creek and to have water to wash with. Dunking my head in a cold current now would be good. I held my breath, listened. The barest of breezes in the pines. The faintest rush. Nothing. Oh well. I had two milk jugs of water for drinking, and I had an old Therm-a-Rest foam pad and a light sleeping bag all stuffed into a milk crate in the back. I'd walk up to the pines and unroll them beneath a big tree. I'd bring a jug, a jacket for a pillow, the gun.

I stretched, my whole body stiff. I hitched myself along the side of the truck to the back and lifted the topper door and jerked open the tailgate. The bull glanced up, but barely, the rest kept feeding, they were used to me now and I was grateful for that, don't know why.

I leaned in and pulled the milk crate back. Beneath the light sleeping bag was an old rucksack. I opened it and stuffed in my bed, a water jug, a fleece jacket. I went back to the front seat and fetched a packet of little smokes and the gun, locked the truck. The engine was still ticking and a cricket was chirping out of the grass close by. The hopeful end-of-summer chirp when the nights are cooling—he was still singing for a mate maybe.

I walked up the hill. The long grass brushed my legs. The elk had spread out, and once in a while one of the calves lifted its head and cried. It cracked me in two. It was a birdlike cry, something between a chirp and the keen of a hawk. And one of the moms answered, tilting up her chin, louder, hollower, more resonant, a call that must have carried miles down the valley. They were close enough to see each other clearly, I was sure. They were conversing, a kind of call and response, an affirmation that rang against the hill.

Are you there?

I am here.

Will you be there now? Next?

I will be here always.

That's what it sounded like. To me.

There would be no moon tonight until almost dawn. What light would come from the stars. They were already asserting themselves. I walked up into the deeper shadow of the trees. My breath huffed and the grass swished against my khakis. I picked a spot beneath a huge old pine with a view of the valley. Sat. I'd unfold and blow up the pad in a minute. It felt good to just sit and listen and let the cool air slip around me. I took a swig from the jug and unrolled the foil pouch, dug out a cheroot, lit it.

Then I put it out.

A car engine. Just a vibration at first, the lowest growl, but insistent. It grew slowly, more and more distinct. Jerky faint wash of headlights sliding up the meadow a mile off. Coming around a curve. Then the two headlights themselves, high beams, not shy of the dark. Second gear probably, a truck taking its time, picking its way toward a known destination.

Unlike me. When I came up this road an hour ago I had no place in my mind. And if you listen you can hear the difference in the sound of the two engines.

The headlights jounced, the motor revved then dropped, a rising and falling in cadence with the rising and falling of the road.

Never labored, patient, coming on. I glanced down to my right but the elk had vanished. Maybe they could hear the difference too.

The truck came over a slight swell and then my own truck was caught in the glare. It looked old. As stranded as a boat on a mudflat, throwing a bulky shadow ahead of it.

The pickup stopped, idled. Spotlight flicked on, one of those lights cops and poachers use. The beam jerked over to the truck then moved back and forth along the shoulders, then twenty feet or so on either side. Looking for someone, looking for me. Maybe a tent, a figure on the ground.

Without thinking I pushed the rucksack flat back against the trunk of the tree behind me and rolled to the side of it myself. Pulled the brim of my cap low and pressed myself to the bark. The .41 mag was in the pack. I pulled it back to me and slid loose the drawstring and stuck my arm in the opening and fished the gun out from under the sleeping bag. The steel was colder than the nylon. I thumbed open the cylinder out of habit and ran the pad of my finger over each chamber, feeling with growing relief again the stamped brass of each bullet. Onetwothreefourfivesix. Had the box of forty-two more, but not here, they were still in the truck. Probably paranoid. Probably it was the rancher who lived on up the road just checking out what new visitor was in his territory.

Then I knew I was wrong. Because the lights went out and I heard his door chunk open and a few seconds later I heard glass breaking.

■

Windshield glass, that's a sound like nothing else, an ugly, buffered crunching that is too soft, a fractured thudding that doesn't even have the tinkle of breaking ice. Without thinking again I shoved the pack forward and raised the revolver in two hands and braced my fists on the taut pack like a sandbag and thumbed back the hammer because it's more accurate that way than pulling it back with the trigger, and I waited three seconds for my eyes to find the shapes again in the sudden total darkness and then I put two shots into the body of his truck.

The gun jumped. Concussions wiped the night clean of sound. Flame shot from the barrel.

It felt good. To blast away.

At two hundred yards I knew I'd be lucky to even hit the truck. Fuck it. I shifted over to my right and muttered *Fuck off* and aimed about where my windshield would be, where he would be, then raised it higher so the bullet could drop, somewhere over the back of the hood, just to let him know I was serious. Should scare the shit out of him. I thumbed back the hammer and pulled the trigger.

The thudding and breaking ceased. Silence. I waited.

He'd be crouched. I couldn't make out the shadow of any figure in the dark. This could take a while. He would be patient this time. Grant. Brother, barn burner, anonymous threatener and killer.

I didn't wonder what the fuck he was doing here, it seemed like a natural conclusion. Not conclusion, better hope not— development. If I'd thought the shots at the house might be a warning, a scare tactic, now I knew they weren't. He had missed, period. Jason had called him of course. Or he'd followed me from the house. They'd been keeping track. I'd been so lost in my musing while driving I'd never noticed the now and then glimpse of Grant's pickup a few curves back. And there, with a couple of hundred yards of cool country night between us, I could feel he had the meanness of a true coward.

He would be crouched now, behind one of the trucks, and I also knew without considering that he would be armed perfectly for the job. He would have a handgun as I had, and he would also have a rifle, or several, and I had an idea what they would be: an AR-15 .223 for the middle distance flat shot, one of the best setups for killing a man, and a .30-06 or a .308, bolt action, his elk gun, and if I knew the man and I didn't but could feel his malevolence like a smell even at this distance, if I knew him he had night vision scopes on one or both rifles. Because that's where he and his brother really made their money: poaching, and there was no better time to do that than at night.

I went to visit my uncle and aunt in southern Vermont, I was maybe twenty-six, and one night I got drunk and walked up the road, just maple and birch woods on either side, fields, and came to Sam Frazer's, a guy my age I'd known since I used to visit when I was a kid. An old farm house, the light in the front parlor was on and I knocked. He was a town selectman now, and his wife had just left him and he was glad to see me. He'd been drinking, too, and we got more drunk together, then drove into the field west of his house and I tried to shoot a buck in his headlights. I was so drunk that I'd duct taped a flashlight to the receiver of the little .30-30, and taped right around the lever so I couldn't work the action. Well. I'm glad now that the whole herd ran off before I could get my act together.

I imagined that Grant was much better at shooting things at night.

There was no sound coming from the trucks and no shadowed figure moving between them or moving at all. He was waiting. He had broken the glass to draw me out of wherever I might be sleeping nearby and it had worked. Now he was crouched with some flat shooting rifle and a night scope and he was cursing himself for not getting a bead on the short stab of flame from the barrel of my handgun. He would wait. He would maybe expect me to work my way down, to get closer, and that would be fine because he would be scanning the hillside which was all open meadow between us.

My heart was thumping against my ribs. Fuck. I knew, I *knew* there was a man down there waiting to kill me. I think I knew from the moment his truck stopped that certain distance back and froze my own pickup in his headlights. Something about the jerky rhythm of the spotlight, something about all of it that was malevolent and evil, and worse because it was practiced, because it was clear this sonofabitch had done this before and who knew how many animals he had killed this way, who knew even how many men. Because a man who burns down another man's barn, a barn full of horses, seemed capable of most things.

But this way, the coward's way, in the dark from cover. Fuck. Which made us two killers. That occurred to me with a shock: we were two practiced killers squaring off in the thick of night, and it also occurred to me that I wasn't certain he was a murderer but I knew that I was. How much less cowardly to jump out of a bush and surprise a drunk man with his dick in his hands and crush his skull?

So it seemed to me that this was a fitting showdown. Two cowards in the cloaking dark, cloaking their shame which I was sure neither of us felt.

I was pressed against the fragrant bark of the old ponderosa. My heart no longer hammered. Good. If I ever got close enough and had to actually shoot the bastard, being a little calmer would be helpful.

I wouldn't shoot him. One Siminoe was enough. Wasn't it? What was I supposed to do now? He was trying to kill me. I was sure, I could feel it like the heat of an engine.

I breathed. The crickets chirped. His idling truck down in the road was a low murmur, a faint ticking. Probably needed a valve job. Something rustled in the duff under the trees, a quick scratching that froze me. It peeped, sounded surprised, jumped, gone. Drama everywhere. Let out my breath, lay still, listened. Felt my phone bulging in my pocket, pressing my thigh, shifted it to the side. What if it rang? And gave me away like a beacon. It wouldn't. Before I turned up the rancher's road I had thought of Sofia, wondered where she was, and pressed on the phone to call and of course there was no reception. Not here.

Okay, relax. He is a hunter as you used to be, he is accustomed to the Long Wait, probably enjoys it in some primal way.

All he needed was one cough to hone in. Honed in he could probably keep the scope on the spot and wait for me to shift which I would eventually do, and bang. Not a good situation.

I began to taste bourbon on my tongue. Jim Beam to be precise. I am not a hunter by nature, not this kind of hunter. I always moved. I liked to move through trees, to the edge of a meadow or rockfall, crouch, listen, wait a little while, get stiff while ungloved hands got cold, move on. Never had this kind of patience. Why I loved to fish creeks, it was a rhythmic enterprise, wading and casting, never still.

After some time, maybe minutes, maybe an hour, it occurred to me that something needed to happen. If I waited long enough he would kill me. He had the rifle, I had a handgun. It was like a mismatched fight where one boxer's reach is twice as long as the other's.

Fuck it. My worst bar fights came with this impulse to get it over with. Fuck it anyway. I had three shots left in the pistol, I'd have to get very close.

I grasped the rucksack in one hand, backed on hands and knees further into the shelter of the trees and stood up. Go. I moved fast. As fast as I could. Came out of the grove at an angle to my right, out into the open meadow at a crouch, and ran. The pack was in my left hand. Zagged left, legs in freefall, stepped into a hole, prairie dog, stumbled almost fell, sear from the left knee, braced for the hot rip exploding my chest. Cut right again, almost falling down the hillside, a shadow a large shape in the dark fuck! humped—a humped giant, a rock, a boulder beside the road, I collapsed behind it. Thank you God for dropping a boulder in the middle of this valley. Breathed.

Breathed. What must be the crack and echo of his shot reverberating down the valley, right over my head. But it wasn't. Nothing. Quiet again, I made myself listen for more than the drum of my heart. There was no echo. Had been no crack of a shot. What the fuck? I peeped around the side. Two trucks, their shadows. Pulled back, lay on my side, breathed. The moon like an orange lightship was clearing a high wooded ridge back toward the highway. First time I'd noticed. Fuck. I scanned the slope I had just come down and realized that in the ruddy light he could have seen me easily without a night scope. Was he being perverse? Waiting for me to walk right into him?

"Grant!" I yelled it. Risked the shout. My truck was only thirty yards away. He knew I was here, behind the rock. No way he didn't know. Might as well talk to the sonofabitch.

"Grant! You want to kill me? Like a night bear?"

Silence.

"Well come on!"

As soon as I said it I thought, That sounds like a line from a movie. I didn't mean it, not for a second. Why would I frigging say that? Movie script reflex. I would much rather have him climb in his truck and drive away and leave me alone.

The grass heads stirred in a light breeze. The moon up there climbing the swell like the hull of a boat. Fuck it. I left the pack and crouched and ran. Straight at the grille of my beaten truck. Flung myself against it. Breathed in gulping rasps. Lifted the gun and pivoted around it.

He was in prone position waiting. Oh shit. Wait. No rifle but the shank of a lug nut wrench inches from his fingers. Which were still. Flung on his back, eyes open and glassy, shining back the blood moon. A Siminoe, no doubt, the toppled bulk of him, shot in the middle of the forehead, like an execution. He looked like a bully even dead, even in the dark. The thrusting jaw, the grizzled fuck-you of the three day stubble, the hands of bone and wire.

I felt dizzy, whiskey sick. I sat down, leaned against the front left tire, two feet from Grant's exploded head. The back of it was. The blood pooled around it in a dark halo, seeped into the flannel of the shirt at his shoulders. Unbelievable. How many elk had I missed with a rifle at closer range than this? No way. Two hundred yards maybe, in the dark, with no sight picture only sound. No way.

Way.

"Unless you shot yourself," I said out loud. "It was just too much fun smashing my windows, wasn't it, and listening to my desperate warning shots, how could it get better than this? Bang."

No rifle. I killed a man for vandalism. I got up. Swayed on my feet. Almost vomited, didn't, maybe I should. This killing stuff was getting old.

I found the dirt with one foot then the other. Walked. The ground bucked. Wait. Stopped, swayed, turned my head to the side and gagged. Not much there, still. Felt better. I turned around and walked back to my own truck, opened the driver door and found the heavy LED flashlight under the passenger seat. Left the door open just like a drunk. That's how I felt, my head. Foggy like too many of the whiskeys I'd tasted before, too many beer backs, whatever's on tap, just do another. Guts slithering around each other, not staying in place. I walked back to his truck, his driver door also open, and slid my thumb along the patterned steel of the flashlight, found the rubber button and clicked the light on. And there it was, leaning against the far seat, not leaning but strapped with a shock cord, butt on the floor, a ranch rifle with a night scope. And there it was again: a semi-auto, must be a .45, stuck barrel down in the middle console. He'd have one on him, too, I'd bet my barely used, newly abused truck.

I was tempted to trot back and prove myself right, but you know what, I didn't feel that good. Wanted to vomit and get it over with, stick my finger down my throat but didn't. I sat, half leaning half sitting on his driver seat, and stared into the faintly lit night, let the exhaustion blur the farther woods beyond the creek at the lower edge of the meadow. The creek. There was one there, no doubt. Because the ground rose again on the other side of it, only one place for the water in this little valley to go. Just there.

Made myself walk, made myself look. Stumbled over open ground. Tripped on a gnarl of sagebrush. It was a creek in a deep arroyo. I hauled myself up like a drunk at a busy crosswalk, prevented myself from taking another step over the edge. Thumbed on the flashlight and scanned across the gap, then down into the bottom where thick willows choked a thin dark trickle of water, probably fifteen feet down at least. It was a badly eroded wash with walls like crumbled cliffs. It was perfect. Damn, Grant. I will give you a burial-at-creek like your brother.

I wasn't wearing a watch but it was fast. If I were a betting man, which I am, I'd put money on less than thirty minutes. I dug out the work gloves from under my seat. It occurred to me that I should dig a shallow grave under the pines and try to get rid of his corpse for good, but it was also very clear that I didn't have the time or the tools or the strength at the moment. I had a little folding army shovel and I was trembling with exhaustion. It also seemed to me that I was acting just like a bona fide murderer. I didn't feel like a bona fide murderer is supposed to feel. Once the nausea passed, I was moving like a man with a mission. I pulled his truck past mine, then backed up to the corpse so I wouldn't make a long slide. Learned my lesson about blood and stayed away from his oozing head, got his feet up onto the tailgate, etc. I felt, well, pretty good. Grant is, was, like his brother: he was a hurter. A guy who hurt people and animals and things. I just didn't feel that awful that I had shot the sonofabitch by mistake. I was more worried about getting discovered by the rancher than by what I had done, which made me wonder for a second if I was a psychopath.

His feet wouldn't stay up on the tailgate so I got his lariat which was coiled and hanging from the rifle rack in his rear window and

I hogtied his ankles and ran the rope through a tie-down ring in the front left corner of the bed and hauled, got him halfway there. I tied off the rope and walked back and lifted him by the shoulders and half slid half rolled him into his own truck like the carcass of an elk. There.

I climbed in, pulled on the knob of the headlights and drove slowly up the road twenty feet and swung left, the beam cutting the field, and found the obvious clear path between the clumps of sage to the gap in the trees and came across. Easy. Into the faintest moon-shadow beneath the tall pines, and at the lip of the arroyo I slowed way down and shoved off the headlights and jerked the floor lever back into four wheel drive low and let her crawl, and I stepped out. That simple. Grant and his truck crawled to the black edge and top-pled in. A crunch, shriek of bent steel, a bounce, glass and panels busted, a perforating pop like an exclamation point, then nothing. I walked to the edge. Grant's truck was miraculously on its wheels but canted up on the edge of the bouldered bank, must have rolled once, and the man himself I didn't see until I turned on the flash-light: down in the willows thrown, feet tied to the line, half on his back, one arm flung straight, mouth agape, he looked like a crazy person hailing a cab. To wherever the spirits of men like Grant go.

The rest went faster and it was all practical. Glad I had the flash-light. There was blood on the hood and fender of my truck. I washed and scrubbed it off with most of the one gallon jug. I backed up my truck and lit the stained and scrabbled spots in the road and I took out the small army shovel and scraped dirt from ridged gravel on the shoulder and spread it over the pooled blood and the drag marks. Spread two dozen spadefuls and then kicked it around and smoothed it with my feet. When I was done it looked like: road. Okay. Moved fast. The solitude of the night couldn't last forever, just a hunch. I stood off in the grass and stripped off my clothes. Everything. Got a clean flannel shirt out of a fruit crate I leave in the truck and rolled everything inside it, including my boots. Had a hole in the right toe anyway. Tied the bundle tight and hopped tender footed to the truck and set it in the bed just forward of the tailgate. From the crate I pulled out clean jeans, a paint spattered canvas shirt, and my surfer flip-flops and got dressed. Then I drove back up the road and when I got to the highway I turned left and drove back to Alamosa and slept in the front seat in a Love's truck stop convenience store and at dawn I drove into a self-service car wash and power sprayed the whole rig, and stuffed the bundle of clothes into a mostly full restaurant Dumpster, down underneath a stack of flattened cardboard. I spent another two dollars using the soapy jet to fill my gallon jug and with paper towels scrubbed down my seats and dash. At eight sharp I found my phone under a cigar pouch under the passenger seat. The phone was set to hum and there were three messages from Sofia and one from Irmina and two from Steve. Good, Sofia was okay. Now was not the time to chat. I called a come-to-you auto glass company and told them to drive to the back of the car wash. In half an hour a young stoner—good—in a powder blue polo shirt installed my new windshield and by 9:10 I was on the highway again toward Antonito and New Mexico. Like clockwork, all of it. Like I'd done this before. That scared me as much as anything: that I seemed to know exactly what to do.

I passed the ranch road, on my right. It ran off down a little open valley between wooded hills and it looked beckoning and half remembered like a dream.

At Tres Piedras I stopped at a squat adobe roadside café called Ortega's. I sat in the darkened dining room and hoped to have huevos rancheros for breakfast. The waitress was young with glossy dark hair swept up into a ponytail and silver stud earrings. She wore denim shorts and flat sandals and she was skittish as a deer. She put down a heavy ceramic bowl of salsa and chilies as if she were putting out bones for a lion. Quick clatter onto the thick wood of the table, then flight. Flight to three steps back. Coffee? Looking at me sideways, a glance over her shoulder to make sure of her escape route.

"Please, yes, cream and sugar."

I wondered if I smelled of death. Or looked like it. I left my napkin on the table and limped back to the bathroom. Killing was hard work. All the running and lifting and sleeping in the truck had left my knee stiff. I looked in the mirror, the first time since—since what? I murdered a man. I murdered a man ten days ago also. Last night, was what? More of an accident.

I studied my face. My eyes had the shadows underneath that I got when I wasn't sleeping well. My beard was as salt and pepper as ever, no lion's feeding mask of blood, not even a fleck. Because by the time I had started really handling Grant he had bled out. Did I smell? If I did I couldn't tell. I just looked like a traveler who was tired. And my expression didn't look to me particularly culpable. I checked: did I feel culpable? No. I felt worse about myself after trying to shoot that buck at night in Vermont. Which I never hit of course. Mysterious. Maybe I was worried sick about getting caught—was that tightening my smile, contracting my spirit?

Not really. Here's what I figured: if Sport or Wheezy ever caught up with me, which I was sure in one way or another they would, then— Wait, why would they? Because some bow hunter would find Grant's truck and body in the next few weeks. If not then, a rifle hunter later in the fall. Or the rancher rounding up his cows. I hadn't seen any recent signs of cows, there were some old manure patties, leathery and desiccated and crumbling, probably a couple of years old. Still. Someone was bound to find his truck, even if his bones were scattered by lions and coyotes, which I imagined was happening right now as I leaned to the sink and turned on the faucet and splashed my face, my tired eyes. Maybe Jason would find it and call in an anonymous tip. They would find the truck one day, probably soon, and even if it was next year or the next they would find the skull, and the bullet rattling around in there would match the caliber of the very gun I was on record as buying in Portland twenty years ago. No, there was an exit wound, the back of Grant's head had blown off, but I had definitely hit his truck. They would find a slug. And then Sport would call me up.

So what? They would not have a murder weapon because I was planning to get rid of the pistol after breakfast. I would drive out into the pine woods north of Española and bury it under a venerable piñon, one of those that had kept its secrets since probably Cortés had stared silent upon a peak in Darien. They would not have an eyewitness and if I'd been careful, they would not have a hair of my head or any DNA at all to put me at the scene.

And anyway, if somehow they honed in, I would claim self-defense. Willy had also gotten those threatening calls. Grant had tried to shoot me through a kitchen window. The bullets in the walls of the house would match his rifle. What was Grant doing down here in the middle of nowhere but stalking me? They would see the spotlight on the truck and maybe, if some hunter didn't take it, they would find the .223 with the night scope.

If you killed a man in self-defense, why didn't you call the sheriff right away?

Who would believe me?

You went to great lengths to hide your crime.

Not really. I left everything pretty much right where it was. Just moved it over a little. Got the mess off the road.

It wasn't very convincing. I was starting to feel like a professional criminal, one of those dumb ones who was never very good at covering up or at flight. One of those who came back to the pen like a roosting pigeon. One thing about getting old, I mean if we get a little wiser as we get older: we learn what we are good at and what we're not. And we learn that a man is usually only passably good at one or two things.

I took a leak and went back to the empty dining room. A mug of coffee with a rooster glazed on the side was steaming on the table. The girl was nowhere in sight. I heard a ranchera song on a radio coming from what seemed a long way off, though it must have been just in the kitchen. I waited. There was no cream on the table, she had forgotten it, so I stirred a packet of sugar into the mug. Soon she would come back and take my order.

Nothing happened. The music played. The song finished. A voice from another planet, muted by distance, announced a big sale at a Ford dealership in Española, the ringmaster's rolling of the Rs the way only a Mexican radio drummer can do it. Another song. Had they all fled? I could imagine. Mr. Death walks into your low ceilinged café and if you have time you flee out the back.

It occurred to me again that I might reek. I had been working hard all night, physically hard, like a stint at manual labor, I had been handling corpses, corpse, and I was the one item that I had not scrubbed and sprayed. I might smell like a zoo, worse. A charnel house. The smell of death is particular. Maybe I had scared the shit out of the Ortegas. Maybe they were huddled in the shed with their shotgun like the farm family in an old Western. Left the radio playing and the soup on.

Nothing happened. I almost called out. Hey! Anybody home! I'm hungry! Fee fi fo fum! Almost banged my tin cup on the table except that it wasn't tin and it was full of black coffee with no cream. Is this what happens after you murder two people? Things get slippery? Reality bends? There's a disruption in the order, the sequences don't fall the way they used to, the waitress doesn't take my order, steps go missing like the treads in a ruined stair?

I left five dollars on the table, drank the coffee in four gulps, went out the screen door which banged behind me.

■

Just then, as I bumped back onto the paved highway, the cell phone rang. It was Sofia.

"Where are you?" I said.

"Back home. This place is crawling with Feds. Where are you?"

"Feds?"

"Yah. Where are *you?* You okay? I've been calling you. I called your gallery guy, Steve. He said there was a shooting. He said he hadn't seen you after."

"I'm on my way back. Be there in a couple of hours. What do you mean, Feds?"

"Grant left. No one knows where. Maybe he's the one who shot at you. Everybody knows he burned down the barn and threatened everyone. Then they busted his camp. Dell's camp."

"Whoa. Slow down. What do you mean busted Dell's camp?"

"Fucking poachers. They all were. It was a poaching ring. I mean they say the bow camp was a cover. All professional hunters every one. Every year. Some big haul of like black bear gallbladders, mountain lions, trophy heads, what all." She was breathless. I could tell she was crying and trying to hide it.

"What the fuck did you stumble into?" she said. "What a hornet's nest. I'm glad, I mean I'm glad you ki——"

She stopped.

"Yeah. Well. These kind of stories don't just end," I said.

"Telling me. Fuck. *Fuck,* Jim. I miss you. I mean. I know we only just—"

"I miss you too."

I did. A lot. Especially right then, hearing the warmth and the rasp and the pain in her voice. Her voice was full of colors, like her eyes. It was a current that tugged and flowed with the force of her. I could have painted it. It would be a river full of fish, and red leaves fallen out of the woods, and this time she would be swimming alone with the grace of a mermaid but she would not have a tail she would be all woman, and there would be a big elk on the bank, a bull, his flank would be bloody and stuck with arrows but he wouldn't care much and he would be lowering his head to drink in her water.

I had my elbow on the window frame and I pulled it in and rolled up the window so I wouldn't have to strain to hear her.

"A lot of stuff happened," I said. "I'll tell you one day."

Now she was crying openly. I didn't interrupt her. It came in waves, the way crying does, and then it blew through.

"Sport found me at the coffee shop," she said.

"Yeah? What did he say?"

"He's so goddamn smooth. He was real concerned. For both of us. He bought me a dry double cappuccino which is creepy, I mean that he knew what I took, kinda like saying, Hey, I know a lot more about everything than you think I know—even though I told him no, I would definitely be buying my own, and then he sat down at my table and said that at some point, which was just about now, obstructing an investigation of homicide, which is withholding any knowledge of a homicide, becomes accessory to murder which is treated by the law the same as murder. He said that now was the time to come clean with any information, any at all, about Dellwood Siminoe's death, and I would be treated, you know, as a witness, but that after this point it was accessory and that I could spend most of the rest of my life in jail. Which was not fun. Oh fuck."

She collected herself, breathed. I could see her face as if she were in front of me, exasperated, with herself for weakness.

"Hold on," she said.

I waited.

"Okay. He was smooth, Jim. I mean really really smooth. I couldn't ask him to leave or leave myself like he had me in some kind of spell. He painted a picture for me of the daily routine at the women's pen in Pueblo. The disgusting food, the stench, the fights. It went on and on. I was frigging transfixed. It was sickening, everything he was saying. Then he says, And that's just one day. The lights don't go out and you lie down in your concrete cell and you can't sleep and then the next day is the same. And that's two days. A week is an eternity. But the second week starts with a day like the first and the second and the third and then you are not done with the second week and the lights stay on and you only have twenty more years like that and you definitely go mad. A madness that is not even human. Why you can always tell a con from half a mile off, that thing in their eyes, that stare they try to cover up which is the madness of the first day becoming the second becoming the third. Jim, it worked on me like a spell, what he was saying, like I couldn't move and kept listening like I was hypnotized. Which made me want to throw up. Which I refused to do because it seemed, well, self-incriminating, though it was touch and go for a minute and I indulged myself in an image of his nice clean hiking boots covered in my vomit."

I felt nauseous just listening to her. I rolled the window down again. Sport may have been playing her but he had the prison thing pretty well nailed. Hearing her I remembered that I'd rather die than go back for another year. Years.

"Whew." I took a deep breath.

"I forgot."

"What?"

"That you did time in—"

"Yeah. I think you should talk to him," I said.

"What?"

"Tell him what you know."

"I don't know anything!" She practically yelled it.

"Well."

"You *listen!*" She was crying again. She was hysterical.

"Listen you big fat wonderful motherfucker, I don't know a goddamn thing! What happened the night Dellwood died. I went to sleep. I remember you got up to pee, I woke up a little, and then I fell right back to sleep and that's all I remember. I remember waking up with you in the morning! Do you hear me? What I told them, what I'm telling you!"

"I know I know."

"I'm coming to Santa Fe."

"Well."

"Shut up, I'm coming. I need a vacation."

"Well."

"I miss the fuck out of you and I need a vacation."

"Okay. That'd be good."

"You are going to paint some big fat twenty thousand dollar canvases of yours truly naked and put some goddamn fish in the things somewhere and take me out to fancy dinners every night."

"Well."

"Say Yes. Just shut the fuck up and say Yes, dear."

I started laughing. Man. That was the other thing about women. The great ones made me laugh and laugh.

"Okay. Yes."

"Right. Good. I'm not coming for a couple of days. I have a life you know, stuff to do. You aren't the center of the frigging universe!"

"Whoa!"

"I've got to get a restraining order on Dugar for one thing, I think. He keeps mooning around after me declaring a love for me that is deeper than human love, deeper even than sea elephant love. He wrote me a poem called 'Mammal Amor' in which I think a dolphin fucks a beaver. I don't know I didn't read it, just caught a few words as I crumpled it up."

I was laughing. I told her I would get my money from Steve so I could take her out to Pasqual's and The Compound every night. I hung up. Before I did she ordered me to write her number on the vinyl of the dashboard, if I lost my phone and her number along with it she would hunt me down and cut my nuts off. I swore I would. I did.

I drove south onto the high piñon plateau above Española. I felt almost okay again. As okay as a man can be who kills like a pro and has a sporty detective scaring the shit out of his—what? His lover. Don't scare yourself, I said to myself. Be in the moment. Maybe find someplace to pull over and go fishing.

There was a spot just south of the Ojo Caliente hot springs, a long quiet shady run under ancient cottonwoods that looked cool and dark from the road. But when I got there it was Indian summer hot and midday and I knew the trout would be in a trance, so I drove on.

There are two paintings in the Tate Modern in London that I saw years ago and that together made a deep impression on me. One is by Paul Delvaux and it depicts a milky nude stretched on her back on a divan in a courtyard surrounded by classical stone buildings. The light is sepulchral and ominous. The palest things in the picture are the girl's skin and the cold columns of the mute buildings. Around and above the square are the bulwarks and cliffs of a severe mountain scape, a scape of the dead. Nothing is living up there in the gloom, no bird or bush or forest, nothing but a waxing sliver of crescent moon that can barely sustain the weak light it breathes down on this silent scene. Around the girl on the divan are: an erect skeleton who seems to be walking toward her, in no hurry—why would he hurry?—a pretty young lady in a red hat, expressionless, who is walking at the viewer and seems to be about to walk out of the frame without noticing, and another imploring nude, who is at the head of the divan and raising one arm emphatically and about to step into it as if she were calling a rescuer. Our heroine by the way is perfect. Every time I look at the thing in the big catalogue book I bought at the gift store I get the stirrings of desire. Her skin is flawless, her hips round, her waist small, her full breasts lifted and spread by her arms which are folded up behind her head. And her exposed armpit is shadowed, cupped by her breast and the lovely smooth muscles of her shoulder and upper arm. Whatever light there is must be coming from the skinny wan moon, but it must be magnified on the way down. There has been no attempt to hide her pubis. The hair there is the same color as in her armpit. One leg is stretched straight, the other hanging off the near side of the bed, half bent. It's a sexy pose.

Is she dreaming? Doesn't seem so. The deathlike quiet seems to extend to her spirit, her mind. She could be dead. The first time I saw it I had just galumphed through three galleries of paintings with barely a pause and I was suddenly transfixed. Was she? Dead? Or sleeping? I needed to know. Her skin, as I said, was flawless, *seemed* alive, did not have the waxy sheen or grainy gray of a corpse. Was it ruddy? No, that was the gloom. Okay, if she was not dead she was deathlike, she suggested death, as did the night, and whatever death was not yet here it certainly was on its way.

Standing before the painting I realized that I had been holding my breath, and that I was attracting stares. Well. I was right in front of it, and it was a graphic nude and I was an imposing man with a beard with flecks of gray. Dirty old man is what they must have been thinking, though why in this age of Internet and cheap nudie bars a dirty old man would go anywhere near a museum is a sensible question. I was not. I was not even old, I was maybe thirty-four. I had been asked to come to London to join an arts festival, I was staying in a four star hotel in Bloomsbury, and I felt like a king.

The painting disturbed me profoundly. I got the sense that the scene was taking place during a terrible war, a war that had left little in the world alive, but I couldn't be sure of that, either. I couldn't be sure of anything. What it made me feel in the end was something that was not fully realized until I saw the second painting.

This one was more famous, I think, the way the curator's card spoke about it, and I was surprised that I'd never seen it. It was Picasso's *Nude Woman in a Red Armchair*. The card said it was Marie-Thérèse, Pablo's seventeen year old lover. Apparently he was head over heels in love with her. I could see why, even through the stylized geometry of her round and semi-reclining form. She was all round. She was in a red chair as advertised and she was frankly uncovered. Her tilted face was round. The sweep of the hair framing her face was round. Her head was leaning into her right hand, her other hand up to her chin in reflection, and her hands and her arms were round round round, and her ear, her hips, her thighs, and whatever thought she pondered was light and pleasant and round. Her pearls or beads. Everything about her, especially her breasts, which were circles, it all rounded and came back to her simple fresh beauty, as if the lines and the light could not bear to be anywhere else, everything was round but her lovely cat eyes and the V and crease of her vagina. Well. She made me instantly happy. Her contained exuberance was contained, barely, in the simple circle of her being. She also aroused me. She was not perfect like the other, not in a classical sense, her limbs were short, she was pudgy, she might even waddle a little as she walked. But. She was devastatingly sexy. That was it, maybe. The painting was so simple. Simple joy, simple sensual heat, simple love in her presence. I felt what Picasso must have felt. She was clearly an uncomplicated soul and I imagined that she reduced all the world before her to its simplest and most fiercely living elements. I imagined that the world talked back to her in the clearest colors, the cleanest music. How else to live in love?

Now back to the other, the dead or sleeping woman. I wended my way back to her through several large rooms. As soon as I caught sight of that pale form, the very realistic length of her limbs, her shadowed armpit, the closed but beautiful eyes, I was aroused. A much different arousal—dark, tinged with what? Guilt maybe. At the voyeurism of studying this woman who could not know I was watching. At the shame of being stimulated by a body that might be a corpse. It was a dark and groaning and maybe violent feeling, violent in the sense of being drawn, exquisitely, toward death and what it does to all things in its proximity. The way it both chills and sanctifies them. The way death is both near and infinitely remote, the way it freezes and somehow kindles the heat of something grotesque and maybe irresistible and sexy, which is life at its most desperate. Phew. What I realized standing there, is that this dark yearning is what happens when we idealize any-thing: the form of a woman, a landscape, a spiritual impulse. We move it closer to the realm of the dead, if not outright kill it. The living joyful exuberant woman becomes statue marble and dead, or pornographic and equally dead. The spiritual impulse becomes religion. And dead. To my mind.

That is when I decided that whatever I did as an artist, I would try to go toward the living and not away from it. Even, especially, in the most abstract paintings.

A funny memory to have as I drove that morning toward Santa Fe, me, the recent purveyor of death. I kept checking my mirror for a black El Camino, but the road behind me was empty.

■

I wasn't ready to go back to—what? Everything. Not right away. I checked into a Super 8 on the strip in Española and spent two days watching TV and napping and soaking in the hot springs, which weren't that hot, and eating Chinese food. I let the phone run out of juice and didn't recharge it. I didn't drink. I wanted to. I kept an eye out for Jason and his car and never saw him. On the third day I drove at dawn into Santa Fe. Went straight up to the room, took the cell phone out of my coat pocket and left it on the charger. I went back downstairs and got in my truck. Fishing gear was still in back just in case and I drove out Washington past the pink church and north into the country toward Tesuque.

The road skirted the base of the mountain and dropped off the mesa. It narrowed and followed the creek. Along the stream the big old willows and elms, the cottonwoods grew over the road and their leaves were already starting to turn and some had already fallen. I could follow a road like this forever: narrow and winding, tunneled with old trees and littered with yellow leaves. Dappled sunlight slid up the hood and over the windshield. The morning was cool. Clouds massed in the west over the mountains, but here it was sunny. At the church I took a right and wound up into the juniper. Sad to leave the big twisted poplars and the stream, but. Pretty up here, too. The sky opened and I saw two hawks floating in it, big raptors. The road turned to dirt and leveled out and I downshifted and slowed. The washboards could loosen your teeth. The driveways along here led to double-wides, leaning barns, yards with rusted horse trailers, dirt corrals. At a mailbox painted with a leaping fish, my fish, I turned in to a sage field and wound toward a grove of piñons and a small adobe.

She was standing on the step, waiting. Smoke threaded from the chimney. The sun was behind me, rising into the morning, everything was full lit with a warm russet light. That time of day. Her long black hair was loose, hanging to her waist, the silver flashed at her ears, her eyes were sharp with concern. The sight of her. She was not tall but she looked tall. She stood with her arms crossed over her stomach, comfortable, waiting. She knew. She probably knew hours ago, days, that I would be here. She never claimed to be psychic, but she was. She knew things people shouldn't know, like that a good friend would show up today.

Where have I been? That's what I thought. For weeks, months now? Where the fuck have I been? On some journey. I can't say for what. Just the sight of Irmina cracked me open. The simple love, my oldest friend.

She reached out a hand as I came up the steps and took mine and turned and led me inside. The house smelled warm of woodsmoke and stew maybe. At the kitchen table, she let go of my hand and faced me. We were inches apart. For a moment I felt fully occupied by another soul, and then released. She trembled all along her length, like a tree struck at its base by an axe.

"Sit down," she said. "I made coffee."

I sat. She swayed in her long skirt to the counter. There were two cups already on the red Formica of the table. She brought the pot and poured them full. She sat across from me. My hands cupped the heat of the mug and my eyes lifted to hers. She shivered.

"Jim," she said. Just that, the simple utterance of my name. A confirmation. I existed. Here I existed, just as I was. Then: "What in the world have you been up to? Wow."

She drank her coffee and never took her eyes off me. It was odd, I did not feel pinned and wriggling on the wall, scrutinized, never with her. I felt held and fully seen. There's a big difference.

"It won't bring her back," she said.

I nodded.

"You are burning up."

I nodded.

She smiled at me, her eyes worried.

"Do you remember when we all went to the zoo?"

"Of course."

I wouldn't forget it. I had a show opening in Denver, at the Museum of Contemporary Art, and a patron who had a pied-à-terre right on Cherry Creek offered us her condo for the weekend. We invited Irmina and all piled into my cranky, loud four door GMC pickup and drove over La Veta Pass and up the interstate to Denver. The condo was on the second floor of a fancy new four story building sided with corrugated sheet metal and accented with blocks of primary colors. We pushed open the door, and I remember that it smelled rich—smelled like wool Persians and fur throws and glove leather. Smelled like freedom, the freedom from financial worry I knew I would never have, the freedom to buy a twenty thousand dollar calfskin couch.

Cherry Creek, the actual creek, was a clear gravel-bottom stream that ran between two bike paths and which we could hear rushing over its ledges below, along with the deeper thrum of traffic and jingle of bicycle bells, and the tatters of conversation from people walking on the path just below us. I remember pulling the sliding balcony door wide and being carried by the sounds. It brought me back I guess to San Francisco, to the last time I had spent much time in a big city. The lostness of myself back then, the first stirrings of enchantment with art. I stood on the balcony and I thought, Here you are, not lost now. You have a show at a top museum, sonofabitch. I looked down at my Little One, clinging to the balusters of the railing and pointing down to a pair of mallards in the creek. I looked over at my dear friend who was blinking in the bright early afternoon and taking in the almost musical flows of traffic, and I looked over my shoulder like Orpheus, back to my beloved, to count Cristine among the bounty, reckoning her among the other gifts like an object of gold. Never do that. Never say: I am so frigging lucky.

Her back was to us, she was at the sideboard pouring out a decanter of single malt scotch into a tumbler of ice. She was wearing a halter top and her skin was soft copper. She had a beautiful back, strong and slender, and seeing it, unprotected, under the black curls that spilled to the faint wings of her shoulder blades, seeing it I almost forgave her everything. The rages, the drinking, the absences. I loved her more right then than I had ever loved anything but Alce. I thought: She is regal. And she was, in a way. She was a Marquez from Mora County and her family had been in those valleys since something like the fifteen hundreds. When she turned I knew by the shine in her eyes she was already on her second scotch.

"Damn, this is good," she said. "Best I ever had. You want one? You guys?"

She shook the ice to chime against the glass and toured the room, holding the drink with the nonchalance of a Gatsby flapper. Stopped at an end table, picked up a photo of what must have been the patron and her family on top of a wooded mountain with lakes or inlets behind it, maybe Maine. They were fit and tan and had very white teeth. "The people you're mixing with now. Swank," she said, turning the frame toward me. "Look, the daughter's t-shirt says YALE. My my." She set it down and went to an art deco framed print on the wall: Dartmouth Winter Carnival 1981, a ski jumper sailing off a hill, a church spire in the valley below him. Cristine tapped the glass with a tapered fingernail, right at the jumper's head. Her silver bracelets jingled. "Careful, young man," she said. "You think you are an eagle now, unh huh. There are things out here none of this snow can prepare you for."

I said, "I was thinking maybe we could take Alce to the zoo."

"The zoo?" Her eyes blurred. She had to shake her mind free of the Ivy League winter.

"We have four hours until the opening, and it's pretty close to here. They have polar bears. Polar bears that play in the water. Where you can see through the glass."

She twisted her lips into a smile. "Alce will go crazy." She knocked back the rest of the tumbler. "White people, white snow, white bears."

We got back in the truck and drove to the zoo. I opened all the windows against the reek of booze. I bought the tickets while Cristine fished a beer out of the cooler in the truck. She couldn't take the can through the turnstile, so she downed the whole thing in a frat boy chug. Even then she was glorious: her smooth forearm flexed, her strong shoulder swelled with layers of smooth muscle, the wide silver bracelet glinted at her wrist. No big deal, I told myself, she's on vacation.

For an hour we were a perfect family. It was mid-afternoon on a mid-May school day and not crowded, and we walked four abreast, hand in hand on the wide paths. We gawked at the peacocks wandering freely, at the elephants bathing in dust, at the leopards stretched along the limbs of a huge tree in such a trance of stillness they seemed emitted by the dappled shade. I thought, Relax.

It will never get better than this. You are about to open a big show, everyone you care about is okay. You have a family.

Alce was floored by everything. In total thrall. She tugged us along like the streamer to a little kite. The hyenas transfixed her. The Komodo dragon wanted to eat her through the glass and she wanted to be eaten. She ran ahead, a double size pink cotton candy flagging her like a showy flower. She got it sticky all over her face and took it into the bird house and some kind of tropical finch landed on her shoulder and surprised them both. Maybe it wanted the candy. The bird twitched and they both let out a squeak and the finch flew off and Alce burst into hysterical laughter. Cristine picked up her daughter and squeezed and said, "You are like St. Francis, you know that? The birds can't help themselves. Me neither!"

We strolled up to the polar bears. We could hear sea lions barking nearby. I wondered if the smell of prey so close drove the polar bears crazy. Probably not, they were probably prodigiously fed.

"Let's check out the underwater window first," I said. "Yeah, yeah!" chimed Alce. The bears were playing. Luck. Two huge white adults and one little one swam through the green water in a parody of walking, then dove with the sudden graceful fluidity of a loon. From ten feet away we gasped. Ten feet from the big plate glass. The bears were playing keep-away with a rubber fish the size of a twenty pound salmon. Alce ran forward. She forgot all about her cotton candy and dropped it on the way. A family was already there, pressed against the glass, three towheaded kids Alce's age and older, and a mom with streaked blond hair and gold scallop earrings and a lily patterned summer dress. Alce pushed through the two boys, completely focused on the bears. "Hey, hey," called Irmina, laughing, "*Cálmate Alcita,* be polite." "*Mummy!*" cried the littlest, "the *Mexican* girl pushed me!" The mother was just turning from the glass. Alce said, "*Am* not! I'm not Mexican!" "You are, too!" insisted the boy. "I heard you speaking Mexican!"

"Was not!" shouted Alce, her face wavering between crumpling and setting for a fight.

"You're a *spic* like Sergito!" the boy taunted, shoving Alce back, his eyes flashing toward his mother, not quite sure of his ground, knowing it was a bad word.

That was all it took. Cristine stepped fast between them and crouched so that she was level with the boy and put her hand on the boy's chest. "*What* did you call my daughter?" she said, very cool. "Do we shove other children?" I knew, coming from her, what the gesture meant, her hand across the boy's rib cage. It meant: let's stop right now, let's reassess. Let's gather ourselves and feel fully who we really are. Forceful and gentle at the same time. Whatever else she was, she had a special way with children.

The lilied mother didn't: know what Cristine meant, nor care. The kid was in too much shock to speak. The mom lunged for her son and swatted away Cristine's arm like a forceful volley at the net. "How *dare* you!" she blurted. She had no idea. No idea what she'd just asked for. Cristine stood slowly and wound up away from her and pivoted from the torso and slapped the woman full force, open handed across the face. It almost knocked her over. Even the bears heard it, probably. They swam down to the glass curious. All three kids wailed. An overweight guard in a silly khaki safari outfit hurried up. Alce stood there in the midst of the ruckus, her face sticky with pink, and watched it all unfold above her, uncrying, her jaw set like a boxer.

I finally broke my own trance and stepped between the women, the two camps, and separated them like a bouncer in a bar fight.

The guard in khaki repeated over and over, "That's enough! That's enough! Plenty of bear for everyone!" I knew how she felt. Cristine and the other mom stared at each other, both breathing hard, neither crying, both stung beyond tolerance, both gathering their children to themselves. Pretty evenly matched in tiger mom fury and courage, I have to say. The Waspy woman's cheek was scarlet but the skin was unbroken. Probably lucky for all of us. She was smart, too, I could tell. She was calculating very fast the percentages—of gain and loss in pressing charges, in dragging her children through more of this kind of day, and suddenly she knelt down, looked her three kids full in the face, each one, tallying the damage, it was livable, and stood, and very haughty, uttered, "Let's go! Alex, Jessie, Connor. Now!" and they were gone. Leaving us with the liturgical guard, intoning, "That's *enough*. Plenty, plenty of polar bear for everyone!"

Amazing, given Cristine's pugnaciousness and my volatility that we stayed together for ten more years. After Alce died the marriage broke like an egg. Cristine moved to Tempe and I hear she married the heir to an oil fortune, an alternative therapist who uses flashing lights and spirit journeys to heal his patients. I hear she is content.

"How could I forget?" I said now.

Irmina broke into a wide smile. "I remember how Alce never cried, and how all the way home she kept looking up at her mom with like a new appreciation, like, Holy cow, Mom knocked the shit out of the mother of those mean kids. Wow. After the other family left she didn't know whether to look at the bears or at Cristine." Irmina laughed. "After that I think she kind of saw Cristine as the sheriff."

"That's what she told me. Why did you bring it up?"

"She learned to fight from her mom."

"Well."

The parking lot, the bag of pot, Alce kicking the gangbanger. Well. I knew she learned to fight from both of us. I could feel the tears running on my cheeks.

Alce always adored Irmina. Made Cristine jealous sometimes. I suddenly understood that Alce's death was like losing a daughter for Irmina, too. That she had been grieving alongside me every step of the way. I'd been so leveled by my own blind loss. Fuck, Jim, self-centered doesn't even begin to describe it.

I reached across the table and took her hand. It was small and warm.

"I've been an ass."

She raised an eyebrow. "More like a crazed bear I think."

"You miss her as much as I do."

Whatever she was feeling, it moved like a flock of fast small birds, the way they whir into and out of a bush.

She squeezed. "I know," she said. "I know how much you love me."

"You do?"

Her smile lit the table.

"You want some ribs?"

"Venison? Sure."

There were no other kind with Irmina. She shot a deer whenever she needed one, in season or out. She was always careful never to shoot a doe with fawn. Her neighbors knew, I guess. Out here the state game wardens were tracked like weather events, like tornadoes. Phones rang down the county roads, anything not quite legal went into the sheds, the lofts. Clap went the barn doors. *Hello, Warden! Nice day! How's the wife, the kids?* A way of life.

She got the pan off the woodstove, I went outside into her little sculpture garden. The clouds had moved in and darkened the sky and the sun was a smudge in an ominous overcast. Sometimes a stormy morning can feel like dusk and unsettle the hills. Nothing cast a shadow. In among the sage and the wild rose were some of my fish and birds. They were jumping and swooping. Steel and wood. I could smell the plants. The air was still, a perfect outbreath of day, caesura, pause. Like evening. I could hear the buzz and thrum of hummingbirds going to the feeders but didn't see them. Was this it? All I had needed the past few months? The perfect stillness? The needing nothing for just a minute? Or did I just need to be seen? Seen right through without fear. I walked over to the edge of her piñons and a jackrabbit shot from under a saltbush and zagged off into the false twilight. Most of us are never seen, not clearly, and when we are we likely jump and run. Because being seen can be followed by the crack of a shot or the twang of an arrow. I took a leak in the flinty dirt. I didn't know what any of us wanted.

We ate venison ribs in a green chili sauce and late kale from her garden. I wanted badly to tell her everything, from the first fight with Dell. I wanted to see her eyes when I told her I had killed two brothers. That they were orphans, that they were cruel, bad men, but that they had fought for each other their whole lives until I came along. Irmina, more than anyone I had ever met, seemed to be able to feel the balance of energies in the universe. If there were a god who cared about the death of a single sparrow, I knew a woman who could feel it. I wanted to see what the men's deaths meant to her, to the hot and cold currents, the colors that swirled around her. Maybe I wanted to be absolved. But I also knew better. The way Sport was leaning on Sofia, I knew it was better to keep the stories to myself. You tell a story and no matter how well it is sequestered it still lives. It may be in hibernation, like those microbes trapped in the Antarctic ice. So I told her about the paintings instead. I described them one after another in order, making up the titles I couldn't remember. *Ocean of Women, The Grave in the Garden, Two Horses Carrying a Girl.* She watched me closely, and at some point in the telling she closed her eyes and I knew she could see each one, the images in her mind more faithful in their way than the paintings themselves. I told her about giving the picture of the beaver ponds to the trucker, and about the painting of the toiling men in the valley I had titled *In Hostile Country. Horse and Crow. The Two Boats.* I told her about the birds following the more distant longboat. I understood as I told it that she was already way ahead of me, that her understanding outstripped the details, that she let me tell it because I needed to. When I finished I said,

"I don't know why I put both of them on the same sea."

"They are on the same sea. We all are."

"What about the birds? Following her?"

"The fish are probably giving her an escort. The birds are eating the fish."

"Huh. Never thought of that. Maybe I should take it back and put in the fish."

"Leave it alone. You have your gun?" she asked.

Startled: "In the truck," I said.

"Is it—?"

I nodded.

"Give it to me."

"No."

"Yes."

"No."

"You're not a bear, I take it back. You're a big dumb ox."

"Thanks."

"Well, okay, go. Go back to town. Someone will be waiting for you. Before you leave my property get rid of it. Promise me."

"Okay."

"You're sleepy, huh?"

"Yah. All of a sudden."

She smiled. "Go take a nap in the hammock. Your favorite spot. Then go."

I hugged her. I may have been a dumb ox but I hugged her like a bear.

I did. I lay in the hammock under her ramada and fell asleep to the buzz and whir of the hummingbirds. I didn't dream. When I woke it was late afternoon and the sky was still heavy with clouds. I felt refreshed and went straight to the truck. I didn't say goodbye again, didn't have to.

Near the end of her driveway, in a stirring of breeze that smelled like rain, I walked off a few hundred yards into the mesquite with my little folding shovel and I buried the gun. I buried it deep and covered it carefully. On private property. Then I walked big circles all through the brush. I drove back through Tesuque and stopped at the Village Market for a beer. It was happy hour and packed with rich hipsters, young and old in silver concha belts, and a lot of local manitos too. Everyone seemed to be getting along. That was like the old days. A band was setting up. Must be Thursday or Friday. I ordered a Buckler, a non-alcoholic beer, and enjoyed sitting at the bar without a single agenda. Nothing to do but sit and look, listen, drink. There was the line from one of the poetry books I kept thinking about, from T. S. Eliot's *Four Quartets*. I felt in the zippered breast pocket of my coat and pulled out the wrinkled slip of paper.

> *You are not here to verify,*
> *Instruct yourself, or inform curiosity*
> *Or carry report. You are here to kneel*
> *Where prayer has been valid.*

I loved that. No one had ever said it, not to me. Was he saying we are here to pray? To tell you the truth, right now that was all I really felt like doing. I could spend the rest of my goddamn life on my knees. It occurred to me that every painting lately was a prayer. That fishing, with Alce, her memory, was also a kind of prayer. Praying really was all I knew how to do. I read the lines three times, folded them back up and tucked them away.

The beer was cold and it tasted hoppy and good and I didn't miss the alcohol. The portrait of the girls was done, it was really good, the gun was gone. That surprised me: losing it in the field was like taking off a heavy pack. For a moment you think you will float away. I thanked the bartender and went back into the cool wonderful heaviness of a desert pregnant with rain.

It was that time of day when late afternoon is just tipping into evening. Probably an hour till dusk. It felt like it might rain any second. I'd head back to town and go to the plaza for a simple dinner. In the parking lot against the trees of the west edge was a black El Camino and standing next to it the outline of a man.

He was leaning against the car and he was tall and bearded and wore a baseball hat, and even in ambush, if that's what this was, he looked relaxed and loose jointed and as familiar as a childhood friend. His eyes were shadowed but they could only be blue, mineral blue and hard with mischief. Fuck. I felt under my seat as I opened the truck door, a reflex, and remembered that the gun was gone, buried. I was on my own. I stiffened tall, looked back toward Jason, raised a hand. He didn't move. There was a length of pipe behind the seat. Why didn't I bring the shotgun, too, when I had driven away from the Paonia house? I totally forgot it, that's why. I waited a beat, got in the truck, started up and pulled out.

I rolled down the window. The evening smelled of juniper smoke from a dozen stoves and the sweet fragrance of the first fallen leaves. I drove back along the creek under trees that obscured the sky and one leaf, then two, hit the windshield. It would have been gorgeous but it wasn't. He was two hundred yards behind me. Whatever distance it was he kept it to the inch. What it seemed like. If I lost him on a curve, when I moved out onto the next straightaway he slid back into my mirror at the exact interval. Like I was towing a can on a string. It was unnerving, more than if he'd ridden up on me. The message was: I'm in complete control, you can't shake me. If I can mark this distance with such precision on a twisty back road, I can take you any time I want. And he could. I knew he could. It was a muscle car and on one of these stretches where there were no houses, no farms—and there were plenty of these deserted reaches—he could close the gap in a heartbeat and pull up beside me and blast me with probably the shotgun I wish I had myself.

I gunned it, then slowed, then gunned it. He was right there. Out of every curve. My pulse sped up like the truck, I could feel it pounding in my temples. He seemed to be saying: We aren't fucking around anymore. Your time, Pops, is up.

If he came up on me and didn't kill me with the first blast, he could easily make me wreck, then walk up as casual as you please and execute me like a wounded elk. I passed a goat farm down in the creek bottom off to my right, a tight left bend then a short climb and my spirit yearned toward it: like, I wish I were you. Just tending my goats and making dinner with my family and having trouble paying my bills. I wish I were you and not me in this truck right now with that black thing blessedly out of sight for half a minute. The mundane quandaries I yearned for right then. Any predicament but this. Jason's strategy was bell clear. I could feel the panic rising as I tried to control my speed. There was no point in accelerating. I thought: I could pull into that goat farm, or the next house, I could run for the door.

But he could catch me easily in the yard before I got to the stoop. Even if I made it, then what? Endanger a whole family? Call the cops, Wheezy? Jason would melt away, plug me in the dark when the circus was over. Fuck. I could try to straddle the center line so that he couldn't pass me. Wouldn't work. There was too much shoulder on both sides, gravel sure, but he was too good a driver, and anyway he was good enough he could shoot out my rear tires and send me into the ditch any time he wanted.

I felt for a packet of Backwoods and with one hand gripping the wheel—I realized I was clenching it hard and forced myself to relax a little—with my free hand I dug in the console for a packet of cheroots, and unwrapped it clumsily and brought it trembling to my lips and pushed in the lighter knob on the dash. Was I trembling or was it the rush of wind, the frost heaves in the road?

I was scared. Something was definitely different. In all my encounters with the trucker there had been a sense of possible reprieve. That word. I kept saying it, like my whole life now was a search for the nectar of it. That a life could come down to that, it seemed pathetic. Grant me, grant me, oh Lord, relief. From all my fuckups.

Before, between us it had been: confront, measure and maneuver. What was different now was the feel of the pursuit. It was not a game, it was deadly serious now. I knew. You know this stuff. As many bar fights as I had been in, as many brawls, you know when it's more about roughhouse, about breaking furniture and knockdowns and bruise and blood and welt—and you know when it turns, when it becomes deadly and serious and cold, when the bottles begin to break on the table edges and the knives come out. I knew. As clear as I knew Jason could close the gap in four seconds. He was going to kill me.

Every good and stupid thing I'd done in my life came down in the end to this.

I went through a tight left curve and topped a little rise and came down into a barren stretch of sparse sage and mesquite and the black thing swung across the rearview, slipped square into the center of the mirror exactly as if I were pulling a water-skier on a towrope. I wish. I am towing my own death behind me. That's what I thought. I have been hauling it behind me ever since the night I went fishing up the Sulphur, pulling it like a carcass.

And then there was the other impulse, the one I always have: just to get it over. Pull over out here in a deserted stretch and get out and face the music, or whip the truck one-eighty at one of these wider pullouts and come back to him, straight at him and aim for a head-on and let the chips fall.

That wasn't such a bad idea. I had lost him on the last tight curve and was emerging again into a wide treeless valley. I could. He could round that bend with the cold calculating precision of a Formula 1 driver and gape at nothing but my lights and radiator grille barreling at him like a meteor. I wanted that. To do it just to break his icy composure, the one that was more and more apparent after the false reprieve of every curve, that was chilling my guts from an eighth of a mile back.

There was another way. I had done it once to a state trooper who flagged me on a high pass up in the Green River country. The cop had passed me going the other way and hit his lights, which meant pull over, I'm going to spin around and come give you a speeding ticket, and instead I goosed it, it was a twisty pass, and I took the second ranch road, a rocky track that cut up into some outcrop bluffs, and I rattled and bounced onto another track and shut the motor and took a nap until nightfall. The road had been damp from recent rain and it probably saved me, because I didn't raise any dust. Back then I couldn't afford the ticket. Had he been less lazy he might have called for backup, and they might have figured I might have a warrant and searched for me, but he was probably at the end of his shift and heading home, and I drove out that night and down to I-70, down to the big wide Utah desert, humming and thinking of dumb ways to spend the money I'd just saved myself. Simpler times.

But I knew this road. This one. I didn't know every track coming off it, where they went, but at least I knew where they met the Tesuque road. Not like I could sit down and draw a map of them, but I'd driven this stretch so many times, my whole life it seemed, and I could confidently say: There will be a gravel road coming up on the left after this bend. Or: a dirt track after this grove of cottonwoods on the right. Could just feel it coming.

I did. Feel it like a gift. And not dirt. A dirt or gravel turnoff would raise a cloud of dust and signal my entry like a semaphore.

Up ahead I, we, would enter two switchbacks back into the river bottom, with tall cottonwoods and old willows on either side, and just after, there was a county road off to the left. It was perfect because there was one more broad right-hand bend beyond it, just before the road opened out and climbed onto the last mesa before Santa Fe. And it was paved. For the first half mile or so. I knew, because I'd taken it once, looking for a new place to picnic with Cristine that wasn't crowded with tourists. We'd only gone up it maybe a hundred yards, and found a grove of poplars beside the creek, with benches someone had cut crudely out of logs, and we'd stopped happily and had our meal and made love on a blanket further back in the trees beside the stream. Perfect. If I jammed it I could make the left, and get into the trees while he was still coming out of the last turn. And the empty road ahead wouldn't bother him, because I would be, he would think, just out of sight on the final arc of the wide bend. Good. And even better, there were two more side roads, just after this on the right, in a space of about half a mile. Two decoys. I took a deep long shuddering breath and made myself wait until I had entered the first twist of the switchback, had lost the black chimera in my mirror, and stomped the gas.

The truck shook and roared. Took the next two turns way too fast. It was too top-heavy, not built for this. The seat belt straps held me against a centrifugal force that tugged and leaned me into the passenger seat, the whole rig trying to hold the pavement and make the leftward trajectory, the tires squealed, then a sound like the shriek of a shot stoat and the rear right tire went off the shoulder and hit soft dirt and gravel sprayed into the undercarriage with a loud rush and we lurched and I thought it was over, he would have his wreck, and then the caroming rig pulled us back into the road, all four tires, and I threw the wheel right for the next turn. We were going downhill. We were accelerating now. Fast glance at the speedometer, it was needling past seventy-five, way way too fast for these curves, Jesus, and I just held the wheel over. I tapped the brakes once and felt the rear tires break free—*No!*—and then hold as I jammed the gas pedal to carry the turn, my left shoulder pressed into the door and frame, fuck, we would never make it, not this right swing. Again the squeal. A weightless sickening lift—abrupt silence as all four tires broke contact. Here we go, oh Lord. Here the fuck—full slide, sailing for the trees on the left. Not sure. I must've eased on the gas, pressed harder, and something in the chemistry of rubber and tarmac: the wheels, first the rear, gathering again under the truck as in the leap of a predator, all haunches, the rear grabbed and propelled us to the shoulder and then the front grabbed and the steering kicked in and we were thrown to the right and I felt both left tires spin and grind in the dirt just off pavement and launch us into the middle of the road, in time for the next left.

I let off, let off completely of the gas and found my seat and coasted through the next two corners and shot out of the switchbacks at close to seventy with both hands tight on the wheel and the cheroot miraculously still in my mouth and lit. Somewhere in there, just before the turns, I had lit it, couldn't even remember. I thought, Okay, man, you have the distance. You earned the time. Now jam it. I did. Just ahead on the left was my road, the turnoff, and I flew toward it like an arrow and took it in a full slide, I was fucking getting used to this, and careened up it and hit the roof hard, top of the head, as I took the bumps into the makeshift campsite and stuck the gap in the poplars where we had parked once before, stuck it like a cork in a bottle and slid to a stop and turned off the engine. And breathed. Okay wait. I thought I would hear him. Wait till he passes, give him twenty thirty seconds so he is well past, then back fast out onto the country road, probably Forest Service access, whatever, wait because it turns to dirt just ahead, don't let him see the plume, and then go up it. Go up it fast but not screaming, and get lost in the hills while he looks for you on the highway ahead and on the other side roads first. Because he is methodical. He will eliminate first one then the other and you will be long gone, forked off onto whatever myriad tracks up ahead.

I didn't hear him. Maybe it was the blood pounding in my ears. I didn't hear anything. But I figured a minute had passed, plenty long enough, too long, and then I started the truck and backed out and continued on up, jounced over the line where the road turned to dirt, washboarded as it climbed, and took it with a mission but not too fast, not enough to raise a huge plume. Also, the sky was darkening with more than evening, the clouds were thick and black and a wind had kicked up, and it thankfully carried my dust ahead of me to the north. I drove.

I drove up into juniper then aspen with a growing sense of relief. I was climbing a ridge and the track contoured along it so that through the trees to my right I could see now and then the valley below and the darkly wooded piñon hills that fell into it, and the sky darkened and the wind picked up and tore leaves out of the trees that blew across the track. The track got narrower and rougher. Good. Be hard to follow up here, to drive up it at all in the El Camino.

Up ahead, up behind the highest ridge, lightning flashed like distant cannon fire. It flashed through the heavy clouds in silent pulses, muted and buffered by distance, and sometimes sustained like the rolling cannonades of a battle in another province. It was not quite full dusk yet and no longer day, not with the black thunderheads and the soundless vespers of the thunder. Another limbo time. Good. This one felt good. A space to let my panic drain away, an interval that asked for no decision, good or bad, just asked me to drive up a road I had never taken and somehow find my way back to town.

And then two things happened. The road topped out in a smooth track through aspen, thickly ferned at the edges and uncobbled with the rocks of the climb, beautiful, some kind of haven fragrant with ferns and fallen leaves and the charged and humid wind. I released a long breath, felt a gladness surge.

And I glanced in my side mirror and saw headlights swinging through the trees then square up on the track and flood my rearview. Fuck. And the track ahead dropped steeply away. I could see through the pale trunks and limbs of the trees that it was dropping into a cut-rock canyon below, probably the upper reaches of the same creek as in the picnic area, no it wasn't the headwaters at all, I could see now in the murky light that the cut of the canyon continued on through steep hills into who knew what distances now shuddering with lightning.

It felt like death. Like nowhere to go but there. Between the hard beams of the headlights behind and the vague flashes of the storm ahead. I almost cried. Almost seized and gave up. Almost offered my throat. Hard to describe the collapse: how the strength emptied from my limbs like water, how all conviction of anything worthy, any worthiness left on earth much less in my own life, how it didn't surrender but simply absented itself, leaving only a chalk outline: this was your reason to live and now it is gone. He could kill me here, a perfect place, kill me any way he wanted to, and bury me in the scented ferns and run my truck off a ledge into the steep woods like some parody of my killing of Grant.

And then he did something shocking: he blared his horn. Leaned on it, then a double tap, then leaned on it again. Less like the trumpeting of a charging army than like Hey, motherfucker, Get a move on—I didn't trash my shocks to climb all the way up here to have you just fold. Just cry Uncle. That's what it seemed like to me.

Maybe it was just a head game, a triumphant shout of *You are all mine now you piece of shit.* Who knows. It woke me up. I stomped the gas and threw dirt behind me and revved off that little bench and the track fell away and the nose of the truck tipped and dropped hard and jounced into a rut and I tapped the brakes and slid just a second, and then I was diving steeply, bouncing down a hunter's trail straight for the bottom of the canyon. Didn't need the headlights, I could still see well enough. But with the windows open and the wind whipping through I heard the first rumble of thunder and then raindrops spatted against the windshield, big ones, heavy, singular, and they stopped. One opening salvo. I barreled downhill, holding to the track easily, it wasn't too rocky, which was maybe not a good thing, because he could take it too without too much trouble, maybe not as fast. Right then no grander thought. Just Drive. All the adrenaline surging back through arms, chest, the strength too, no reason for any of it, but suddenly a boundless desire to get through this, to live.

For a minute I thought he'd had enough. Hoped. Didn't see his lights, figured maybe he didn't want to risk the climb back out of here. That rising euphoria. The black bird of false hope, not a phoenix, but one of those raven-vulture things squalling out of the trees. Fuck. Did I think he would come this far, *him*? And give up? And just as I thought it, his lights dropped, dropped into the rearview from above and burned the mirrors like a pursuing chopper, and we came out of the aspen as suddenly, into the sparse low trees of the junipers. The loss of high canopy opened up the sky and gave more light ahead and fine rain sprayed across the windshield and it was true dusk and I heard a clap now of thunder, loud and close. And just as suddenly I bounced hard and barreled down a sandy bank, past a beaten down turnaround on my right and a rough rock outcrop on my left and hit the creek. I splashed into it with a loud crash of spray that plumed over the windshield and washed into the window and doused my head.

Whoa. Water. I revved and slipped. Wha—? Fuck. Deeper than I thought. The tires spun on the bottom. I was about in the middle of the stream and I wasn't moving. The water was over the floorboards, oh fuck, and it was muddy. In the half light I could see it was muddy and I looked left upstream and saw the current sliding around the wall, emerging from the little gorge in foamy sheets that carried sticks and limbs and bits of leaves.

Oh fuck. The intake manifolds were clear, barely, the engine would run until they swallowed water. But the creek was rising and if I didn't break free of this now the motor would sputter and die, and just then I heard a slide and the blast of horn and the lights flooded the creek, me, and then cut. I craned around. The headlights cut off and so did his engine. I could hear it. Could hear it don't know how, over the sliding of the surging current and my own motor. Heard his car door slam and craned further and saw his car at the very edge of the water, saw him standing on the sandy gravel of the track beneath the outcrop, then lean back against the black car. He wanted me to see him. See him leaning there arms folded while I drowned, that's why he cut the lights, that's what I understood. Fuck, I would move. I was moving. Oh, Jesus, I was slipping sideways. The pressure of the current. If I floated free the truck would tip and roll and the current was swollen and swifter than I could handle and I would probably drown. Oh fuck, fuck, not like this! That was the final blast of thought, loud as a car horn: I don't want to die, not like this. Oh shit.

I pressed the gas and heard the tires spinning underwater, an unreal whining sound, and felt them grab and slip, and the truck was, it was sliding little by little downstream, and I craned around again to look back, for what? At him, desperate I guess, and saw the figure leaning, him thinking, Hah! Let God, let God take care of it, sonofabitch, and as I did there was a crack, a crack loud now of thunder right overhead, and on top of it a crash a loud fork of lightning zagging onto the ridge above us, behind it the boom. Then the sound no one ever ever forgets. Like a jet engine. More than roar, like the earth cracked open and howled without voice.

That roar. A gust of wind hit me, from straight upstream and I turned my head and saw a billow of torn leaves and dust erupt from the canyon and blow through the mist of rain. Maybe fifty yards above me. Or thirty. In that instant the image burned like a shadow on old film: the mouth of the little gorge filled with a wall of water. Or mud.

In the flash, seeing it all, not the lightning, maybe it was, or just the acuity of terror: it was clear in the dusk as if etched: a mudwall of water and in it as if frozen: a tree, yellow leaves, a sheep, the white sheet metal of an old stove. Why did I do the next thing? Never know. I leaned far out the window as if ducking my head into the flood and yelled. He was behind, beneath the outcrop—he couldn't see it, he was a sitting duck. In five seconds the wall would bury him.

FLASH FLOOD! I screamed it, as loud as I could, and saw him startle, bolt for the door handle and jump into his car.

That was all. Reflex. I slammed the accelerator and the truck roared, bellowed I remember just like a beast. The rear end fish-tailed and we must have slid into a shallower shelf of rock because the whole thing grabbed and tore into the bottom and gunned as if shot out of the water, tearing into the gravel of the far bank and lurching, almost like an animate—an animal—up the ramp of the far side, slamming up onto the bench as the roar swallowed the entire world and I felt it whomp the rear end, the wind and spray of it, and the hard rain hit at the same moment. A fierce wind rank of rot and death and mingled with clean mud and water tore through the cab and pummeled my face and I felt the ground shudder and the flood pass behind us.

I was shaking, just like a poplar, uncontrolled. Pulled the emergency brake hard and shoved the door and stood on the mud, and shook, and turned, and searched the near dark now of the far bank as if I could conjure him out of it. Why did I think: *Please, oh God, let him be there?*

He was. The car was on its own bench on the far side. Oh, man, lights still off but it was there, up at the lip of the sand ramp that had descended to the creek. Where he had been seconds ago was now subsumed in foam and clotted wood, sticks and logs circling there in an angry vortex, in the eddy formed by the rock, what would have been his own mudwater grave. I shook. I winced down my eyes to see more but didn't. Didn't see him, couldn't, his shape anywhere, he must've been in the driver's seat watching also.

Then the headlights flicked on, I could hear over the wash and tear of current against the new-ripped bank the uptake of the engine and the lights swung back into the turnaround, lit the piñons and pushed forward in a tight arc and then nothing but taillights rising slowly up into the black backdrop of the trees. He was gone.

I stood and shook and it rained on my bare head, somewhere in there I had lost my hat, and I cried like a baby. Bawled. Not sure for what. For everything. Shook and howled and the rain came down hard and the lightning exploded right on top of the thunder and rolled away, shook me to the roots, and I knew.

I knew: that whatever I was, my soul was no more substantial than a tattered leaf, one of those torn off a streamside tree in the flood. That I was nothing, that whatever I had done in my life amounted to just that, shreds no heavier than leaves, and that also whatever I had done, I had done it like a blind storm-ripped thing, or like a blind animal nosing from scent to scent and was whomped and carried most of my life by the wrath and high spirits of a power without malice, and that I had done my best and loved my daughter. I had loved her. I had loved Alce the best I could, the best I knew which was nothing to brag about, but I had loved her hard, as hard as a heart could, as hard as this flood tonight. I loved you.

I wept and I said it over and over, I loved you. I loved you.

The storm might have lasted two hours. I stood in the downpour and filled with cold water like a cracked shell. I shook apart. And then I could no longer feel anything except that I was freezing, to the bone, and that whatever pieces of me were left were shivering now with hypothermia. I thought of what Mitchell my doc friend had told me about dying that way, and I would not. I would pull into the partial shelter of some big juniper and pull out my sleeping bag that might or not be soaked, and unroll it in the truck bed under the topper and try to sleep. Sleep till morning and let the creek subside and cross it again and go home. To the hotel. To a meal and a hot bath.

I did pull in under a big old cedar, to buffer the impact of the rain on the topper's roof, if nothing else, and crawled around in the back and found the milk crate in which I kept the sleeping pad and bag and they weren't there. And remembered: they are in my rucksack, still stuffed in there from my last brush with Grant. Okay. I felt around for the pack, felt up in the front corner where it often ended up and nothing. Where the fuck? I was kneeling, shivering on all fours in the back of the truck, the rain whipping against the camper shell, knees hard on the corrugated bedliner, thinking back, tracing. And then it hit me: I left the pack. That night. I left it behind the boulder, the big rock I had dived behind when I thought Grant would plug me. I left it.

I froze there on my knees and went over it again: remembered that I had taken it with me out of the trees, and down the grass hill as I ran zigzag, expecting to be torn apart by a bullet any second, and dived for the boulder, and taunted Grant, what I thought would be him and was instead an already cold corpse, and then I charged him, charged my truck and I left the pack. Oh my frigging God. Left it behind the rock like a calling card at the scene of a murder. And then I laughed. Like a maniac. I laughed so that it rebounded in that tight dark space and shook me harder than the cold. I laughed because I had thought I was such a wise guy, covering up all the signs with the little shovel and dirt, washing the truck the next morning, replacing the windshield, felt almost like a pro, which had creeped me out. Well, I need not have been so proud of myself nor so creeped out. I was a stone cold amateur. I had left a sleeping bag right there like a DNA-covered flag. I was an idiot. No different than I ever was. God.

Something about that realization warmed me. The return to my old dumbass self. I found the tattered wool sweater I sometimes wore fishing in the crate with my gear, and I stripped my sopping shirt and tugged it on and it was wet but it warmed me instantly. In my wet vest I found a fruit and nut bar and tore open the cellophane with my teeth and devoured it. Better. And then I curled up and the shivering subsided and I went dark. Don't even remember falling asleep, just went blank and woke with the loud chortling sound of water and the scream of a robber jay and the descending six note call of a canyon wren. I crawled out of the covered back of the truck and blinked. The sun streamed through the heavy branches of the juniper, already warm. The creek ran low in its bed and clear. Like nothing had happened, except that there was a pile of dead wood wracked against the bank on the far side, dropped there in the eddy that had formed where Jason might have died.

I didn't give him a second thought, don't know why, he didn't seem right now my biggest worry. What was? I felt lighter, the way I had last night after burying the gun. Was that just yesterday? Already seemed like another life. Except that this time the relief wasn't from getting rid of some hardware, some incriminating thing, this time I felt washed clean somehow and unburdened of something bigger.

I waded across and spent a few hours dismantling the tangle of driftwood blocking the ramp, enough to get through. I was thirsty and drank straight from the creek, fuck it, I was sure I'd already had giardia, then I started the truck and turned around and nosed into the stream which ran easy and clear, and crossed it on the old ford. And the rough road out of the canyon was mostly already dry, amazing, and I chugged and churned up it like any happy hunter. I was starving.

They were waiting for me as Irmina said. Three squad cars. Two were Jeeps. I saw the bar lights reflecting red and blue in the hotel windows before I turned in to Don Gaspar and I thought they looked festive. Perpetrator's holiday. Wheezy leaned against one of the SUVs drinking coffee and talking to Sofia. Sofia. Huh. Steve was there, too, in conversation with a uniformed officer, high ranking by the look of the stripes. It was like homecoming. Only ones missing were Sport, Willy.

I pulled up behind the cop cars, double tapped the horn, stepped out, waved. Sofia jumped forward and a deputy caught her. Steve squeaked like a groupie. They were on me. Two big local cops, I knew their families most likely. *Hands on your head, turn around please. Okay hands on the hood. Please spread your legs.* Fast frisk, hard against the junk. Wheezy wheezed,

"Okay, good, thanks, step back." This to his boys.

"No arrest?" I said.

Wheezy's sad smile. "Not today."

He looked me up and down, glanced over the truck. I followed his eyes. My knees and shins were skinned, there was mud all over my shorts, and there were leaves stuck in the gap between the camper shell and the truck cab.

"Rough night?"

"No arrest?" I said. "What then? You wanna come up to the room and have a Coke? I made a new painting, think you'd like it."

His smile.

"We already tossed the room. Nothing violent. I saw the boat painting. Nice. The brothers again?"

"Probably. Art is weird."

"That's a fact." His smile widening. "You made two. Steve here has already hung the horse and the crow. I'd buy it if I could afford it. Couldn't get to him before he put the sticker on it."

"I can tell him to give it to you. Seriously."

Shake of his big head. "Conflict of interest."

"You wanna toss the truck?"

He nodded.

"You're wondering about that gun again?"

No reason to cat and mouse him. They either had enough to put me away or they didn't. He wasn't smiling now. Tipped back the last of his Starbucks, held out his hand and one of the cops took the cup. Wheezy nodded.

"Yep, the gun again."

I said: "If I did the things you think I did, be pretty dumb to keep the gun, wouldn't it?"

"Criminals can be really dumb. Not saying you are, don't sue me. Okay, you're gonna have to sit in the car while we do this, if you don't mind. Not detaining you, just creating a little space. Also, I figured you may not be ready to talk to your posse yet." He tipped his head toward Steve and Sofia.

I nodded. Note to self: when you are in the pen serving twenty to life make sure you make him some killer pictures.

"You got some new information I guess?"

He held up a hand, held the cops off.

"Yup, found somebody you might know. The shooting up at the Pantelas' was an escalation that frankly didn't please anybody in the department. And then both your trucks dropped off the map. Got a warrant from a sympathetic judge and tracked your phone until we lost the signal. Tracked it back the next morning. That left only three ranch roads that were real roads, that a man might head down to camp if he were tired. After that it was a cinch. Three miles up the northernmost road was a lot of beaten down grass and sage off the shoulder and fresh tracks headed straight into the mesquite. Straight for a gully. Arroyo I guess you'd call it. If we had missed the tracks we wouldn't have missed the buzzards."

Buzzards. Hadn't thought of that. I wanted to tell Wheezy that criminals weren't really dumb, they just sometimes didn't think of everything.

"Guess what was down there?"

"A bunch of crows."

"That, too."

Now he looked at me really serious.

Wheezy said: "Grant had a loaded and racked .223 ranch rifle in his front seat. With a night scope. He had a spotlight out his window. He was wearing a .45 with a tac light and red dot sight. He had a .41 magnum slug in the side of his truck, shot from long range. Very long. He was hunting somebody, somebody he may have shot at a couple of days ago, we're still waiting on ballistics. Somebody whose life he may have threatened on the phone. As he had threatened this somebody's neighbor just minutes before as the neighbor tells it in a sworn statement. It is my understanding that his killing was most likely an act of self-defense. You with me?"

"I think I understand."

"It is also my understanding that whatever happened on that creek in Delta County in the middle of the night could also be reasonably construed as self-defense. Bad blood, a fight the day before, signs of a scuffle. Dellwood much bigger and stronger than even, say, you. And armed, by the way: both a .44 and a Bowie knife on his belt. Actually, just the sheath, clear that Dellwood had already drawn the knife first on whoever hit him with, say, a rock. It is my further understanding that whoever might have killed the Siminoe brothers might come clean and make a very compelling case of self-defense in both deaths. I have had long chats with the lead investigator in Colorado and the DAs both here and in Colorado—"

"Sport."

"What?"

"Sorry. You talked to Sport."

Wheezy winced at me, wheezed a few breaths and refound his thread.

"And"—*wheeze*—"and furthermore, the longer whoever it is killed these men delays in coming forward with the truth, the less compelling the case for self-defense becomes. It would behoove this individual to come back with me to the station and write out a formal statement just as soon as we toss this gentle soul's truck and probably not find the handgun that would, if we could find it, probably exactly match the slug buried in Grant Siminoe's truck."

He wheezed hard, licked his lips, and locked eyes. "Think about it," he said. He put out his pudgy hand and touched my elbow.

"It's not a betting proposition, Jim. I'm not joking. There's a clear path here. You own what you've done and what you never did"—he paused, let that burn into my viscera—"you do your time or not. Whatever happens at trial"—*wheeze*—"and that's not up to you. Remember what I said about secrets eating away at us. They do. I mean it. Can eat a man's life away like a cancer. I've seen it more than a few times."

I nodded. Christ, he almost had me jumping to confess. He was either a really good man or a really good cop. Maybe both.

"You get a lawyer yet?" he said.

I shook my head.

"Why not?"

"I've been busy."

He nodded. "Get one. Okay, go sit in the car." He nodded at the cops and I followed them back. I couldn't look at Sofia and Steve just then. I had a lot on my mind.

∎

Didn't take them long. They knew all the places to hide a pistol in a pickup. Good for me that I thought to bury the box of shells as well. No incriminating notes, no pools of dried blood. They did come up with a few crumbs of broken windshield glass which they took out with tweezers and put in a Visqueen envelope. Wheezy held it up to the light of midday and looked uncharacteristically thoughtful. He glanced at me, back at the glass, worked the scenarios in his mind, I could tell. That tightened my guts. He would be back up the highway maybe this afternoon, looking for matching crumbs at the site of Grant's shooting. Does window glass match up like bullets? When they were done with the inside of the truck they took imprints of the tires.

Huh. They could place me there, I was sure, already had put me nearby with the phone. Proximity. Probably not enough to convict. A lot might depend on how close they could put me to Grant's body. And what he'd said about self-defense. Would a DA really want to get into a complex murder trial and then have the suspect turn around and claim a clear case of self-defense?

Can you please explain to the court why you didn't come forward before?

Because I just can't stand courtrooms, no offense. Jails aren't much fun either.

But. But. Always the but. Would the but haunt me? Like Wheezy said?

Wheezy pocketed the envelope, stepped over to the squad car, motioned me out, held up the truck keys.

"Want me to have them valet park it?"

"I think I better change hotels."

"Nah. The guests love this stuff. Think of the stories they can tell."

"Newspaper?"

"Nope. Not protocol to report executed search warrants. Think how that would mess up investigations. Go upstairs, take a hot bath. We left the bathroom nice and clean."

I got out of the car, stretched, took a long draught of cool, high altitude autumn air.

"Nice place to paint, that roof room," he said. "We were up there, of course."

"Can you match broken window glass?" I said.

His head came around. All his cheer fell away. He studied me. I was thinking that one crumb on the shoulder of the ranch road that matched the pieces in his envelope would place me unequivocally at the scene. Not proximity, but ground zero. Not to mention if they found the pack while they were looking for the glass.

"We can try. It's not a precise science. It's like tire tracks: the most you can say is that the pieces are of the same type and match two million other trucks on the road."

I took the keys.

"Things can pile up," he said. "What they mean by the weight of evidence. It just piles and piles up and you carry it all with you until you're walking around like a hunchback. You, not me."

He wheezed. He shook his pant leg out of his shoe. "Try to be good," he said and walked off.

What Bob had said at the gas station. Be good. I was good. I think. Being good, on the other hand, is really hard.

I watched Wheezy go, and then watched as he turned around abruptly. He came back.

"Just had an idea," he said. "I'm going to take a little trip now"—wheeze—"back up to the scene of Grant's demise. Go look for a little broken glass. Why don't you come? You know, see some new country."

New country. He and I, we both knew it wasn't new for either of us. His eyes were dancing.

That's what they do, don't they? I thought. They get the killer back to the scene of the crime and they watch him like a hawk and wait for him to trigger and slip up and give it all away. And just after I thought that, I thought, *What the fuck! Of course I'll go with you!*

I'll go, because if I don't you'll stumble on the rucksack, my personal warrant to the pen, stumble on it while you're looking for crumbs of windshield—and why you didn't find it already I'm not sure, it must be under some brush, you must have been focused on the mess in the gully. Of course I'll go. And if I can distract you somehow, or you can distract yourselves, I'll slip over to that rock and get rid of the pack. Not sure where, or how, but I have two hours of highway till then to figure it out, make a plan.

I kissed Sofia fast and told her I was glad to see her and that I'd probably be back by nightfall, don't ask. I nodded to Steve. I got into Wheezy's unmarked Crown Vic and when I craned out the window and lifted a hand they both waved awkwardly. Wheezy drove. I leaned my head back against the front passenger seat and I thought, I have no frigging plan. No plan. Then I must have fallen asleep.

I can't say I had a plan when I woke up. Nothing came to me in a dream. He was joggling my shoulder, he was saying, "Hey tough guy, hey Jim"—the second time he'd called me by my first name—"rise and shine." And: "Jesus, you snore like a freight train! You must have been whipped."

He got out and stretched, and wheezed the fresh high-plains air as if it were clearing his lungs which it wasn't. I heard the two squad cars pull in behind us. Must have rained here, too, recently, I smelled the grass of the valley and the damp earth. I got out, stretched with the fat detective as if we were warming up for a yoga class.

We weren't. We were twenty yards east of the boulder which was just off the shoulder of the road. All they had to do was walk by it looking for glass and they could not help but see the rucksack behind it. My heart began to hammer and I could feel my face flush with heat. He was watching me with a casual sideways glance as I made myself take in the ribbon of ranch road running up into the pretty meadowed valley where the elk had been. And the ponderosas on the hill, and the trees along the creased bottom where the arroyo would be. Made myself take it in like a tourist.

"Pretty," I said.

He grinned. "Pretty like a postcard or pretty like one of those places you can't get out of your head?"

I shrugged. He turned and spoke low to the deputies who began to comb the dirt of the road and the edges of the shoulder. Looking for window glass. They began just ahead of our car and very slowly moved west, toward the rock.

"Let's take a walk," he said, pointing to the gully.

"Just a sec," I said, maybe too quickly. "I've got to take a leak."

He studied me for a beat, said, "Be my guest."

I glanced around as if looking for a place, as if I were shy, settled on the boulder with an expression that was meant to convey, Oh look there, a perfect piss spot! Maybe none of it very natural—and isn't this why they brought us out here after all? To test and rattle us? Fuck that, I walked forward, and I passed the furthest deputy who was crouching and picking up a crystal crumb with a pair of tweezers and moving it toward a clear envelope, I walked and made myself go one step at a time, go slow. As if I weren't walking straight toward my own conviction.

I looked back once, again as if I were shy, and Wheezy was in intense conversation with the deputy who was holding up the little envelope with the glass. Perfect. They were in a kind of huddle, so I speeded up, I covered the last fifteen feet in a near jog. If they just kept talking, bent in conference—I could grab the rucksack and hurl it like a hammer throw far into the grass, further up the hill. They wouldn't be searching the hill, they were looking along the road for glass. That would be enough, get it just out of sight. I could come back tonight and get it. Yes. If they just kept talking, the others bent to the road—if. It was my only chance. All I needed was to get the pack maybe ten or twelve feet further back and into the tall grass.

I stepped fast up to the boulder and stepped around it, reached for my fly.

There was a bush, a saltbush growing right up against the hump of rock. Just about the color of the rucksack.

It wasn't there.

There was nothing there. Grass, the bush. The rock. Nothing.

My mind sped up, ran. Wait—wait. Maybe. I might not have left it here. Maybe. Where else? I ran through the whole scene again, the sequence from first seeing Grant's spotlight. I did, I took it with me down the hill because I remembered clearly how heavy it was, how it swung as I ran and how I'd wished I'd left it up in the trees as I came down the hill, thinking, *Dumb. Should've left it.* And I remembered yelling to Grant to come get me, come and get it over with, and I remembered charging my truck and finding him, and after that I had no memory of the rucksack, not one. I had left it here.

Had they already found it? Fuck. No. No way, I would already be in jail.

Wheezy must have noticed, because when I was done peeing, actually peeing out of sheer nervousness, he looked at me strangely and brought a deputy with him and they searched carefully all around the rock and up into the grass of the hill.

CHAPTER FIVE

My Lover Is a Train
OIL ON CANVAS
11 X 14 INCHES
COLLECTION OF THE ARTIST

Brothers
OIL ON CANVAS
50 X 80 INCHES

Pim decided to hold an unveiling party when he got back from Detroit. The police had assured him that he was not under any threat, but that extra security for the party might not be a bad idea. The Pantelas were the kind of couple that would make a show of shaking off any kind of mishap or misfortune, could send out one hundred and fifty evites for a party five days hence and a hundred and forty-three people would show. I would be the guest of honor and Julia asked me who I'd like to be there. I told her John "Wheezy" Hinchman, Santa Fe PD, and Celia Anson. The Pantelas adored their portrait of the girls, and even better, Julia called to tell me that Celine and Julie couldn't get over it. Her voice was bright, without a hint of trauma, a marvel of resilience. She told the girls that what had happened that afternoon was a hunting accident, that everybody had gotten excited over nothing, and they had digested that and accepted it, the way children do. She said the painting made them laugh and laugh and they had endless discussions about what the chicken and colored blackbirds were doing on each other's heads. The best theory was that being atop a small person, especially one linked to another small person, kept the foxes away and gave them a changing view of the world that was way less boring than, say, being in a tree. Julia's laugh rang over the phone as she told it. I told her that I thought the girls simply had a strong association between the painting and bubble gum cigars.

I said, "I told Steve to keep a box of them on a pedestal next to my wall of latest paintings."

"Paaw! You didn't!"

"Yes, and just for fun, he did. Go look. He put them in a Cohiba box, pink and blue ones, and one of his customers said it was a terrifically ironic comment on tradition, authenticity, self-congratulation and self-mockery in contemporary art and asked how much."

"Oweee! Knowing Steve, he probably sold it."

"No, he wasn't fast enough on his feet. He didn't have clearance to put my name on it. That's when he got the idea of inventing an artist, like in that Banksy movie. Dunno. I think he's working on it. The backstory et cetera. It's like inventing a cover dossier for a CIA agent or something. He's afraid of the liability issues but he can't get over the temptation of not splitting the sale price with anyone."

"You make me laugh."

"Yup. We started a tradition with those cigars. He says it's a hit with the patrons. Gets them in a buying mood like balloons at a car dealership."

I hung up feeling happy. Pim also decided that he'd like to keep me in the hotel another week, until after the party. It was only fair, he said. I wasn't going to argue. I was painting every day up on the roof and I was painting well. I had Steve send half a dozen thirty by forty canvases and I tore through them in four days. I don't paint with a lot of detail, especially in landscapes it's mostly about color and movement, and I painted into the afternoon without pause. I felt lighter in my spirit. Sofia stayed with me in the suite and delighted in letting the valet dudes park Triceratops. Which they did with alacrity, as she always blessed them with very small fitted tops. The management politely asked that she please not pull out or in too early in the morning or too late at night because of the roar. She loved the hotel. She put in dedicated time reading on the wide porch, and in the big tub with lighthouse candles and whirlpool jets. We went to Ten Thousand Steps one afternoon and got sunburned and turned into raisins and on another day I showed her the stick hobbit shelters up on the mountain, and we followed the creek on a deer trail up through the aspen and all the way to the high ridge. In the evening we liked to walk up Canyon Road and tour the galleries. Unlike me, she was methodical, and she found a lot to appreciate. She even found a blue coyote red moon painting to love.

"Look, look you big lug. This one. Stand here. No, here. Close your eyes. Now imagine there had never been a blue coyote in the world. There was water, there was darkness, there was the Void, and then the Word and then there was a blue coyote! Voila!"

She poked me. "You can open your eyes now."

"Oh, sorry."

She was sort of right. To me. It was a good painting. That's probably how it happened for Heberto Nuñez-Jackson. He painted the first one out of the Void and it was really compelling and he did it again and it was also pretty good and he got addicted to that relationship with Creation: him, the darkness, the coyote, blue. And the red moon broke his own heart one day. I got it. And then you have a habit and all you ever wanted in the world was to feel this thing about what you create, and then presto your coyote paintings begin to sell like hotcakes. And the people in the ski lodges and big adobe houses who buy them don't really care if their blue coyote has a hundred cousins, maybe they actually like it, it makes them feel part of a trend, a phenomenon in art that is repeatedly reinforced. And so everybody is happy.

"What do you think?" she said, standing before it and gesturing with her hand like a game show model. "The only, the first. Look! The composition, the color. It's really good. How is it different than a thousand of your Diebenkorn Ocean Park paintings?"

I looked.

"It just is."

"Ohhhh, snobbism. I never, ever thought I'd see that in Jim Stegner."

"Not a snob. I believe in truth. Which is also excellence, by the way."

She narrowed her eyes at me. "You mean raw, clumsy honesty is the same as excellence?"

"I didn't say that. Truth is excellence. Honesty is not the same as truth."

"Huh." She frowned, willing, maybe, to give me the benefit of the doubt for at least a split second.

"Truth needs honesty, but that is not all it needs."

"Speak."

"Well, an artist can be honest in her rendition of say a hummingbird, in how she sees it, in her application of technique, but she may not be true to the bird."

"You mean in skill?"

"In skill, in her ability to see. To really see the bird. To see the bird as it bears its spirit forward into the world. In empathy. When all of that is there you can feel it. It knocks you over."

"Huh."

"There is something in even this coyote, this dawn of the world Genesis coyote, that is not true. He did not see into the heart of the coyote. And so I reject it. That's not snobbism."

"Huh." She smiled at me. She said: "He speaks, who knew? He's sort of a guru."

"You didn't think I had opinions on art?"

"Pretty much I just saw you as a sex object," she said.

"Hah!"

One night we walked all the way to the top of the road and I took her into El Farol for dinner. I'd about gotten over the shame of my incident with Celia. I had played it over and over in my mind and I could not see the man's moves as expressing anything other than malicious intent. He needed to be stopped and I stopped him. Right? Maybe. A salsa band was rocking in the packed low-beamed room. We sat at a small table in a corner and ate little plates of sautéed eggplant and duck empanadas. Who would make an empanada out of a duck? Someone straining for originality like Nuñez-Jackson. Tapas is a fancy way of saying a morsel of food for a fuckload of money, but I didn't mind, I was feeling flush. Pim wired the money for the portrait before he had even seen it. Steve forked over the promised 60 percent in cash, twenty-one grand, though I could tell it hurt him.

"You sure you want this in small bills like a felon?" he said, holding out a courier bag full of twenties. Then he turned white. He actually paled.

"Oh, sorry, Jim. Dumb dumb stupid."

"I am a felon, get used to it. A felon who pled down to misdemeanor."

"Yes, before. A long time ago, well. But. I'm sorry."

I took the bag and slung it on my shoulder. "It's been a weird month," I said.

He chewed the inside of his mouth, hesitated. I knew him so well.

"What? Spit it out," I said.

"Well, I've been hanging your paintings as they come in, in order. The west wall. And."

He took a big breath, it expanded him, there was hope for all of us, and then he slumped. He looked beset, excited, too. Not sure I'd ever met anyone who could telegraph so many battling emotions at once.

"And what?"

"Your work has changed. Whatever is going on out there on the road, with our nice detective friends, whatever. Something has happened to your painting. I've known you since you were a kid. And—" I knew what he was going to say next: "I've been in this business a long time." He continued: "When Alce died things changed, too, it got darker sometimes, but not like this. Back then it seemed you fought your grief by getting more and more whimsical. I'm not saying the work is better now, but it has deepened. The patrons are noticing it, too."

"You raised the prices."

He shrugged.

I thought about that. Sour disgust. And then for some reason a huge sadness overtook me, right there in his office, holding a bagful of money. All my lightness vanished.

"I couldn't paint my way out of it," I said. "Of Alce."

"I know."

"I tried everything."

"I know."

I stood there.

"I was drinking, fucking people. I didn't protect her. She came to me for help before she died and I just yelled at her."

Steve looked at me. He didn't say a word, for once.

"Okay," I said, and adjusted the bag on my shoulder. "Thanks."

"I've gotten some calls from some producers," Steve said. "And magazines."

"What?"

"Go, get out of here. Spend some twenties. I'll tell you later."

That was the long way of saying I had a pocket full of money and I didn't mind cutting loose and spending it on the two of us, Sofia and me. Also, Steve was up to something. He is always up to something. I hadn't been this flush since the book about me came out. That had lasted a little less than a year and I pretty much blew it all gambling and doing other stupid shit. This time it felt different. This was a better cutting loose, with Sofia, and for some reason when it's all cash it spends easier and lighter. I liked it that way. At the little table in El Farol we leaned forward and talked into the music the way you would talk into the wind. Sofia had been several times to the gallery on mornings I was working in the sun room, she'd walk over and study the wall of my paintings. She and Steve got along like two train engines on fire. I made that painting fast one morning, on a small canvas, their two locomotives flaming and chugging happily toward each other under a benign mesa. With her training at RISD and all her reading and the traveling she'd done in the best museums, they could talk to each other in a way I never could. "You and Steve," I'd said, holding up the picture. "Wow," she said and laughed. "Those billowing plumes of black smoke, that's art talk," I had said. She laughed harder. "It's for you," I said. She was very touched. *"I think I can I think I can,"* she murmured and kissed my ear. Now in El Farol we drank espresso, full caffeine, we weren't on any schedule, and leaned into each other and she asked about the horse and the crow and I tried to tell her about their evolving conversation.

I said, "Paintings can take on a life of their own. It's like stuff happens in them when you're not looking. The crow and the horse started out as adversaries—I mean the crow would love to eat the horse, if he ever, say, jumped off the cliff and became a carcass. But instead they began to talk. I think maybe the crow cursed the horse. I told you that I thought the crow was telling the horse that he had a choice, that he didn't have to jump after all. Well, I think that's sort of like Eve biting the apple. You were talking about Genesis. I think it's like that, the crow is like the serpent. He is giving the horse the awareness of choice. And with a full knowledge of choice comes a foreknowledge of death."

"How do you mean?"

"Well, when we have no choice, everything just happens. Everything is compelled by instinct or by some shit from outside us, some imperative, and then, well, we never have to think about where it's all headed. We react and it's headed where it's headed, that's all, and we are where we are. Just being. There is nothing but the fullness of being, the moment we are in. What the animals have, why they are blessed."

"Huh. Why Dugar wants to have sex with sea elephants or beavers maybe."

I laughed. I dug in the pocket of my barn coat and pulled out the slim volume of Rilke.

"Listen to this."

I flipped through the *Duino Elegies* until I found the page I'd turned down—it was at the beginning of the Eighth Elegy. I started to read it out loud, but the words were beaten around by a loud Venezuelan merengue, so I just handed it to her. Her eyes weren't that great. She squinted and shifted around in her chair so she could hold it up to the patterned light from a stamped metal wall sconce.

> *The creature gazes into openness with all its eyes. . . .*
> *Free from death.*
> *We alone see that: the free creature*
> *has its progress always behind it,*
> *and God before it, and when it moves, it moves*
> *in eternity, as streams do.*

She rocked her head as she read, not with the rhythm of the salsa but with the poem. She read it again, came around and put the book face down on the table.

"I always thought you were more like an animal, the way you worked. The way you don't think, the way you are just in it."

"And?"

"Turns out you are thinking all the time. Fuckin A." She laughed.

"I'm serious," I said. "I don't think the crow is doing the horse a favor, and I wonder if painting isn't a way just to be like an animal for a few hours. To be in the stream of eternity or whatever. To feel like that. Same as fishing."

"It's not the same as fishing! You were on a roll and now I realize you're the same old retard. Phew."

And then she didn't say anything. She frowned and she was very thoughtful. I wondered if she was thinking about what did that for her, put her in the stream, I wondered if she missed working on her own art.

On the fourth day after Sofia's arrival I did a big portrait. I guess it's a portrait. I asked Steve to send up another fifty by eighty stretched canvas, same size as the one I'd done of the girls. I'd enjoyed working on the larger size, and I wanted to be ready in case the mood struck me again. Steve loved it, because the bigger pieces commanded quite a lot more money. So he had Miguel deliver it to the sun room. But first he asked me if I'd called a lawyer yet, and when I said no he had a small fit and then had a prominent local defense attorney's card hand-delivered to me on the roof, with Steve's scrawl in red marker right across it: *Call him you idiot!* I put it in my shirt pocket and forgot about it.

The management, meanwhile, was getting into the swing of having a famous New Mexican artist working in their penthouse. They began to make hay with it. A young reporter ambushed me twice at the main entrance after the St. Francis leaked to the *Santa Fe New Mexican* that the famously reclusive Jim Stegner, celebrity artist, was staying in the Artist Suite and actually painting major new work in the rooftop conservatory, the same "colorful" artist that had recently been in the news as a person of interest in the killing of a notorious animal poaching kingpin and horse abuser in Colorado. And a POI in the curious death of the kingpin's horse abuser brother. I refused to talk to the journalist, I hurried by, but a few days later I picked a copy of the paper off the front desk to take with me out on the gallery with a large cup of coffee, and I settled into one of the big chairs, thinking, *Life doesn't really get better than this*—when I flipped to regional news and there on the second page of the section was a photo of me, bearded, in my spattered cap, smoking a little stogie and fishing. I spilled the coffee into my lap. The impulse was to cover the picture. The story told about my stature in the art world and the killings, and said I was accompanied by my comely young model. At least they didn't put *model* in quotes. For a moment I was blind, literally, with rage. I felt ill. Two men were dead, a sickening fact, more sickening if you knew them, way worse if you had spattered the last jets of their blood on the ground. I recognized the picture as coming from Steve, it was one we had used for some promotional stuff in the last couple of years. I went straight through the lobby and took the elevator and called him up from the room phone.

"I haven't seen so much buzz about your work in a decade—" He started right in, didn't let me get a toehold.

"It's super duper, Jim. I'm jacking up prices so often my arm's getting tired."

He went on to say that the Albuquerque paper, the *Journal*, had picked up the story from the *New Mexican*. Now the local news show, *Albuquerque Channel 9*, wanted to do a segment, as did *Art-Speak*, the New Mexico PBS weekly art show.

Steve was so excited he was talking over himself. He said, "So 9News called this morning, they want to do a piece next week for the morning show. Vigilante artist or something. They are just beside themselves that you are one of our most famous artists and that you had this rough past and are now maybe a killer. Of course they can't say *vigilante* because, after all, you are innocent until. But they can hint at it. And they just flipped over the clip from that radio interview in San Francisco. You scare the crap out of them I can tell. Maybe they want to skewer you but they won't. Listen, this is your moment. You won't believe how much *Horse and Crow* has gotten to. Kind of a grudge match between Pim and Sidell with a few others piping in. I've put in a call to the Harwood Museum—"

"*Stop.*"

"What?"

"Shut the fuck up."

I couldn't begin to tell him how it really felt, how awful, so I said, "Do you realize what that picture in the newspaper is going to do to my privacy? I'm going to have to leave town."

Indraw of breath I could hear through the phone, then a long moan. "*Aoooouuww!*"

"What?"

"Don't do that, Jim. You have no idea. Have you been online? Of course not, you're so damn antique! A blogger who does a lot with the New Museum just wrote about you: 'Art and Blood in the Wild West.' The blog has gotten a storm of comments. The comparisons to Van Gogh again, some mention of mental illness, but I wouldn't worry about it—"

That slugged me like a punch. Not the antique thing but the blogger thing.

"I've even been talking to the hotel, they want to give you like a month free! To keep painting on the roof. They are calling it the Artist's Residency. They're thinking of continuing it after you."

I was now speechless. So officially steamed and disgusted I could not speak.

Out of the silence, timidly, Steve proffered: "You know, you need to take advantage of the hotel's offer, stay. If you go back to Paonia it will follow you, the story, and I won't be there to protect you."

"Ouaaoauuw—"

"Jim? *Jim?*"

"You're a goddamn psychopath. I'm convinced now."

"Who's talking, Vigilante Man?"

"I want to throttle you. Seriously. No gun, no rock."

"Don't say that! Jesus." Pause. "You don't mean that?"

"Steve."

"What?"

"Is this what you want? Seriously. To drive me at last over the edge?"

"What edge? One you haven't been over already? Do you know what it's like trying to keep track of you and your edges?"

"I mean it. Do you want me in living hell?"

"Is that how you think of me?"

"I don't know how to think of you."

"You aren't miserable, Jim. I've known you practically since you were a baby. Trust me. I'm being serious now. You are happier now than you've ever been. We'll get through this patch, this little media frenzy, we'll try to make you rich, we'll get you a museum show, some of the national attention that has been eluding you lately, and then you can slip quietly back home, wherever that is, and go fishing. Meanwhile we'll pray that our friend Detective Hinchman—what do you call him, Wheezy?—and what's his name who just called from Colorado, Detective Gaskill, pray they don't find any eyewitnesses or guns or anything. We'll keep you out of the pen and you can paint and fish and entertain. Sofia is a dish by the way."

It was monstrous. Steve was going to take the killing of two living breathing brothers and make hay. *I* was going to make hay, if he had his druthers, if things went according to plan. I didn't say a word, for what seemed like a long time. I was out of words.

"Jim? Jim?"

"I hate your guts," I said. I meant it. Right then.

"Me, too. My guts. I hate myself so much sometimes I just want to give myself a big kiss."

"It's all I know how to do," I said. I think I was starting to choke up. "Don't you *get* it? I couldn't stop if I tried. Painting. Do you want to kill it? Me?"

"Jim? You're really upset!"

"Oh, fuck, Steve. *Fuck.* I am of a mind to stop painting altogether. Have Miguel send over the fifty by eighty ASAP."

I hung up.

The painting I made was a reprise of the little girls except that it was two little boys. I made it for no other reason than it was building inside like an overstretched balloon and would burst. I put the boys standing in the bright kitchen with flowers behind them but not the same ones as for the girls. I put sage and Indian paintbrush, yellow alfalfa, clover, goldenrod, the scrappy stuff you'd find along the shoulder of any road. A thorny black limbed mesquite with a line of ants climbing the trunk. The energy of the girls had been like two chicks breaking out of the same egg, hungry, ready to be skeptical, and surprise! a candy necklace. They held hands, the habit of protection, but seemed to be saying, Hey this is fun, give us something else ridiculously delicious. The boys were holding hands, but they were turned slightly askew, as if ready to stand back to back. And they looked scared. On the smaller, on the left, call him Dellwood, I put a model ship in a bottle, in a wooden stand right on top of his head. Don't know why. On the other I put three crosses and from the center one I hung a pale bird, ocean gray, hung from the neck and drooping dead like the pheasant by Lucas Cranach. An albatross maybe, which must have occurred to me because of the ship. I painted fast, not seeing anything, hard to describe but I mean I don't think I was seeing in any conscious way anything I was painting, and for the first time in a long time I painted scared. The picture scared me. The boys scared me, their predicament, whatever it was. No one should have to carry around a ship in a bottle. In fact as I made the ship I found the whole project of bottling up a little ship to be so monstrous I was actually painting in a kind of spiritual pain that was not at all the pain of labor as I imagine it, of birthing forth, but the pain of killing someone.

I was shaking. I finished the picture maybe faster than I've ever finished anything of that size before. I was shaking all over. I stood back and I thought, Is that what you are trying to do? Put the brothers in some bottle and cork it? Is that what the painting is? The ship you are carrying around on your own head, your albatross and the spiky crosses too? What they say about dreams: you are every character? Is that the brothers and also you?

The thought that we were somehow the same made me gasp. When you kill do you also conjoin somehow? In some horrible communion you will never shake? Is that why soldiers come home and scream at night and kill themselves? Because they have become their targets?

I sat in the folding chair they'd brought for me. Only one end of the conservatory was glass. The easel and I were out of the sun in an end of the big room shaded by a wall and by a curtain. I put my head in my hands and shook. When Alce came to visit me she spoke to me softly. The brothers had never spoken and I suspected now it was because they were burrowed too deep inside, inside of me, they were becoming me, and you can't speak to yourself except by speaking to yourself, which was a circular kind of conversation and what I suspected now I was doing with these paintings. I wanted a drink. I tasted bourbon and I wanted one badly and didn't want to fight the easy ride down to the hotel bar. What time was it?

Sofia was out somewhere thank God, maybe at the gallery, maybe in the plaza shopping for a necklace, I told her to get one. I left the painting on the easel, I had my coat, the keys were in the pocket, I hustled down to the lobby and fetched the truck and drove up the Paseo to the Old Santa Fe Trail and drove straight south under the long ridge and turned up it at Double Arrow, the same road to Pim's, climbing the washboarded dirt too fast and rattling my teeth. It was a bright clear cold morning. At the gate across the road I punched in the four numbers I remembered and pulled over in a shallow pullout under some tall pines. As soon as the engine cut and I heard the wind feathering in the needles and smelled the sunwarmed bark I felt better. I crunched over fallen needles into the woods. The juniper trees were a blue-green and they riffled in the stronger currents of wind. Their dusty berries littered the ground. A squirrel squealed and chattered. Squawk of distant crows, echoing the empty spaces, ridge to ridge. I walked uphill breathing hard and came to a small clearing. The Buddha was there cross-legged on his stupa, a little bigger than a normal man. The dirt had been cleared around him and laid with polished stone flags. I had heard that Buddhists walk clockwise around the Buddha with their hands at their chests in gratitude and prayer, it was about the only thing I knew about Buddhism and right now I needed all the help I could get. I got on the flagstone path and pressed my hands in prayer and I walked. I walked around three times. I prayed.

Forgive me.

Forgive me everything.

I want to love all things. I don't know how. I don't know how.

Please help me.

I walked and prayed harder. I heard the wind in the trees like water, like a creek.

Please give the brothers peace. Wherever they are, some measure of peace. I wish that for them. Please please please God whoever you are. Please let Alce be joyful, let her spirit fly in joy. Please oh please God. Buddha, forgive me, grant me some peace. Please. Alce, sweet girl, forgive me. Forgive me. I wish you were here I wish I wish we could go fishing this afternoon.

Oh please. Let me live somehow in peace. In truth. Thank you for not killing me before I could ask.

It was all a jumble. Like that and repeated and jumbled. I knelt on the rock in front of the statue and lifted my eyes to his eyes. How I remembered them: the color of a calm sea, without judgment, seeing things exactly how they are, seeing me. Like Irmina but without concern or worry. Conveying a deep and cool peace.

I sat on the knoll with the pines whispering and the Buddha looking down on me. I sat all afternoon, sat as the air turned frosty in the dusk and I was shivering with cold but not shaking with fear anymore, and I got up stiffly and walked back down the hill. I drove back barely seeing the gravel ahead, but just before the stop sign at Zia Road I saw the El Camino parked against the trees. I went through the intersection digesting the image, then pulled over and began to back up fast, half turned backward in the seat, two wheels on the soft shoulder. Fuck him, haunting me like a hit man. What was he trying to do? Why didn't he just plug me? But his headlights flared and he peeled out and turned down Zia and was lost to sight at the first curve.

CHAPTER SIX

When I got back to the hotel there was a TV camera, a news girl, and three print reporters holding out little recorders. They told me their papers as I walked by: the *Albuquerque Journal,* the Inrock alternative weekly, and the magazine *Art in America.* The news girl was wearing a red knit rolltop sweater, tight black pants and stilettos, and her lipstick matched her top. Definitely local. Her hair was sprayed into stiff curls at the edges of her cheeks. She looked Navajo and a little tense, like she was on her first big assignment. The print reporters started right in.

Mr. Stegner Mr. Stegner can you confirm that you are a suspect in two murders?

Do you have a lawyer? Who is it? Why isn't your lawyer making any statements?

Are you working on any paintings now?

The hotel says you like to go fishing in the afternoon. Where did you go?

Well. Steve had clearly not gotten the hint. I shrank away from them. I knew that if I waved my hand and said *Sorry,* that would suit their purposes as well as an interview. Reclusive fisherman-artist-maybe-turned-vigilante refuses comment. We caught him returning from an afternoon fishing.

I needed a smoke. I couldn't smoke anywhere in the hotel except the roof and I didn't want to lead the wolf pack up there. The anger, the hatred of this spectacle boiled up. The girl had advanced uncertainly and held out her mic and said, almost pleading, *Mr. Stegner, can I have a few words?*

Something about her diffidence struck me, and that she hadn't hit the right note yet with her dress and makeup. She was probably from one of the pueblos. She needed a break. I felt for her. What the hell.

I pivoted like a bullfighter. The extended digital recorders recoiled. Having a rep as a suspected violent killer has its advantages. The reporters clammed up in unison. I walked right up to the news-caster. She stiffened, blinked, realized she probably had her story and unleashed a guileless and grateful smile. Okay, I was ready. She cleared her throat, looked down at a folded page of notes in her left hand, and spoke into the mic: "Here, just getting back from the river, we think, is our famous Taos artist Jim Stegner. He is a dedicated outdoorsman and a fanatic fly fisherman and tonight he has perhaps just returned from a long afternoon on the Rio Grande. Were you fishing?"

She smelled of perfume, a little loud. I thought how hard it is to play a role, any role. Sometimes it took half our lives to get it half right. I looked at her, I looked at the camera and stretched a grim smile. Probably looked like a hyena. How I felt.

I dug in my coat and took out the foil pack, a lighter, and lit a cheroot. I offered her one. Wave of hand. I smoked. Whoa that felt good. I scratched my chin under my beard. The print reporters gathered tightly around just off screen, held up their little recorders.

"Yes," I said. She nodded. She hesitated. She smiled. It was not a fake smile, it was real, a little too vulnerable, and I thought, *Get out of this business.*

"My father used to take me fishing on the Animas when I was little. We used worms." She wrinkled up her nose.

I stared at her through the smoke. Suddenly I could see it, her and her father—who was heavy but agile and wore an oversize t-shirt that didn't hide the tribal ink running down his arms—I could see them stepping down the bank with a bucket, throwing out bobbers. The image paralyzed me.

"You look shocked," she said. "Are you okay?"

I shook myself. How long had I been staring at her with maybe my mouth hanging open? I took a long draw and let out a cloud of smoke to cover for a sec while I got my wits back. I had seen a stark image of this woman as a girl stepping into the water, the covered stones, holding her rod high, following her father. Stark because there was nothing else in the world but the swift dark current and the two of them.

"I—I—"

I was speaking, but no words came. She glanced down at the folded paper. She looked a little bewildered. She said quickly, "You have been through a rough time these last few weeks, these last few years. I know what an escape fishing can be. Painting must be that way, too. Has it been extra stressful?"

I didn't answer. The camera was on me and she was reading straight off the paper.

"Your work in the last month is extraordinary. Prolific, and disturbing, and in some ways different than anything you have painted before. It seems to be getting some in the art world excited. Can you say that these allegations of murder have inspired you in some way?"

The image of her as a young daughter fishing was gone. She was very thin and tall for a Navajo. She probably wasn't. Everybody down here was mestizo in one way or another. She was probably Chicana and Ute or something. The Ute were up by the Animas. Suddenly I didn't feel charitable anymore. Her eyeliner was too heavy. I thought: TV will make you cruel and it will ice the humanity inside you, and you will grow into something your father won't recognize, and all this will happen because you chose it.

I felt mean.

I dropped the cheroot. I grunted something that came out as a roar, I guess, because all of them flinched back, and I turned and fled through the big hotel door and almost fell inward as the doorman pulled it open and I nearly ran across the smoothly tiled lobby. I had the impression that everyone there was watching me as I went. The rapt focus of fans at a sporting event.

I couldn't find my card key and I pounded on the door and Sofia let me in. She had paint smudged on her face and in her hair and her arms were open.

The painting she made me was the first one she'd made in three years. She called it *Backstroke*. She was excited and proud. It was a bearded man swimming lazily on his back in an ocean devoid of women or drama. Sitting on his belly was a family of four otters, all smiling the way otters smile. It was very good. Clean and full of humor and life.

The morning TV magazine story ran three days later, a full fifteen minutes. 9News wanted to be the first, and they put the pedal to the metal. How did they pull this shit off so fast? There was a brief bio, a sort of photo album collage of me surfing as a grom (tyke surfer); Pop's death in news clippings; me with my buddy Jan looking handsome and disturbed as a junior in the yearbook, unkempt dark hair blowing, blue t-shirt with a hole in the shoulder, the expression far off, like trying to focus on a bird who is moving into a greater distance; running away to sister in Santa Rosa; the San Francisco MOMA where I went one day to stay away from the neighborhood cops after a fight, seeing Winslow Homer and Van Gogh and Matisse for the first time; the fascination then passion, art supplies, enrolling in the SF Art Institute; a photo of the painting that won the jury prize at the spring contest; Taos; me and my truck, me with fishing rod, me and Cristine and Alce, me at easel in studio, everything you'd expect, most of it out of the book Steve had commissioned, then: news flash, famous painter shoots bar patron! TV news now, shots of Santa Fe State, me in orange jumpsuit smiling, my release, growing fame, slew of paintings, their images, what a couple of critics said, the book about me, the exhibits, then: the radio interview in which I crush the interviewer's hand. Gone viral. An artist who spoke for the working classes, a loose cannon, a big, passionate, physical man. Then: death of famous painter's daughter, mug shots, TV news now of an ambulance, a gurney, I turned away. Divorce, gambling. Second marriage, Maggie as a pinup with bunny tail, Paonia, a current shot of my house—that made me sit up—they were trespassing clearly, then: news flash: murder on the Sulphur.

And then it slowed down and Cindy De Baca began to narrate the chain of events, the cracking of a poaching ring by the Feds, U.S. Fish and Wildlife, the brothers, their dovetailed operation between Colorado and Arizona, documented cases of horse abuse, animal deaths, ASPCA allegations, the fight between me and Dellwood, the little horse. Then: death of Dellwood. The old brawler-artist the local fishermen call Hemingway is a person of interest. A barn burning, an interview with Willy who clearly did not want to talk but wanted to set the record straight. Then: an ambush, shots through the window of Santa Fe society family, my biggest collector, suspect brother Grant, then murder of Grant. Is Jim Stegner the Vigilante Artist? Did he see himself as the Eliminator of Bad Men? That was the question. And: *In a twist that could only occur in a volatile art world, Stegner's recent paintings are in such high demand they are going for double what his work previously commanded. And requests for shows are increasing. In the last week, the Harwood Museum in Taos has . . . We may ask ourselves: should allegations of murder dramatically increase an artist's stock?* Then Wheezy chiming: *There are, as of now, no allegations.* De Baca: *What?* A shot of her shoving her mic into Wheezy's face *And now we ask Detective John Hinchman, Santa Fe PD homicide and lead investigator on the Grant Siminoe murder case: Why isn't Jim Stegner a suspect?* Wheezy finishing a paper cup of coffee just like a screen detective, grinning heartily into the camera: *Because, Cindy, he is not a suspect!* Tight on her face, her look of moral shock. Okay, now I officially did not like her. Wheezy again: *And by the way, Cindy, the death of Grant Siminoe has not been classified as a murder.* Forgiving chuckle. De Baca: *What! A man is shot in the head and his truck and his body crashed into a gully in the middle of the night?* Perfectly pitched incredulity backed by the common sense of all New Mexican viewers. *Why? Why??* Wheezy, grinning, patient didact: *Well, in this business we call them extenuating circumstances.*

Then a survey of my paintings since the first murder. The dates of the killings, and other seminal events like the arson, flashed at the bottom of the screen while the paintings that were finished at about the same time revolved across the top.

I couldn't stop watching. It was completely compelling. The Albuquerque station was clearly gunning for an Emmy. Sofia sat beside me on the plush couch with her mouth half open, speechless. It struck me how riveting the story, how maudlin: that she was dumbstruck. An event as rare as a full solar eclipse.

The centerpiece of the whole story was the interview just outside the hotel, if you could call it an interview. Given that I'd said two words it was surprisingly impressive. I mean it made an impression. It confirmed everything the story had been building to—a grand insinuation, pretty much case closed, that murder finds a man, especially a rugged artist-vigilante, reticent and mercurial, and lights a great fire under his art, and his art, well, is pretty much genius. *BUT*—it cannot and never will justify breaking the law—*AND CERTAINLY NOT MURDER! NOT EVER!* That seemed to be the takeaway. I found the remote on the floor and flicked off the tube. Sofia turned to me.

"Wow."

"Yeah, right?"

"We're gonna have to get you better sunglasses, Jim. Wrap-arounds. Or maybe just a full burka."

"Huh." I was just sort of staring at the black flat screen that mirrored the light from the windows, staring at it as if it were a quiet pool that mirrored the morning and had just revealed the flash of like a three foot trout.

"Maggie was really pretty. So was Cristine. Makes me feel a little insecure, to tell you the truth."

"Huh."

"Jim!"

"Wha?"

"Snap out of it! Say something. Jesus. That was crazy."

"It was crazy."

I thought: It was. For one, to see your life wrapped up in a quarter of an hour. It was like going to your own funeral. Was that me? Nah. No way. For two, was I such a crazy bastard? Had I been that impulsive and violent my whole life? I felt so gentle most of the time. I really did. I swear.

The room phone rang. It would be Steve. Steve wondering why my cell phone was probably buried under trash in my truck. He had, remarkably, stayed out of the program, except a shot of him in pressed jeans and pink oxford waving like a beauty queen and disappearing into his office, the door closing. I was amazed. Uncharacteristic discipline for him. How could he resist? He'd been smart enough to know that the skyrocketing value of my work did not need his interpretation, that in this case discretion and modesty for once contributed to the mystique. They perpetuated the narrative of the outsider artist suddenly besieged by a fascinated popular culture and resisting it with all his might. Playing hard to get. His dealer, too. The mainstream seemed to love that: something authentic for once! Something that didn't cave and crave at the first glare of regional television. The public treasured their Joe DiMaggios, their J. D. Salingers. I didn't answer the phone, I couldn't do that right now. Steve would be needing to crow. To somebody. My dramatic emergence from the sticks was thrusting him into the spotlight and it might make him a rich man. I mean, I was already a well known artist, but this was different. When Sofia went for the phone I stopped her.

She was in the middle of the big plush carpeted room. She seemed a little stunned herself. She stood there.

"I know," I said. "Getting drunk is looking pretty good."

She blinked. Then that impish smile crept across her face. She folded her fingers around the bottom of her shirt and lifted it off. She wasn't wearing a bra and her wonderful breasts lifted as her arms went over her head, then they fell and buoyed like launching boats finding their float. I laughed. She had a way of cutting not to the quick but to my joy. Maybe it's the same thing.

"You wanna get distracted you crazy vigilante?"

I shook my head.

"Not in the mood?"

Shook my head.

"Let's go get some breakfast," I said. I was shaking all over. "Let's walk over to the plaza and have café con leche and eat huevos rancheros and pretend."

"Pretend what?"

"That life is simple. That we can do what we want."

CHAPTER SEVEN

The Pantelas were used to throwing big parties, but this took the cake. Cars were parked all the way down the driveway in the pines and out to the gravel road where they lined both sides. Couples in engraved cowboy boots that weren't meant for walking held each other's hands and tottled up the hill. We drove with Steve who promised to leave when we did, who slowed his Range Rover and opened his window and waved and made passing comments to everyone as we passed. This was his moment.

The pueblo house was built for autumn. Around the carved front entrance and all along the ledges at the tops of the stick ladders were bundles of Indian corn and strings of crimson chilies and piles of flame colored squash. My hand itched to paint it. Everything except the security guy on the main roof in fatigues, a shooter with an M4 assault rifle. There would be others, no doubt, keeping a perimeter, and probably some in plainclothes inside. That Pim had planned the party at all, so soon after the shooting; that he had let the target—me—anywhere near his kids again. But that was Pim: it was his way of saying: We don't let the bad guys rain on our parade. We don't let them win. For a moment, as the three of us were about to step inside, I wondered if he would be furious at me for putting his children in danger, ever, and I realized in the same moment that this was his way of forgiving me.

Leave it to Steve to time our entrance. We were an hour late. We came through the door past two more uniformed security men who checked our invites, and the crowd parted and something like a guffaw of pleasure and fascination billowed out of it, a little like a gust whomping the alders. Or the loud gasp at a hanging. I scared most of them I was sure, and the paintings inspired love, and I was a genius and under investigation for two murders and I was the dark celebrity of the hour, and here was the beautiful young lover-model we have all been reading about and and and. The mixture was high octane. The sea of admirers parted in a crush. Drinks were spilled.

The painting, under a drop cloth, was at the other end of the red carpet that was not red but blue, another Central Asian runner, maybe Kirghiz, woven with geometric green birds. The painting was on one of my easels against the big windows with the big view of the valley and the wooded ridges, and the light was already going graciously to dusk so as not to backlight the canvas.

A tray passed, balanced by a waiter, Knob Creek bourbon and water—my favorite, how did they know?—the bottle on the tray, and I took one without thinking and downed half the glass before I realized that I'd just thrown away almost three years of sobriety, every day hard earned as a day at the mills. I mean if you are into counting days and years. It was a moment of horror. Does that count? One slug? Yes.

Suddenly I felt I was in a nightmare. Did I just do that? Holy shit. The full impact hitting me at the same time as the sweet warm unutterably delicious booze, hitting my gut and then my blood and brain like the all smothering and transporting kiss of an old and favorite lover. Oh Jesus. In a panic I grabbed Sofia by the arm, hard.

"What?" she whispered.

"Don't let me do that again. I mean it."

"What?"

"I just tossed back a whiskey, oh fuck."

I felt something like panic zing through her. We had talked about my fitful dance with booze, how nothing good could happen for me when I drank.

She reached for my hand. "You're okay, it was a mistake. Reflex. You didn't even know. Don't worry." She squeezed. "Really. Forget it."

I glanced at her. She was smiling. Okay. I shuddered. Somehow I believed her.

Pim made a toast. He stood by the easel, held out his cut glass tumbler, someone else rapped the crystal of a wineglass with a spoon. He wore an alpaca vest with silver buttons, jeans. Ruddy tan, salt and pepper full hair, boyish, bushy eyebrows, hunter's clear gray eyes and the lined drawn cheeks of an endurance athlete. Easy in a crowd. Could it be that most of the people who loved him also envied him so much they hated him? I thought probably so. Maybe my biggest collector.

"Some of you have champagne? Good. Good for a toast. I can't drink it, it makes me giddy and I'm giddy enough already."

Murmur of laughter.

"Julia, are you——? Ah, here."

She appeared by his side, raised a glass of white wine to the crowd, smiled—Here I am, you knew I'd be here, I'm always a little late, aren't I? I love you all and you love me always anyway. What her smile said. It struck me that Pim was running for something, for office. Julia, too. What was it? King and Queen of Santa Fe? Art Mavens of the American Southwest? And my paintings, one after another, my paintings in their aggregate were crucial to their winning. With my sudden fame their accession was a lock. This was a coronation as well as an unveiling. That was suddenly clear to me. The sense of nightmare was morphing into another kind of dream, something compounded of dread and excitement.

What I mean is: you get this pressure, this internal pressure that builds like a swelling lake and you paint. It's all you want to do, all you know how to do. And if you focus in the right way, a way you had to learn, you let yourself go. You lose yourself and just about vanish and the painting asserts and fills and flows over the dam and down into the streambed of everything you have ever experienced and thought, and carries you both on a current that takes you into a country that neither of you have ever seen. Where you have never been.

And then what? You go through this journey of losing everything, this vertiginous process and create this somehow magical thing and you wake up and remember your name and dip your small brush and sign it, which is odd when you think about how you got there, and then maybe you have a dealer and a way to make a living doing it again and again, and the dealer sells it to Pim, and he displays it and maybe loves it, but is not at all equivocal about how it fits into the swelling pile of his net worth, nor into the marvelously growing balance of his prestige and status. And then you kill two men. And the rich get richer.

It's kind of a long train of thought, but it all occurred to me in a flash as I saw the two of them half raise their glasses and as I listened to Pim launch into his toast. This is where the process ends, that's what came to me with the whole, big, round, comprehensive knowledge of a dream. And spacetime rippled like a big sail losing then catching the wind. The way it does in a dream sometimes.

Dunno. Maybe it was the jiggerful of booze.

I scanned the crowd around me. Celia Anson caught my eye and waved, relieved. She began to make her way toward us. I saw my other big collectors, the Sidells, up against the windows talking to the hanging-stone artist. Invited I knew in the spirit of amicable competition. Speaking of hangings, where was Detective Wheezy Hinchman? I went onto my toes and searched the way I looked sometimes for trout rising along an evening bank. I saw Fazil, the owner of the torture gallery next door to Steve's, and I saw Steve in animated conversation with the owner of the La Paloma Hotel, another rich collector but of dubious taste.

Sofia squeezed my arm. She was a knockout tonight, dressed elegantly in a new black silk shift and silver chain belt, watching me closely, with the rapt attention of a volcanologist: she was very close, right at the base of the mountain, and her interest in the smoking peak was equal parts science and self-preservation. She stretched and said loudly into my left ear:

"Hand that feeds you, buddy."

I shook my head against her lips. "What?"

"Relax! It's a scene. You can't paint in a vacuum. You need these people."

These people. I took in the room, and the faces blurred and she was telling me that they loved my work, loved me.

They *do*? That's what I thought to myself. They do? After what I've done? Nobody knew. They knew. A lot of them knew. I felt queasy, I felt like turning around and rushing back out the door.

I sucked in a big breath and found Steve again in the crowd. He does. He really does. Julia was at the front of the room, listening to her handsome husband with huge indulgence. She did. She really loved it. Pim must. I'd seen him go apeshit over a painting. It wasn't just an investment. I knew how much he adored his daughters, more than anything on earth maybe, and he had asked me to memorialize this time in their lives. So what if the Pantelas had everything and wanted more?

"Not everybody can paint," she said into my ear like a megaphone. "Some people just get to love it. Buy it, treasure it. The way it should be."

"The way it should be."

I felt her squeeze my arm hard again and I felt the adrenaline wash out into my limbs. She squeezed and the fight fluttered out of me. Whatever I was about to say in front of everyone, I had lost it. Was I really *not* going to fuck up and not blow my life apart right here at this autumn art party? Really?

A new phase. Maybe. Damn. Celia grabbed my other arm as if she'd just reached a life ring.

"There you are! How exciting." Lush kiss low on my cheek.

"Fazil is such an asshole," she said much too loudly. "Would you kill him for me? You look so different with your clothes on!" She started in on Fazil and all the twisted dealers in town and she was clearly sauced or getting there. She said excitedly that there were reporters here from Albuquerque and *Bullett,* and I lost her words to the clamor in my head, and when they came clear again she was saying that some blogger for *ARTnews* asked—*in reference to you Jim, to you!*—if the tendency among talented artists to believe themselves above the law might extend to a crime like murder—

I lost the sound. The room went mute and began to tilt. What the fuck was I doing here? A burst of loud applause roared through my vertigo and I saw that they were ushering up the little girls, their Costa Rican nanny was, and of course they were in their sailor suits. Pim handed his glass to Julia and reached down to lift one of the girls. The nanny hoisted the other. They swung them up onto a table that had been placed next to the covered easel so the crowd could see. Instantly the hands found each other, came together. They wouldn't look at their mother, they didn't know where to look. Someone yelled, "Cheese, girls!" Cameras flashed. Smiles fluttered over their faces like butterflies in the last cold sunlight before a killer frost. I could see that they were terrified. Julia went to them, smoothed their hair, their dresses, whispered in their ears, leaned over to Pim, was clearly telling him to get his stunt over with.

"—life does imitate art. Can't help itself. Without further ado, I give you Jim Stegner's latest great painting."

Well, that wasn't exactly true, but. He handed the nanny his glass this time, carefully rolled up the drop cloth, then jerked it up and free with a flourish. Cameras flashed. The crowd shifted and shifted back like an ocean swell. Cheers went up, laughter, applause, the girls tucked closer together, eyes closed, and shivered as if weathering a hailstorm. For a long moment the tableau held. Then Julia spoke sharply to the nanny and the two of them lifted the girls down and shuttled them out.

Here's the strange thing: I felt the energy of the painting move into and through the people around me. A compression and release, maybe the way an explosion moves through water. The sight of the painting. That's what it was, without a doubt. The spontaneous laughter, the clapping, the sounds, the childlike glee on some of the faces, the sudden serious focus, maybe recognition, on others. What it is about painting, how it can hit people exactly like music, and hit people so differently.

Pim was grinning like he'd just landed a five pound German brown.

"Jim! Where's Jim Stegner? Can we get our favorite artist up here? Can you say a few words, Jim?"

Filament of panic, lit like a bulb. All eyes turning now to me. A kaleidoscope of hooting owls, huge dark owl eyes lit with love. Goddamn, lucky thing I'm not a mouse. They weren't scared at all now. How could the man who had painted the twins this way be a murderer? A loose cannon? Well.

Pim was extending a hand, as if to help me from the dock to his yacht. I was on the edge of an open aisle to the painting. Not a red carpet but the blue kilim runner.

Sofia grabbed a handful of my butt and pushed. What the hell. Die Another Day.

Pim put his arm around my shoulders. He raised his glass and two hundred glasses lifted. "To one of America's greatest painters!"

I thought: None of this would be happening if I hadn't killed two men. We might be having an unveiling, but there would be less of a crowd, it would be a lot quieter, no writers from *Bullett*. That queasiness, the nausea, washed through the warmth of the booze and rose into my craw. I remembered getting hit by a rogue set wave surfing. Clawing out through the crashing whitewater on a big day to sit well out past the break on the safe calm of the swell and then seeing the thing rise in a wall beyond me, out where I did not think a wave could be, rise and stiffen and begin to collapse. The tumbling wall of my immediate future. Just then a pair of eyes that weren't owl at all, and weren't smiling, just a man, looking straight at me, serious, it was Sport, holy shit. Wearing a gray Harris tweed jacket and a predatory expression. Not mean, just patient. Watching the prey. Not still so much as withholding action, for the moment. The way, it occurred to me, I had watched Dellwood from the willows. And next to him was Wheezy. Wheezy at least seemed about to laugh. He couldn't get over it, any of it.

Another jolt of panic. Had they found the rucksack? Or the gun? Had one of the hunters stepped forward as an eyewitness? Had they come to arrest me in front of all my hometown admirers? I didn't think so.

"Go ahead, Jim," Pim prompted. "Give us a word."

I shook myself off like a dog.

"Thanks," I said. "Thank you all for years of support. And friendship. I'm not sure what else to say."

I couldn't breathe. I needed to get out of here. My mouth felt like parchment. I looked on the table beside me for something to drink. There was nothing. I took a deep breath, let the pounding of the pulse in my ears subside. Did I? Think I was above the law? No. If anything, I always thought the law would probably have its way with me no matter how I chose to live. I said:

"I never thought I was above the law, above anybody, ever." I looked at Sport. "The law is relentless. I—"

A gasp from the crowd. Pressure drop in the house, just like before a big thunderstorm.

There's this scene in one of those asteroid movies, where the fleeing, hapless victims—where the fuck are they running? Where could they go, after all?—where they just turn and stand transfixed on a mountainside and watch the hurtling rock the size of like Australia falling out of the sky. That's what the guests looked like. Like I was about to reach impact and maybe take them all with me. Some, have to hand it to them, were fascinated and incredulous at once. Not every day you get clobbered by a rock. Ask Dell.

Still couldn't get a full breath. Suddenly I felt sad. Incredibly sad. I looked around the room, scanned face to face. So many faces I knew. I cleared my throat.

"Does anyone have some sparkling water or something?"

A young woman waiter in a short tux jacket and red bow tie came swiftly out of the crowd bearing a tray of tumblers garnished with limes, offered them up, and was gone. I took a long sip, set the glass on the table by the painting, took in the faces, the silence freighted and palpable as fog.

"You know I lost my daughter a few years ago. She was my best friend."

I saw her again, stepping down the bank ahead of me, excited, holding up her rod, turning over stones at water's edge. I thought how she would have loved this party. We would have fished together this afternoon and come straight from the river. She would have caught more fish. She would have teased me about it.

I saw her casting. The long living loops of line. Saw her step to the turn of the bend, look back, her face a question: *Are you there? Are you coming?*

I am here. Now. I—

"I didn't protect her," I said. "I let her go away."

Silence.

"I can't bring her back."

I clawed at my collar. I needed cold fresh air.

"I've got to go. Is it too dark to go fishing?" I turned to the big window where a smoky harvest moon was breaking over the eastern ridge. Turned back.

"A moon. There's a moon—I better try."

A murmur filled the room like water. Some of the faces looked stricken. I heard someone whisper, *He's leaving? Already?*

And another, hushed, *It's so sad. It's awful.*

I walked fast down the runner and out the door and out the drive and down the road. Sofia came right behind me. In a few minutes we were washed in headlights and Steve pulled over and picked us up and knew enough not to say a word. All the way to the hotel.

We did go fishing. We drove, the two of us, all the way to the Taos Box. While Sofia slept I fished in the cold and the dark, the stretch Alce and I used to fish together. I fished above the falls, and below in the big pool that silvered in the moonlight. I caught a few fighters and I fished until daybreak.

Not Too Scary
OIL ON CANVAS
20 X 30 INCHES

At the house in Paonia I put a cattle guard in the driveway where it crosses over the ditch from the county road, the road that goes to Willy's. It's one of those grates a car can drive over but an animal won't cross. So the little roan wanders the whole property, all forty acres, drinks at the pond, leaves piles of manure on the little swimming beach, wanders by the house and looks in the west window when I am painting. No shit. She likes to watch me paint. Or maybe it's the smell. Something. From where I was standing at the easel, I could see her now: head down past the dock, tugging at the brown wheatgrass. A little helmeted kestrel sat in the young cottonwood above the mare, waiting I guess for her to kick up a mouse. Behind the bird and the horse, up on the mountain, the swaths of aspen on the ridges were a shimmering yellow that did not have a name.

We'd been back almost two weeks. It was mid-October, into the first rifle season on elk, and once in a while, especially at dawn and dusk, the shots came off the mountain, sporadic and muffled by distance. I didn't mind them. It was the sound of a changing season. Bob Reid and his son would be up there now. The first time I pulled in for gas he came around to my window and looked straight at me, way longer than most people would find comfortable. He was asking himself, I guess, what he felt about everything. Then he shook his head like, What the hell, and reached into the breast pocket of his shirt and pulled out his can of Skoal. He took a pinch and said, "Dip?" And I knew we would be okay.

Willy was glad to see me and helped me get the roan settled on my place, and helped me put in the grate. He had been designing his new bigger barn and was almost ready to break ground. He never mentioned the killing of Grant, which I was sure he'd read about, and he never mentioned either of the brothers again.

The cops weren't so tactful. Sport called me the day we got back, to let me know, I guess, that he was keeping tabs on me and knew exactly what I was up to all the time. He didn't have much to say except that the investigation was still very much open. He was all business. He said that any time it occurred to me to come down and add some new information it would probably be better for everyone in the long run. The long run. I never could, ever, wrap my head around that concept. I guess the short run always seemed hard enough.

The painting I was doing now was of two birds, redwings, sitting on the head of a scarecrow. A cloudy choppy sky, veils of rain, not virga. That's all. The scarecrow looked resigned, like he had been handsome and imposing once, but was now in tatters and just happy to be outside looking over a stormy beautiful afternoon. I signed the canvas and took it down and leaned it against the wall. Sometimes when a painting is hot off the press I get it off the easel fast so I won't be tempted to mess with it in passing.

"Nice," she said from behind the counter.

Sofia had on hot mitts and she turned back and leaned down and pulled two bread tins out of the oven and set them clattering on the stove top and I heard the hinge of the oven door and the door bang shut.

"There." She blew a strand of curly hair off her face. She said: "Bread. You want some hot, with honey?"

I shrugged. I felt uneasy. Sofia had moved right in. I was glad, mostly. There was not one thing wrong and that spring inside was coiled pretty tight. I had seen this version of domestic bliss before and it had never worked out. Maybe that was it. If I could just let things be what they are. I was trying, would try. It's okay, Jim, to be content for once, you might even like it.

"Smells delicious."

"And?"

"I'm going up the Sulphur, till dark," I said. "Maybe we can have trout for dinner."

A shadow crossed her eyes, but she summoned a smile and said, "Sounds good." She held up both oven mitts like boxing gloves and said, "Wanna box? I am having the feeling you need the bullshit knocked out of you again."

She stood there, her curly hair exuberant, flying in every direction, her gloves up, and I laughed. Whew. Sofia knew. She was patient. She would, if I let her, probably knock the bullshit down the road.

"See ya," I said.

"Byyyyyye."

The best time of year, period. Anywhere. Mid-October on the Sulphur may be the most beautiful thing I had ever seen. The creek was low, showing its bones, the fallen spruce propped high on the rocks like a wreck, the little rapids now shallow, the pools cold again and slate blue. The wooded canyon had gone to deep shadow but the pink rimrock high up was brilliant with long evening light and the sky was that hard enamel blue. When a gust blew downstream the willows along the gravel bars loosed their pale yellow leaves to the stones and the water. I listened. Hard to hear above the rushing current, but almost every evening I'd heard a crash and seen a yearling bear scrambling up the bank away from me, and I often heard the knock of elk, antlers against a tree, and smelled them nearby, and by nightfall it would be freezing and I would have to quit because my cold fingers could no longer tie on a fly.

I was standing in what I'd named Cutbow Channel, knee deep below a long run of swift water. The rocks in the bed were every color of green and rust and slate. I breathed. The scents of the spruce and the fir stirred downstream, and the smells of water and cold stones.

Above the channel was a corner where a few boulders had made a swift drop and a massive fir tree had fallen across them like a gateway. To get beyond it you had to clamber over rocks and the trunk of the tree, and when you did, the creek opened up: it widened and slowed and spread between wide gravel bars. Nobody ever fished this far in, and it felt remote, out of time, and I called it Heaven. I stopped knee deep at the long riffle beneath it and dug out a vanilla cheroot from the pouch in the vest, and lit it and watched the smoke trail easily downstream.

The current lapped and gabbled here, raising its voice and pressing my legs. I cradled the rod in the crook of my left arm and unhooked a bead head prince off a foam patch on my vest. Fingers already cold. I'd switch out the copper John I was using as a dropper along the bottom. I could feel my pulse quicken. It was a perfect evening, no moon, and a perfect fly, they would not be able to resist the flash of the white wings. Could almost feel the tug of a hit, imagine it, even as I was threading the eye and twisting the tippet and pulling it tight with my teeth.

"Ow—fuck!"

Hard pressed under my jaw the cold prod. Steel. I knew without thought that it was a gun.

"Prince nymph, good choice. What I'd use, probably."

I couldn't see him. He was behind me with the handgun held out and up against my throat. His voice was graveled, as if he hadn't spoken in a while.

"Can't lose tonight. Nobody feeding up top, all gathered up in the deeper pools, idling, just waiting for that thing to tumble by."

His voice in the back of my ear. Could smell the chew on his breath, not a bad smell, Copenhagen. Couldn't look though, couldn't turn my head, because there was the cold muzzle hard against the bone. The quickening of my heart.

"Hi, Jason."

A long silence while the snout of the handgun held pressure against my head.

"Isn't that civil?" he said at last. "Dunno. I'm thinking maybe you should say thanks."

"For what?"

Slight push of the gun. So that I bent my neck, head away.

"For not blowing up your shit right in the middle of the party, your hour of glory. Or after, while your girlfriend slept in the truck and you fished all night like you were on some fucking vacation."

The hot smell of the words as much as sound.

"I brought you something."

The pressure relieved a little. I couldn't see him but I sensed him switching hands. And then his right hand came to my side. I looked down. It held the rucksack.

"This yours?"

"Yes."

It swung back out of sight behind me, and I heard it hit the stones of the bank.

"Pretty fucking dumb. Right? They'd a found it, you'd be in County waiting trial. Man." I heard him blow out his breath. "It was never about the law. I told you we take care of our own business."

Then the gun was hard against my temple and his left hand slid under my cap, knocked it into the water, and he grabbed a fistful of my hair. He was forcing me to look upstream. Beyond the fallen tree, sunlight cut down through a draw and lit the gravel bar. The light that would last minutes before the sun went over that piece of ridge. I thought, This is the last thing I will see in my life. I didn't want to die. Right now I didn't. I had wanted to die many times in my life before but now I didn't.

"You know I hiked in from the Snowshoe," he said. "No way any-body knows I'm in here. Nice hike. Places in there I bet nobody in history ever fished. You should've tried that sometime. Lotta blowdown though. No, I guess not. Not with your trick knee. It's the left one ain't it?"

His boot on the back of it, my left knee, the soft crook, his boot against it shoving slowly, harder, harder until it buckled and I went down on the knee in the creek and the current was against my chest and sweeping hard against the rod. I tried to keep the rod out of the water, but the current levered against it and I needed my right hand for balance. I crooked the rod tighter in my left arm but the current tore it away.

Ahhh!—both hands grabbed for it, reached, and I almost toppled, it was gone. The tip came out of the chop as it went. It was the Sage five weight, the one I had used forever.

"Whoops," he said.

I watched the rod. Where it had been. My heart broke. What it felt like. It was the rod I had fished with Alce the years we had fished. The one that had been my solace after, the one Sport had taken for testing and given back. I might not have counted on a paintbrush or a bottle of bourbon to save me but I had counted on fishing. I was on both knees now against the current and the swift water was nearly up to the top of the waders above my sternum. I had been so excited to fish I had forgotten to snug on a waist belt for safety, plus the creek now was so shallow, and if the water went in over the top of the waterproof overalls and filled up the legs in this current, that would be another way to die.

"That feels bad, huh? I know what a rod like that can mean. Probably what you taught your little daughter to fish on, huh?

"Huh?" Push against the temple.

I wasn't even angry. The hot anger I'd depended on in fights. I felt tears running on my cheeks.

"Kinda like a ship without a mast, ain't it? Or a rudder. Maybe it's a rudder."

Push of the gun.

"I don't know."

"You don't know."

"I don't know anything."

I didn't. On my knees in the icy creek about to drown with my rod gone, and my daughter gone, and my father, and my mother, and the one patch of light on the gravel gone, and my tears falling in the cold current, I didn't. Know shit. I didn't know why they had left, all of them, why I was still here, why my fly rod had been pulled away and sunk. Why I had killed two men. Nothing left. I couldn't fathom it. He reached around and yanked the cheroot out of my teeth—I didn't know I was still smoking it—and he flicked it into the current.

"Better not smoke while you listen. I'm going to tell you a story. Don't worry it's short. Those waders must be getting pretty leaky and cold by now. My experience, those lightweight summer deals don't stand up too good to that kind of pressure. Those ones I used the other day? Simms. A little hot on a warm day but they don't leak."

He spat out his chew. The black gob hit the water beside me.

"You should use a waist belt. A guy could drown out here by himself."

Shove against my temple.

"I think I better have a smoke. Chew is good, but smoking is more social."

He kept the gun to my head and I could tell he was retrieving the pack from a breast pocket with one hand and shaking out a smoke and I heard the snick of an old Zippo as he lit up. I could feel trickles of cold water seeping in at the waist, the legs.

"Whew. Good. Better."

His smoke trailed downstream. It smelled good, it smelled like life.

"You know Dell and Grant had a sister. Did you know that?"

Shook my head. His words were another sound with the rush of the current and my own thoughts. They went by my head like his smoke, then I saw them re-form. They had a sister.

"Gwen. Funny name. Gwendolina. Like something out of King Arthur, isn't it? Well, she was parceled out to foster care just like them, but she was older, and she didn't know them like they knew each other coming up. So when they each ran away from where they were caged, well. She must not have known where to go, or how to stay in touch. And they didn't know where her foster family was neither—"

Long outbreath of smoke—

"Cruel, huh? Like slavery. But on one of those runaways, well, she had me. I mean got knocked up. It was a religious family where she was at, down in Montrose, and so they beat her bad and let her go to term and then guess who popped out, and guess who went up for adoption and nobody took? Little old Jason. Poor little old guy. Well—" Draw on the smoke, could hear it, hear him blow it out, my aching knees numb now, the gun right there, hard and still—

"Well she died. They had to tell the boys, because after all she was their older sister. How did she die? they wanted to know. Under mysterious circumstances. In a group home of about eight kids in Montrose, she was just about to turn seventeen. Under mysterious circumstances. I guess she was really pretty. Pretty and smart and drug addicted off and on, things she shot up. Well. To Grant and Dell, that was the last straw. That wasn't happening to them. They were in different homes but they had their ways of getting in touch and they broke out and stayed out until they were the age of majority or whatever the shit they call it, till they were legally adults. And you know what?"

I didn't. I mean I couldn't get my thoughts in line. I could hear the water and my own thrumming pulse and his words but. I couldn't, I didn't know anything. Shove of the gun against my temple. "You know what?"

"No," I said.

"They didn't forget me. It took them four years, but they kept at it, kept at it the way they stayed on the blood trail of a shot elk. They worked every angle and they sprung me. I was eleven. They were what, just kids themselves, twenty-two and twenty-three. Brought me over to Delta for middle and high school, had me legally adopted, taught me to ride and fish and hunt. They didn't forget did they?"

Shove.

"Didn't let me go."

Shove. My tears running, hitting the current, I watched them hit right there below my face.

"And you know before they got to me it was pretty rough." His voice rising now.

"It was pretty fucking rough in that place I was in, in fact there was some shit going on in there I don't know if I would have survived. God's truth."

Shove, harder.

"And they sprung me. And they brought me into a real home, a family. A fucked up home at times. A hard drinking, hard fighting fucked up home, and maybe when they got going they didn't treat their stock so good, I didn't agree with that and I was working on that, I was, but it was a fucking home. And some of the other shit, maybe some of the other shit with the hunting outside the law, that wasn't me either, and I told them: That's not me. I'll bring you hay, I'll help you load up, maybe set up camp but that's as far as it goes, I've got other fish to fry and it's not me and they could respect it. See, there was respect."

Hard shove.

"Now there ain't shit. Is there? Because of you."

The gun was gone. Sudden relief of pressure, absence, only then feel the ache, how hard it had been. Nothing. The current. Burble. I straightened my back from where I was bent over the water and turned my head, neck stiff, looked up.

He wasn't wearing the shades. He was standing calf deep in the water in his jeans. No cap. The cigarette was in the corner of his mouth burnt down almost to the filter, the downstream breeze taking the smoke away. His blue eyes looked down on me, tears running out of the corners.

"I ain't gonna cry in front of you. Give you the satisfaction. I ain't."

He wiped his face with the back of his sleeve, shook his head. The gun was still up.

"All this time trailing you I thought about what I wanted to do to you. Killing you would have been easy. I could've done it five, six times, clean. Easy. Grant got too excited I guess. He was always a little like that, a little too much of a hothead. Then what? I kill you and you go dark. You don't even know. Or I give you a few minutes to repent and beg and shit your pants and then I kill you, like in the movies. Like now. Well. You're not begging and you haven't shit your pants as far as I can tell. Good for you."

He snagged the pack out of his shirt pocket, shook out another cigarette, dug into his jeans and thumbed open the Zippo, lit up. Let out a long stream of smoke.

"Then I thought, Well, I can string you up by the feet like an elk and maybe even skin you alive. That'd be sort of fun. And with each strip I slipped off I could ask How was it—selling all these paintings and making shitpiles of money off my uncles' killings. Pretty fucked up, ain't it? That the world works like that. I even thought about cutting off your hands. It'd make painting and fishing pretty tough. You could still fuck, though. So I could cut off your dick, too. I could. Easy as gutting a trout."

He stared down at me. The gun was aimed at my face.

"That's not really me, though. I never pulled the wings off a fly or tortured a cat, nothing like that. I think it would give me nightmares. Even you. Screaming like that and all the blood. Fact is, I realized that any of that would hurt me more. That's what came to me as I was driving around stalking you like prey. Call it a Jesus moment. You'd be dead and I'd be driving down the road the rest of my life wondering if Tweedledum and Tweedledee would ever have enough to put me in a cage. And wondering why all the things I did to you didn't bring my uncles back and why I still didn't have people to call at Christmas, and why there was still that big hole where a family should have been, and why maybe I felt worse about everything."

Suck on the cigarette, exhale, toss it in the creek.

"It's a quandary, ain't it?"

He raised the gun and pulled the trigger.

I flinched, jumped. Water erupted a foot to my right. The crack reverberated in the canyon like five guns going off at once. *Fuck*. Echo. Echo. The gun there where he had fired it, straight armed. The whole canyon awake now, altered, like a top that wobbles and regains balance.

"Still works."

He was staring at me and his eyes had gone hard again and they were lit with violence.

"And then I think, J, just keep it fucking simple. You think too goddamn much. Just shoot the fucker and let the chips fall."

My pulse hammering now. *Alce*. Just the name, no other thought.

He stared at me.

"I think it's better like this. Maybe I walk away. Not too far. You can be one of my projects. Like a hobby. We'll see how you come along. We will never ever be very far apart. You took away my family and you're gonna carry around a piece of hell wherever you go. More of the hell to add to the one you already got inside you. Shit yeah, I see it. Like a house fire you can see through the front windows, before the whole shittin place goes up in flames."

He reached across and shoved the automatic into a Cordura holster sewed to the side of his own rucksack and turned away, turned back.

"Get you another Sage. They're having a sale down at Leroy's. You already got that fancy Winston rod, huh? But it ain't the same, is it? Not like the old standby."

He hitched his thumbs into the pack straps, tugged one tighter and turned in to the willows.

"Hey. Hey!"

He stopped, looked back.

"I—"

He stared hard, like he was rethinking whether to shoot me.

"I'm sorry," I said.

He stared at me.

"I know," I said. "I took your family away. I know about things you can never put back."

I wiped my own face with my sleeve. "I fucking know."

I got off my knees and straightened slowly. A gust of wind blew willow leaves onto the stones of the bank.

"What do you want me to do?" I said.

His blue eyes were very still. He looked as if he were barely breathing.

"I'll do anything you want. Do you want me to go down to the courthouse? Turn myself in?"

He turned full around and looked at me hard, his imagination tightening the screws. I heard the current ripping along the rocks, the wind. The canyon was in full shadow now, it was that time of day, the cusp. Then I saw a sharp light move in his eyes.

"Something with kids," he said. "You do something for some lost kids. Or old folks, I don't give a shit. You bust your ass."

He met my eyes. "For the rest of your fucked up life," he said. "I mean it. Like a goddamn saint. And then one day I still might wake up in the morning and decide to shoot you in the fucking head. Goddamn you."

I started to say Okay and he shrugged the pack higher and turned his back and disappeared into the trees.

I walked to the bank and stripped off the waders and emptied them on the stones. I sat on a rock and let the feeling come back to my legs. I sat for a long time as the canyon filled with dusk. I let his words sift. Something had just happened and I wasn't sure what. I put the wading boots back on and picked up the rucksack and walked downstream to the truck.

Acknowledgments

Many dear friends and family gave generously to the making of this book. Kim Yan was, as always, my first reader, and I am deeply grateful. Lisa Jones, Helen Thorpe, Rebecca Rowe, David Grinspoon and Donna Gershten gave crucial, passionate input, as did Nathan Fischer, Pete Beveridge and Caro Heller. Leslie Heller kept the idea alive for many years. Sascha Steinway and Mark Lough were immensely helpful all along. Lawrence Norfolk gave me a brilliant notion. Jeff Streeter, Jason Hicks and Max Marquez lent generously of their expertise, as they have in the past. And Eric Aho and Jay Mead read closely and gave the best advice. Thanks also to Louise Quayle and Matthew Snyder for their wonderful work.

This book would not have been written without the stewardship, intellect and integrity of David Halpern. Nor would it exist without the inspiration and brilliance of Jenny Jackson, who is a truly great editor.

What a pleasure and a privilege. Thank you all.

Peter Heller is the best-selling author of *The Dog Stars*. He holds an MFA from the Iowa Writers' Workshop in both fiction and poetry. An award-winning adventure writer and longtime contributor to NPR, Heller is a contributing editor at *Outside* magazine, *Men's Journal* and *National Geographic Adventure* and a regular contributor to *Bloomberg Businessweek*. He is also the author of several non-fiction books, including *Kook, The Whale Warriors* and *Hell or High Water: Surviving Tibet's Tsangpo River*. He lives in Denver, Colorado.

A NOTE ON THE TYPE

This book was set in Scala, a typeface designed by the Dutch designer Martin Majoor (b. 1960) in 1988 and released by the Font-Font foundry in 1990. While designed as a fully modern family of fonts containing both a serif and a sans serif alphabet, Scala retains many refinements normally associated with traditional fonts.

Composed by North Market Street Graphics,
Lancaster, Pennsylvania

Printed and bound by Berryville Graphics,
Berryville, Virginia

Designed by Soonyoung Kwon